MAKING A KILLING

**Also available by Warren Dunford
from Alyson Books**

Soon to Be a Major Motion Picture

MAKING A KILLING

BY WARREN DUNFORD

alyson books
los angeles | new york

MANUFACTURED IN THE UNITED STATES OF AMERICA.

THIS TRADE PAPERBACK ORIGINAL IS PUBLISHED BY ALYSON PUBLICATIONS, P.O. BOX 4371, LOS ANGELES, CA 90078-4371.
DISTRIBUTION IN THE UNITED KINGDOM BY
TURNAROUND PUBLISHER SERVICES LTD.,
UNIT 3, OLYMPIA TRADING ESTATE, COBURG ROAD, WOOD GREEN,
LONDON N22 6TZ ENGLAND.

FIRST EDITION: NOVEMBER 2001

01 02 03 04 05 a 10 9 8 7 6 5 4 3 2 1

ISBN 1-55583-657-7

LIBRARY OF CONGRESS CATALOGING-IN-PUBLICATION DATA
DUNFORD, WARREN, 1963–
    MAKING A KILLING / BY WARREN DUNFORD.—1ST ED.
    ISBN 1-55583-657-7
    1. SCREENWRITERS—FICTION. 2. GAY MEN—FICTION. 3. CANADA—
FICTION. I. TITLE.
PR9199.3.D867 M35 2001
813'.54—DC21   2001031594

CREDITS
COVER DESIGN BY MATT SAMS.
COVER PHOTOGRAPHY BY SUPER STOCK.

For Trudie Town,
who always loved a mystery,
and for my mother, Rita Dunford,
who bought me my first Agatha Christie

Many friends have played an influential role in the writing of this novel—providing research notes, editorial advice, and ongoing encouragement. Among them: Rick Andreoli, Bruce Appleby, Jennifer Barclay, Debrann Barr, Martha Beaudry, Joanne Bigham, Martha Bouchier, Rob Bowman, A.A. Bronson, Ann and John Brookes, Daniel Brooks, Mary Burack, Sally Catto, Karen Cumming, Lloyd Davis, Hart de Fouw, Dino Dilio, Monica Ditchburn, Damon D'Oliveira, Lee Doran, the Duckworth family, Linda Durkee, Judy Filman, John Firth, Thom Fitzgerald, Stuart Fleming, Michael Thomas Ford, Sharon Freedman, David Fullman, Andre Goh, Martha Hale, Richard Hayter, James Huctwith, Ed Janiszewski, Joan Jenkinson, Jeff Kirby, Mark Krayenhoff, Linda Kroboth, Karen Lim, Preben Guy Lordly, Michael Lewis MacLennan, Barry Marshall, Lynn Harrison McLachlan, Jeff Morgan, Brenda Morrison, Mrs. Morrison, Ira Mulasi, Janis Orenstein, Barry Patterson, Jeremy Podeswa, Suzanne Pope, Shaun Proulx, Susan Lynn Reynolds, Soosan Robertson, Timothy Roney, Michael Rowe, John Schell, Anya Seerveld, Joey Shulman, the Simmons family, Ed Sinclair, Darrin Singbeil, Patricia Jo Steffen, Loreen Teoli, John Theo, Robert Thomson, Shelley Town, the Weese family, Joan Williams—and my father, Gerald Dunford, and his wife, Olive Dunford. Particular appreciation goes to my agent, Hilary Stanley, and also to Attila Berki and John Terauds for giving me my Big Break, Michael Schellenberg, Cheryl Cohen, Shannon Proulx, and the team at Penguin Canada, and Scott Brassart, Dan Cullinane, and everyone at Alyson Books. Thank you very much.

"Look at him—broke, spooked, as good as fired."
"Those are his circumstances, Mrs. Faulk.
Not the man himself."

—Tennessee Williams, *The Night of the Iguana*

FRIDAY, OCTOBER 9

If you read this and I have become a New Age cult zombie, please help me.

Being of sound mind and body as I type these words, I declare that I do not intend to join Ramir's cult tonight. And if I do join Ramir's cult through brainwashing or sheer force of peer pressure—then whoever reads this note has my full endorsement to kidnap and deprogram me as soon as possible.

Not that having a free will is doing me much good. But at least I have my *own* neuroses and not some wacko cult leader's.

For more than two months now, Ramir has been begging me and our friend Ingrid to come to an intro night for the Seven Gateways to Spiritual Success. We've always managed to politely yet firmly decline.

But I guess I've been particularly vulnerable lately—after getting fired from *Five Fun Fish,* the pseudo-educational kids' TV show that's been my main source of income for the past two years.

They always say cults prey on the weak.

Anyway, last night Ramir, Ingrid, and I were out for dinner at our habitual Hungarian restaurant, and I admit I might have been whining—worrying yet again about the wreckage of my career. "My agent just signed me up to write for another kids' show—something about a spunky cat who explores the world. *Travels with Willie.*"

"That could be fun," Ing said, always eager to be optimistic. Then she winced.

"It gives me the willies even to think about it," I said. "I don't want to get permanently stuck in kiddy schlock. I keep wondering if I'm a one-hit wonder. One movie. One book. And it's not as if either was a big hit in the first place."

"They were both really good," Ingrid said for the ten-thousandth time, and Ramir nodded in agreement the way he always does.

The three of us have been best friends for the last four years—supporting each other through various career ambitions, love affairs, and other personal traumas.

"But the cat show doesn't start until next month," I explained, "and that means I've got four weeks to myself. And I've realized that I need to jump through my window of opportunity before it closes for good."

"So what are you going to do?" Ramir asked.

"I'm going to write the best screenplay of my life. Something totally commercial. A shameless box-office smash that'll help me get rich quick. Because a big-budget movie can pay a writer a million dollars. And once I have some cash behind me, I won't need to feel insecure like this all the time."

I could tell Ingrid was doubtful of my strategy. "So what are you going to write?"

"I'm still not sure about that part. I want to come up with a really catchy plot. Some sure-fire hook. But I can't think of anything. It's like I've hit a wall."

That's when Ramir lunged in for the kill. He set his raspberry soda on the table and radiated an expression of serene wisdom. "You know, Mitch, a lot of people say Dr. Bhandari has given them a creative breakthrough. You should really come to a meeting."

"Okay, I'll go," I said. I don't know what made me say it.

Ingrid glared at me as if I'd gone insane. Then Ramir grabbed hold of her hand. "You should come too."

"Tomorrow's no good," she said. "I have to finish another painting for the show."

Damn her quick thinking. Because in five minutes Ramir is picking me up to escort me to the cult.

I will now print out this document and stick it to my fridge— in case I inadvertently participate in a ritual mass suicide.

FRIDAY, OCTOBER 9
—LATER—

The house looked spooky.

It didn't help that the raging thunderstorm was a cliché right out of a horror movie. The sky was black and pelting down rain. And there was not a soul to be seen on the winding Rosedale street lined with stately old mansions, ominous trees, and lamp-posts with moon-like globes.

As Ramir climbed out the driver's side of his Land Rover, I tilted back my umbrella and examined the house. Full-blown Victorian Gothic—like Dracula's castle or some gloomy mansion in a book by a Brontë sister. Three storeys of dark red brick topped by a steeply angled roof of gables, turrets, and chimneys.

"You're sure they don't do devil worship?"

"It's phenomenal, isn't it? Some famous architect built it back in the 1880s."

"You'd think a cult would pick a headquarters that's a bit more cheerful."

"Mitch, I told you, the Seven Gateways isn't a cult."

"No cult ever admits it's a cult."

We hurried up the circular driveway, leaping over puddles in the chilly autumn damp. The path was lit with old-fashioned gas lamps. Tiny flames danced in the raindrops.

"I wish you'd calm down," Ramir said. "You're going to have a great time. I've got a special surprise all set up."

"I don't want any surprises tonight."

"Have I ever steered you wrong?" In fact he had. Hundreds of times. But he smiled in that way that's so infectiously enthusiastic, you can't help but go along.

We climbed the stone steps to the front entrance. A brass plaque on a pillar gleamed in the rain:

THORNFIELD MANOR
NINE THORNFIELD ROAD

I'd never been in a house with a name.

Ramir opened the massive carved door as casually as if he were entering his own home.

"Don't you think it's sort of suspicious that a spiritual guru lives in such an expensive place?" (Ramir had finally confessed Dr. Bhandari's price list: $250 an hour for psycho-spiritual therapy, plus an additional $5,000 to learn each of the Seven Gateways.)

"Dr. Bhandari used to be one of the top psychiatrists in Toronto. Anyway, there's nothing wrong with making money, Mitch. If you believe there is, then you'll never make any yourself."

"You don't have to join a cult to learn that. You can just watch *Oprah.*"

We stepped through a small vestibule into a massive front hall painted ivory. A grand staircase rose before us, and a marble fireplace was angled in the corner. Doors led off in every direction. This was the kind of house that had inspired the game of Clue.

"It really is incredible," I had to admit.

"Wait until you see the rest," he said, smiling with more proprietary pride. Ramir is 30—blessed with boyish good looks and a café-au-lait complexion. He was born in Trinidad, but he moved to Canada when he was 5, and deep down he's just as suburban as I am. But as an actor, he's always playing up his ethnic versatility and exotic allure.

"I warn you," I said, "I'm still not signing up for anything."

"You just have to relax and get into the flow of the universe, Mitch. Once you do that, I bet you'll get a great idea for your script right away."

A young man rushed toward us from one of the many doors. Short with reddish-blond hair, freckles, and a tight-clipped reddish beard—a cute Jesus. He wore a snug black sweater that showed off a gymnast's physique.

He stopped two feet in front of us—just a bit too close for comfort.

"Say it," he said to Ramir, nodding and grinning. He had an adorable tiny nose. "Come on, say it."

Was there some kind of secret password?

"*Greetings from KerrZavia,*" Ramir nasally droned. His standard opening line on *Station Centauri.*

Jesus laughed in appreciation. "I love it when you say that."

Ramir flashed his winning smile. Unfortunately, on the TV show in which he stars, all his best features are buried beneath an inch of latex and makeup.

Jesus was still nodding and grinning. "So how are things going on the show?"

Ramir went into his standard PR mode. "Terrific. We just finished the last episode of the season. We don't start shooting again until April."

"I even watch the reruns," Jesus said. "Do it one more time?"

"Only because it's you." Ramir returned to his nasal alien voice: "*Greetings from KerrZavia.*"

"That's so great!" He hugged Ramir energetically, and they glowed in mutual joy.

"Kevin, this is my friend Mitchell Draper. It's his first time at a meeting."

"Welcome, Mitchell," Kevin said, and he immediately engulfed me in an identical hug, his short muscular body pressed tight against my tall gangly one. Which actually felt extremely good. He looked me in the eyes, warmly and steadily. "Tonight has the power to change your future."

"Terrific," I said, hoping to sound a tad cynical. But in truth I sort of liked the idea of changing my future.

More cult zombies were coming in behind us. Kevin took our jackets and rushed off for more hugs.

I whispered into Ramir's ear, "Have you had sex with him?"

"He's straight."

"That's never stopped you before."

Ramir put his arm around my shoulders. "No need to be jealous, Mitch. You know I love you the most." (The two of us slept together once back when we first met, and Ramir likes to keep up the pretense of flirting.)

I shook his arm off.

"Who is Kevin anyway?"

"Dr. Bhandari's personal assistant. He lives here in the house."

"They live together?"

"Not like that. Dr. Bhandari is straight too."

"So when do I get to meet the mysterious Dr. Bhandari?"

"He stays up in his meditation room until just before the meeting. Come on, everybody else is in the back."

Ramir guided me toward the stairs, then to the left and through a maze of rooms and hallways. We stepped through tall double doors and entered, to my amazement, a grand ballroom—already abuzz with 50 or 60 disciples.

The room was stunning. The extra-high ceiling was detailed with a multilayered pattern of squares and diamonds—all white. Rows of elegant white chairs covered the hardwood floor. The left wall was a line of French doors adorned with sheer curtains.

"Can you believe somebody built a room like this in their own home?"

"I've never seen anything like it," I said.

The disciples stood in intimate clusters of three and four, some hugging, some clutching each others' hands in earnest confessions. A few loners were seated with their eyes closed—reliving past lives or astrally projecting to Pluto.

Actually, they all looked remarkably uncult-like. No shaved heads or violet robes. Most wore business suits or expensive designer casual wear. It made sense when I thought about it. They'd have to be rich to afford Dr. Bhandari.

"Am I the only new recruit?"

"Of course not. But most of the people here have gone through the Gateways already. They just like to come to the intro nights for sharing."

"I'm an only child. I hate sharing."

From the far side of the room, a woman came sailing toward us. Luxurious auburn hair, intelligent wide-set eyes, luscious mouth.

Gabriella Hartman.

My heart leapt to my throat. For years Gabriella Hartman had been a sex symbol on nighttime soap operas and TV movies. She'd starred in a bad sitcom and was the spokeswoman on an infomercial for hair-care products. Now, in her late 40s, she'd risen to the status of cult figure as Commodore Lisa Rutledge on *Station Centauri*.

Ramir loves dropping her famous name, but in two years he'd never found an opportunity for Ingrid and me to meet his illustrious costar.

Gabriella enveloped Ramir and pressed him to her breast. "Darling, I am so *delighted*! You *convinced* him!"

Did "him" mean me?

"And he *does* look like a young Bruce Dern," she said. "Only with more hair."

She *was* talking about me.

Then Gabriella turned and clenched both of my hands in hers. "Mitchell Draper," she said, "it is *such* a pleasure to finally meet you."

"I'm Mitchell Draper," I said, not believing she'd actually uttered my name.

She clapped in delight. "Now I'll *never* forget you."

"I see you on TV every week. Ramir talks about you all the time." I was in my babbling mode. I'm always easily starstruck.

"He talks even *more* about *you*," she promised. "Isn't it *ridiculous* that we haven't met before now? Ramir tells me you're a *brilliant* writer. Now, what was the name of your film?"

I cringed. "*Hell Hole*. It was a horror movie. It came out last year."

"I think I've heard of that," she said. Which is what everyone says who's never heard of it.

"It only played for a week in movie theatres. But it's supposed to be doing better on video."

"And you wrote a novel as well?"

"Sort of a roman à clef. Nobody's heard of it either."

"Mitchell, my dear new friend, I know *exactly* how you feel. Ramir was saying you're trying to come up with your next script. Those follow-up efforts can be the most daunting. The notorious 'sophomore jinx.' So much at stake. So much fear and self-doubt. I know from personal experience. That's why I think it's so *wonderful* that you're going through the Gateways."

"Actually, I haven't made an official decision."

"But Mitchell dear, you *must*."

"I'm just here to check things out."

"May I tell you the absolute *truth*, Mitchell? I credit Nigel Bhandari for reviving my entire career. And no actress has been washed up more times than I have, as the tabloids so love to report. Would you believe that I received my role on *Station Centauri* the very day I went through the Second Gateway?"

"What happens in the Second Gateway?"

She winked at me. "I know what you're up to."

"What am I up to?"

"You won't trick me into giving away any *secrets*! And I hope our gorgeous Ramir Martinez hasn't been spilling the beans." She tweaked Ramir's chin.

"Not a word," he swore.

"And tonight will be *particularly* powerful, Mitchell," she said, "because I'm going to be making a special announcement about a creative breakthrough of my own. Are you *burning* with curiosity?"

I nodded eagerly, as I was supposed to.

"We'll chat again later, do you *promise*?"

I promised. She flitted off.

"Did you like your surprise?" Ramir asked, grinning. "You always said you wanted to meet her."

"Is she always like that?"

"Like what?"

"So...larger than life."

"Mitch, you're being a bitch." Ramir loves to say that.

"Sorry. It's nice that she was so supportive." But I never dreamed I'd be getting the high-pressure sales treatment from one of *Entertainment Weekly*'s 101 Stars Who Just Won't Give Up. "Do you really talk to her about me?"

"Of course. All the time."

"What do you say?"

"That's personal," he said, flirting again.

"I bet you called her this afternoon and coached her. So anyway, what *do* you learn in the Second Gateway?"

"I can't tell you."

"Of course you can tell me."

Ramir primly shook his head. "You have to sign a nondisclosure agreement."

"Now that's *really* creepy."

A gong donged. I noticed Kevin standing at an old-fashioned cymbal dangling on a cord—like a butler summoning us to dinner.

"It's time to get started," Ramir said, and he took me by the arm.

There was no escape now.

"Let's sit near the front," Ramir said, leading me to the third row.

At the head of the room, a massive white marble fireplace was framed by slender windows. A white lectern and a single white chair waited for our leader.

"There's not going to be any audience participation, is there?"

"They might ask a few questions."

"They're not going to drag me up to the front, are they? I won't have to levitate or walk on burning coals?"

"Mitch, I wouldn't have brought you if I didn't think it was worthwhile. I'm not a total flake, you know."

"I'm sorry. I guess I've been going too far."

"Just listen to what they have to say."

"But I'm really not going to enroll in anything. I couldn't afford it even if I wanted to."

"Don't worry about the money," Ramir said, implying personal financing. *Station Centauri* pays him $10,000 per episode—22 episodes per year.

"I couldn't let you…"

"It's just that you haven't been yourself since Ben left."

That caught me by surprise.

At the end of August, my boyfriend Ben had moved to Vancouver to go back to university. It was a total shock. He hadn't even told me he'd applied. Admittedly, I was sort of a mess for a while. "But I'm over that now," I said.

"I've been worried about you."

It was strange to think of Ramir being worried about *me*. I thought it was Ingrid and I who were worried about *him*. "There's nothing the matter with me."

"I just know how helpful Dr. Bhandari can be. Honest to God, Mitch, the Seven Gateways are changing my life."

"Your life was great already. An amazing job. You bought a new house. You have a new boyfriend every two weeks."

"You know all that stuff doesn't matter."

"At least you're a legitimate success, not some permanent wannabe."

Ramir stared me in the eye. "Mitch, I have to tell you something important. I should have told you this before, but I didn't want to talk about it to anybody when it happened."

"What is it?" I knew it must be serious.

"Back in the summer, they almost fired me from *Station Centauri*."

I felt my throat clench and my stomach sink—just a fraction of what Ramir must have felt. "Why?"

"It was after my father died. I couldn't memorize my lines. I was always late. I was fucking up all the time."

I remembered that period well.

"So the producers gave me a warning. Then Gabriella dragged me into her dressing room and told me about Dr. Bhandari. I came with her to an intro night. And I straightened out the next day."

We sat in silence for a moment.

"Why didn't you say anything?"

"I couldn't. My whole world would have fallen apart if I lost the show."

I stared straight ahead. I hadn't had a clue.

"So listen to what Dr. Bhandari has to say, OK?"

The rest of the crowd took their seats, and silence quickly settled. I noticed that everyone else had closed their eyes. Including Ramir. So I succumbed to the peer pressure and shut mine too.

I was still shaken by Ramir's revelation.

After his father had the heart attack, Ramir fell into a frenetic depression, obsessively going to the gym, taking steroids, then ecstasy, then various other illegal substances. That's why Ingrid and I thought the Gateways were just another crazy addiction.

I felt a rush of guilt. What if Ramir were right? What if the Seven Gateways to Spiritual Success really were the answer? Why did I automatically want to presume the whole thing was a fraud?

I opened my eyes and glanced around at all the peaceful, meditating faces.

I checked my watch. We'd only been sitting there for two minutes. I closed my eyes again.

I thought back to the stack of anticult pamphlets my mother had given me when a Mormon family moved in down the street. She'd given me a similar series of pamphlets when I told her I was gay.

I thought about Ben, who was now enrolled in Environmental Studies at the University of British Columbia.

For a brief moment, after he told me his plans, I'd imagined moving to Vancouver with him. There's lots of TV and film production out there. Maybe I'd have more luck.

Then Ben said he intended to go by himself, and I realized he was dumping me. He pointed out that he'd been suggesting we move in together for more than a year, and all that time I'd kept saying I needed to live alone so I could write. I thought living together had become a mutual running joke, but it turned out he'd been deadly serious.

At first, I was noble and understanding, and we carried on as normal. But about a week before he left, we had a huge yelling match during which he implied that I have unrealistic ambitions and that maybe I should reconsider my career.

We decided not to communicate for a while.

I checked my watch again. Six minutes.

But what if Ben had been right about my writing? I couldn't help wondering, after my dismissal from *Five Fun Fish*. The producers said they wanted to "try a fresh approach." Which was a polite way of telling me I'd lost my flare for witty repartee between a macho shark and a slutty tuna.

I've written three other scripts since *Hell Hole,* and my agent hasn't been able to get a producer interested in any of them.

And now I'm destined for *Travels with Willie.*

I was hit with a fresh wave of panic. The pressure to come up with a brilliant screenplay idea. The meditation obviously wasn't working.

Actually, I've occasionally experimented with meditation on my own to help deal with my chronic neuroses and panic attacks. But after five minutes, I get bored and turn on the TV instead. I watch The Shopping Channel. Even though I never phone in to buy anything. But somehow the incessant chatter seems to drown out the chatter of my mind.

The gong sounded again. My eyes immediately popped open.

And there, at the lectern, was Dr. Nigel Bhandari. At least I presumed it was him.

His skin was a soft brown—just slightly darker than Ramir's. Thick black hair, lightly flecked with grey at the temples. He wore a camel-coloured cashmere turtleneck.

"Welcome to each and every one of you," he said. His speech had a formal British/East-Indian rhythm. His face was sensual and calm, his cheeks almost cherubic.

I leaned forward in eager anticipation. Finally I'd find out what made Ramir and Gabriella so devoted to this man.

"I would like to begin this introduction to the Seven Gateways as we always do. I would like to invite those of you who are already experiencing the gifts of the Gateways to please tell us of your current successes and to make decrees for the future."

He smiled—no, actually he beamed—at his audience. And he sat on the white chair beside the lectern. Was that all he was going to say?

Automatically, a woman in the front row stood up. "This morning when I was washing the dishes, I felt so happy. Normally, when I'm washing the dishes, I get bored or annoyed. But today I just washed the dishes—and it was so peaceful!"

She sat. And everyone applauded.

Hmm. Wouldn't a woman rich enough to see Dr. Bhandari be able to afford a maid to do the dishes? Or at least she could buy a dishwasher.

A man stood. "I decree that within six months I'll be CEO."

Short and to the point. Everyone applauded.

"I called my father today." Everyone craned their necks to see Kevin standing at the back of the room. "If any of you remember the story, my father was really angry when I left my teaching job to volunteer here at the Gateways. But I decreed I was letting go of all that. And we got along really well today. At the end of the conversation, he said, 'Maybe those Moonies are doing you some good after all.'"

People laughed with knowing condescension and applauded. Kevin sat.

Then Ramir stood, and the crowd gazed attentively upon his tall, leanly muscular frame—built through five sessions a week with Kristoff, one of Toronto's hottest personal trainers. "I decree that I am starring in a major feature film."

The crowd applauded and Ramir sat. I gave him the supportive pat on the leg you're supposed to give when someone beside you stands up and says something.

An eager young male executive explained that being fired from his job meant that his Higher Power must be saving his time for something more valuable. Then an eager female executive announced that she'd had her first short story accepted by an obscure literary 'zine. As if *that* would actually help her publishing career. But I shouldn't be so bitter.

This went on for an hour—numbing to both mind and buttocks. People decreed about business deals and being reunited with adopted daughters. They spoke about the beauty of leaves turning red on a maple tree and receiving unexpected cheques in the mail. They made new decrees and explained the results of old decrees, while Dr. Bhandari sat there at the front, nodding sagely.

Not a single person made a single reference to the Seven Gateways.

Then, after a long, oddly peaceful silence—maybe it was over?—Gabriella stood in the front row. She turned and gazed meaningfully into every corner of the room.

"As many of you know, I am not only an actress, I'm also a *singer*. I did a few Broadway shows in my time—*Luther* and *Nobody Loves an Albatross*. And of course I had a number-one hit on the radio."

The crowd applauded. Gabriella's smiling lips performed facial calisthenics.

I remembered her big single from the mid '80s—a wailing middle-of-the-road ballad called "Babe, You Make My Heart Break."

Gabriella placed a hand over her famous breast. "In the past few months, I've been feeling *called* to bring the power of song back into my life. I've always been *fascinated* by Celtic music. And now, I decree that the music of the Emerald Isles is flowing across the ocean and pouring right from my heart."

After Gabriella had been applauded, Dr. Bhandari stood again. "Thank you, everyone, for your generosity this evening in sharing your experiences. I would now like to announce a very special upcoming event. On Friday, October the 30th, we will be hosting our annual gala for The Centre for Spiritual Success. Tickets will be $500 per person. And the highlight of the evening will be a special musical performance by Gabriella Hartman."

Gabriella rose again and nodded graciously to incite more applause.

"I haven't been to one of their parties yet, but I've heard they're amazing," Ramir whispered. "You'll have to come."

There was no way I was spending $500 on a ticket.

"We will now have a 10-minute break," Dr. Bhandari said, "and then we will reconvene for meditation—each according to your own Gateway. The new guests are invited to join me for a special introduction."

Everyone stood and began to mill about.

I pulled Ramir to a quiet spot by the French doors. Rain was still streaming down the panes.

"What were all those people talking about?"

"It's subtle. You're supposed to see the simple changes the Gateways bring to your life," Ramir said. "That's what it's about. Helping you appreciate what's wonderful about your normal everyday existence."

"I thought Dr. Bhandari would give a better explanation of the whole thing."

"He does that in the next section."

"Is that when he starts the hard sell? When he's got us locked in a tiny room?"

"Mitch, there's no hard sell. You should have realized that by now."

"So how does he get people to join his cult?"

"The Seven Gateways is not a cult," said Dr. Bhandari. He'd been standing right behind me.

My stomach lurched. "I was just teasing Ramir," I said. "I know it's not a cult."

"It's not a word we care to repeat."

"Sorry. Sorry."

Ramir took charge. "Dr. Bhandari, this is my best friend, Mitchell Draper."

He shook my hand. "Good evening, Mitchell." His rich brown eyes seemed heavy with wisdom, but strangely sealed off. "May I tell you, Mitchell, my explanation of why these evenings are so powerful?"

It was a rhetorical question, but he seemed to expect an answer. "Please," I said.

"Everyone receives precisely what he has come for."

"That's great," I said, not really sure what he meant.

"The second part of the evening should tell you more of what you want. But, Mitchell, if there is anything further you wish me to explain, please feel free to call or drop by the house for a visit."

"Thanks. That's nice of you."

"I sense you would benefit greatly from the Seven Gateways."

I bet he says that to all the boys.

"Now, Ramir, I would be grateful if you would do me a special favour."

"Of course," Ramir promised, prematurely.

"It's a very large favour, in fact. I would like you to help organize our upcoming gala."

Clearly, Dr. Bhandari didn't know that Ramir had a hard enough time coordinating his sex life.

Ramir seemed taken aback. "Uh, umm, it'd be an honour."

"Perhaps we can discuss this on the phone tomorrow morning."

Dr. Bhandari moved on to his other devotees.

Ramir turned to me, sparking with excitement. "You have no idea what a compliment that is."

"Asking you to volunteer is a compliment?"

"It is when you're in charge of an event like that. You wouldn't believe all the famous people who've gone through the Gateways. And Gabriella's manager will be flying in from L.A. He's got connections to everybody in Hollywood."

"So there's a business angle to it too."

"Of course there's a business angle. I mean, I love *Station Centauri,* but I still want to get into a movie. I don't want to be stuck in sci-fi for my whole career. It's like you and your kids' shows."

"Intergalactic Travels with Willie."

Gabriella rushed to Ramir's side. "You said yes, I hope? Oh, how *wonderful!* It's going to be an absolutely *magical* evening." She grabbed my hands again. "You'll come too, won't you, Mitchell? I'll need everyone to send their positive energy."

"I'll send you all I've got."

Gabriella's arm flailed into the crowd, and she drew a woman toward her—a Chinese woman, clad in black leather, with jet-black hair frizzed out in a perm. Fuchsia lipstick burst against her golden skin. She looked like a groupie with a rock band.

"I want you to meet Jane Choy, one of the world's absolute *best* psychics and a dear, dear friend of mine."

"Nice to meet you," Jane said. While her fashion sense was garishly North American, her accent was distinctly Chinese. She looked fidgety, restless to get away. She barely glanced at me.

"Jane is guiding my singing career. I *never* make a decision without her."

Jane nodded as if she'd heard this before. "Gabriella's always trying to butter me up so I'll give her better predictions."

Suddenly, Gabriella and Ramir were yanked away by another *Station Centauri* admirer, and Jane and I were left in that awkward cocktail-party situation—suddenly missing the mutual friends who had provided our communication link.

"So is this your first time at a meeting?" I asked.

Jane finally focused on me. Her eyes locked on my face. Then her gaze lifted upward. She became transfixed, staring at something above my head.

"Is there something in my hair?" I asked, raking my fingers through the clump. "I'm always getting stuff stuck in there."

Jane shook her head, like a dog shaking off water.

"You should come see me for a reading," she said. "I'm getting very strong vibrations."

"Vibrations?"

"I feel a mystery around you."

"A mystery?"

She let out a burst of manic laughter, as if I'd said something hysterically funny. "You think this is some big line, right? Some gimmick to get new clients."

"No, not at all." Though clearly she could read my mind.

"I don't do this for everybody." She handed me a business card. "You call this number. Tell Vilma I said you should come see me right away. But don't expect a discount!"

"I'd never dream of it," I said. Now I was being pursued by *two* New Age quacks. "So, are you sticking around for the second part?"

"No way. I want to get out of here. This house spooks me."

As Jane rushed from the ballroom, I slid her business card into the back pocket of my pants.

Ramir came back to my side. "Isn't she wild?"

"She wants me to come see her for a psychic reading."

"That's weird. I wonder why she didn't ask *me*."

The gong sounded again, and Dr. Bhandari spoke to the crowd from beside the double-door entrance. "Would all our first-time guests please join me here?"

17

I looked at Ramir in a panic.

"It's going to be fine," he promised and gave me a shove.

☆

Ten sacrificial lambs congregated around Dr. Bhandari. We smiled nervously at each other—all harbouring secret loathing for the friends who had brought us.

Dr. Bhandari smiled placidly. "If you would all come with me to the drawing room."

He set out through the maze of the house, and we followed our shepherd obediently. Once we'd made it back to the front hall, he opened a door to the most normal-looking room I'd seen so far. The furniture looked genuinely antique, but the fabrics were bright and contemporary—lavender and chartreuse. White walls. The ceiling was a weave of plaster diamonds with ornate cornice mouldings. Hanging in the centre was an old-fashioned gold chandelier.

A dozen white chairs from the ballroom were lined up in four short rows facing yet another fireplace. I sat at the back.

Dr. Bhandari stood before us. He closed his eyes and breathed. He opened his eyes and smiled beatifically. "The Seven Gateways to Spiritual Success are actually seven techniques of meditation, corresponding to the seven chakras of the body. Using these seven meditations, I have developed the first methodology for making dreams come true. By aligning internally, we connect with the universe and transform thoughts into physical reality." He smiled again, demonstrating his enlightenment.

"Before we discuss the details of business, I want each of you to enjoy a taste of the Seven Gateways. To begin, I would like you each to make a decree to the universe. State your dream, in the present tense, as if you are experiencing your dream right now. For example, 'I decree that I am flying my own airplane,' or 'I decree that I enjoy a loving and supportive relationship with my spouse,' or 'I decree that I possess cosmic consciousness.'"

The biggest suckers chuckled at Dr. Bhandari's cosmic in-joke.

He motioned to a woman in the front row. She hesitated a moment and cleared her throat. "I decree that I will learn to speak Spanish."

"In the present tense, please."

"I decree that I am speaking Spanish."

"Good."

Was I the only one who found that odd?

"I decree that I am living a healthy nonsmoking lifestyle."

"I decree that I am facing my fear of driving a car."

Being in the back row, I was the last to decree.

"Mitchell?" Dr. Bhandari prompted.

I was reluctant. I felt silly. My decree would sound ridiculous. But it was the reason I'd come. "I decree that I am writing an exciting blockbuster screenplay."

"Are you certain that is what you genuinely want, Mitchell? Or is there something deeper that you feel is missing from your life?"

"No, that's what I want."

Why was he picking on *my* dreams and nobody else's?

"Very good, then. Now, I would like to lead you in a brief, most basic meditation. Everyone, please, sit up straight. Uncross your legs. Hands on your knees. Close your eyes. Now simply follow your breath. Feel it coming in your nose, down your windpipe, filling your lungs, expanding your chest. Now let it go..."

He repeated himself.

Oh God, no wonder he was giving this away for free. This was Meditation 101, available in any how-to book or early-morning yoga show. Any minute he'd be swinging a pendant on a gold chain, intoning, "You're getting sleepy, ver-r-ry sle-e-epy."

I wasn't concentrating. I wasn't relaxing. I was thinking about how much money Ramir was wasting on this overprocessed spiritual pabulum. And how there's no way he'd listen to any serious critique. I felt worried about him all over again.

I opened my eyes and looked around at my fellow neophytes, all with eyes closed. Dr. Bhandari's eyes were closed as well, the model of peaceful enlightenment. I gazed around the lavishly

decorated room. Clearly, this house had cost a fortune. A lot of
people must have walked through the Gateways to pay for all
these antiques.

I wondered about the home's previous owners—the decades
of WASPy Rosedale matrons sitting in this very room for afternoon tea parties. How bewildered they'd have been if they'd
known someday people would be sitting in the same room discussing chakras.

I looked at the ceiling and examined the chunky gold chandelier—the kind with five arms, each holding a glass dish. Four
arms held white dishes with stripes, but the fifth dish was decorated with a floral pattern.

Dr. Bhandari caught me gazing around. He made a gentle
motion with his hand, bringing his fingers down over his eyes,
indicating that I should shut mine.

So I obeyed and followed the rest of his instructions. Breathe.
Breathe. Breathe.

CUT TO:

INTERIOR. DARK ROOM—NIGHT

Looking up at the fine crack of light at the top of a
door frame. From the angle, the viewer must be lying
down. Restless camera motions. The sound of heavy,
rapid breathing.

A TALL FIGURE steps into frame, looming above. The
room is so dark, the TALL FIGURE's face can't be seen.

A low grunting sound.

The TALL FIGURE bends forward, swiftly lowering a
hand.

The camera jerks and everything goes black.

CUT TO:

My head snapped up.

Everyone in the room was staring at me.

I could only have been asleep for a moment.

"Was I snoring?" I asked no one in particular.

"You grunted," a revolted woman informed me.

Dr. Bhandari stood at the front of the room, eyeing me with an expression of concern. "Are you all right, Mitchell?"

"I had a dream."

"Dreams are often the voice of the subconscious mind, responding to what we decree. Was the dream related to your decree?"

I thought about what I'd seen. "No. No, I don't think so."

"Would you like to tell us your dream?"

"Um, I don't think I remember it."

Dr. Bhandari nodded patiently. "See if it comes back to you in a moment." And he moved on to somebody else.

Of course, I remembered the dream perfectly. I just felt too stupid to talk about it. It was so odd. Like a flashback scene in a horror movie.

I wanted to get up and leave. But Ramir would never forgive me for being so rude. And I didn't want to walk home by myself in the rain.

Still, something about Dr. Bhandari definitely made me uneasy. The whole place gave me the creeps.

Then I remembered what Jane Choy had said about feeling a mystery around me. And what Dr. Bhandari had said about why the meeting tonight would be so powerful: *Everyone receives precisely what he has come for.*

And I started to wonder if I might have the makings of a screenplay after all...

SATURDAY, OCTOBER 10

First thing this morning, I called Ingrid and gave her a full report on the cult meeting.

"All the way home, Ramir kept trying to convince me I should join."

"But you didn't."

"Of course I didn't."

"At least you weren't brainwashed."

"Would I know it if I was?"

"You seem normal enough to me, Mitchell. This is going to sound horrible and selfish, but all I can think is that now that you've gone to a meeting, Ramir's going to be after *me* even more."

"Be afraid. Be very afraid. He was talking about the big gala concert, and he said he wants you to paint banners to hang around the stage."

Ing wailed plaintively.

"And then there was Gabriella Hartman's crazy psychic…"

"Have you decided if you're going to call her?"

"I don't like the idea of anybody reading my mind. I have a hard enough time doing it myself."

"I just hope Ramir gets over this New Age phase soon."

"He seems pretty serious about it. He thinks it's doing him a lot of good." I didn't think I should repeat what he'd confided about almost getting fired.

"Anyway, Mitchell, can you come over this morning? I want to take some Polaroids of you so I can get started on the next painting."

"How about this afternoon? I should see if I can get some work done first."

"You have an idea for a script?"

"Possibly. Knock on wood. Because I think this might be the big one."

☆

I spent two hours plotting out my brilliant new screenplay idea. A mystery about a famous TV star who gets sucked into a bizarre New Age cult. During his initiation ceremony, he unwittingly participates in a human sacrifice. Which creates a serious dilemma. Should he obey his new spiritual doctrine? Or should he go to the police and risk becoming a human sacrifice himself? The big climax happens when the TV star rescues his new girlfriend just as she's about to have her heart removed. A mysterious tall figure is reaching down from above—just like in my weird little dream.

Then I came to my senses and realized that Ramir would cut out *my* heart if I wrote anything remotely like that.

Cult exposés are overdone anyway.

For a while I poked at another story—about a famous TV psychic who foresees the grisly death of her sexy new boyfriend. Can she wield her psychic abilities to rescue him from the deadly hands of fate? I could interview the psychic Jane Choy for research.

Then I realized the plot was too similar to *Eyes of Laura Mars*. So I tossed the idea into my ever-thickening reject file.

Stuck again.

I stared at my orange walls and felt increasingly oppressed.

Last year, in anticipation of my imminent fame and fortune as a novelist and screenwriter, I left my cockroach-infested hovel above a Hungarian schnitzel house and moved to this luxury high-rise.

My new place is a one-room rectangular box, almost identical in layout to my previous apartment, except now I'm on the 16th floor, and I have a balcony and an actual kitchen. Sometimes I wonder about the wisdom of my decision. I pay more than twice as much in rent, and I still sleep on a pullout couch.

Initially, the walls were a pleasant shade of ecru—otherwise known as apartment beige. But after Ben dumped me, I decided I needed to make some major changes to reflect my exciting new bachelor lifestyle. I went to the paint store on a whim and immediately picked a sophisticated shade of terra cotta.

When I unveiled my weekend of sweat and toil to my neighbour down the hall—Cortland McPhee, who's a famous interior designer—he described the colour as rotten pumpkin. He said that with all my black furniture, it looks as though I'm hosting a perpetual Halloween party.

I'm planning to repaint. But not until after I've finished my month of writing. By then maybe I'll have come up with such a brilliant screenplay, I can move to Hollywood and leave some other poor fool to try to cover over the orange.

SATURDAY, OCTOBER 10
—LATER—

At 3 o'clock I headed out to Ingrid's—stopping to check my mailbox and lingering a moment to savour the lobby of my apartment building. With its dark wood paneling and bold modern furnishings, it looks more like a hotel lobby. And I've always had a weakness for hotels.

Otherwise, the building is just a big brown slab from the 1970s—known as a popular address for people in transition. Working in town temporarily. Renovating the family mansion. Divorcing. Dying.

The location is another key advantage. On prestigious Prince Arthur Avenue—just a block north of Bloor Street—right between the funky artsy area where I used to live and the chic designer area to which I aspire.

So all in all, it feels like a good transition place for me too.

But today I headed back to my old neighbourhood—the stretch of Bloor between Spadina and Bathurst—a hippie mixture of coffee bars and Hungarian restaurants, health-food stores, and third-world knickknacks.

About a month after I left the strip, my friend Ingrid Iversen moved in—almost right across the street from the coffee shop where she used to work. Her doorway is squeezed between a dry cleaner and a card shop. The ultimate in convenience for removing stains and sending thank-you notes.

I pressed Ing's buzzer and waited—gazing in the front window of The Paper Gallery. On display was a row of eight painting easels, showcasing an array of kitschy, handmade greeting cards. Petite black-velvet paintings of sad clowns, bullfighters, and Elvis Presley.

Daphne, the store's owner, was lackadaisically arranging cards in one of the wall racks. No customers at the moment. I knocked on the glass, and she gave me a perky little-girl wave—a shoestring of red licorice dangling from her mouth.

Finally, Ingrid buzzed open the electric door lock, and I entered the dim corridor, skirting around the staircase that leads to the two levels of apartments above. At the back of the ground floor is Ingrid's place. The door was unlocked, so I stepped directly into her kitchen.

"It's me!" I called.

"Hi, Mitchell," Ingrid said, rushing toward me. She's eccentrically lovely with delicate birdlike features and an unruly pile of artificially coloured red hair pinned atop her head. She gave me a hug, and I got caught in her big white work shirt.

"I'm still spinning," she said. "I just got off the phone with Geoffrey Abrams." Her Toronto art dealer. "We were talking about the show in Germany."

"No wonder you're spinning."

"It turns out the dealer from Berlin is going to be in town next Friday. They want to come here for a meeting to choose the pieces for the show."

"They're picking them already?"

"It's actually sort of late to put together the catalogue. And they decided on the date for the opening—Saturday, February 11th."

"Eva Gabor's birthday."

"How do you remember that?"

"It's a gift," I shrugged.

"She was always my favourite on *Green Acres,* so maybe it's a good omen. You have to make sure you can come, Mitchell."

My heart fluttered. It'd be so thrilling, witnessing the international art scene firsthand. Exploring Germany. Exploring Germans. But my burst of excitement was immediately tempered by the reality of my recent firing from *Five Fun Fish.* "I have to figure out if I can afford it."

"You have to. I'd be a mess without you and Ramir there."

"You'll be great no matter what."

Ingrid's art career has been on a steady ascent for the last two years. She's had two solo shows in Toronto and her work's been in three group shows in New York. And now she's preparing for her solo European debut—her chance to establish an international reputation.

"Do you want to see the new painting? I just finished it last night."

She led me back through the apartment. The place was originally built as an auto-body shop, and it still bears a distinct resemblance to a two-car garage. It's a concrete-block box, painted white, with a band of windows running along the roofline. She's divided the loft-like space into four quadrants: for eating, living, sleeping, and painting (with the bathroom tucked in the corner of sleeping).

Her latest creation was leaning against the far wall in the painting quadrant—where a garage door to the back lane had been bricked over and whitewashed. The painting showed the back of a naked woman, who was painting a wildly abstract canvas of a nude man.

"It's me and Pierre," she said. Her ex-husband, recently back in her life. "It's supposed to represent the new us."

"The *nude* us," I said. "It's beautiful."

Her paintings are all elegant swirls when you first look at them. Then, after a moment, the short, curving brushstrokes coalesce into incredibly detailed portraits. I pointed to the rectangular mini-canvas—contrasting the swirls with its violent hard-edged lines of colour. "I really like the little painting you're doing in the painting."

"It's weird, isn't it? I don't know how it happened. It just sort of came out in a burst."

I examined the swirly part of the canvas more closely. "It's a bit blurry there around Pierre's middle."

"He asked me to protect his privacy. Not that he has anything to be ashamed of."

"I never said he did."

"He wouldn't let me take a Polaroid of him without any clothes, so he had to pose for me every time." She grinned naughtily. "Which means I didn't make very fast progress."

"Mixing business with pleasure?"

"Trying. He's been working a lot of overtime at his new job. His boss asked him to go in today, even though it's Saturday."

"I guess that gives you more time in the studio."

"But it's nice having him around—being able to talk to him about what I'm working on." She scrunched up her nose. "Sometimes when I look at him, it's hard to believe there were all those years when we didn't even speak to each other."

Four years, to be precise.

Ingrid Iversen and Pierre Belanger first met at the Ontario College of Art. Both aspiring painters, they got married when they were both 24. Then Pierre had an affair with a former professor, and Ingrid ended up divorced and alone at 26. (Enter me and Ramir.) Pierre moved to Paris, then New York, where he shifted out of painting into advertising. He came back to Toronto two months ago to start work at a big graphic-design firm.

"So it's getting serious?"

"It could be. I don't know." She pulled at her hair like a mad-woman. "It's too much to even think about."

There was a rapid-fire knock on Ing's door in the kitchen, and Daphne from the card shop came busting in. Daphne looks like a street urchin with bleached-out pixie-cut hair and Egyptian-style eye makeup. Thick black eyeliner flares out to her temples.

"I'm so excited! I had to tell you right away. I sold your first Human Bean card!"

"Which one?"

"The purple girl blowing out the yellow birthday cake."

"You didn't tell me you were making Human Bean cards," I said.

Ing invented the Human Beans back when she was working at the coffee shop. They're manic squiggly-lined cartoon characters with heads in the shape of giant coffee beans.

"I just did about a dozen to see how they go."

"Remember how I always used to say you should put them on greeting cards?"

"I think they'll be a big hit," Daphne said with her chronic hyperenthusiasm.

"I hope so," Ing said. But selling a few cards wasn't of quite the same magnitude as establishing an international art career.

"Do you two want some candy?" Daphne thrust forward a clear plastic bag bulging with multicoloured jelly worms and licorice babies, sour soothers, and chewable denture plates.

I stared into the sack of unhealthy delights. "You even have those big red feet."

"They're from Sugar Mountain. I love that store."

I put a foot in my mouth. Ingrid took a single kernel of candy corn.

"Do you make cards too, Mitchell?"

"I limit my artistic humiliation to writing."

"Excuse him," Ing said. "He's having some writer's block about his new screenplay."

"I'm not talented at anything," Daphne said proudly. "But I'm a really great fan. Anyway, I'd better get back to the store in case I get another customer."

Daphne dashed out.

"Does she ever eat anything other than candy?" I wondered.

"Once I saw her with a date square."

"Her metabolism must be even faster than mine. Do you think her store's doing OK?"

"Not very well from what I can see. I think her father helps her out. He's a dentist, believe it or not. So are you ready to get to work?"

"Can I keep my clothes on?"

Within seconds, I was leaning against the wall with my arms stretched out to either side and my head thrown back as if I was about to be hit by a bus.

"You look perfect, Mitchell. But would you mind just opening your eyes a bit wider. Like you're surprised. A little more. Like you're really stunned."

"I can tell this is going to be very flattering."

"Just let me get the lighting right."

The concept of the painting is that I'm standing in front of a pull-down classroom-style movie screen, while a beam of light points at me from an old-fashioned movie projector. Ing was adjusting the beam to achieve the appropriate skin-tone effects.

"Am I supposed to look like a deer caught in the headlights?"

"I shouldn't have even told you what I was doing."

"Maybe you're trying to say I've been run over by the movie industry. Hollywood roadkill."

"Don't be ridiculous, Mitchell. I'm just using you as a model. You used me in your novel and I never complained about all the stuff you made up about me."

"I never made up anything about you. Your parts were total nonfiction."

"Well, my paintings are total fiction. Could you keep your arms up and stay still?"

As Ingrid dealt with technicalities, I listened to the Jane Siberry CD playing in the background and moved just my eyes. The room was overwhelmed with canvases ready for Berlin. Nearly 40 to choose from, even though they only need 18 for the show. Some were hanging on the walls, more were leaning in six-deep stacks. It fascinates me to see how Ingrid's painting style has evolved, growing more confident and sophisticated. Lately, she's been focusing on portraits—of her mother, her sister, her nieces, Ramir, me sitting on the dock at a cottage the three of us rented last summer.

She snapped the camera, pulled out the undeveloped photo, and then immediately began loading more film. "How'd your new script go this morning?"

"I ended up ditching it."

"No wonder you're so frustrated. Do you at least have a direction you're interested in, or a character, or some kind of theme?"

"The other day I was reading this screenwriting book that talked about the five essential ingredients you need if you want to write a commercial hit." I counted them off on my fingers. "Sex, murder, and rich people are the top three. Celebrities and the supernatural are always good if you can squeeze them in."

"So you just need a story that has all five."

"That's what I've been trying to come up with."

"You could always write a sequel to *Hell Hole*."

"Sequels are too derivative."

"I know it doesn't have any sex and murder, but what about that idea you told me about a few months ago? The quirky love story. About the office temp and the bike courier."

"I want to stay away from all that quirky, ironic stuff. It's not commercial enough to make any money, and it's not serious enough to get any artistic respect. That's why I need to go mainstream."

"You can't just *decide* that kind of thing, Mitchell," Ing said. "You have to write from your heart."

"I've written three scripts from my heart, and not one has gotten me anywhere."

"You could be one of those writers who doesn't make it big until your tenth."

"I can't wait that long. If I write another script nobody wants, I might as well quit and get a job in some corporate communications department."

"It won't come to that," Ing said. "You haven't even reached your peak."

"What if I've already passed my peak? What if it was all a fluke in the first place?"

Ingrid pursed her lips and shook her head. "You can't get away with playing the martyr with *me*, Mitchell. We both know you're not giving up."

We heard the kitchen door open again, and Pierre came in, carrying full plastic grocery store bags in each hand. "Hey there," he said, and Ingrid rushed over to greet him.

He's handsome, I have to admit that. Tall and dark with a noble Québécois nose and a sexy little goatee.

"Hi, Mitchell."

He dumped the bags, and he and Ingrid did their elbows-on-each-other's-shoulders kissing ritual. I looked away to give them privacy.

I still feel slightly peculiar about Ingrid having this new man in her life. Even though technically he's been around longer than I have. I stared at *The New Us* and wondered how different my relationship with Ingrid might become if she and Pierre actually

31

do get married again. She's always talked about having kids. Everything would change after that.

"At least they didn't make you work late," Ing said.

"But they want me to go in tomorrow. There's a big deadline on Monday."

"I thought we were going to that play tomorrow afternoon."

"Maybe we can go next week," Pierre said, reaching into a shopping bag.

"OK. Fine with me," Ing said lightly.

"I stopped by St. Lawrence Market and bought salmon. I thought I'd make dinner."

"Great."

It felt odd—witnessing coupledom's daily balance of compromises and rewards. I thought about Ben. But I shouldn't be so jealous. "I should get going," I said, "let you two catch up."

"Why don't you stay and eat with us, Mitchell?" Ing said. "I'm sure there'll be enough."

"Salmon always gives me indigestion."

"Can you hold on a minute, though? I want to take one more shot."

I returned to my ludicrous pose by the wall, while Pierre watched with amusement. Ingrid moved the light a few inches to the right. Then she brought over another lamp from the corner.

"So do you like the design firm where you're working?" I asked. I always try to act casual and chummy with Pierre.

"I thought it'd be more interesting than it's turning out to be. One of the big clients is a bank, so this weekend we're designing five different versions of the same brochure. Very boring. But we'll see."

"They're nice people, though," Ing said. "Last night we went out with a bunch of them from his office. We played pool. I actually beat Pierre."

"And we won't let that happen again," he said, redolent with secret romantic teasing.

I looked away and noticed one of Pierre's paintings hanging on the wall near the kitchen. A city street in Paris. The material of millions of clichéd canvases sold on French sidewalks. But his version was stark and modern, black and white.

I motioned to it. "I really like that street scene."

"That one's really old. I haven't painted anything in over a year."

"Daphne asked Pierre to make some cards too," Ing said. "I think you should try it. It'd be a good way to get yourself back into painting."

"Maybe I will. Give you some competition." He smiled at her with that same teasing intimacy. "Did you see the painting she did of us?" Pierre put his arm around Ingrid again and gave her a gentle squeeze. "It's great, isn't it? I've always been her biggest fan."

I always thought that was me.

"I think your right arm was up a bit, Mitchell. And put your right foot forward."

"It sounds like we're doing the hokey-pokey," I said. But Pierre didn't notice that I'd made a joke. Even though it was a bad joke, I admit. I stretched my mouth wider and looked my most stunned.

She clicked. "Got it! That's going to be the best one."

I dropped my arms and resumed normalcy immediately. "I should get going."

"Have a good night, Mitchell," Pierre said, busy putting away the groceries. "Nice to see you."

Ing walked me out to the door to the street. "Thanks for being so patient, Mitchell."

"Just make the painting of me brilliant, OK? I want to be the star of Berlin."

"I'll do my best." She kissed me on the cheek. "I hope it didn't sound like I was lecturing you before. You'll come up with the right story. Just take it easy on yourself, OK?"

SUNDAY, OCTOBER 11

"What do you think of this one?"

With an elegant finger, Cortland McPhee pushed an 8-by-10 photograph across my dining table. "We have to show something of the banquet hall, and this is the best picture I have in the file."

I stared at the photograph. The room belonged in a castle. It was huge—glowing with burnished wood and gold filigree. An impossibly long table was laid with 20 elaborate place settings. A rather absurd contrast to my plain black IKEA furnishings. "It's gorgeous," I said. "Like something out of *Citizen Kane*."

Cortland took the compliment in stride and lit another cigarette. "It's a bit heavy-handed, I suppose, but I was evoking the mood of the Italian Renaissance."

"Why would they want an Italian palazzo in the middle of the Caribbean?"

"Bizarre, I agree. But Ned Montague always said he was a modern-day Renaissance man. So I gave him a Renaissance house."

Cortland himself looks as though he's been transplanted from another era. He's somewhere in his late 50s—rail-thin with thick silver hair swept back from his forehead in a flawless swoop. He wears perfectly cut British shirts and vests that you'd swear he purchased from the *Brideshead Revisited* mail-order catalogue.

"The Montagues were my first major clients. I'd worked for years under other designers. But they were the first to have faith in me on my own."

On my laptop computer, I took Cortland's dictation that "the ceiling is based on a 16th-century ceiling in the Palazzo Gonzaga in Mantua" and that "three 16th-century tapestries adorn the walls." As Cortland flipped through his folder of photos and slides on the house, I quickly rearranged the notes into a poetic photo caption appropriate for a $75 coffee-table book. The tome is titled *Life of Beauty: The Palatial Home Designs of Cortland McPhee*.

Cortland and I met four months ago when he moved into the apartment at the far end of the hall. We started chatting one day at the elevator and, after mentioning that he was off to a doctor's appointment, he casually added that he was dying of a brain tumour. Moving to this high-rise rental was part of his grand plan to simplify his life before his death. He'd sold his elegant Yorkville townhouse to clear away some bad investments, updated his will, and prearranged his funeral.

Immediately upon learning that I'm a writer, he offered to pay me $40 an hour to help him finish his book as quickly as possible. At first I was skeptical, wondering if he was just a washed-up dreamer (because I've worked for enough of those) or if he was secretly looking for sexual favours. Then he showed me the publishing contract, his grandly decorated apartment, as well as the carefully organized file drawers full of pictures of his work. And he increased the hourly rate to $50. So I said yes.

And the book is genuinely fascinating. It's a collection of lavish photographs showcasing 24 extraordinary mansions and castles catering to the rich and famous of Toronto and Chicago, Switzerland and Saudi Arabia, California and the Caribbean.

Today we were working on a chapter about the 10-bedroom, 10-bathroom Montague House, located on a posh strip of beach just north of Bridgetown, Barbados.

Cortland pulled another 8-by-10 photograph from his file folder. "We'll label this one 'Illustration 12-10. The terrace.'"

"'The magnificent terrace,'" I elaborated as I typed into my laptop.

Cortland pensively dragged on a cigarette and resumed dictation: "'The line of seven arches creates a sense of control and symmetry in vivid contrast to the lush vegetation that surrounds.' Did you catch all that?"

"Just give me a second." I finished keying it in, then went back to repair my typos.

"You can't see it in this shot, but the swimming pool is right there in front of the terrace, and beyond that is the sea—stunning turquoise. Unfortunately, the whole enterprise was so costly it nearly bankrupted the dear Montagues. They run it as a guest-house now just to pay for the upkeep."

"It must be an amazing place."

Cortland blew an elegant smoke ring. "I finished that house in 1979. That was when I was at my peak—1978 to 1988. Of course, I was always very good before that and after that. But those 10 years were when I was at my very best."

"Do you want me to mention that in the introduction?"

"Let people figure it out for themselves." Abruptly, Cortland snatched up my wineglass. "You, my dear, need more Merlot." He always brings a bottle of wine to our writing sessions. He fussed about in my kitchen. "In the dining-room section, you should make sure to mention the table. Quite a fabulous piece. I picked it up from a dealer friend in London. A refectory table, walnut, from northern Italy, mid-16th century. The chairs are 17th-century. Beautiful things with intarsia decoration—"

"What's *intarsia*?"

"Mosaic woodwork. Very Italian Renaissance."

I typed "intarsia" and yawned discreetly.

"Bored with me already?" Cortland asked.

"I was up later than usual last night."

"Touring the baths? The discos?"

"Nothing that fun. I was catching up on my diary. I've had a very full couple of days."

"All work and no play…you know what they say. Are you putting me in that thing too?"

"I write down everything that happens."

"Then I suppose I should make an effort to be more interesting."

Cortland brought in the glasses of wine. His left hand trembled uncontrollably, and the goblets skittered onto the table. "Another of my delightful symptoms. Forgive me."

I grabbed a napkin and wiped up the spill so we could pretend it hadn't happened.

"I received another business call this morning," he said. "One of my society ladies, begging me to redo a guest bedroom. But I told her no, I've shut up shop."

"It's not as if you're on your deathbed." Was that in bad taste? It must have been all the wine.

"I need to devote all my energy to the book." Cortland raised his glass. "To finishing the damn thing before my memory dissipates completely."

"Your memory is perfect."

"That could change at any moment, so the doctor warns me. Of course, I've heard what some of my lady friends are saying behind my back. They think it's AIDS and I'm camouflaging it as a brain tumour. After all these years of me telling them their houses look like shit and their hair is ghastly, you'd think they'd know I'm telling the truth. In any case, a brain tumour strikes me as refreshingly original. A gay man dying of a somewhat natural cause. A nice change of pace, don't you think?"

I still find it disconcerting—Cortland's matter-of-fact approach to his own mortality. "I can't imagine what it must be like."

"Let's hope you never find out." When Cortland turned to me, his mouth was a tight line. "Have you made any headway on your script?"

"Temporarily. Then I threw it all out. Did I tell you Ramir's joined a psycho-spiritual therapy group?"

"A cult? Don't tell me you're joining it too. You're not that desperate, are you?"

"No, but I had this idea for a screenplay—about a TV star who gets involved in a cult that practices human sacrifice. It sounds stupid, I know, but it's staying with me for some reason. Maybe I *am* getting desperate."

"I know your *real* problem, Mitchell. Sexual frustration."

I smirked. "And you're going to tell me again how you've always preferred younger men?" I've learned that the best way to deal with Cortland's outrageousness is to be just as outrageous in return.

"It's true, there was a time I would have made a pass. But after that last round of radiation, I'm in far too fragile a condition. Now, how many months has it been since your boyfriend left?"

"Nearly two."

"He rode a motorcycle, didn't he? A bit on the rough side. I've always liked that sort of thing myself."

"Ben wasn't rough. Just…pragmatic."

"But you're at such an exciting age, Mitchell. The 30s are a man's best years for sexual experimentation. Everyone's over all those silly hang-ups they had in their 20s. Now they're ready to jump straight into bed. An attractive fellow like yourself, you should have them lining up at your bedroom door."

"It's not that easy. I've been monogamous for two years."

"You'll bounce back in no time. Wanton promiscuity is like riding a bicycle."

"I've never been very good at that either."

"If you're going to be having gentlemen callers, Mitchell, you really should let me do something with these walls—get rid of this overripe tangerine."

"I'm starting to like it. It feels cozy."

"You're just trying to provoke me, I know."

"Besides, I'm not getting distracted by anything until I've finished my new script. It's like you with your book." I drained the refilled glass of wine. "Cortland, can I ask you a serious question?"

"Any question that doesn't involve brain surgery is not a serious question."

I ignored his morbidity.

"You said you had that peak—those 10 years—and that was the highlight of your career. But, I mean, that was sort of a long time ago now. How did you stay motivated?"

"The show must go on," he said. "One has no choice."

"But after you were successful for a while, didn't you wonder what to do next?"

"You really are serious, aren't you?"

I nodded. "So what did you do?"

"That's the thing that nobody ever mentions about success. You work so hard to have your dreams come true, then once they do, you don't know what else to dream."

"And what if the first set of dreams hasn't turned out so well?"

"My darling, you fret about things far too much." He ruffled my hair and gave me a patient, fatherly smile. "You're just having a dry spell. We all have those. The only thing you can do is keep going. You do more of the same thing. Or you pick something else—at random perhaps. You can't think about it too much. And sooner or later, life gets interesting again and you forget all your worries. I promise you, Mitchell, once you come up with an idea for your screenplay, you'll feel much better." He tapped my computer. "But right now we must get back to work on my book. I have to guarantee my *own* immortality."

SUNDAY, OCTOBER 11
—MORE—

After Cortland and I finished the chapter on Montague House, he went home, and I felt sleepy.

I decided I should take a procrastinatory nap before taking another stab at the killer-cult idea. I collapsed on the couch and rested one of those tiny tube-like silk pillows over my eyes. The kind that's filled with lavender, promising total relaxation through aromatherapy. Mostly it makes me think I'm sniffing my grandmother's linen closet.

I felt my mind soften and go fuzzy in preparation for dozing.

CUT TO:

INTERIOR. DARK ROOM—NIGHT

Looking up at the fine crack of light at the top of a door frame. From the angle, the viewer must be lying down. Restless camera motions. The sound of heavy, rapid breathing.

A TALL FIGURE steps into frame, looming above. The room is so dark, the TALL FIGURE's face can't be seen.

A low grunting sound.

The TALL FIGURE bends forward, swiftly lowering a hand.

The camera jerks and everything goes black.

CUT TO:

I was sitting up on my couch. The eye pillow was lying on the floor. My throat was dry, my heart was pounding as if I'd been running for my life.

I'd only been asleep for a few moments. How was there time to conjure up that weird little nightmare again? It was like one of those jerky handheld-camera sequences from *The Blair Witch Project.*

Was it a murder scene? Somebody being strangled? What could it mean?

Maybe I *had* been brainwashed at Dr. Bhandari's. Or maybe it really was the beginning of a screenplay, as he'd suggested.

Not that I had any idea what to do with it.

Then I was hit with one small bit of inspiration. I went to my closet and found the pants I'd been wearing the other night. I pulled Jane Choy's business card from the back pocket.

Maybe she could explain all this. Or better yet, maybe she could look four weeks into the future and tell me the brilliant story I've already written.

MONDAY, OCTOBER 12

It was raining again.

Huddled under my umbrella, I stared up at Jane Choy's broad yellow-brick house on Palmerston Avenue. Not as spooky as Thornfield Manor, but there was still something strange about the place. Its walls were almost completely consumed by ivy. And at the peak of its roof, a single black spike pointed up to the dark and looming heavens.

The front walk leading to the house was a long puddle, so I crossed the soggy grass and climbed three steps to the old-fashioned front porch. I shook the rain from my appropriately black umbrella.

Just as I was raising my hand to knock, the door swung open.

Jane Choy was dressed once again as a garish rock 'n' roll babe. Skintight jeans and a black bustier studded with sequins.

"How did you know I was here?"

"Psychic powers," Jane Choy said, then let out a burst of hysterical laughter. "I saw you through the window." She held up a cordless telephone. "I'm booking an appointment. Go sit down. I'll be two minutes."

She led me into her high-ceilinged living room and pressed a button on the phone. "OK, I'm back."

Her decorating style was expensively multicultural. The long low couch was zebra-striped. Two armchairs were covered in red silk with gold Chinese lettering. A Hindu shrine in the corner emitted dense floral incense. And a giant fish tank—at least four feet wide—dominated the back wall.

"OK, that's good," she was saying into the phone. "If they want to go out for dinner after, we should make it Tuesday."

I stared into the aquarium, home to eight massive goldfish. A village of Japanese pagodas was submerged at the bottom.

"Kurt wants a session too? OK, I'll do him right after Goldie. Three o'clock."

Kurt Russell and Goldie Hawn?

Was she dropping famous names to impress me? Was it some

kind of con job? But she was friends with Gabriella Hartman, so it was possible she knew other celebrities.

I took a seat on the low zebra couch, my knees jutting up to my chest. On the coffee table, beside a collection of five laughing Buddhas, was a formal framed photograph of a scrawny WASP businessman in a pinstripe suit. Her husband?

Jane was still coordinating. "We're staying at the Beverly Wilshire." She then went into great detail about restaurants and reservations—Orso, Spago, The Ivy. All those famous places they always mention in *Vanity Fair*. "OK, Tuesday it is. Have a nice day." She pressed a button on the phone. "Sorry about that." She sat on one of the red silk chairs. "Vilma, my housekeeper, she usually makes my appointments. But next week my husband and I are going to L.A. for a computer convention, so I like to book all the times myself."

"That was the real Kurt and Goldie?"

She nodded vigorously. "I have lots of clients in Hollywood. They come to Toronto to make movies, then they want to see me whenever they can. I like creative people. More open. More interesting than accountants, believe you me." I wondered about the accountant-like man on her coffee table.

"It was just so weird meeting you the other night—"

"You thought I was a real nutcase. Sometimes when I get strong vibrations, I have to tell the person. Means I have a good connection, so they get a good reading. I did that one time with Charlton Heston, and he almost had me arrested."

"But what really made me want to see you is that I've had this weird dream—"

"Don't tell me anything!" Jane shook her big black hair decisively. "Otherwise you'll think I'm a big phony fake. So be honest, tell me the truth, do you believe in psychics?"

"Well, maybe with some healthy skepticism."

"Skepticism is never healthy," Jane declared. For emphasis, she adjusted the position of her bustier. "I have a saying: 'If you don't believe anything, you don't receive anything.'"

"Maybe that's my problem."

"Believing is easy. We can fix that in no time. I like to educate people. Because I'm not only a psychic, I'm a teacher. Every Tuesday afternoon I hold a psychic-training workshop."

"You can teach people?"

"Some people. It's very good to develop your psychic powers. A long time ago, psychics weren't some kind of freak-show 1-800 phone-line type thing. This was a normal way to help people. Now everybody goes to psychiatrists, but mind reading is much better because it cuts through the bullshit."

I noted her theories in case I decided to go back to my TV psychic screenplay idea.

She stood. "Come with me. I like to sit at the kitchen table. My husband says it's the only time I work in the kitchen!" She led me down a hallway to the back of the house. We passed a small jade-green room. Inside sat a giant black coffin. "Don't be scared, I'm not a vampire. That thing's my husband's sensory-deprivation tank. He gets in every night after work."

The kitchen shone with black-lacquer cabinets and red-lacquer walls. We sat at a small round table, cluttered with countless bottles of vitamins, a jar of ivory chopsticks, another telephone, and a portable tape recorder.

"Did Vilma tell you to bring a tape? She always forgets to tell people."

"I brought one. It's 60 minutes." I reached into my pocket for the blank cassette.

"When the tape runs out, your time runs out. You have the money?"

I gave her the cheque for $200, as Vilma had instructed. As thanks, Jane puckered her fuchsia lips and pretended to kiss it.

"Do you mind if I ask how your psychic ability actually works?" My instinct for research popping out. "Do you see visions? Or do thoughts just appear in your head?"

"Mostly I see pictures. I talk to you in the beginning, looking right at you. After that, I look over there on the right side of you. The pictures, they just sort of float up in the air. Then I tell you everything that's going on. I see the past, present, and future. All three at the same time. It's like each person comes in with a movie from the video store. My head is like a VCR, and I start watching the movie. Fast-forward. Rewind. That's how I do it."

"Do you ever hear voices?"

"Oh yeah, voices too. First I see pictures, then I hear noises. Sometimes smells. Sometimes I feel things. They touch me—mostly here on my arm." She pointed to her forearm. "Weird, huh? Lots of people say being psychic is a sixth sense, but I say it's all the five senses combined. By the way, the reason I'm talking so much is because I can't see your aura yet."

I looked from side to side to see if I could spot it myself. "Is that a problem?"

"Totally normal. I have to wait until I see all the colours." She was talking faster and faster—as if revving her engines. "The other thing I should tell you is sometimes my timing is off. Sometimes six months, sometimes a year. But if you ask my clients, they say I'm very accurate. Who knows, you could be the first person it doesn't work for. I'm not God, in case you thought so when I opened the door!"

I laughed obediently.

Her head jerked to the side—like a chiropractic adjustment. "OK, I can see you now. We can get started." She pressed the red button on the tape recorder. Then she squeezed her eyes shut and pressed her index finger to the centre of her forehead, as if she were pushing the play button on her mental VCR.

She opened her eyes.

"OK, I'm going to ask you 'yes' or 'no' questions only. Don't give me any more information unless there's something specific you want to know. Understand?"

"Yes."

"I'm seeing a man with a gold cross on a chain. A minister. Does that make sense?"

I thought for a moment. "Actually—no."

"He's a priest—from Ireland. An Irish priest."

"No."

"He's very upset. Angry. You know any priests?"

I scanned my life for any angry Irish priests I might be forgetting. "No, no priests."

"I'm getting this very strong. Very clear picture. Maybe a relative. Maybe he's your uncle, your grandfather?"

"My family isn't even Catholic."

"He's someplace hot. Jungle. Hill beside the ocean."

"No."

Even Jane was starting to look frustrated. "He's in a hammock. Tied up in a hammock. He's very angry. You're sure you can't remember this?"

It was starting to sound familiar.

"There's a woman with him—older woman, grey hair. Calming him down, giving him some tea."

Suddenly I could see it too. "It's *The Night of the Iguana*."

"A lizard?"

"It's a movie. From 1964. Richard Burton plays a minister."

"Richard Burton?" she said, sounding annoyed.

"I think you're describing the big climax scene from *The Night of the Iguana*. I saw it on TV last night."

"Oh shit." She let out another burst of hysterical laughter. "At the beginning sometimes I pick up crazy things—what book you're reading, what food you bought at Loblaws. I tap into the wrong part of your brain waves. Just crazy. OK, hold on."

She stared intently at my chest. Then looked to the right. "OK. I'm seeing you holding a big gun."

"Yes," I said tentatively—just to be encouraging.

"And now you're trying to fire the gun."

"I've never even touched a gun."

"You squeeze the trigger, and the gun makes a little click sound like it's empty. Like you're shooting blanks. Does that make sense?"

Shooting blanks. "Actually it does."

"OK, now I'm seeing words coming out of the gun. Lots of different words. Lots of different projects. I thought I saw a book a few seconds ago. Let me go with this. The field I see is—communications. Just say yes or no."

"Yes."

"See, I'm not some cheap phony! I get things right too." She laughed maniacally again. "I'm seeing publishing. A book. But there's something else. A TV. A big screen in a movie theatre."

"Yes." But maybe Gabriella had told her some facts about me.

"Let me look at your hand. The other one." She grabbed my right hand and turned it palm up. She pointed to a line. "OK, definitely you're a writer."

"That's true."

"But you're having trouble. You're stuck." She closed her eyes and her expression turned intense. "I see a man around you," she said. "There's going to be an important man."

"That'd be nice."

Then the telephone rang.

"Who the hell is that?" She picked up the handset, read the Caller ID screen—"My husband, late for dinner again"—and turned off the ringer.

She grabbed both my hands, palms up. "When I look at the lines here and here, I see you have a tendency to addictions. Alcohol."

"Tequila."

"You watch too much TV."

"Old movies. And The Shopping Channel."

"You've got long hands. You're tall and skinny. That means good imagination."

"That's good."

"Pale skin, dark hair. You worry too much about other people. Curly hair. You're screwy sometimes."

It was starting to feel perfectly normal that she knew every-thing about me—as if she were an old friend recounting my biography.

"Hazel eyes. I can tell by the shape of your eyebrows that you have psychic powers."

"I do?"

"Not developed. You should definitely take my psychic-training workshop." Was she going to turn this into another high-pressure sales pitch? But she kept talking. "You get visions sometimes in dreams."

"Well, like I said, I've had this weird, scary dream—"

She held up her hand in a stop sign.

"OK, I'm seeing a woman. Red hair. Friend of yours. Looks like a bird."

"That's Ingrid."

"She's working very hard. Very busy. Very happy. She's in love."

"Yes."

"But you don't like the guy."

"I wouldn't say that."

"That's why I have to say it for you. But it's the truth, right?"

"Right."

"I think she could have a family soon."

"She could?"

"Just potential. The year I was supposed to have a kid, I got those goddamn fish. OK, I'm also seeing a man. Brown skin."

"Ramir. He's on the show with Gabriella."

"You think I'm cheating? OK, this man, he thinks a lot about himself. No surprise, he's an actor. Big egomaniac."

I chuckled. "Actually, when I told him this morning that I was coming to see you, he asked me to ask if he's going to get a part in a movie soon."

"He's too cheap to book his own appointment? I don't give it away for free. But your friend's on shaky ground. Not stable. Hard to find his footing."

"I guess that's why he's seeing Dr. Bhandari."

"*Very* shaky ground. Between you and me, I don't trust that doctor guy. Gabriella thinks he's the best thing since sliced bread. But Hartman can be a real fruitcake sometimes. Don't tell her I said that. But Bhandari gives me the big creeps."

"Me too."

She looked over to my right again, staring blankly. I wondered if she'd run out of things to say. "Things are good for you in lots of ways, but you feel like a big failure."

Suddenly my eyes stung with unexpected tears. "That's true."

"How old are you?"

"I'm 30."

"Makes sense. Difficult time."

"It is?"

"From 28 to 30. Sometimes 32. In astrology, it's called the Saturn Return. The planet of Saturn returns to where it was when you were born. Transition period. Means big changes in your life. Deciding what to do. Finding your purpose."

"Can you give me some kind of advance clue?"

"You have to find out for yourself. But it makes sense that you're stuck." Jane looked into my eyes. "I see you looking for things. Like a detective."

"I've been looking around for a story to write about."

"You'll find the right story. A mystery story, like I said before."

"Where will I find it?"

"You don't have all the experiences yet. Just trust the universe, and what you need will fall in your lap."

She looked to the side of me again. "OK, next is love life. I have to ask you a personal question. You're gay, right?"

You didn't have to be psychic to figure *that* out. "True."

"The reason I ask is because I see an important man in your life."

"The same man you mentioned before?"

"Same one." She laughed again with nervous hysteria. "This sounds like a bad movie. You're going to think I'm some old gypsy woman with beads in the doorway. Crystal ball and bad breath. Because I see a tall, dark, and handsome stranger."

"That's my favourite kind."

"He's going to be very important in your future."

"Important how?"

"Lots of ways."

"Important romantically?"

"Also with work. I see a big mystery adventure. Very exciting."

"And I'm going to be meeting him soon?"

She concentrated. "I feel his energy around you. Floating over your head."

"Over my head?"

"He's coming down toward you."

The image echoed through me. "That's sort of like the dream I was trying to tell you about. I see a figure that's above me, reaching down."

"That must be what I sensed over top of you at Bhandari's house."

"That's where I had the dream the first time."

"Didn't I say you were psychic?"

I thought about the dream again. Maybe it wasn't a violent scenario. Maybe it was a sexual scenario.

"So he's a real person? How will I know who he is?"

"You'll know," she said. "When you're on the right path, the universe gives you funny coincidences. That's the way with everything. Follow the coincidences. They help to guide you."

"So I'm going to meet him by accident?"

"Nothing is an accident. The man is very good for you, Mitchell. He'll help you find the right story. You'll be shooting your big gun in no time."

"When someone says 'tall, dark, and handsome,' do you think it means dark hair or dark skin or dark eyes?"

"I think it can be any of the above."

"I was hoping to narrow it down."

Ramir, Ingrid, and I were squeezed into our usual green-vinyl booth at the back of the Little Buda, a.k.a. Little Budapest—the restaurant above which I used to live. It's among the last of the neighbourhood's dying breed of Hungarian schnitzel houses. The decor remains gaudily Eastern European, featuring yellow garden trellises tacked with plastic grape vines.

"You know *lots* of tall, dark, and handsome men," Ramir said. "There's me, first of all." He squeezed my knee under the table.

"You're not exactly a stranger."

"Pierre's tall, dark, and handsome," Ing said.

"I don't think we'll be having an affair."

"Just checking," she said. "What about that waiter at Spiral? You've always liked him."

"*Everybody* likes him. I think that cancels it out."

"Even *you're* tall, dark, and handsome, Mitch." Ramir squeezed my knee again.

"Maybe the tall and dark hair part."

"Don't be so modest," Ing said.

Magda, our eternal waitress, delivered our traditional menu selections: three authentic Hungarian raspberry sodas, two Wiener schnitzels, and one chicken schnitzel for Ramir.

"What if the psychic meant it symbolically?" Ramir said. "Like finding the tall, dark man means getting in touch with your inner child. Or maybe it means you're supposed to start seeing Dr. Bhandari. He's tall, dark, and handsome."

"Does he give you commissions or something?"

"I just believe in what he's teaching."

"So is Dr. Bhandari gay or what?" Ing asked.

"He's married, but I've never met his wife. She's studying in India."

"Sounds appropriately mysterious," Ing said, tapping the straw into her glass of raspberry soda.

"But what's so bizarre is what Jane Choy saw about the tall, dark man. It was so much like the dream I had at Dr. Bhandari's house."

"Did she have any theories?"

"She said the meditation might have opened up my psychic channels, so I was able to see into my own future." I grimaced. "I can't believe I just said that."

"You're becoming a New Age flake yourself," Ramir said with delight. "So did Jane say anything about me getting a movie this fall?"

"She said you were a shameless egomaniac."

"She didn't."

I didn't want to repeat what Jane Choy had actually said about him being on shaky ground. Nor did I want to tell Ingrid the stuff about having a family.

"She said if you want to find out more, you should book an appointment with her yourself."

"Dr. Bhandari said that's not a good idea right now. It's too distracting to focus on the future."

"You're *always* focused on the future," Ing said.

"That's one of the main reasons I'm going through the Gateways. It's a whole different approach. Because once you're in line with the universe, everything happens easily."

"Nothing happens easily," I said. "Only people who are successful already say that, because they forget how hard they worked before."

"Those are limiting beliefs," Ramir said. "If you let go of thinking that way, hard things suddenly get easier. Creativity is a mystical act. It's effortless."

"That happens sometimes," Ing said. "But not all the time."

"Is that how you're getting things organized for Gabriella Hartman's concert? Just letting it happen mystically?"

"Kevin's doing most of the coordination with the caterers and the sound equipment. That reminds me of something." Ingrid and I both knew what was coming next. "Ing, I was hoping you could paint some banners we can hang in the ballroom."

"I already warned her," I said. "You know, Ingrid's really busy too."

She nodded. "The dealer from Berlin is coming to look at all the portraits on Friday."

"We don't need the banners for three weeks, so you'll have plenty of time."

Ingrid smiled and shook her head. "I can't believe you're sucking me into this thing too." She's just as susceptible to Ramir's shameless charms as I am. "Can you imagine if the tabloids ever found out about you and Gabriella Hartman being in the Seven Gateways?"

I imagined the cover of *The National Enquirer*: "'Stars of Cult TV Show Join New Age Cult.'"

"The Seven Gateways isn't a cult," Ingrid repeated, as trained.

"They just like having high-profile converts," I said. "The Scientologists have Tom Cruise and John Travolta."

"And Isaac Hayes," Ramir added.

"The Buddhists have Richard Gere," Ing said.

"The Jehovah's Witnesses have Michael Jackson," I said, "even though they probably don't want him any more."

"Madonna was hooked on the cabala for a while," Ing added.

"I just thought of a great idea for a screenplay," I said. "It'd be about a famous TV star who joins a cult that practices human sacrifice."

I admit I was fibbing about the spontaneous creative inspiration. But I wanted to test the water about that nagging screenplay idea. And apparently the water was very chilly.

Ingrid and Ramir were both silenced.

"You're not really going to write that, are you?" Ramir asked. I could see genuine annoyance in his eyes.

"No, of course not. It was just a crazy notion."

"It might be hitting a bit too close to home," Ing said delicately.

"I mean, it's one thing when you poked fun at *me* in your book," Ramir said. "But I don't want you saying anything bad about Dr. Bhandari."

"I'm sorry. Don't worry, I'm not going to write it." I had no idea he'd be *that* sensitive.

Suddenly, Pierre was sliding into our tiny booth. Ing hadn't mentioned he was coming.

"Hope I'm not interrupting," he said.

Ingrid happily squished over against the wall.

"Great to see you." Ramir welcomed him with the complex faux blood-brother handshake they've developed.

Ingrid kissed him on the cheek. "Do you want to order some apple strudel?"

"Maybe a coffee."

"I thought you were working late."

"I had some big news. I wanted to tell you right away. I quit my job."

Ing froze. "You quit?"

"Don't worry," he grinned. "I got a new one."

"You didn't tell me you were quitting."

"I got a call this afternoon from that agency I turned down when I was looking the first time. They made me a better offer."

"That's terrific," Ramir said.

"I wish you'd told me first," Ing said.

"The new place has more interesting work. And it's $5,000 more a year."

"That's not the point." Ingrid glanced to me and Ramir. "Sorry, you two, we're being rude—we shouldn't fight in front of you."

"We're not fighting," Pierre said.

"You're discussing," said Ramir.

"It all happened two hours ago. I thought you'd be happy."

"I am, I guess." She forced herself to smile. "I just don't like surprises. I'm sure it'll be good."

It now felt safe for Ramir and me to make our congratulations.

"So what were you guys talking about before?" Pierre asked.

"Mitchell was just telling us about a psychic he went to," Ing explained, mercifully avoiding the truth.

Pierre smiled at me quizzically. "Really, Mitchell? I didn't think you were the type to believe in psychics."

"Always full of surprises," I said.

For the first time, I noticed that—with his French lilt—Pierre pronounces my name "Michelle."

Jane Choy was right. I don't like him.

TUESDAY, OCTOBER 13

No sign of a tall, dark, and handsome man at the grocery store. Or the liquor store. Or the Starbucks where I sat for two hours.

Vibrating with caffeine, I gave up and wandered home. In my apartment-building lobby by the mailboxes, I bumped into Cortland, returning from an antiques auction at Waddington's. He asked me to come over to his place for a cocktail. But I said no, I had to work.

He gave me that wry, knowing, paternal look he always gives me. Like he knew I wouldn't be very productive anyway.

Sure enough, I sat here watching TV, sipping tequila by myself.

TUESDAY, OCTOBER 13
—LATER—

I decided I should make an active effort to get in touch with the universe.

So I settled into my wing chair, a notepad on my knee, and waited for a fabulous story to drop into my lap, quickly and efficiently—just as Jane Choy had predicted.

I kept sneaking glances above my head, wondering if there really might be some spiritual force hovering around up there.

I sat and pondered.

Chanted "om-m-m" a few times.

Waited.

Then I stopped because I felt ridiculous, and I turned on The Shopping Channel.

WEDNESDAY, OCTOBER 14

This morning I scratched away at a plot about two tall, dark, and handsome gay men who rob a string of banks in Miami Beach. *Donnie and Clyde.*

Abysmal.

Then Cortland called to confirm our afternoon session of work on his book.

"Over your dry spell yet?"

"Still barren."

"I blame your colour scheme. Your brain is turning to mush from staring at all that candied yam. Why don't I treat you to lunch to give you some fresh visual stimulation? We'll go to the Courtyard Café."

"That place is way too expensive."

"We'll call it a thank-you for all your help on my magnum opus."

"I feel so at peace here," Cortland said as we stepped in the door of the Windsor Arms Hotel. "It's like travelling back in time, back to my glory days."

From the '60s to the '80s, the hotel's Courtyard Café had been the ultimate in chic for Toronto society and visiting celebrities. I always read about it in the entertainment section of the newspaper. Then, in a bizarre twist of real-estate development, the hotel was torn down and, a few years later, replaced with a new-and-improved replica—topped with a tower of million-dollar condominiums.

Cortland nodded his approval as we passed through the tiny dark lobby and entered the reincarnated Courtyard Café, aglow with flattering golden light. Buff-coloured stone walls rise three storeys, creating the effect of an Art Deco courtyard.

Cortland surveyed the restaurant's elegant arena of dark-green leather armchairs and white tablecloths. From the side of his mouth he whispered, "A particularly good day for people-watching."

Seated at our prime table beside a soaring column, Cortland ordered Bloody Marys for both of us and immediately launched into the mythic tale of a local antique dealer who was positioned at a nearby banquette.

"He just wandered into a garage sale one Saturday morning and picked up a tarnished old silver vase for $5. Then Monday morning, he took it to Christie's, and they sold it for $2 million."

I pondered the meaning of the story. "You can sweat and toil forever, then one little bit of accidental luck can change your whole life. It makes everything else seem like a waste of time."

"Wrong attitude entirely, Mitchell. If the gentleman hadn't studied antique silver all those years, he'd never have known the vase had such value."

The waiter brought our breadbasket—giving Cortland the excuse to crane his neck and scan the room once again.

"At the banquette over there, beneath that monstrous painting, you'll observe the world-renowned soprano Jeanette Peabody-Jones. I went to a party once at her condominium. The caterer cancelled at the last minute. Not a speck of food."

I reached for a breadstick. "Did I tell you Ramir's been put in charge of arranging a big party for his cult?"

"Tell him he can call me if he needs any advice."

"Tickets are $500 each. Gabriella Hartman is going to sing."

"She sings too? I've always thought she was a dreadful actress. Aging bimbo who never had the sense to retire and become a real estate agent."

"I wish you could see the house in Rosedale where they hold the cult meetings—"

A petite blonde woman was suddenly standing at the edge of our table. Her jacket had an oversize black-and-white houndstooth check that caused my eyes to cross. "You could try to be more discreet," the woman said in a pronounced Polish accent. "Everyone can see you over here, staring and gossiping."

"Ermina, darling, I didn't see you. Otherwise I would have gossiped about you first."

Cortland rose, and the two of them air-kissed with Olympic precision.

Ermina was somewhere in her late 50s, like Cortland, but there was a very girlish quality about her. She had a small frame, delicate features, and smoothly coiffed honey-blonde hair. She glittered with diamond earrings and a lavish diamond brooch. Two fingers were stacked with gold and diamond rings. (I've developed a new appreciation for jewellery since watching The Shopping Channel.)

"And who is this attractive young man?" Ermina inquired. She had a soft roll to her R's and a flirtatious twinkle in her eyes.

"Ermina Milenska, this is Mitchell Draper, a neighbour in my new apartment building. He's a very talented writer, and he's helping me with my book."

"Very convenient for you, yes?" she said, loaded with mischievous insinuation.

"I assure you my relationship with Mitchell is purely platonic," Cortland scolded, then turned back to me. "Ermina doesn't understand the word *platonic*. She doesn't feel she's been properly introduced to a man until she's pulled down his trousers."

"Oh, you're being vulgar," she said with delight. "That's not at all true."

"Married four times and counting."

"It's you who's counting," Ermina taunted back. "Every time I get married or divorced, you have a new place to decorate. More chances to send me your ridiculous bills."

"Yes, I've earned quite a sum off your head. And the key word, Mitchell, is *head*."

Ermina tittered gaily at the insult. "We should have lunch next week, yes? I'm going to New York tomorrow. Tickets to the ballet every night. But I'll call you as soon as I'm back."

After Ermina had returned to her table, Cortland shook his head with fond remembering. "We've been through a great deal together, Ermina and I. One of my oldest friends."

"I see her name in the paper all the time."

"'The Polish Princess.' She's on the board of the National Ballet and heaven knows how many charities. You could write a quite a film about her sordid love affairs. Though I'm afraid it would have to be X-rated."

"What does she—"

Suddenly, Cortland pressed his thumbs to his temples.

"Another headache?"

"All these memories must be straining my brain."

"The food should be here soon," I said. Though I wasn't sure why that would help.

"I wish they'd let you smoke in this place." Cortland sipped some water, and the pain seemed to pass. "Did I mention that I went to the hospital the other day for another MRI scan? Horrible claustrophobic thing."

"Could they tell you anything?"

"They told me a great deal, I'm afraid. I was at the doctor's this morning to hear the results. Still inoperable. Apparently, my tumour has grown from the size of a cherry to the size of a plum. Isn't it peculiar how they always compare cancer to pieces of fruit? Soon I'll have an entire Carmen Miranda headpiece growing inside my skull."

"You always hear about spontaneous remission."

"All it means for certain is that we need to hurry up and complete my book. I don't want to leave any unfinished business."

I wanted to change the subject, lighten the mood. I noticed a couple standing at the entrance, waiting to be seated. A blonde woman—on the heavy side—with a gorgeous man. Slim and elegant, wearing a navy sports coat with a gold crest. Thick black hair was brushed back from his face, finishing in crests of waves behind him. Even at a distance, I could see that his eyes were almost clear green.

"Cortland, a very tall, dark, and handsome man just came in."

Cortland perked up. "Would anyone notice if I turned?"

"You've been spinning your head every other direction."

"I knew I should have fought you for the seat facing the entrance." He spun, and when he turned back to me there was a wry bitterness in his eyes. "Congratulations, my dear, you've just spotted The Best Kept Boy in the World."

"A kept boy? You mean that guy's a prostitute?"

"Much higher class than that. Of course, I'm referring to a very long time ago, when Mr. Graham Linden enjoyed the attention of certain rich older gentlemen. I don't expect he wants anyone to remember that now."

"You knew him?"

"We met once or twice—back at the beginning of his career, when he was still in his teens. But I was never rich enough for him to take seriously. Graham was that unique species of young man whom anyone would do anything to obtain. He always told people he wanted to be a fashion designer. Then he moved to New York to become a model and lived with a string of fashion designers instead."

The maître d' guided the couple through the restaurant. I observed the man with a different appreciation. As a teenager he must have been achingly pretty. Even now there was the echo of a fresh-scrubbed English schoolboy.

Graham Linden glanced toward our table—green eyes sparkling—but he looked right through us.

"Arrogant bastard," Cortland said with a gulp of his Bloody Mary. "But he's aging well, I must say. He must be nearly 40 by now."

"That psychic I went to the other day said I was going to meet somebody tall, dark, and handsome."

"I'm afraid you're out of luck with Mr. Linden. That woman he's with is his wife."

"He got married?"

"A fellow like that has to watch out for his future."

"Maybe his wife's a lesbian, and the whole thing is a cover."

"By all reports, not. They were childhood friends. She comes from a wealthy family. Food importers. And Mr. Linden was always quite ruthlessly ambitious about maintaining his lifestyle. I heard he deserted one of his famous fashion designers on his deathbed, so he could move on to richer territory. The lover was so distraught, he expired the next day. But now, of course, Mr. and Mrs. Linden are the very picture of marital bliss. Straight out of *Town & Country* magazine."

I looked across the restaurant at them. They were chatting conspiratorially, laughing. Acting more like me and Ingrid than a typical married couple.

But he sure was tall, dark, and handsome.

Our salads were delivered. Cortland reached for a breadstick, but he didn't make any move to start eating. There was a serious look in his eyes. "Mitchell, something just dawned on me. That cult you went to in Rosedale—where Ramir is having his big party— it's not on Thornfield Road, is it?"

"Thornfield Manor. How did you know?"

"What an extraordinary coincidence." He sat back in his chair. "I hadn't put it together until now. Would you believe I actually worked on that house?"

"You worked for Dr. Bhandari?"

"No, no. The previous owners, the Donningtons. Though I did meet the doctor. He knew the family as well."

"You decorated the place?"

"Just a few rooms. And I arranged a party there. A rather catastrophic party."

"What made it a catastrophe?"

"Death at a party is always a catastrophe."

I'd been expecting another lighthearted bit of gossip. "Someone died?"

"Two actually."

"There was an accident?"

"A murder-suicide."

"During the party?"

"The host and his son. One of the most horrible nights of my life."

"And you knew them?"

He nodded tightly. "Mostly I knew the wife, Vivienne. In fact, it was Ermina over there who introduced us."

I glanced across the restaurant. Ermina Milenska was happily absorbed in conversation with an identical society matron.

"So the father killed his son during the party?"

"The other way around—or so it was determined. There was a great deal of speculation at the time."

"And it happened right there in Dr. Bhandari's house?"

"On the third floor. And in the back garden. That's where the son landed when he jumped out the window. Impaled on a fence."

"Oh my God. Why didn't you tell me about this before?"

"I've only known you a few months, my dear. And the Donningtons are not normally my favourite topic of conversation."

I tried to absorb all this, to put the details together. "Ramir made it sound like Dr. Bhandari has lived in that house for a long time. When did it happen?"

"The summer of 1979, I think it was. Hard to believe it was so long ago. It was written up in all the papers. They even did a spread in *Maclean's* magazine."

"I guess I was too young to notice," I said. "You know, Cortland, this might make a good story for my screenplay."

He stared off into the distance for a moment. "Do you think so?"

"Now you definitely have to tell me all the details."

Cortland clasped his hands for his moment, then rested them on his lap. "Well, I'd met Vivienne about a year earlier. I did some decorating for her. Two or three rooms on the main floor. Such a marvelous house to work on."

"It looks like it's straight out of a horror movie."

"Bite your tongue. It's classic Victorian Gothic. One of the only houses in Rosedale with a ballroom. Vivienne had impeccable taste. She wanted all the furniture precise to the period. Of course, the family had buckets of money. Her husband was Jackson Donnington. He owned a very lucrative printing company. And they had two children: a daughter who was 12, I think, and the son, who was about 17."

"The dead one?"

"The dead one," Cortland nodded. "Normally, I never arranged parties. But Vivienne asked me to take charge of it as a favour for their 20th anniversary. She and her husband had spent their honeymoon in Hawaii, so they wanted a tropical theme. Tasteful tropical, of course. And I made the house beautiful beyond belief, if I do say so myself. Orchids and bougainvillea everywhere. Rich reds and yellows and oranges against all that dark wood. Vivienne was thrilled. But I suppose the first sign that things might go wrong was when we were putting up the final decorations in the drawing room—"

"The room that's just inside the front door?"

"Exactly."

"That's where I did the meditation session with Dr. Bhandari the other night."

"Well, the son came into the room wearing his tuxedo for the party. Trevor was his name, if I recall. Just a teenager, but he'd already been causing a lot of trouble. Always fighting with his mother. Terrible temper. They decided afterward he was schizophrenic. In any case, he was carrying his tennis racquet, and he said he was going out to play. So I suggested quite casually that he should change his clothes. Suddenly, he was yelling at me, and he threw his tennis racquet. Viciously. Fortunately, it missed me, but it hit the chandelier. He broke one of the glass dishes."

"This is so weird, Cortland. I noticed that one of them was different."

"The chandelier's still there? Oh good. It was one of the original gaslights. Converted to electricity, of course."

"This whole thing is getting too creepy. So what happened next?"

"The maid swept up the broken glass, and Vivienne sent the boy up to his little garret on the top floor. She always tried to play tough with him, though she loved him dearly. Then the party began. Over 300 guests. Everyone having a marvelous time. Or so it seemed. According to the police, at some point during the night, Jackson went upstairs to check on the boy. And Trevor stabbed him. Then, when he realized what he'd done, he threw himself out the window."

"No wonder the party was a catastrophe."

"But nobody knew what had happened right away."

"The party just went on?"

"Vivienne noticed that Jackson wasn't around. She thought that was odd, but she carried on being the hostess. Then, at about one in the morning, she went upstairs to look for him. He wasn't in their bedroom, so she went up to Trevor's room. And there was

Jackson, lying in a puddle of blood on the floor. The window was broken, so she looked out and there was her son, stuck on the wrought-iron fence that went round the swimming pool. The poor woman, she started screaming uncontrollably. You could hear the sound all through the house. Everyone froze on the spot."

"I'm getting goose bumps just thinking about it."

"You can only imagine how horrible it was to be there. Then the police arrived and took charge of things. And all the guests began coming up with their own theories."

"You mean, people didn't think Trevor did it?"

"Because Trevor and his father were so close, you see. Jackson may not have been the most likable man to other people, but he and his son got along famously. Vivienne always played the disciplinarian and Jackson was the hero. So no one could believe Trevor would kill his father."

"That's the reason people doubted he did it?"

"And then there was a peculiar situation with the knife."

"What peculiar situation?"

"They found it the next morning in the swimming pool below the boy's window, but there weren't any fingerprints. There was some question as to whether the chlorine in the pool could have washed them off, or whether the handle had been wiped clean intentionally."

"So somebody else might have killed them and made it look like a murder-suicide?"

"I can see your screenwriter's mind at work. At first they suspected Jackson's business partner. The two of them had had a terrible row during the party. But then they found Trevor's fingerprints on a chair he'd thrown, and they decided it must have been him after all. That's how things settled in the end."

I started to put the rest of the facts together. "And Dr. Bhandari knew the Donningtons too?"

"He was Vivienne's psychiatrist. Trevor's as well. Vivienne was always interested in that spiritual business. I never paid much attention."

"So was Dr. Bhandari at the party?"

"I don't recall for certain, but I believe he was."

"And he bought the house from them afterward?"

"Vivienne was desperate to get rid of the place. He bought it dirt cheap, furnishings included."

"Then that's all the Donningtons' furniture too?"

"I haven't been back since, but I would presume so. It was all excellent quality."

"How bizarre."

"A short while after, Vivienne remarried. Then she and her second husband were killed in a car crash about 10 years ago."

My imagination was reeling. "Cortland, this could make a really good movie."

"You could turn it into one of those true-crime stories that are always so popular."

"I'm not exactly an investigative journalist. I was thinking I'd fictionalize the whole thing."

"Truth is stranger than fiction, they say. You could be the next Norman Mailer or Truman Capote." Cortland picked up his knife and fork. "But Mitchell, do you mind if we change the subject to something more appetizing? I should eat a few morsels before I grow faint."

I pretended to be listening as Cortland gossiped about Ermina Milenska's legion of young lovers in Paris and Monte Carlo. But really I was thinking about the Donningtons and the tall, dark, and handsome Dr. Bhandari and the strange dream I'd had in Thornfield Manor—and how the universe had dropped all these mysterious coincidences so conveniently into my lap.

WEDNESDAY, OCTOBER 14
—LATER—

I called Ramir.

"Can I take you out for a drink?"

"Why do you sound so weird?"

"I don't sound weird."

"What do you want to talk about?"

"I'll tell you when I see you. Is 8 o'clock OK?"

I arrived at Byzantium at 8:10, hoping Ramir would be there ahead of me, because I hate being in gay bars by myself. Even though it was in a gay bar that I'd met Ben, and I kept telling myself that maybe lightning could strike twice.

In the social stratosphere of Toronto gay bars—all clustered around the intersection of Church and Wellesley—Byzantium caters to the A-list. It's a long maroon hallway of a room with an elegant sliver of red granite serving as the bar. The space for promenading from front to back is so narrow that all the gym-hewn patrons are forced to press tightly against one another, providing a discreet opportunity to assess each others' pecs and lats.

Since my ectomorphic frame doesn't even possess these muscle groups, I took my stool quickly and ordered a Rob Roy to quell my anxiety.

Of course, the Donnington murder story didn't really have anything to do with Ramir's cult. Dr. Bhandari was just a minor player in the tale—easily replaced or removed altogether. I could change all the details. Turn his character into a female. Swedish instead of Indian. A social worker instead of a psychiatrist. No one would ever guess the connection.

But what if Ramir objected to the story on principle?

I'd have a hard time letting go of it—after the universe had practically forced it on me.

And especially since the Donnington story includes four of the five essential ingredients for a commercial screenplay. Celebrities don't really fit. But it's got murder. Rich people. I can probably squeeze in some sex pretty easily. And as for the supernatural, I've got the wife's interest in spiritual teachings. Even if they're not Dr. Bhandari's. Definitely they're not Dr. Bhandari's.

Then Ramir appeared, striding in the door—confident and gorgeous as always.

"Greetings from KerrZavia."

"Greetings from Earth."

He gave me a quick massage-like squeeze on the shoulders from behind, then a peck on the lips.

"The Seven Gateways are starting to work. My agent just set up a big movie audition for next week."

"Something good?"

"The director is Stephen Swann."

"Should I know who that is?"

"El Dorado? Trust me, he's great. It's a Western, shooting in Alberta. I'd play a Mexican bandit, so it's another ethnic thing. But it's supposed to be a really strong script."

I raised my near-empty glass. "Break both legs."

Ramir ordered a cranberry and soda—since Dr. Bhandari requires him to abstain from alcohol—and a plate of exotic Mediterranean dips. I requested another Rob Roy.

"So what's your big secret? Did you meet your tall, dark, and handsome stranger?"

"Not yet. I don't think. But you won't believe the story Cortland told me."

And I revealed the murderous history of Thornfield Manor—including a fleeting mention of Dr. Bhandari's distant, insignificant relationship to the family.

Ramir immediately threw his drink in my face and shouted, "I forbid you to write anything that might even remotely tarnish the reputation of my guru."

No, he didn't do that.

Instead, he shook his head in disbelief. "I can't believe I never heard all that stuff."

"You can understand why Dr. Bhandari wouldn't mention it. A murder-suicide isn't very conducive to an atmosphere of spiritual peace."

"Dr. Bhandari doesn't think like that. He believes in dealing with everything right up front. I'll have to ask him about it."

"Of course, I'm going to fictionalize all the important details. Change the people's names. Move the story to Chicago—because it's more commercial if it's in the States anyway. And I'm going to make the psychiatrist totally different. A Swedish female social worker."

"Keep him the way he is. Then I can play his part in the movie."

That sounded encouraging. "It's just that I wouldn't want you to think I'm trying to libel the Seven Gateways or Dr. Bhandari."

Ramir laughed at the ridiculousness of my notion. "It's not like Dr. Bhandari killed them himself. It's not like that last idea you had."

"That was just a joke."

"But this sounds great, Mitch. It's really got potential."

I sipped my Rob Roy, giddy with satisfaction that I had Ramir's blessing. Or maybe it was just the alcohol.

A cute black guy passed behind us and strategically pressed his rock-hard abs against Ramir's back.

"Why don't you follow him to the toilet and give him your phone number?"

"Why would I do something like that?"

"That's what you did the last time we were here."

"Distant memory. Anyway, not tonight."

"Why not tonight?"

"I'm taking a break."

"What kind of a break?"

"From sex."

"Isn't that physically impossible?"

"Mitch, I've had a lot of sex, so taking a break for a few weeks is no big deal."

"This isn't one of the Gateways, is it? They're not trying to cure you of homosexuality, are they? I've heard that's what the Scientologists do."

"It's not like that."

"And those Heaven's Gate people would have performed a castration."

"There are lots of gay people at the centre, Mitch. It's not about changing you. It's about making you more of who you really are."

"I always thought the inner you was a slut."

Ramir laughed. "Dr. Bhandari says holding off sex for a couple of weeks is good for the chakras. It's supposed to help charge the internal energies for the Second Gateway."

"That mysterious Second Gateway."

"The first Gateways are the slowest because you're just learning the basics. But he says after I've done the second, the third'll be no problem. And then I'll be out of the lower chakras. That's when you really start noticing results."

"You said you were already seeing results."

"Of course I am. I have this big audition. And I'm a lot more peaceful."

"You won't be after a few weeks without sex."

"I don't know why you're having such a problem with it."

"Remember how you always used to tease me when I was celibate?"

"I'm just ready to try something different," he said. "I'd like to settle down. Look how happy Ingrid is now that she's back together with Pierre."

"Can I ask you a totally confidential question?"

"Of course."

"Do you like Pierre?"

"Sure. Why?"

"He just rubs me the wrong way sometimes."

"Did he do something?"

"Nothing in particular."

"Maybe you're jealous," Ramir said.

"Jealous of what?"

"Of Pierre being with Ingrid."

I gave his head a light smack. "I've never wanted to sleep with Ingrid."

"You know what I mean. I was always jealous of you and Ben."

That startled me. "You've had tons more boyfriends than I have."

"Quantity versus quality. You and Ben were really good together. I was jealous."

Ramir looked at me steadily. I felt all the weight of my former crush on Ramir.

"Well, thanks, I guess."

Ramir squeezed my knee. "You're going to meet somebody great, Mitch. I can feel it." He picked up a wedge of pita and smeared it with a dollop of black-olive tapenade. "You should call Dr. Bhandari."

"I told you already—I don't want to go through the Gateways."

"I mean to ask him about the murder. He could probably help you with your research."

"But he was friends with the Donningtons. He might be offended."

"You can't offend Dr. Bhandari. He's too spiritually advanced."

"I'm sure I could figure out a way. Anyway, I'm just going to use the facts for a starting point. I'll make the rest of it up."

"Whatever. But let me know if you want to make an appointment."

"I'll think about it." But for some reason, the mere thought of talking to Dr. Bhandari again scared me to death.

THURSDAY, OCTOBER 15

I woke up at 6 this morning and began work on the screen-play. I scribbled notes for plot ideas on index cards and laid them out on my living-room floor—arranging the potential scenes into three-act dramatic structure.

I need to work the whole thing through:

ACT ONE
Introduce the wealthy, fucked-up family, bursting with raw passions and tensions. Maybe the opening scene can show the troubled son in the midst of a brutal fight with his father. Dramatic foreshadowing. Father dominates son. Son rebels and is punished. Maybe the father can dominate the mother and daughter too, for added impact.

Or maybe the murder scene should be played out right at the beginning in one of those short blurry prefaces to catch the audience's attention. Or maybe the first moment should be the wife finding the bodies during the party. That bloodcurdling scream.

ACT TWO
I'm still not sure about this part. Filling out Act Two is always the biggest challenge in screenwriting. I'll have to bring in some subplots. Explore the son's schizophrenia. (Need to research schizophrenia.) Invent some problems at the father's printing company. Maybe make the mother an alcoholic. The daughter could be a smarmy cheerleader the son despises. Give the son a girlfriend to up the sex content.

ACT THREE
The night of the big glamorous party. Capitalize on all that '70s free-love debauchery. The bold, confident garishness of the Me Decade. Include the fight between the father and the business partner. More family tensions, giving the father a good reason to go up to his son's room.

I've already started fleshing out the climactic murder-suicide scene:

INTERIOR. TREVOR'S ROOM—NIGHT

JACKSON is trying to calm his son, TREVOR, who's in the midst of a vicious tantrum.

                    TREVOR
I don't give a shit about your party.

                    JACKSON
Your mother and I simply want you to come downstairs and make an appearance.

                    TREVOR
I don't care what you want. Just get out of my room.

                    JACKSON
I'm not going to put up with much more of this behaviour.

                    TREVOR
Get out of my room!

From beneath his bed, TREVOR reveals a large knife.

                    JACKSON
                   (exasperated)
Give that to me. You're going to hurt yourself.

Without warning TREVOR plunges the knife into JACKSON's chest.

Stunned, JACKSON stumbles. He clutches his chest and drops backward onto the floor.

The room is silent.

As TREVOR stares at JACKSON's body, his anger crumbles—replaced by guilt and horror. Tears stream down his face.

With revulsion, TREVOR looks at the knife in his hand. He opens the window and pitches the knife into the night. A gentle splash as it lands in the swimming pool.

TREVOR looks at JACKSON on the floor. Blood is spreading across his white shirtfront.

                    TREVOR
I'm sorry. I'm sorry.

Suddenly TREVOR dives through the window. A strange short cry as he lands on the fence below.

The end.
Hmm.
Falls a bit flat.
Even with the violent murder-suicide, the ending doesn't feel satisfying enough. Needs a turnaround. A big surprise. Maybe the son isn't really dead. Maybe the father isn't really dead, but only wounded, allowing a romantic reunion with his wife and a blissful embrace for the last shot.

And to be truly commercial, the story needs more dramatic build-up. Maybe Trevor could be killing other people along the way. Maybe he could poison a nanny. Bludgeon a neighbour. Attack his sister. Maybe he's a budding serial killer.

Back to the cards…

THURSDAY, OCTOBER 15
—LATER—

Ingrid and I stood at either end of her ancient green couch, and on the count of three, we bent over and lifted.

"Why are old couches so heavy?"

"Back up a bit more," she ordered.

"Over here?"

"Over here. By the bed."

"Ow, watch my toe."

"I think we can put a few more paintings against the wall."

"First, can we lift the couch off my foot?"

Ten minutes earlier, at 9 A.M., Ingrid had called in a panic. (This was a mere 10 minutes after we'd hung up from discussing Ramir and Dr. Bhandari and my murder plot.)

"Max Friedrich just phoned from the airport."

"Should I know who that is?"

"The dealer from Berlin. He flew in a day before he was supposed to. And he wants to see the paintings. He's taking a limousine from the airport right now. You have to come over and help me set up. Hurry. I have to fix my hair."

I jumped in a cab, and within seconds we were rearranging furniture in her garage of an apartment—shifting everything into the far-corner sleeping quadrant to create maximum space to display her collection of portraits.

"He's stopping in Toronto on his way home from New York. He's got another flight at noon. And Geoffrey and his assistant from the gallery are still in Montreal." Ing shoved the kitchen table beside the couch. "I thought we were getting together tomorrow afternoon. I was going to buy a bottle of really good wine and make some of those cheese-and-apple hors d'oeuvre things my sister invented. I just don't feel ready. Do I look OK?"

"You look totally cool. Very sophisticated."

She wore a trim white shirt over her Donna Karan black pants. Her wild red hair was pulled back in an urbane version of a ponytail.

"OK, let's start putting out the paintings."

We went to the stacks leaned against the walls in the painting quadrant and began placing all 40 of the 3-by-5 canvases around the perimeter of the room. Against bare walls. Up on tables. In the arms of a giant chair too massive to move.

I noticed my screaming portrait underway on her easel, sketched out with only a few twirls of paint—definitely not ready for viewing by the German dealer.

But Ingrid caught me noticing. "Oh, Mitchell, I'm sorry. I was going to finish it today." She immediately draped the canvas in a paint-spattered white bedsheet. "But I've got the other one I did of you. You like that one too, don't you?"

"Of course I do."

"So you'll definitely be in the show. I'll insist if I have to. OK, there are three more under the bed."

We maneuvered them out, both of us grunting and sweating.

The portraits were now in a giant malformed circle around the studio. Ingrid stood in the middle of the room and called out orders. "Move the one of my mother over here and my sister over there. And Ramir should go over there beside the one of you. That gives a better sense of the progression."

I circled round and round. Then Ingrid grabbed my arm so hard she was pinching. "Do you really think they're good enough, Mitchell? Not just good enough for here. But good enough for Europe?"

We were reenacting our familiar insecurity-coaching dialogue—at which we've had far too much practice.

"Ing, they wouldn't be giving you a show in Berlin if the paintings weren't good. He's going to love them."

"I mean, it's not going to be a big surprise for him. He's already seen most of them on slides. But what if we put...no...what if..." Ingrid took over and shuffled the paintings around herself, according to a logic I couldn't hope to comprehend.

Suddenly the job was done, and she collapsed beside me on the couch—surrounded by all the people of her portraits. She patted the dampness from her forehead with a dish towel.

"There sure are a lot of them," Ing said, looking around.

"You must feel really proud. He's going to have a hard time picking the ones he wants."

She paused a moment. "It's strange," she said, biting her lower lip. "I've been working on these things for over a year. I haven't seen them all at once before."

The door buzzed.

"Don't worry, I'm not going to put my foot in my mouth," I promised. "I won't say a word."

Ingrid scurried down the hall—poking her fingers in her hair—and a moment later, Max Friedrich zipped in. He was a tiny exclamation mark of a man—dressed all in black, which should go without saying. Wispy blond hair and fluorescent-orange octagonal spectacles.

"Ze limousine is vaiting out front. I haf only five minoots." (He spoke with a German accent so profound and stereotypic, I feel obliged to phonetically reproduce the highlights.)

"I thought I'd put out all the paintings to save you from going through the stacks," Ing said. "This is my friend Mitchell."

Max nodded at me, then pivoted in place, observing all of Ingrid's paintings.

"Fairy nice, fairy nice," he said with flat appreciation. "Zo menny. But vee only haf room for 18."

He lifted his spectacles so the frames sat atop his head. (The octagonal lenses looked like tiny orange stop signs directed at the ceiling.)

In all his bizarreness, he was terrifying.

"Make notes for me please on ze ones I choose."

First he flew to the painting of Ramir. Naturally. "Zis one." Ingrid scribbled "Ramir" on the back of an envelope.

Max continued around the circle, assessing each painting for two seconds and anointing the chosen—"Zis one, zis one, not zis one."

Ingrid and I observed his efficiency in awestruck silence.

A moment of breathless suspense as he got to me sitting on the dock. "Zis one." (Though Max didn't seem to notice that the subject was standing right behind him.)

"*Ja*" to Ingrid's mother, her two nieces, and the two gay men with identical bushy beards she'd photographed on Church Street.

"*Nein*" to her sister and brother-in-law. How would she break the news?

Within a minute, Max was up to 17 paintings.

The last canvas on his circuit was the recently completed portrait of the seminude Ingrid in the midst of painting the nude Pierre.

"Zis!" he said excitedly. "Zis!" He was nodding and pointing. "Ze ozers are gut, but zis is great."

"Thank you," Ing said, somewhat taken aback.

"I love zis. I love zis zo much."

"That's wonderful," she said. But I could tell she was as puzzled as I was by his enthusiasm.

"Zis is very exciting."

"I'm really pleased you like it," Ing said, "but may I ask *why* it's so exciting?"

"Is it the nudity?" I wondered.

"No, no." He poked with his finger. "It's ze painting *in* ze painting." He was pointing at the little abstract piece in the middle. The hard-edged slashes of colour somehow managed to capture and summarize the fully detailed painting of Pierre beside it. "Zis is very bold. Zis is your new direckshoon."

"It is?"

"Enough wiz ze curlicues. You must do more like zis. Five? Six? Ten more? Vee can put zem in ze show. Vee vill make room."

"I guess we should talk to Geoffrey about it first?"

Max dropped his orange glasses back into place. "No questions. I vill tell him. I am very heppy. I must go."

And he zipped out.

I checked my watch. "Exactly five minutes. Just like he said."

Ingrid didn't say anything.

I hugged her. "I think that vent really vell."

She didn't say anything.

"You're not upset, are you?"

"No," she said vaguely.

I prepared for more insecurity coaching. "Because it's not like he hated your swirly paintings. You're not thinking that, are you? Because that's the kind of thing *I* might think."

"I'm just…confused. About what I should do."

"You should keep painting."

"But I'm not sure I can do what he wants."

"You don't think you can do more paintings like that?"

"I don't even know how I did that one. I did it without even thinking."

"Of course you can do more. You paint actual people all the time—which must be really hard. It must be easier to paint… nothing."

"It's not nothing."

"Poor choice of words."

"What if I can't get into the right head space again?"

"You will."

"Maybe I *have* been in a rut, doing all the portraits of people."

"He didn't say that."

"But that's what I was thinking to myself when we were looking at all the paintings just now before he got here. Maybe this *is* a good time to explore some new territory."

"That's good then. This was your portrait period. Now you're ready to move into a new period. Your abstract period. It's exciting. It's the perfect time for it."

"I'm just not sure where to start."

I nodded. "I'm familiar with that dilemma."

"You've already *solved* that dilemma. You've got your murder story."

"I still have to write the thing."

"So we're in the same boat."

"Misery loves company."

We looked around at the curlicue paintings again, all of which seemed to have fallen into the shadows behind that little abstract nonrepresentational square.

"Did you want me to help you put them away? Put the furniture back?"

Ing paused a moment, before shaking her head no. "Pierre can help me tonight. I want to stare at them for a while."

THURSDAY, OCTOBER 15
—LATER AGAIN—

After I got home from Ingrid's, I settled in to deal with my own creative dilemma—developing the Donnington plot.

But just as I was scratching my first note on an index card, my agent Rebecca called to inform me that *Five Fun Fish* had finally paid me for the final episode I wrote before they fired me. "I'll drop the cheque in the mail."

"Don't do that!" I said in a burst. "I'll be right over."

I try to take advantage of every opportunity to spend time with my agent. I figure that way we can bond more deeply and she'll feel more obligated to get me work.

"My morning's really tight, Mitchell."

"I was going to call you anyway. Because I've got a really great idea for that big commercial blockbuster I was telling you about. I'd love to bounce it off your head."

Bounce it off your head?

"Maybe I can give you five minutes."

"Thank you. Thank you."

Every time I talk to Rebecca, I sound like an idiot. I know she thinks I'm a total waste of her time.

Briefly, I was represented by a high-profile literary agent in New York City. But, as in every other aspect of my career, I ran into a little problem.

She died.

So I begged my way onto Rebecca Devlin's roster of "Canada's finest film and television professionals"—based entirely on my expertise at churning out crap for another annoying kids' show, *The Big Blue Dog,* now mercifully put to sleep.

The Devlin Talent Group is located on a low-profile stretch of Yonge Street, amid a mix-up of Asian fast-food places and discount shoe stores. I entered the halfheartedly renovated 1960s office building, right across the street from the Church of Scientology. Which didn't strike me as meaningful until today. Not that I'm sure what it means.

I took the elevator up to the ninth floor and walked the hard blue-carpeted hallway, rehearsing my pitch—as thousands of desperate writers have done before me.

"A perfect family copes with the tragic impact of a teenage boy's schizophrenia."

Sounds more like a disease-of-the-week TV movie than a blockbuster feature.

Remember the five essential ingredients for a commercial hit.

"A rich and famous family copes with the violent impact of a telepathic teenage boy's murder-suicide during an orgy."

Not quite.

The agency's reception desk is planted right in front of the door as a kind of guard station. And it's easy to imagine Mandy the Receptionist pointing a machine gun.

All bubbly and positive-thinking, I grinned at her sharp little face. "Hi, Mandy, how are you?" (I always make an effort to suck up to the underlings, in case Rebecca drops dead too.)

"I'm fine," said Mandy suspiciously.

"Rebecca told me to come in."

"She's already in a meeting."

"She said she could give me five minutes. I'll wait."

"Your name?"

She knew my name. I know she knew my name. But I told her anyway.

"OK," Mandy said doubtfully.

She marched to Rebecca's door, knocked, opened the door, stuck her head in, and a second later Rebecca herself came barging out with tilted-forward urgency. As usual, Rebecca wore black, black, and black. Her only accents were red lipstick and a wide silver cuff on her wrist.

Rebecca takes two aerobics classes each day and could level me with a single kick to the throat.

"Come with me."

I didn't need to come with her because she scooped her arm under mine, literally dragging me out the office door and into the neighbouring stairwell—regularly used as her private conference room.

"I've got a guy in my office from Apex Entertainment. Senior Creative Executive. He's here from L.A. working on a big movie. He's hiring one of my costume designers. But I want you to meet him. I told him you're one of the hottest young screenwriters in the country."

"I am?"

"I've been giving him the rundown on your scripts. If you make a good impression, maybe he'll read something. I'm telling you, Mitchell, this could be your Big Break."

I've already had at least six Big Breaks. And they never cease to throw me into a nervous panic.

"He's from Apex? I've never met anybody that legitimate before. Is he scary?"

"Uptight. One of those Hollywood corporate types. But you can handle him no problem." Rebecca slapped me on the shoulder and dragged me back toward her office. "Now get in there and treat him like he's God."

And my first thought when I beheld the holy Hollywood executive was that, in fact, he might be God.

He stood to shake my hand. He was 6 foot 4—even taller than I am. Handsome with black curly hair and a California tan. An interesting crook in his nose. Large, passionate nostrils. He wore chunky black-rimmed glasses that had a Clark Kent effect. As soon as he took them off, he'd bust out in gorgeousness like Superman.

Rebecca played hostess. "Mitchell Draper, meet Aaron Pasternak."

"How are you?" he said, exuding deep-voiced confidence.

I couldn't tell if Rebecca noticed that our eyes had locked, that our hands had frozen in mid-shake. An electrical charge bolted us together.

This wasn't what I'd expected at all.

He was in his late 30s or early 40s. Expensive black jacket with a white shirt open at the collar. Beige chinos. I could see what Rebecca meant about him being uptight, but I found his constricted conservatism highly attractive. Straitlaced and barricaded to hold back a powerful tidal wave of hot sexuality. A kindred spirit.

I checked his left hand. No wedding ring.

"Nice to meet you," I said.

"Nice to meet you too."

"Isn't this nice?" Rebecca said with a grin that was a bit too snidely knowing.

The three of us sat—Rebecca behind her desk, Aaron and I side by side in the guest chairs.

I've always been easily infatuated by chiseled Hollywood handsomeness. And here was the genuine article, imported direct from the source.

"So are you related to Boris Pasternak?" I asked.

He smiled with a sorry shake of his head. "My father says he was my grandfather's second cousin. Not close enough to get me any royalties."

We chuckled together.

"Who's Boris Pasternak?" Rebecca asked, clearly not happy to be left out.

"He wrote *Doctor Zhivago*," I explained.

"David Lean directed the movie," Aaron added. "It came out in 1965."

My infatuation deepened. He shared my ability to remember movie years.

I mentally hummed "Lara's Theme."

Rebecca leaned back in her chair in a take-charge pose. "So, Mitchell, Aaron was just telling me how much he enjoyed *Hell Hole*."

"Lara's Theme" stopped dead.

"You saw it?"

"On video a couple of months ago."

"I thought the only people who rented it were redneck teenagers in the Deep South."

He laughed. Gorgeous teeth. "I've always been a big horror movie fan. The script was very funny. Nice sense of irony."

"There was a lot more irony in my original draft. But the

director cut most of it out. He was a complete idiot." I panicked. "You don't know him, do you?"

"Can't even remember his name." Aaron's uptightness was fading fast. "Rebecca was just telling me about your other work." He motioned to my three scripts lying like vulnerable naked babies on her desk.

I'd loved each one of them, but suddenly they all seemed embarrassingly terrible.

The quirky yet wise story of a grown-up gay son dealing with his right-wing parents in the suburbs.

The quirky yet poignant tale of a teenage boy who has an affair with his art teacher's husband.

"I was just getting to the third one," Rebecca said. "The gay *Cyrano de Bergerac*."

I took over. "It's the quirky yet classic scenario of an ugly guy who helps his gorgeous friend seduce the college football star. The original title was *Queerano de Bergerac,* but I thought that was too much."

Aaron chuckled again. He had very sexy crinkles around his eyes. "That sounds great," he said, "but we're mostly in the market for dramas right now."

Rebecca interjected. "In fact, Mitchell is working on a big commercial blockbuster. He was pitching me on the phone this morning. It sounds fabulous. Why don't you tell Aaron?"

"I'd love to," I said. My moment of truth. My chance to pitch to the authentic Hollywood big time.

What the fuck should I say?

"It's the story of—"

A peculiar chirping silenced the room.

Aaron revealed a minuscule cell phone from inside his jacket. "Sorry, I have to take this."

Rebecca and I pretended we were in suspended animation, while Aaron spoke softly and urgently. Then he hung up, and his manner was back to uptight and professional.

"I have to go. Emergency I have to deal with. I'll take these with me if you don't mind." He picked up all three of my scripts.

"Call me if you have any questions," Rebecca said. "I'm sure we can work something out."

"Good to meet you both," he said. Aaron grabbed his brief-case, but before he departed he stared into my eyes for an extra additional fraction of a second.

Then he was gone.

Rebecca raised her eyebrows and leered at me. "Well, Mitchell, good for you. I didn't have a clue."

"A clue about what?"

"I thought my gaydar was pretty good—what with all the gay guys at my gym. But I couldn't tell with that one. Let's hope all your flirting gets you some work."

"I wasn't flirting."

"Mitchell, trust me, I'm an expert at sexual manipulation, and you had him right under your thumb. Now let's get the *Five Fun Fish* business out of the way." She reached for the calculator on her desk to figure her 10% and subtract all her expenses. "So did you want to bounce your new story off my head?"

She really does think I'm an idiot.

"OK. Well. Um. It's based on an actual real-life event. A rich family is torn apart by a violent murder-suicide. This teenage boy stabs his father, then he jumps out a window and lands on a fence."

"Yuck," Rebecca said. "Sounds depressing." She pulled a ledger from her bottom drawer. "If you're going to write that thing, you'd better finish it fast. Remember, *Travels with Willie* starts in three weeks."

THURSDAY, OCTOBER 15
—MORE—

I found the nearest pay phone, tucked in the doorway of the Charles Promenade, a barren miniature shopping mall a block north of Rebecca's office.

My mind was twirling with hope and disappointment.

I dialed Ramir's cell phone, eager to find out if he'd heard of Aaron Pasternak. His voice mail kicked in, so I hung up.

Thank God Ingrid was home.

"He was the absolute prototype of tall, dark, and handsome."

"Maybe your agent can tell you how to get in touch with him."

"I can't ask her. She was teasing me about it already."

"Maybe you could call his film company and find out where he's staying."

"It's probably the Four Seasons or the Sutton Place. I could call and check. Or I could go hang out in the lobby."

"You hang out in hotel lobbies anyway."

"Unless he rented a condo or a house. It's totally ridiculous. I should just forget about him."

"You know, Mitchell, you're forgetting the other possibility…"

"Which is?"

"He might get in touch with you."

"Never. That would be too easy."

As I walked home, I considered Rebecca's blunt assessment of the Donnington story. Depressing. She was right. A murder-suicide might make titillating gossip over lunch, but as a movie it would be just plain bleak.

On the other hand, an executive from Apex Entertainment had told me he liked *Hell Hole*. And he had three of my other scripts in his possession. There was reason for hope. Of course, he probably took them just to be polite. He'd probably pass them on to an assistant who'd pass them on to a reader who'd immediately pass them into the priority recycling bin.

But he sure was tall, dark, and handsome.

I knew Cortland would gladly listen as I recounted and relived my meeting with Aaron Pasternak. So instead of going to my own apartment, I went down the hall and knocked on Cortland's door.

"Mitchell, thank God! You've got to help me."

As soon as I saw him, I knew something was wrong. His silver hair, usually perfectly arranged, was greasy and askew. It was midday, and he was still wearing his loose plaid pyjama bottoms and a fine white undershirt that showed his bony arms.

"What's the matter?"

"I've been robbed! Someone's taken them."

Stepping in the door of Cortland's apartment is always strangely disorienting, because one moment you're in an innocuous brown hallway on the 16th floor, and the next you're in an English country mansion with cornice mouldings, Indian carpets, and chintz on every upholstered surface.

But today his lovely living room was a mess. Pillows from the overstuffed chesterfield were tossed on the floor. Drawers on the antique desk hung open precariously. Stacks of interior design books cascaded across the floor.

"My sister Beatrice was here. She stole them. I know she stole them."

"Stole what? What did she take?"

He rushed down the hall to his office. I could see into his bedroom. Clothes from the closet were piled in a heap. I followed him into the study, totally custom-fitted with dark oak bookshelves, filing drawers, and a massive banker's desk. The normally pristine room was strewn with papers. File folders spilled open across the dark-green velvet couch. Photographs lay everywhere.

"She wants everything. She can't wait for me to drop dead." He went to the filing cabinet and began pulling out papers in clumps, totally destroying the carefully established order.

Was he acting like this because of the brain tumour? Because of his medication?

"Calm down, Cortland. What do you think she took?"

He stopped digging and turned to me. "I have to find them."

"What did Beatrice take?"

"The photographs."

"Which photographs?"

"She can't have them, the hateful bitch."

"Which photographs?"

"The ones at the Montagues'," he spat.

"Montague House? The place in Barbados?"

"Of course."

"Just sit on the couch and let me have a look."

But Cortland didn't sit down. He hovered beside me. "They're gone. I know it."

"I'm sure they must be here somewhere." I tried to sound calm and rational—even though I was beginning to panic about what I should do. Call his doctor? Call his sister?

I went to the file drawer for "M-N-O" and found the Montague file right where it should have been. "Here it is," I said. "There was a piece of paper stuck in front of the name. That must be why you couldn't see it."

"Thank you, Mitchell. Thank you very much." He collapsed onto the velvet couch, squeezing his eyes closed.

"I'll put it right here on your desk." I cleared an empty space among the loose photographs. "Do you want me to help you straighten up?" It would take hours to put everything back in proper order.

Cortland pressed his thumbs to his temples. "I have a terrible headache."

"Maybe you're pushing yourself too hard with the book."

"I'll finish the damn thing even if it kills me," he snapped, then winced at the pain.

"Do you want me to get you some Tylenol?"

He nodded.

I went to the bathroom, shook out three pills and filled a crystal glass with water—as I'd done so frequently during our writing sessions.

"Leave me alone now," he said, lighting a cigarette.

"Do you want me to help you get into your bedroom?"

"Leave me alone, Mitchell, please."

"Get some sleep," I said. "I'll come back later to see how you are."

☆

Back in my apartment, I was bewildered. What if Cortland were dying at that very moment? I imagined the tumour exploding in his brain like some deadly time bomb.

I wondered about phoning Beatrice. I've only met his sister twice, and she hadn't seemed that hateful to me. In fact, the last time she'd followed me out into the hallway and pressed her phone number into the palm of my hand, whispering that I should call if even the slightest thing seemed wrong.

Then my phone rang—the short double ring that indicates someone's at the intercom downstairs in the lobby.

I wasn't expecting anyone. Maybe it was a courier. Maybe it was Beatrice.

"Mitchell, it's Aaron Pasternak."

I was stunned. "Hi."

"Remember me?" he barked into the speaker. "We met at your agent's office."

"I remember." How could I forget? Had he read the scripts already?

"I was taking a chance you'd be home. Can I come up?"

"Of course," I said. "It's apartment 1611."

Ingrid had been right.

What could he want? I suppose I could guess.

I was excited, terrified. Still distracted about Cortland. I circled around my apartment. The floor was covered with my maze of index cards. I couldn't scoop them up. I'd lose all that work.

I ran to the washroom. I hadn't showered since my sweaty furniture-moving with Ingrid. Oh God. Wet washcloth. I scanned my face for whiteheads, spritzed my neck with cologne, and drank a mouthful of Listerine.

I shoved a stray pair of underwear under the couch.

I stood back five paces from the door—a natural distance to have to walk if I were actually doing something natural—and waited for Aaron to knock.

He knocked.

I opened the door and there he was, smiling in all his hand-someness—white teeth against movie-star tan—one hand hidden behind his back.

"I wanted to apologize for running out in the middle of the meeting," he said. "I brought these."

He revealed a bouquet of a dozen red roses. No man had ever brought me roses. Not even Ben.

"That's so nice of you," I said. And totally beyond the bounds of professionalism. "Please, come in."

He looked around my apartment. "It's orange."

"Big mix-up at the paint store. I'm redoing it next month."

"It's cozy."

"That's what I'm trying to convince people. And please excuse all the notes on the floors. It's the script I'm working on. Have a seat. I'll just put these in water." I raised the roses in a gesture of appreciation and thwacked myself in the chin.

"I must have caught you in the middle of something. You seem sort of stressed."

"No, I'm always like this. I've just had a very…busy day so far."

He followed me into the kitchen. I took my only vase from beneath the sink and filled it with water.

"I hope you don't mind me dropping in. Your address was on the front page of your scripts."

"No, I'm glad you did. Honestly, I was wondering how to get in touch with *you*."

"Good," he said. "At least we're on the same wavelength." He ran his hand up my arm. The implications were very clear.

"Do you want to sit and talk a bit first?" I suggested.

He laughed. His crow's feet crinkled in the sexiest way. "Forgive me, I always like to dive right in."

A genuine Hollywood executive was coming on to me. I felt a panicky combination of anxiety and arousal. I hadn't had sex with anyone other than Ben in two years. With Aaron just dropping in like this, I'd had no time to psyche myself up. What if I was terrible? What if I wasn't even able?

"Did you want something to drink? Beer? Iced tea? Tap water?"

"Water's fine."

I poured two glasses from the Brita pitcher in the fridge. He took off his jacket and hung it on the back of a chair at my dining table/desk. His white cotton shirt stuck to his back in a damp oval. Even that I found attractive.

He sat on the couch.

I sat beside him.

A moment of dead air.

"So do you come to Toronto often?" I asked, attempting to sound normal.

"I was here for the film festival a few years ago. But this is the first time in a while. Nice place."

We paused for a moment to sip our waters.

I noticed that his hands were wide and masculine. Slightly hairy below the knuckle. His fingers were thick, the nails perfectly manicured.

I relied on my old reliable interview tactics: "So what does a Senior Creative Executive actually do?"

He smiled. Those eyes again. "Everybody always asks me that. It changes a lot. But we've got a picture going into production, so I'm here supervising—making sure all the talent's in place. For example, this morning I sat in on casting, and then I had that meeting with your agent because we're replacing our costume designer."

"What's the project?"

"It's a remake of an old Marilyn Monroe picture, *Niagara*."

"I love that movie. 1953." The classic suspense thriller was filmed on location at Niagara Falls, an hour and a half from Toronto. "Who's playing Marilyn?"

"Drew Barrymore. Her company is co-producing."

"That'll be amazing."

"That's what we're hoping. We start shooting in three weeks."

93

So he'd be staying in town for a while. Potential for a long-term relationship.

A momentary pause.

Was it sex time yet?

"So how does a person actually become a Senior Creative Executive?"

"Everybody asks me that too. I produced a couple of movies a while ago—*The Penance* and *The Sound of Your Voice*."

"1993 and 1996."

"I'm impressed."

"They were both really good. Actually I only saw *The Penance*, but I heard the other one was really good. I'll rent it. So are you still producing anything yourself?"

"Not right now. I got tired of begging people for money. That's why I took a job at the studio. But I always like to hear about new scripts." He motioned to the cards on the floor. "So is this the big commercial blockbuster your agent was talking about?"

"I'm not sure if it's really a blockbuster. It might be too depressing."

"Tell me about it anyway."

"Really? Well, it's based on something that actually happened. It's about this schizophrenic teenage boy who stabs his father and then throws himself out the window at his parents' anniversary party."

"And it's a true story?"

"It happened here in Toronto—back in the '70s. A friend of mine was there at the party."

"What was the family's name?"

"Donnington."

"I just wondered if I'd heard about it."

"You might have. But I'm going to fictionalize everything so no one'll be able to sue."

"Sounds pretty heavy."

"Maybe it's *too* heavy. Do you think it could be a blockbuster?"

"It could be—if you handle it the right way. Have you written any of it yet?"

94

I pointed to the floor. "That's it."

"Are you doing some research? Interviewing people?"

"I hate that part. I always get embarrassed, telling people I'm a writer. They always ask what I've written, and then I have to tell them, and of course they've never heard of anything."

"I knew about *Hell Hole*."

"You're an exception."

He smiled at the shameless flattery. "You should show me an outline when you've got something on paper."

"Seriously?"

"If you want to. It sounds like it might have potential."

I took a breath and absorbed this moment. A genuine Hollywood executive thought my idea might have potential. Hardly a guarantee. But at least it was encouragement.

I stared into his brown eyes, examining his tall, dark handsomeness. Did it all mean something? Was the universe somehow at work? Or was I simply being a career-climbing whore?

Aaron leaned forward, elbows on knees. He looked at his watch. It was 2:15. He turned toward me and whispered in a throaty voice, "Mitchell, this is going to sound bad. But I have a 3 o'clock meeting."

"And you can't be late."

He laughed and nodded.

I gently took off his glasses and set them on the table. Superman.

Then, faster than a speeding bullet, he had me flat on the couch.

THURSDAY, OCTOBER 15
—EVEN MORE—

Aaron and I had a fabulous time. Fast but fabulous.

Jane Choy was right about that big gun.

He left at 10 minutes to 3, rushing off to his next engagement.

But other thoughts had been pressing at the back of my mind. As soon as Aaron was gone, I dug in the bowl on top of my fridge to find the key Cortland had given me to his apartment, held on a silver loop from Tiffany's.

What if he'd keeled over dead while I was practicing my promiscuity?

I knocked first, just to be polite. If there was an emergency, I'd call 911 first, then notify Beatrice. But a moment later, Cortland answered. His hair was washed and styled, and he wore one of his custom-tailored white shirts.

"You look perfectly normal," I said.

"Of course I'm perfectly normal," he exclaimed and he motioned for me to follow him toward his bedroom. "Just a little spasm of the brain. They warned me to expect them."

Miraculously, he'd already finished tidying his apartment and putting his files in order. "All I needed was a nap and a hot bath."

On his grand four-poster bed, complete with lace canopy, were laid out three pieces of Louis Vuitton luggage, each loaded to the brim.

"Are you going to the hospital?"

"Don't be ridiculous. I'm flying to New York."

"You're going to New York City? Today?"

"I'm joining Ermina. You remember the Polish Princess from the restaurant the other day? She flew down this morning, staying at The Pierre. We're going to have an impromptu long weekend, just like the old days."

"Do you think that's a good idea? You know, after…"

"That's what makes the timing so perfect. It practically guarantees that I won't have another episode until next week."

"I guess that's good. I hope you enjoy yourself."

"Who can help but have a wonderful time in Manhattan?"

I sat on a silk-upholstered bedroom chair, ready to inform him of my own good time—when a long-bodied black cat entered the room.

"Cortland, a cat just walked into your bedroom."

"Skinny little creature, isn't it?" he said, ignoring the cat completely.

"I thought you didn't approve of pets."

"I don't. They're for tedious shut-ins who aren't motivated enough to entertain themselves on their own."

"So why do you have a cat?"

"Apparently, Beatrice thinks I have now fallen into that pathetic category. She delivered it this morning, along with a supply of food and a litter box. I don't know what she was thinking. As if I, of all people, need a black cat crossing my path all day."

The cat arched its back and rubbed itself against my leg.

"I've always liked cats," I said. I scratched the soft tuft of black fur on his head. The cat bared his teeth and slashed at me with a paw, leaving three tiny trails of blood on my hand. "He doesn't seem very friendly."

"He's a she. Do you want some antiseptic?"

I wiped away the gashes. "I guess she's not rabid. Is she?"

"Poor thing must have been terrified when I went on my rampage. I found her hiding in the closet."

"What's her name?"

"It's rather unfortunate, actually. Pisces."

"I guess that means she likes seafood."

The cat rubbed against Cortland's leg, and he scratched behind her ear with surreptitious affection. Pisces then made a loud and distinctly pronounced "meow," stretched every limb individually, and curled up in a ball at the foot of Cortland's bed.

"You still have my key, don't you? Would you mind popping in to feed the beast? Just until Sunday. Unless you're too busy entertaining your new beau." Cortland smirked and, with a flourish, he dropped three silk ties into his suitcase.

"Have you been spying on me?"

"I was at the garbage chute when I noticed a rumpled gentleman hurrying out of your apartment. Very handsome, I must say."

"I was planning to tell you about him anyway." So I gave him the full rundown on my Hollywood executive. "He's driving down to Niagara Falls tonight to check out the locations where they're shooting. But we're having dinner on Sunday night before he goes back to Los Angeles. He's staying at the Sutton Place."

"The Sluttin' Place, as they called it in my day. Ah well, it should give you some interesting new tidbits for your autobiography. You'll have *The Diaries of Anaïs Nin* in no time."

"But the biggest thing is that I told him my idea about turning the Donnington story into a movie."

"And?"

"He liked it."

"My, my," Cortland chuckled. "The Donningtons brought to the big screen. How extraordinary that would be."

"He said he wants to read my outline. So you can bet I'll be working on it like crazy until Sunday."

"You've become a shameless opportunist, Mitchell Draper. I'm impressed."

"It's not just that. I really do like him."

"Now don't you be foolish and fall in love, young man. You should be very afraid any time love rears its ugly head. It's the most dangerous thing that can happen to a person."

"I'm not going to get smitten," I said, not entirely convincingly. "Anyway, Aaron thinks I should do some investigating into the Donningtons."

"Didn't I suggest the same thing myself? But first, you should follow me." Cortland led me into his study. "I found this when I was cleaning up my files. You know how obsessive I am about keeping things." He handed me a folder of papers, bulging at least four inches thick.

"What is all this?"

"My notes from when I was working with the Donningtons." Cortland pursed his lips in a self-satisfied smile "Maybe your morbid little mind will find something inspiring."

THURSDAY, OCTOBER 15
—MORE AGAIN—

I bade Cortland bon voyage and came back here to my apartment. I quickly cleared off my dining table/desk. Then I opened the file folder, as reverently as if I were opening a treasure chest that contained all the secrets of the universe.

At the top of the pile was a letter on Cortland's creamy business stationery, addressed to Vivienne Donnington at Nine Thornfield Road. I scanned the contents quickly. Cortland outlined plans for redecorating the drawing room, the dining room, and the conservatory.

In fact, the bulk of the paperwork consisted of Cortland's notes for furnishing those three rooms. Invoices for chairs, credenzas, Indian rugs, and paintings. Since Dr. Bhandari had bought the place completely furnished, those were probably the same pieces that were in the house now.

Deeper down in the pile, I found a formal party invitation, requesting the honour of my presence at the Donningtons' 20th anniversary party, scheduled for Friday, July 13, 1979.

Friday the 13th? Clearly, they shouldn't have tempted fate.

Then there was another letter from Cortland, giving an advance summary of details for the party for 300 guests. Next were estimates for the rental of tablecloths and glassware. Rough sketches for tropical flower arrangements. The bill for flowers alone came to $8,000—and this was over 20 years ago.

I found a copy of the handwritten guest list (Vivienne's writing?) and scanned the names for anyone familiar. There was Ermina with the number "2" in brackets beside her name. I guess she'd come with her husband of the moment. And there was Dr. Nigel Bhandari with another "2" in brackets. Did he bring his mysteriously absent wife? No mention of Cortland, but I guess as the party coordinator, he didn't need to be invited.

Slipped between the bills, I found two stapled pages from *Maclean's* magazine, the weekly chronicle of Canadian news. It was the article Cortland had told me about. The glossy paper was crisp and slightly yellowed. "Gruesome Murder-Suicide in Toronto" was the headline.

My eyes went first to the pictures. The large main photograph was a portrait of Jackson and Vivienne Donnington. The caption read: "The final photograph of the anniversary couple, taken on the night of the fateful party."

Here they were, smiling before my eyes: my main characters. They were standing in a double doorway—the entrance to the ballroom?—festooned with red and orange flowers.

Vivienne was a classic dark-haired beauty, a gardenia set behind her ear. She had fine features that looked as though they'd been sculpted in marble. Jackson had side-parted sandy-brown hair. His face showed a polished friendliness, but his smile was regal and proud.

Jackson wore a tuxedo with a garish tropical-pattern bow tie and cummerbund, while Vivienne wore a white Halston-like gown. Both had bright Hawaiian leis looped around their necks. They smiled confidently, oblivious to the fate that would soon befall them.

In the bottom left corner of the page was a shot of Jackson and a victoriously smiling man—holding up a trophy at some kind of banquet. The caption said the man was Bill Zale, Jackson's business partner and "an early suspect in the deaths."

On the bottom right was a school-portrait-style photograph of "the schizophrenic teenager who killed his father, then himself," Trevor Donnington.

I zeroed in on his face. Dark curly hair. Nice-looking for a 17-year-old. I wondered how he would have looked now.

I read the article, noting every detail that might help me in telling the story. The Donningtons were from a well-established Toronto family. Despite the high profile of their deaths, the funeral was a low-key affair in St. James' Cemetery.

Trevor was emotionally troubled and had been thrown out of several private schools before attending Jarvis Collegiate for the last year of his life. He was very close to his father, which made the murder all the more shocking. But his temper had been known to flare out of control. And a broken vodka bottle had been found in his room. The boy had been drunk on top of his other problems.

The day after the party, a police investigation commenced. Just as Cortland had explained, there was some confusion about the lack of fingerprints on the knife. It wasn't clear whether the chlorine in the pool had eroded them or if someone had wiped the handle. The article went into great technical detail about the instability of fingerprints and other skin oils when submerged in water.

According to the story, the police spent several days interviewing all the guests to search for other possible suspects. There was another mention of Bill Zale of Donnington-Zale Lithography, "one of the most successful firms in the Canadian printing industry." Bill had argued with Jackson during the party and seemed a likely culprit.

But the murder-suicide theory was quickly confirmed.

There was a brief aside that the Donningtons also had a 12-year-old daughter named Laura. On a whim, I pulled out the Toronto phone book. There was only one listing under that name: "Donnington, L." On Hampton Avenue. I checked my handy pocket map book. The street was located in the wholesome enclave of Riverdale. Very nice, but a few steps down from the prestige of Rosedale.

Could it be the same Laura Donnington? I jotted down the phone number.

I went back to searching through the file.

Floor plans of the three-storey house. Which might come in handy for the set designer once the movie goes into production...

At the back of the folder was a large manila envelope. I slid out a pile of 30 or so 8-by-10 colour photographs—all obviously taken on the night of the tragic party.

The first photographs were of the decorated house before the guests arrived. Cortland's eye for beauty at its best. Rich Victorian furnishings, brought to life with vibrant tropical flowers.

The rooms looked familiar from my visit last week. Even though the photographs showed the elaborate wallpapers and dark woods of the Donnington era—not the stark white of Dr. Bhandari.

A shot of the fabulous ballroom showed a long table laden with a Hawaiian-style buffet. No roast pig on a spit, mercifully.

There were several shots of the crowd. The ballroom jam-packed. People gyrating unbecomingly with disco fever. Random tipsy strangers, smiling for the camera. The VIPs of decades before. Maybe they were still VIPs, but with new hairstyles rendering them unrecognizable.

I stopped at a portrait of Jackson and Vivienne. The same shot they'd reproduced in the magazine.

The next photograph showed a teenage boy and girl, posing self-consciously on the staircase. Trevor and Laura. With their dark features, they resembled their mother more than their father. Laura wore a little grass skirt and smiled broadly with big front teeth. She hung onto her brother's arm adoringly.

Trevor wore a black tuxedo with the same brightly coloured bow tie and cummerbund as his father. This shot must have been taken before he'd been banished upstairs—before the broken chandelier incident with Cortland.

I looked into his deep brown eyes. He had a serious intensity in his stare. Almost too focused. There was something dangerous about him, but maybe that only came from retrospect. No surprise that he was tall, dark, and handsome. Like every other man I encounter these days.

He looked familiar somehow.

Hard to imagine that within a few hours of this moment, he'd have killed his father and himself.

Or maybe he didn't.

I went back to the magazine article—to the mention of the police investigation. Investigations are always good for dramas.

Even if it really were an open-and-shut case, that didn't mean I had to tell my version of the story that way.

I stared at Trevor's picture. What if—in my fictionalized version—Trevor isn't really the killer? What if somebody else killed both him and his father and then disguised it as a murder-suicide?

Making it a mystery gives me a way in. The gruesome killing scene becomes an exciting beginning instead of a depressing ending. I could turn the story into a whodunit. The plot becomes the investigation.

Aaron would love it.

My heart pounded with excitement.

I sat on the floor and began rearranging my index cards.

Then another idea dawned on me. Maybe it was the spirit of Trevor Donnington who Jane Choy saw floating above me, reaching down. Like a muse descending. Maybe it was Trevor who appeared to me in that weird dream.

Maybe Trevor wants me to tell the true story.

But that's just *too* ridiculous.

I have to get to work.

FRIDAY, OCTOBER 16

"So you think you're possessed?"

"When you put it that way, I realize it sounds ridiculous."

I'd spent the day making notes, plotting and theorizing. Now Ramir and I were lounging on the black leather couch in his basement—completely renovated to become a high-tech home theatre. A giant video screen was mounted against the far wall.

We were eating chicken curry with rice while watching the 9 P.M. broadcast of *Station Centauri*. A semiregular tradition—whenever Ramir doesn't have a date. Which might become more frequent now that he's celibate. Mostly we end up talking through the show until his scenes come on.

"So you think this crazy dead kid wants you to reveal what really happened?"

"It was just a little whim that crossed my mind," I said. "Remember what the psychic said about a tall, dark, and handsome man hovering above me in the spirit world?"

"I thought this Aaron guy was the tall, dark, and handsome stranger."

"I'm having a hard time keeping track too. But the first time I had the dream, I was sitting in the Donningtons' house, looking up at the chandelier that Trevor broke."

"Maybe during the meditation Trevor's ghost actually entered your body," Ramir suggested lasciviously. "At least you think he's cute."

"I don't know why you're acting so skeptical. You're the one who got me into this whole flaky world."

"What if you're Trevor's reincarnation? Like *The Reincarnation of Peter Proud*."

"Released in 1975. I can't be the reincarnation of Trevor. The two of us were alive at the same time."

"What about the transmigration of souls? Or maybe you're like the little kid in *The Sixth Sense*."

I ignored that, and we watched a brief scene in which the KerrZavian Ramir complains about the diminishing water resources on his home planet.

"But seriously," I said, "what if Trevor really was innocent?"

"You want to clear his name and put the real murderer behind bars?"

"The idea crossed my mind."

"Admit it, Mitch. All you want to do is impress your new Hollywood boyfriend."

"OK, that's part of it."

"Sleeping your way to the top. Or bottom in your case."

I punched his arm.

"So if Trevor didn't do it, who did?" Ramir asked.

"Maybe it really *was* his father's business partner."

"Even though the police decided it wasn't him."

"I know it's a long shot. But I have to come up with some interesting theories if I want to give Aaron an outline on Sunday."

Ramir put his empty plate on the table.

"You know, I asked Dr. Bhandari about what happened with the Donningtons."

Why did my stomach suddenly lurch? "What did he say?"

"He said it was a terrible tragedy."

"Anybody would say that. But does he mind that I'm writing about it?"

"He didn't seem to. He said he'd released the energy from the house. That's why he never mentions it anymore."

It seemed like an odd reason. "Did he say he'd talk to me?"

"You said you didn't want to, so I didn't ask."

"Maybe I should."

A scene with Gabriella Hartman came on. She was wearing her tight little uniform, her hair pulled back severely. She was bossing around a Saturnalian alien in the space station.

"She acts more normal on TV than she does in real life."

"Mitch, once again, you're being a bitch."

"Remember ages ago when she was on *The Vixens* and she suddenly went missing. Everybody thought she'd been kidnapped."

"And nobody knew if it was a publicity stunt or the real thing."

"Does she ever talk about that?"

"Not a word."

Ramir took a sip of soda water and twisted around to lie on the couch, his head resting on my lap. Which struck me as rather overly intimate.

"Don't you think that's rather overly intimate?"

"We're friends. It's comfortable."

"I think you've been celibate too long."

"Just because I'm celibate doesn't mean I don't need some physical affection."

Even if it was strange, it felt nice. I put my hand on his head and smoothed his hair.

"You want to hear something weird?" he said. "I auditioned for *Niagara* a couple of weeks ago."

"You did?"

"I didn't get it, obviously."

"Does that mean you met Aaron?"

"Just the casting people."

"I don't think he has a lot to do with casting."

"I'm not blaming him. I've just been having really bad luck lately."

"Maybe you'll get this new Mexican bandit thing you were telling me about."

"Honestly, I did a great audition. Dr. Bhandari taught me this new meditation technique that's just for actors. You visualize the character as a separate person and then you let him float into you."

"Sounds sort of like me and Trevor."

Ramir suddenly put his hand over my mouth. "Hold on, I'm in this scene."

We were silent out of respect. We watched as a gang of Ramir's fellow KerrZavians stole frozen water supplies from a cargo ship.

"I come in at the end," Ramir said.

We waited.

"I come in...right...now."

Another commercial appeared.

"They cut me out."

"Maybe the episode was running long."

He sat up. "Shit. I hate it when they do that."

"I'm sure it wasn't anything personal."

"They cut down my part in last week's episode too."

"But you were in all those scenes at the beginning."

Ramir took a deep meditative breath and closed his eyes. "I just need to keep myself focused. You're right. It doesn't mean anything."

We sat silently and watched the commercials. I could imagine what he was thinking, but I didn't want to say anything.

There was a clattering sound upstairs.

"What was that?"

"The front door," Ramir said casually.

"Who's opening your front door?"

"My mother."

"Why's she coming to your house at this time of night?"

"Getting back from a prayer meeting."

Like mother, like son. "But why's she coming here?"

"She doesn't like staying at her apartment." The condominium that Ramir had bought for his parents last year. "She says it reminds her of Dad."

I looked at him quizzically. "Does she stay here a lot?"

"A couple of days a week. She cleans the place, does the laundry. Who do you think made the chicken curry?"

"I thought *you* did."

"I never have time any more. Anyway, tomorrow she'll go to my brother's. Then she'll spend a few days at my sister's."

"Why didn't you ever mention it?"

"I didn't think of it."

"But you're still paying the mortgage on the apartment in Mississauga?"

He nodded. "I understand why she doesn't want to go there. I mean, that's where we were when Dad had the heart attack—right there in the kitchen—when the ambulance came and everything."

"Then why don't you sell the place?"

"That doesn't feel right either." Ramir pushed the mute button on the TV remote control. "You know, when I was getting dressed this morning, I went to the closet to get a shirt, and I saw this old straw hat of my father's on the top shelf. He used to wear it when I was a kid. After he died, I asked my mum if I could have it. I don't know why, but this morning I put the hat on. And I sat on my bed and cried for 10 minutes straight."

He sounded unemotional. Just reporting the facts.

We were silent for a while, watching the muted TV. Then I turned my head and saw tears streaming down Ramir's face.

"I miss my dad," he said.

I put my arm around his shoulders and held him.

SATURDAY, OCTOBER 17

For four hours this morning, I worked on the outline, translating the cards on the floor into two pages of something resembling prose on my computer.

And I roughed out another version of the killing scene:

```
INTERIOR. TREVOR'S ROOM—NIGHT

JACKSON gently knocks on his son's bedroom door.
TREVOR sits mournfully on his bed.

                    JACKSON
Hi, Son. How are you feeling?

                    TREVOR
Thanks for coming up to see me, Dad. I'm feeling
much better now.

The MYSTERIOUS KILLER bursts into the room and
stabs JACKSON, who collapses on the floor and dies.

The MYSTERIOUS KILLER wipes the knife handle with
a paper towel and throws the knife out the window so
it lands in the pool.

                    TREVOR
                  (concerned)
Dad, are you all right?

The MYSTERIOUS KILLER shoves TREVOR through
the bedroom window. TREVOR plummets through the
air and is impaled on the fence below.

The MYSTERIOUS KILLER cackles with evil glee.
```

Of course, I'm still not sure who to *make* the Mysterious Killer. The sleazy business partner. The devoted wife. The wife's trampy best friend. The cheerleader sister. The snooty interior designer. (Cortland would *love* that idea.)

I found myself wishing Cortland were home, so I could discuss all my theories. In lieu of the man himself, I visited his cat.

I figure getting to know Pisces might be useful research if I do
end up writing for that vile traveling kitty show.

Cortland's apartment felt eerily silent. I wondered about turning on some music, but that felt too intrusive. And besides,
Cortland's collection of opera only confounds me.

"Pisces? Where are you hiding, Piscey-Miscey?" (Perhaps it's
inadvisable to record dialogue spoken to a cat.)

But no matter how friendly and alluring I sounded, the pussy
didn't come bounding out to greet me. She must be suffering from
severe paranoia. Dropped off at a new home, then abandoned.

Her food bowl was empty, though I'd filled it this morning
with one of the cans Cortland had left. Tuna packed in spring
water. I debated loading it up again, but I worried it might be
dangerous to overfeed a cat. In my childhood, I'd accidentally
overfed my Uncle Barry's rare tropical fish and burst their intes-
tines. I didn't want to witness that again.

At last I heard one muffled "meow" from the direction of
Cortland's bedroom. I followed a rustling sound and found her in
the custom-fitted bedroom closet, buried in the laundry hamper
beneath a pile of white cotton sheets.

I cooed a few gentle words, but when I reached in to scratch
behind her ears, she burrowed farther down beneath the bedding.
At least she didn't claw me again, making me bleed on a pillowcase.

Then I happened to gaze around Cortland's closet. Really I
wasn't snooping. And I was startled to see four shelves loaded
with bottles and jars and tubes. Skin-care products. Hundreds of
them. Eye gels and face creams and honey-almond-apricot skin
scrubs. Twelve bottles of the same hydrating lotion. Quantities
that would take decades for a single person to use.

Most of them were brands I recognized from The Shopping
Channel. The Connie Stevens Time Machine. The Marilyn Miglin
Iolight System. Joan Rivers Results. Serious Skin Care by that
fashion model who's married to Sylvester Stallone.

No wonder Cortland's skin always looks so youthful.

But then the outrageousness of it all began to register. Cortland teases me all the time about watching The Shopping Channel—even though I never actually order anything—and here he is, a complete moisturizer addict.

SATURDAY, OCTOBER 17
—MORE—

Bonding with Pisces wasn't a particularly satisfying method of procrastination, and I didn't think it was appropriate to experiment with Cortland's beauty secrets—even though I was dying to. I shouldn't even tell him that I'd discovered them.

So I used my time-tested method of procrastination: I called Ingrid and invited her out for an early lunch. I could talk through my plot and get her input. And she said she wanted me to take a look at her new abstract experiment for Berlin. She was transforming the miniature "painting in the painting" into a full-scale canvas.

Just as I was about to press Ingrid's door buzzer, I heard a knock on the window of Daphne's shop next door. Ing was peering out from between the row of card-bearing easels, motioning for me to come inside. Her face wore a serious frown.

We'd just talked 15 minutes earlier. What could have happened in 15 minutes?

I stepped inside The Paper Gallery. All the walls are lined with wire shelving, and there's a crowd of spinner racks in the middle of the floor—providing each handmade card with maximum visibility. There are hundreds: Ingrid's Human Beans, ironic Mona Lisa reproductions, line drawings of Toronto landmarks, plus innumerable hand-painted pumpkins—just in time for Halloween.

Surrounded by this riot of art, Ingrid stood with her arms folded tightly across her chest.

"What's wrong?" I asked.

Daphne grimaced behind the counter, mugging and bugging out her Cleopatra eyes. "We're having sort of an awkward situation."

"It's not awkward," Ing said. "I'm just pissed off."

"At me?"

"At Pierre. We had a fight just after you called. That's why I came in here."

"The neutral zone," Daphne said.

"How could you have a fight so quickly?"

"I asked him what he thought of the new painting. Basically, he said it was terrible."

"That doesn't sound like very constructive criticism."

"But he's right. It doesn't work on a bigger scale. It loses all its energy."

"But you were just experimenting. It's not fair to start judging already. Do you still want me to come have a look?"

"There's no point. I'm doing it over. But then Pierre said I shouldn't even be listening to Max Friedrich. I should just do the show with my curlicue things."

"Don't you sort of *have* to listen to Max?"

"That's what I said. And then Pierre said I've always been too easily influenced by other people's opinions. And you know that that's true."

"It's not *always* true."

To alleviate the angst, Daphne thrust her goodie bag toward us. "Do you want some candy?"

Ingrid listlessly reached for a Sour Patch Kid. I took a marshmallow banana, but it was stale and crunched into sugary dust in my mouth.

"So you just walked out?" I asked.

"Not soon enough. First, I said some stupid things about not needing his advice like I did when we were in school—because I've got other professional people to help me now. Which made him really mad, like it should have." Ingrid pushed a spinner rack and set it whirling. "I don't know whether I should apologize to him or he should apologize to me."

"I think you're both just in cranky moods today," Daphne said.

"But what if he's right? What if I'm not being true to myself? I mean, just last week I was telling you to listen to your own instincts about your screenplay. And now I'm not even doing the same thing myself."

"Let's go," I said, taking her arm. "I'll buy you lunch. You can have a glass of wine. I can give you some distraction. We can talk about my script."

"Does that mean you're over your writer's block?" Daphne inquired, delaying us at the door.

"I think so." I crossed my fingers and pointed them to heaven.

"So what's your movie going to be about?"

"I'm hoping it's sort of a post-modern twist on the classic Gothic murder-mystery."

"I love Gothic stuff," Daphne said. "All those creepy houses and damsels in distress and brooding lords of the manor. Can you tell me the story? Or do you two want to go eat?"

"I'm not really that hungry," Ing said.

"Would you mind? I was actually hoping to get some feedback. And from both of you would be even better."

"It's not like any customers are going to interrupt."

"I warn you, the story line's still got a few problems. That's what I'm trying to fix. But I was playing around with titles this morning. What do you think of *A Killing Upstairs*?"

"I like it," Ing said, nodding.

"I'd go see it," said Daphne.

Feeling the nervous adrenaline of pitching my story, I leaned against Daphne's counter to steady myself. "OK, so imagine the first scene of the movie is in a big creepy mansion at this incredibly glamorous party. This is where we see the opening credits."

"*A Killing Upstairs*," Daphne announced in a deep, froggy voice.

"The wife is in a beautiful ball gown, climbing the grand staircase. At first we think she's looking for her lover, so they can have a little rendezvous. She searches in every room of the house. Finally, she goes up to the third floor, and just as the credits finish, she finds her husband's body in a puddle of blood on the floor. Then she looks out the window and sees her son impaled on a fence in the backyard. And she screams."

"That's so gross," Daphne said. "I love it!"

"It looks as though her son stabbed his father, then jumped out the window to kill himself out of remorse."

"That's so *nasty*!" I was loving Daphne more and more.

Ingrid nodded. "It really is a good opening, Mitchell."

"But the story really kicks in the next morning when we meet the main character, the police detective. Something tells him the boy isn't really the killer."

"Maybe he reminds him of his own son," Daphne suggested.

"Or of himself when he was a teenager," offered Ingrid.

"So the detective starts investigating—talking to the wife and the dead boy's little sister. But his boss declares it an open-and-shut case and assigns him to another murder."

"Is the boss the typical grumpy chief of police?" Daphne asked.

"I don't want him to be a stereotype," I said curtly. "But like that, yes."

"Let me guess the next part," Daphne said, thrilled at the game. "The detective is so obsessed with the case, he investigates on his own, right?"

"Right."

Ingrid picked it up from there. "Is his wife worried about him too?"

Daphne mimicked the loving wife in a squeaky girly voice: "'Honey, you're jeopardizing your career. Think of the children.'"

I shut my eyes. "Oh my God. The whole setup is just a big string of clichés."

Daphne tapped a finger on her nose. "That part does sound a bit familiar."

"But if you're trying to write a commercial blockbuster," Ing said, "that means you're *supposed* to have clichés."

"It can't be one *continuous* cliché." I wished I hadn't eaten that marshmallow banana.

"It's not *that* terrible," Daphne soothed. "It just needs a little creativity."

Ingrid looked as sickened as I felt. "Oh, Mitchell, we've done the same thing to you that Pierre did to me."

"No, I'm glad you told me. I need to fix it. It's just that I need to fix it by tomorrow so I can show Aaron the outline."

Suddenly, Ingrid and Daphne turned away from me.

Pierre was standing in the doorway. "I wondered if you were still here," he said.

Ingrid stiffened. "I told you I was going to wait for Mitchell."

"Hi, Daphne. Hi, Michelle. I guess you've heard about our little fight by now."

We smiled tersely.

"Would you come back to the apartment?" he said to Ing. "We need to talk."

"I promised Mitchell I'd go for lunch."

"Just five minutes. Please?"

"I want to cool down first."

"I know I went too far about the painting."

"It's not that you weren't right. It's the way you said it."

"I'm sorry. Just come back for a couple of minutes, and we can get this behind us."

A relieved smile settled across Ingrid's face. "Do you mind waiting?" she asked me.

"Sure, it's fine," I said.

Then she and Pierre were out the door.

"Problem solved," I said brightly, though somewhat sardonically.

That left Daphne and me standing there. But she quickly saved us from awkwardness. "You know, Pierre just made some cards for me too."

She led me through the spinner racks to the far wall and pointed to a vertical row of miniature paintings. Dark and finely detailed scenes of a French village perched on a hillside.

"They're beautiful, huh?"

"They really are."

Obviously, Pierre's got lots of talent of his own. But for whatever reason, his art career never took off. No matter how supportive he might be to Ingrid, he still must feel a little competitive. It must be hard for him to see Ingrid's success, while he'd been sidetracked into advertising. The jealous Svengali.

"They haven't been moving very well yet," Daphne said. "I should put some in the window."

Beside them were the bright and boisterous Human Beans.

"We keep selling Ing's cards. At least one a day. Which is really good. But I still feel so bad for her."

"For Ingrid?"

Daphne nodded her blonde head sadly. "The two of them have been fighting so much."

"They have?"

"Every day."

I didn't know that. "About what?"

"About the apartment being too small and paying bills and who's making dinner. Ingrid tells me all about it. And I've been getting Pierre's side too. It's tricky. I'm not very good at playing the diplomat."

"I haven't heard a word about it."

"Don't tell her I said this," Daphne whispered, "but I think most of it's her own fault. She's not handling the relationship thing very well."

"How do you mean?"

"She wants it to work really badly, but Pierre doesn't think she's giving him enough attention."

"It doesn't sound like Pierre's being very helpful himself."

"But it's hard for him. Would you want to be in his position?"

"Which position?"

"You know. Barging in on you and Ingrid and Ramir. Any boyfriend would feel neglected against friends like you."

A customer came in, and Daphne returned to her spot behind the counter, cutting off our relationship analysis.

I twirled a spinner rack and stared at a collection of miniature collages made of tinfoil and toothpicks.

Maybe we do make Pierre feel excluded. Maybe I haven't given him a fair chance.

But if Ing is so miserable, why hasn't she told me?

When the customer departed, Daphne gazed upward, philosophically licking a grape Chupa Chup lollipop. "You know the problem with your movie, Mitchell?"

"Everybody's seen it a million times?"

"Everybody's sick of police detectives."

"I guess they *have* been worked to death."

"When you think about it, how many people actually know a cop in real life?"

"I don't."

"Neither do I. And who'd really want to?"

"I guess I'd have to spend time with one of them for research."

Daphne shuddered. "They always look so full of themselves when you see them walking down the street."

I extrapolated: "If writers don't really know police officers, no wonder police stories are always clichés based on clichés."

"Exactly. I mean, I really like your party scene and the murders and everything. But police detectives just aren't Gothic enough."

"A different genre. A different historical period."

"And Gothic stories usually have a woman as the main character."

"A *female* police detective?"

"What if the person doing the investigation is part of your story already? Like the mother of the crazy kid. Or the sister who wants to prove her brother's really innocent."

Fabulous ideas cascaded into place. "Oh my God, Daphne, that's perfect!" I kissed her on the cheek, knocking the sucker from her mouth. "Thank you. Thank you. Tell Ingrid to call me. I have to get back to my computer."

SATURDAY, OCTOBER 17
—LATER—

Further resistance was futile.

I dialed the number for "Donnington, L." on Hampton Avenue.

The line picked up. Shit. I was hoping she'd be out on a Saturday night. I was hoping to just leave a message.

"Hello," a surly woman snapped.

"Is this Laura Donnington?"

"Speaking."

"I'm wondering if this is the same Laura Donnington who used to live on Thornfield Road."

"Three guesses why you're calling." And she hung up.

No one's ever hung up on me before. Except when I had that telemarketing job for two days.

I sat staring at the phone in shock.

At least I could presume it was the *right* Laura Donnington. Otherwise, she wouldn't have hung up on me. But if it *was* her and she wouldn't talk to me, it would put my whole investigation at a standstill. Back to fictionalization.

I was still sitting there, thinking this through, when the phone rang.

"Hello, Mitchell Draper speaking," I said, which is how I always answer the phone to give myself an air of professional credibility.

"You'd better not harass me," Laura Donnington said. "I have Caller ID."

"I don't want to harass you. I just want to ask you a few questions."

"My brother killed my father. What else is there to know?"

"Actually, there are several things—"

"Like what?"

"Well, um, you see, I'm a screenwriter and—"

"You want to turn Trevor into a freak like in *Halloween* or *Friday the 13th*?" She hung up again.

119

I phoned her right back. "Actually, I'm planning to make Trevor innocent."

That gave her pause. "How are you going to do that?"

"I'm turning the story into a whodunit. Change it so somebody else killed your father and pushed your brother out the window—then put the blame on Trevor."

"Everybody knows Trevor was guilty." And she hung up again.

I stared at the phone expectantly.

Sure enough, it rang again.

"How'd you hear about Trevor in the first place?"

"I should have told you that part right away. We have a mutual friend. Someone you might remember—Cortland McPhee. He's an interior designer. He worked on the house with your mother."

"I remember him," she said. "He gave me a necklace once. How is he?"

"Great," I said. It didn't seem the right moment to mention a terminal brain tumour. "Actually, he's in New York this weekend with Ermina Milenska. I think she was a friend of your mother's."

"Auntie Ermi. She was always really pushy."

"I've only met her once myself, but I think I know what you mean."

"So you're making a movie about Trevor?"

"I don't know if it'll actually get made. I'm just doing some research. I'll fictionalize everything. Change all the names when I actually write it."

"Why bother changing anything? Everybody always gets the story wrong anyway."

"That's why I want to talk to you. To make sure I get it right."

She paused. "So you want to interview me or something?"

"That's what I was hoping."

"Let me think about it." And she hung up.

Well, that was a positive sign. Sort of. She'd neglected to mention exactly *when* she'd call back. I steeled myself to wait several weeks for rejection—as I had so many other times in my career.

I turned on The Shopping Channel for comfort—they were pitching a new juice maker—and sat down in front of my com-

puter to type out my conversation(s) with Laura. I figure it's a
good idea to record all my research to use as reference—if and
when I actually write the script.

Much to my shock, 15 minutes later the phone rang.

"Tomorrow's Sunday. I'm always home," Laura said. "Come
around noon or whatever time you want."

Right away I called Ingrid.

"Is everything better between you and Pierre?"

"We had a good talk. And then we sort of—well, made up, you
know. Anyway, I'm sorry I ran out of Daphne's like that. It was
such a stupid teenager thing to do."

"Love makes everybody act like a teenager. But things are
really OK with you?"

"Of course they are." Nothing else. No outpouring of further,
more intimate revelations. "But it was still rude to ditch you.
I'm sorry."

"Well, if you want to make it up to me, you could do me a
little favour."

"Why am I already starting to get worried?"

SUNDAY, OCTOBER 18

Ingrid and I were in the back of a taxi heading to Laura Donnington's house.

"I can't believe you talked me into this," Ing said.

"You told me you thought it was an interesting story. Now you get to learn about it firsthand."

"I don't want to ask some woman I don't know about how her family got murdered."

"She sounded really casual about the whole thing on the phone."

"How can you ever be casual when your father and brother die that way?"

I wasn't sure about that point myself.

We were speeding across the bridge over the Don Valley, the massive river ravine that cuts a vertical dividing line through the city. Rosedale—the posh neighbourhood where Laura Donnington had grown up—is planted on the west. Riverdale—where she lived now—sits on the east.

Ingrid twisted uncomfortably, rearranging her black leather jacket. "I should be at home, trying that painting again."

"This won't take long. But it'll be better having you there with me. A sympathetic female presence. What if she starts crying?"

"Then I'll start crying too. You know what I'm like."

"What if she gets mad? Or what if she turns violent?"

"You want me to be your bodyguard?"

"You don't have to protect me. You can just run for help. Quickly."

"If you're going to start investigating murders, Mitchell, you can't be a chicken. Hercule Poirot and Miss Marple didn't worry about their personal safety."

"But we're doing this together. It'll be more like *McMillan and Wife*."

We enjoyed a moment's distraction, staring out the cab windows at Riverdale's assortment of Greek restaurants and home-decorating shops. Five young women with baby carriages had created a traffic jam in front of a chic gift boutique.

"Pierre and I were talking about moving out here," Ing said.

After their fight?

"But your studio is so great. And you had such a hard time finding it in the first place."

"It's not really designed for two people. And the studio is *my* place. It might be good to move somewhere else—a new beginning for both of us."

"I guess that makes sense."

"Maybe buy a house. It'd be nice if we want to settle down."

Somehow that left me feeling even more unsettled. Why didn't she want to tell me the whole story of what was going on with Pierre?

The cab turned right onto Hampton Avenue, lush and canopied with giant gold-leafed trees. Undeniably, it would be an appealing place to live. But I counted down the house numbers as though we were approaching a dreaded explosion. "Here it is."

I paid the cab driver, and we climbed out.

We stared up at Laura Donnington's house. It was a handsome semidetached—rosy red brick with brown-painted wooden steps leading up to the front door. But it was decidedly ordinary compared to the mansion in which she'd grown up.

"The dread is hitting me full force," I said.

"It's like you're one of those trashy tabloid journalists —hoping to make a fortune off somebody's dead relatives."

"Don't put it that way. My ethics are confused enough as it is."

"Would you kill me if I ran away?" Ing asked. "You could meet me at The Second Cup after you've finished."

"I've done favours for you, Ingrid. Remember all the art gallery openings I've gone to?"

"I don't think this is exactly a fair trade." And for no apparent reason, she started giggling. I glared at her impatiently. Then I burst out giggling as well. I grabbed her hand, and we headed up the front walk, both bent over with our ridiculous nervous laughter.

Before we could compose ourselves, Laura Donnington

opened the door—regarding us with a combination of surprise and disgust.

"You didn't tell me you were bringing anybody else," she said.

Laura wore a thick brown turtleneck sweater, which only emphasized the thin, strained expression of her face. She had oversize front teeth—though not quite buck—and thick brown hair cut to her shoulders. Her bangs were heavy, and the hair on either side of her head fell forward, threatening to hide her face entirely.

"This is my friend Ingrid Iversen. She's helping me with my research."

"Hi," Ing said.

"I wish you'd warned me."

"I should have. I'm sorry."

Laura paused to consider, scowled, then allowed us in.

Ingrid and I stood transfixed by a large painting above the fireplace. A family portrait. The kind of formal painting you'd expect to see hanging in a museum, revealing the extravagant vanities of the Victorian upper classes. But this painting portrayed the four members of the ill-fated Donnington family, wearing the finest attire of the 1970s.

"If you've been doing your research, I guess you already know who they are," Laura said.

Ingrid gave me a distressed flash of her eyes. I could tell she was wondering, as I was, if she'd want such a morbid reminder hanging in her living room.

Vivienne Donnington, with her windswept black hair, exuded '70s glamour in a navy pantsuit. Jackson—collegiate handsome—was formal in a wide-lapelled navy jacket with a big-collared baby-blue shirt. The 12-year-old Laura wore a long burgundy velvet dress. Trevor, the 17-year-old accused murderer, sported a white shirt with a wide burgundy tie.

"My mother had us pose for it about six months before they

died," Laura said. "She told us not to smile so we'd look more interesting. But the painter gave me a smile anyway."

The childhood Laura wore a carefree grin. It looked especially peculiar, because her expression now was so sullen.

"My brother only went to one of the posing sessions. He couldn't sit still long enough. He and the painter got into a big argument."

Despite this, Trevor was portrayed very attractively. Compared to the photographs I'd seen, he looked more relaxed, with his shoulder-length dark hair feathered back, a belligerent turn to his lips and cocky humour in his brown eyes. (Maybe that was budding insanity.)

"Were you and Trevor very close?"

"He was my big brother. Of course we were close."

"Sorry. Dumb question."

Laura squinted into my eyes with the same serious suspicion that had greeted me at the door. "I guess you might as well sit down," she said.

Laura headed for a big brown corduroy chair beside the fireplace—an oversized mug of coffee already on the table in front of her. Ingrid and I sat on the brown suede couch opposite—coffee-less.

The living room was nondescript. Lots of pine and earth tones. A grandfather clock ticked loudly by the door to the kitchen. But there was no evidence of the major wealth she must have inherited as the sole heir of the family estate.

"So...shall we get started?" I suggested, feeling awkward.

"I have a question for you first," Laura said. "If Trevor didn't do it, who do you think did?"

"I have no idea. That's why I wanted to talk to you. To make sure I understand everyone's motivations."

"Why not just make up their motivations? They won't care. They're all dead."

"But would *you* care?" Ing asked.

Laura stared at Ing through her falling-forward hair. "I was just an innocent bystander. I didn't have anything to do with it."

"But you remember what happened that night?"

"Of course I remember. I wish I could block out all the memories like some people can. I didn't know all the background at the time. But when I was older, my mother told me to help me understand what happened."

"I want to know everything," I said. I adjusted the writing pad on my lap so I could take notes. "I read that your father's business partner was one of the suspects."

"That's what my mother thought all along. She never believed Trevor did it. But the police decided it was Trevor, and they closed the case. There wasn't any arguing after that."

"But was it something you could imagine Trevor doing?" Ing asked.

"My brother was a paranoid schizophrenic. He probably had no idea what happened that night. He might have thought he was killing Hitler or Charles Manson. He probably thought he was flying, not jumping out the window."

"So he was having delusions?"

"They'd started about two years earlier. He was normal before that. I mean, he was always hyper—lots of energy. Then he'd have these mood swings. They thought he was manic-depressive at first, and they put him on lithium. After he died, they diagnosed him as schizophrenic. That's when it usually comes on—when you're 17 or 18." Laura stared into her coffee. "So what else do you want to know about him? He loved playing tennis. He read a lot. He spent a lot of time in his room by himself."

"Did he have many friends?"

"He'd scared everybody off by the end. He'd been thrown out of a bunch of private schools. My mother sent him to Upper Canada College, then to St. Andrew's, and then that boarding school out in Lakefield. Finally, he said he'd only go to Jarvis Collegiate. Which my mother didn't like because it was a public high school, and she wanted us both to go to private. But other kids from Rosedale were going to Jarvis. So she let him switch."

"Did that work better?"

"He stayed all year at least. But he was always in trouble. He'd get angry for no reason. That's why it was so confusing. He was either yelling or quiet. Mostly he'd just sit in his room and write in his diary."

"He kept a diary?"

"He wrote down everything that ever happened. They told us afterward that that's an early sign of schizophrenia."

"Mitchell writes everything down too," Ing said.

I knew Ingrid would be teasing me about that point later. But Laura didn't seem to think it was funny. She looked at me intensely, staring into my eyes.

"Did you ever see anything he wrote?" I asked.

"Not his diary, but some other things. Weird, scary stuff— short stories and poems. He said he wanted to be a horror writer like Stephen King. His favourite book was *The Shining*."

"That was my favourite book when I was a teenager too," I said.

Laura stared at me peculiarly but didn't say anything.

"Did you keep any of his diaries?"

"I don't have them locked in a suitcase in the basement, if that's what you're hoping." Laura laughed darkly. "About a month before he died, Trevor decided we were searching through his things when he was at school. He had this secret hiding place in his room. There were some loose floorboards under the window, and there was a hole underneath. That's where he kept everything he wrote. He showed me once. So anyway, he took a metal garbage can up to his room and set all the diaries on fire. He could have burned the whole house down. My mother was furious."

"Did he normally get along all right with your parents?" Ingrid asked. She was proving to be a better interrogator than I was.

"He and my father were best friends. That's one of the reasons my mother couldn't believe Trevor did it. She and my father were always trying to figure out how to help Trevor. She had him seeing a bunch of therapists."

"And one of them was Nigel Bhandari?"

Laura pushed back her hair. "How do you know about him?"

"We have a friend who goes to see him now for therapy," Ing said.

"Your friend's in the cult?"

"He prefers not to call it that," I said.

"Have you ever been to any of Dr. Bhandari's meetings?" Ing asked.

"I'd never go to one of those crazy groups. I just read about him in the paper sometimes."

"Did Trevor get along with Dr. Bhandari?"

"Trevor didn't like any therapists. But my mother wanted him to see Dr. Bhandari because she was really good friends with him herself."

"Is that why she sold him your house?"

"Nobody else wanted it. Not after what happened. She said she wanted Dr. Bhandari to clear the negative energy. She was going through a whole spiritual phase when it happened. She thought Dr. Bhandari might be able to help Trevor's soul or something. I don't know—maybe they did an exorcism."

"So you and your mother moved somewhere else?"

"We went to my aunt's in Oakville at first. Then my mother got married again six months later."

"Did your life get back to normal after that?"

Laura shrugged. "I was never close to my stepfather. Even with my mother, things were different. They were both killed in a car accident 10 years ago." Laura stood abruptly. "I need another coffee. Do you want some?"

Laura headed to the back of the house, and Ingrid and I followed her into the kitchen. All maple cabinetry and black granite countertops. Attractive enough, but devoid of character. She poured from a Mr. Coffee decanter.

"I drink about 12 cups a day, and it never keeps me awake," Laura said. "They always joke about me where I work."

"Where do you work?" Ing asked.

Laura opened a package of almond biscuits and dumped them onto a plate. "I'm a bookkeeper at a medical clinic. Three afternoons a week. Mostly to get me out of the house."

I wondered about her personal life. It didn't seem as if she was married or had any children. Did she have any friends? It didn't seem like very much fun, being independently wealthy.

"Are these yours?" Ing stared into a shoebox on the counter. I could see it was filled with drawings on small sheets of notepaper.

"Those things? They're just stupid."

"They're good," Ing said. "Did you ever study drawing?"

"It's just a hobby. It's not even a hobby. I don't even think about it."

I went over and looked more closely. Illustrations in black ink. The kind of art that should be on tarot cards or in a book of Edgar Allan Poe stories. Screaming corpses rising from coffins. Gravestones cracked down the middle. An old-fashioned window, smashed to pieces. Like the window her brother had jumped through at Thornfield Manor?

"I do them when I'm watching TV or when I'm on the phone. Then I just shove them in that box. I don't know why I even keep them."

"They're very powerful," Ing said.

For a moment Laura looked pleased. Then confused at being pleased. She looked down, and her hair fell forward. "So do you want me to give all the gory details of what happened? That's what you really came for, isn't it?"

Laura led us back to the living room, carrying her coffee and the plate of cookies. This time she sat on the couch with Ingrid beside her. I took the big chair by the fireplace.

Laura squinted again, and it was as if she was looking inside herself, not at us. "I was excited for weeks about the big party. My mother let me help plan it. Or she pretended to anyway. I went to a meeting with her and that friend of yours, Mr. McPhee. The house was beautiful that night. Flowers hanging everywhere. This Hawaiian band was playing luau music. My mother gave me a little grass skirt to wear. I had a flower necklace. It was tacky, but I loved it. My father said I was his little Hawaiian princess. I danced around, saying 'aloha' to everybody."

"Cortland told me your brother didn't actually come to the party."

"He was supposed to. My mother bought him a new tuxedo. He looked really handsome. But after he got dressed, he and my mother had another fight. Mom told him she didn't want him to come to be around if he was going to act that way, and Trevor stormed up to his room and hid the way he always did. I was sort of mad at him too because he'd promised he'd dance with me at the party." She shook her head, as if disgusted with herself. "When I went up to bed, I remember thinking it was the best night of my life."

"Was your bedroom on the third floor too?"

"On the second. It looked onto the street. I had a little balcony over the front door so I could snoop on everybody in the neighbourhood. My brother used to have the room beside mine. But when he started getting weird, he said he wanted more privacy. They gave him one of the old servants' rooms upstairs."

"And nobody saw Trevor during the party?" Ing asked.

Laura shrugged. "My mother tried. She went up with some food from the buffet. She knocked, but Trevor didn't answer, so she left the plate outside his door. Afterward, they found the empty plate in his room. He'd eaten anyway. His last meal." Laura picked up an almond cookie. "They found a vodka bottle too—all smashed. They said he'd drunk most of it. That's another reason the police thought he went so crazy."

"But you said your mother thought your father's business partner was involved. Bill Zale. I read that he and your father had a fight that night."

"I didn't see any it myself. I was in another room, I guess. But my mom said Bill was drunk and he started yelling, asking everyone where my father was. Dad took him upstairs to his office so they could talk in private. It was something about money. Bill wanted to take control of their printing company, even though it was my father who was really in charge of it. Anyway, after Bill left, Dad came back into the ballroom."

"So people saw him?"

"He was still alive, if that's what you're asking. But like I said, I didn't know any of those things were going on. I was still having a great time. My mom sent me up to bed just after midnight. Probably by then my father and my brother were already dead."

"Did the police pin down when it actually happened?" Ing asked.

"Sometime between 11:30 and midnight."

"So they thought Bill came back to the house?"

"That was my mother's theory. But at first she didn't even notice Dad was gone. She thought he was off talking to people in another part of the house. It wasn't until about 1 o'clock that she went up to their bedroom to look for him. And he wasn't there."

Laura paused a moment.

"Then she went up the back staircase to the third floor to check on my brother. The door to his bedroom was open, which was strange because Trevor always kept the door locked. And he wasn't there, which she couldn't figure out either. Then she noticed there was a breeze coming into the room. She thought Trevor had left the window open. She was just going over to close it when she realized there was a chair turned over and everything was messed up, like there'd been a fight. That's when she saw my father on the floor with blood all over his chest. She was in shock at first. She didn't know what to do. So automatically she went to close the window. And then she realized the window wasn't there. It was all broken glass hanging from the frame. When she looked out, she cut her hand. Then she saw Trevor. And she started screaming."

I took a breath. The scene was so vivid.

Ingrid glanced at me, her eyes glistening with tears.

"I sat straight up in bed. I'd never heard my mother scream, but I knew it was her. I was the first one to get upstairs. I was wearing my pink nightgown—Laura Ashley. I always liked Laura Ashley clothes because we had the same first name."

I smiled tightly at the sentiment, but I wanted her to go on.

"Trevor hadn't let me into his room for a long time, so it was weird to go in there. Right away I saw my father lying on his back

131

on the floor between the bed and the wall. There was blood all over his white shirt. I could see the slit in the cloth where the knife went in. I said something stupid like 'Is he OK?' and my mother turned away from the window, and I saw the blood on her hands. For a moment, I thought she was the one who'd killed him. Then she said, 'Your brother! Your brother!' She tried to push me out of the room, because she didn't want me to see. But I wouldn't move. Then our housekeeper, Mary, rushed in and she saw Daddy too. She practically dragged me down to my bedroom and told me to stay there. A moment later, I heard Mom and Mary go running down the back stairs to the kitchen."

Laura took a slow sip of coffee.

"I figured there must have been something going on in the backyard, and obviously it had to do with Trevor. So I went to my father's office, which was on the second floor too, right underneath Trevor's room. I opened the window, and just as I did, all the bright lights in the backyard turned on, and I saw him. We had a wrought-iron fence with spikes on the top that went all the way around the swimming pool. Trevor was face down, sort of bent over, lying on top of the fence. He was wearing a white T-shirt and jeans—that's what he always wore around the house. And he had bare feet. And his shirt was bright red. You could see that two of the spikes had come out right through his back. My mother ran into the backyard, and she tried to move him, tried to lift him off. But he was stuck there, stuck on the fence."

My stomach churned.

"I guess I was in shock," Laura said. "I sat at my father's desk. He had a big brown leather chair. Everything on his desk was pushed over, knocked out of place—the ink blotter and all his pens. They figure the desk got banged when Dad was fighting with Bill. I remember straightening everything up, the way my father always kept it. He liked things to be perfect. Afterward, the police said I should have left things the way they were. But I wanted it all to be neat and tidy for my dad."

"It must have been horrible for you," Ing said.

"There were sirens, and the police came and then the ambulance. They asked me questions over and over again—because they couldn't find the knife at first. We knew my brother always kept a big butcher knife from the kitchen beside his bed. He said he wanted it in case there were burglars. So he could protect us."

"But then they found the knife in the pool?"

"Not until the next morning. The police figured Trevor threw the knife before he jumped, or maybe it fell when he fell. But there weren't any fingerprints on the handle."

"I read about that."

Laura emptied her coffee mug. "The strange thing is that they found his fingerprints on the doorknob to my father's office. His were the last ones. They thought Trevor must have heard Dad and Bill Zale when they were arguing, and he came down to see what was going on."

"So why did your mother think Bill killed them?"

"She thought Bill must have come back to the house when Dad was upstairs checking on Trevor. Then Bill stabbed my father and killed Trevor to keep him quiet—pushed him from behind so he fell out the window."

I wondered if that made sense. A fall from a third-floor window wouldn't have definitely killed Trevor—if it hadn't been for that nasty fence.

"But the police decided it wasn't Bill after all."

"They couldn't find any of his fingerprints up in Trevor's room. But they found Trevor's fingerprints on a broken chair that he must have thrown at my father. Anyway, a few days later, they decided Trevor was guilty. My mother became a total mess. She saw Dr. Bhandari a couple of hours every day. I remember the morning after it happened, when the police were still there, Dr. Bhandari took me out for a walk in the ravine. Emergency grief counseling. Then my mother drove me to my aunt's place out in Oakville. I never went back to the house again. I've never even seen it since then."

"You've never been curious?"

"Sometimes I think about driving along the street, but I never do. Sometimes I dream I'm back there at the party. I come downstairs and everybody's still there, dancing and having a wonderful time, and I start waltzing with my father like we did that night. And Trevor comes downstairs, and I dance with him too." She rubbed her eyes with the heels of her palms. "Oh God, this is like another therapy session. Maybe you should leave."

"I'm sorry if we upset you," Ing said.

"It's OK. It's nothing new."

Ingrid stood to leave, but Laura sat where she was. "Do you really think Trevor might be innocent?"

"Do you?" I asked.

Laura shrugged again. "Trevor and my father really loved each other. All that stuff about the knife with no fingerprints. About Bill Zale. My mother really believed Trevor didn't do it. But maybe she had to think that way to protect herself. Denial and all that. But it'd be nice if he wasn't guilty."

"It must be so hard to talk about this," Ingrid said.

Laura looked at her derisively. "Do you think this is the first time I've told the story? Do you know how many therapists I've been to? Those pictures I draw—they're a joke. All those corpses and haunted houses. It's because I can't do anything else."

"It's good if it helps you work things out," Ing said.

"My psychiatrist says it's healthy—that I'm exorcising my demons or something."

"Have you ever thought of showing them to people? Maybe putting them on cards?"

"*Greeting* cards? I can't imagine anybody sending one for a birthday."

I was inclined to agree. But Ingrid persevered. "I have a friend who has a card shop. I think she might like them. It'd be easy to glue them onto card stock. I can show you how."

Laura seemed doubtful, but they went into the kitchen together to look at the drawings again. Maybe Daphne could use the cards for a Gothic Halloween window display.

☆

I went back to the portrait above the fireplace for one last look at Trevor. I stared up at him and wondered if it was totally ludicrous to presume he was innocent. But it was interesting to hear that he kept a diary. Even more interesting because I'd destroyed my own childhood journals as well—in my own fit of existential depression. But instead of burning them, I'd torn the paper into tiny squares and then mulched them into pulp in the bathtub.

I sat in an armchair and contemplated—wondering how I could work all this into my screenplay.

A few minutes later, Laura and Ingrid returned from the kitchen and joined me in staring at the painting.

Laura pushed the hair back from her face. "You look like Trevor, you know."

"Me?" I said.

"That's what I thought as soon as you came in the door. That's why it's so weird talking to you."

Ingrid nodded in agreement. "I didn't notice it at first, Mitchell. But it's true—once you compensate for the age difference."

I looked at the painting again. I remembered thinking that Trevor looked familiar when I'd first seen his photographs. But I didn't think he looked *that* familiar.

"I hope your movie works out," Laura said. "It'd be good if they're not totally forgotten."

I looked at the painting one last time and gazed hard into Trevor's eyes, wondering if his spirit really was trying to tell me something about what had happened all those years ago—and wondering if I was totally losing my marbles.

MONDAY, OCTOBER 19

When I got home from Laura's yesterday, I came back to my computer and worked for the rest of the afternoon.

The outline took shape more easily than anything I've ever written. By 6 o'clock, a perfect two-page draft was printed and ready in my leather portfolio case by the door.

I sat patiently waiting for Aaron to call, as promised, as soon as he got back from Niagara Falls. I have to admit I let my mind wander along a path of fantasies. Solving the murder case. Clearing Trevor's name. Police medals of honour. My screenplay produced by Apex Entertainment. Turning the screenplay into a book. Talk shows. Literary prizes. Millions of dollars.

I jumped when the phone rang.

"Are you still free for dinner?" Aaron asked.

As if I would have made other plans. "Should I come to the Sutton Place?"

"I switched hotels. I'm at the Four Seasons. Room 1402. How fast can you be here?"

"Very fast."

I grabbed my portfolio and power-walked along Prince Arthur to the hotel.

I did notice the irony of returning to the Four Seasons, where I had once before come to meet a movie producer—who then ripped my work to shreds and nearly got me killed because of her ridiculous plot to seek revenge on the mob.

But that's another story.

Without glancing at a soul, I sped across the sumptuous hotel lobby. A dim wood-paneled elevator whisked me to the 14th floor, where I circled around a plush Wedgwood-blue hall to 1402. The door was held ajar by the deadbolt. I pushed it open and called hello.

No answer.

I released the deadbolt and closed the door, locking it behind me.

It was a suite. Pale-green carpet. Peach upholstery on the

couch and antique-ish chairs. White sheer curtains.

No sign of Aaron.

Suddenly, I pictured myself finding him crumpled in the bath-tub, naked and stabbed to death. The police would burst into the room and charge me with murder.

Obviously, I've been too focused on violent movie clichés.

I stepped farther into the room and noticed a set of frosted-glass French doors on my right. I pushed them open, and there was Aaron in the centre of a king-size bed. He was draped in a white terry-cloth bathrobe, in delectable contrast to his tanned skin and hairy chest.

"You're alive," I said.

"So far."

I dropped my portfolio on the floor and joined him.

Fast-forward through the resulting sex scene, which involved a few lines of witty dialogue but no pivotal plot developments.

An hour later we were sipping minibar champagne and shar-ing a tin of cashews and a Kit Kat bar while lolling blissfully in a nest of silky cotton sheets.

"The falls are gorgeous, but the town is the tackiest place I've ever seen."

"You'll have to live there when they're shooting?"

He nodded in mid sip. "But it's only an hour-and-a-half drive."

"Maybe I can take the bus and come visit."

"I'd probably be happier to come back here to civilization." He fluffed a pillow behind him. "So how are things progressing with your script?"

"Really well, I think. This afternoon I interviewed the daugh-ter of the family—Laura Donnington."

"Right to the source, huh?"

"She gave me a lot of good background details. And I have a connection to the psychiatrist her brother was seeing."

"You'll have the script written in no time."

"In fact, I've already finished the two-page outline."

"Did you bring it?"

"By coincidence, I did." I reached for it on the floor.

"I've never been pitched to in bed before," Aaron laughed. "At least not this way."

"Am I being too tacky?"

"No, go right ahead."

I pulled a sheet over my crotch, so my fragile ego wasn't totally exposed. "I've come up with a working title. *A Killing Upstairs.*"

"That's pretty good for a start."

"And I've turned the story into a whodunit. 'A clever post-modern twist on the classic Gothic murder-mystery.'"

"I'm with you so far."

"The main character is Lana Donnegan—I changed her name a bit. She's beautiful, intelligent, successful, 30—all the typical heroine stuff. Anyway, she's been having strange recurring nightmares. So she goes to see a psychic who tells her that a tall, dark, and handsome man is floating above her in the spirit world. Then she has the dream again, and she realizes that the spirit must be her dead brother who everybody believes killed his father and himself over 20 years ago. Now she thinks his spirit has come back to haunt her, because he wants her to prove that he's innocent."

"So it's a ghost story?"

"It could be. Even she's not sure if she believes it."

"I like that." Aaron sat forward in bed, looking like an eager little boy. He was so adorable, it urged me on.

"So Lana begins investigating the crime. She's trying to prove that it was a double murder and not a murder-suicide. So she starts talking to all the people who were there on the night of the party. I'll fill that part in as I'm interviewing people myself. And we follow her along as she finds clues and makes deductions. Then at the climax, she gathers all the people together at the house, and that's where she reveals the true identity of the murderer."

"So who was the murderer?"

"Right now I'm saying it was the husband's business partner. But I might change that as I go along. I want to make it a big glamorous whodunit. An all-star cast like *Murder on the Orient Express*

138

or *Death on the Nile*. Nobody's made a picture like that in years."

"Because the budget for the actors is so big."

"Is that a problem?"

"No, it's a good idea. It could work as a hook."

"So you think it might have a chance?"

Aaron glanced at my two pages and handed them back to me. "You should keep working on it—write up a whole treatment. About 20 pages. I can have a look when I come back from L.A."

"When's that?"

"We start shooting in two weeks."

"So you mean Apex might produce it?"

"We can test it out. Maybe I can use a few connections—see if I can get you some development money."

"Exactly how much development money?"

Aaron laughed at my shamelessness. "Well, if it's cast right, a picture like that would probably have a $20 or $30 million budget. So if it goes into production, the fee for the writer would be about $800,000."

I choked on my champagne.

"That's only if it goes into production. But I might be able to get you $25,000 in advance."

"That's fine," I said. "More than fine." Even though $25,000 was a tiny fraction, it would still save me from *Travels with Willie*.

"See, it always helps if you sleep with the right people."

I lay back and looked at the ceiling, my mind swelling again with fantasies. $800,000. I'd practically be a millionaire. It's exactly what I'd envisioned.

"What are you thinking?" he asked.

"Nothing," I said lightly.

"One thing I've already figured out about you, Mitchell Draper, is that you're never thinking nothing."

"It's that obvious?"

Aaron stretched his arms behind his head. "You know, if you lived in L.A., you'd probably do really well for yourself."

"You think so?"

"Uh-huh."

"I've never even been there before. I can't imagine *moving* there. Actually, I *have* imagined it. I just can't imagine doing it."

"No matter what anybody says, you have to live there if you want to get a writing career moving. You could get work in TV, no problem."

"I wouldn't know where to start. I wouldn't know anybody. Except you."

"Everybody in L.A. is in the entertainment business, so you always have something in common."

I was starting to get excited. Imagining it as a real possibility. "Of course, I've heard about L.A. all my life on TV shows, so I sort of feel like I know it already. What part do you live in?"

"Santa Monica."

"That's fancy, isn't it?"

"It's nice enough. But my place isn't anything special."

"Is it a *big* place? With a spare room?"

I admit I was being dangerously pushy.

"Listen, Mitchell, maybe we need to talk about something."

"About what?"

"Just so we're up front."

"Up front about what?"

"I'm not exactly single."

"You're not?" I tried to hold my face together.

"I have a lover back home."

"Well...that's great. I'm happy for you."

"I don't normally talk about it. It's just that Ryan and I have an arrangement."

"Ryan? That's his name?" All men named Ryan are genetically perfect. "So what's your arrangement?"

"I can see other guys, but only when I'm out of town."

"Very reasonable," I nodded.

"So do you have a boyfriend?" he asked casually—as if it wasn't strange that he was asking me this when we were already naked and post-coitus.

"I did," I said. "Until a few months ago. He moved to Vancouver."

"Did you two fool around on the side?"

"No. Old-fashioned. Monogamous. Not that everybody has to be."

"Anyway, the point is that if you came to L.A., we'd just have to be friends. That's OK?"

"Fine," I said. "Sure. Whatever."

"But we can still have a good time now, right?"

"Right." I smiled. And he kissed me on the shoulder.

I didn't want to make it seem like a big deal. I didn't want to look uptight. Because it wasn't as if Aaron had been leading me on. It was my own romantic fantasies that were letting me down. Yet again.

We ordered dinner from room service. We watched part of *Chinatown* on TV, and we talked about *Niagara*. And we had sex again. And I acted perfectly normal.

I stayed the night, but I barely slept.

MONDAY, OCTOBER 19
—MORE—

Aaron had a 9 A.M. meeting and then he was heading directly to the airport. So after a hurried breakfast, I departed—amid his promises to call me as soon as he gets back into town and my promises to keep him informed about any developments on the script.

He acted as though everything is perfectly normal. And maybe it is. Except now I don't have a boyfriend again, and I have a potential paycheque of $800,000.

It was all so overwhelming, I didn't know how to feel.

I've decided that next time Aaron and I talk, I'm going to clarify my position. I think it's better if we keep things strictly business between us from here on in.

I'd just better make sure this treatment is the best thing I ever write. And the best way to ensure that is to do more research.

I figured Cortland might be able to give me some more ideas. I decided I'd drop in on him, because he was supposed to come home from New York last night and he always wakes up early.

Just as I was about to knock on his door, I heard strange music coming from inside his apartment. Pop music. The Backstreet Boys. Music so banal that Cortland would never tolerate it in his presence. Could I have stumbled on burglars? Burglars who like boy bands? Or was I just envisioning another movie-thriller cliché?

I wondered if I should get my key to his apartment. But I didn't want to barge in on crooks who were arrogant enough to turn on the radio. They might be armed and dangerous.

Maybe I could scare them off.

I knocked sharply—prepared to run at the first sign of a gun barrel. But when the door opened, standing there with proprietary nonchalance was a towering black woman in a baggy green nurse's uniform. Her nametag said ROSEMARY.

"Can I help you?" she asked.

"I'm looking for Cortland. Is he OK?"

"He's resting right now."

"I'm a friend of his. My name's Mitchell. I live down the hall."

"I can tell him you dropped by."

Cortland's voice bellowed from deep within the apartment. "If that's Mitchell, please escort him in."

Rosemary permitted me access.

"What happened?" I whispered to her.

"He was coming home from a trip someplace. He had a seizure on the airplane."

"But he's OK?"

"Seems to be."

She led me through Cortland's apartment as if she knew the way better than I did. I noticed the black figure of Pisces dash across the floor from the bathroom to the bedroom.

"What about his cat? Did anybody feed her this morning?"

"All taken care of."

And there was Cortland in his red plaid pyjamas, ensconced in his grand lace-canopy bed. His skin was grey, his face hollow. And, of course, he was smoking a cigarette.

Pisces sat crouched in the corner, observing the situation apprehensively.

"This is a surprise," I said.

"For me as well. Now, Mitchell, pull over that chair and talk to me. I'm in desperate need of stimulating conversation."

"Call if you need me," Rosemary said as she departed.

"So you got sick on the plane?"

"Apparently. I can't remember a thing myself. But the doctors have ordered complete bed rest. Thus Beatrice has hired a battalion of round-the-clock nursemaids. In any case, let's not dwell on misfortune. Ermina and I had a glorious time in New York. Lunch at The Plaza. Dinner at Le Cirque. I even took that ferry that goes around Manhattan. My final farewell to the magical island."

"I'm sure you'll be back on your feet in no time."

"We shall see. Now fetch that little parcel over there." He pointed to an elegant blue shopping bag on his dresser. "I brought you a little present."

"You didn't need to get me anything."

"What's a trip to New York without buying a few frivolous gifts?"

I reached into the bag and removed a narrow blue box. Inside were three perfectly folded white linen handkerchiefs with *M.D.* embroidered in gold thread in the corners.

"Oh my God. These are beautiful, Cortland. I've never had real handkerchiefs before. I always use Kleenex."

"We'll make a gentleman of you yet." Cortland idly took out one of the linen squares and dotted the initials with his forefinger. "They're from my very favourite men's shop—an exclusive little place on the Upper East Side."

"They're wonderful. Thank you."

I attempted to hug him as he lay there in bed. His chest and shoulders were bony and frail, and I could feel him cringe. I quickly sat back down in the chair.

Cortland motioned to the telephone that was lying on the bed beside him. "I was talking to my publisher just now."

"You shouldn't be thinking about the book when you're sick."

"All the more reason. He told me he's still concerned about the ending. He thinks the book just peters out with that house in Connecticut. He said he'd like to finish with a spectacular climax. I told him I'd like to do the same thing myself."

"I'm sure we'll come up with a good idea next week."

"At least it's something to occupy my mind. Otherwise I might die of boredom, trapped here in bed. Now tell me, how are things proceeding with your Hollywood dreamboat?"

"Not so dreamy. It turns out he lives with his lover in Los Angeles."

"Oh, you've hooked one of *that* sort, have you?"

"But he still wants to keep seeing me. And he's still interested in the Donnington story."

"That makes things a trifle complicated."

"He thinks he might be able to get me $800,000."

"Good Lord, Mitchell. You'll be rich after all."

"That's only if it goes into production. And most scripts never get that far."

"You'll have to tread carefully."

"Mostly I have to write a really good script. Ingrid and I went to visit Laura Donnington yesterday. She's sort of strange."

"Who wouldn't be after the childhood she had? Did she remember me?"

"She asked how you are. I said you were great."

"Liar."

"But she made me think Trevor might really be innocent. That it could have been somebody else who killed him and his father."

"You're not going to propose that *I'm* the killer now, are you?"

"It did cross my mind."

"I assure you, Mitchell, I had a foolproof alibi. I was in the drawing room with Ermina the entire time—gossiping fiercely."

"Laura said her mother thought it was Bill Zale. But do you know if the police had any other suspects?"

"Well, they interviewed everyone who was there—asking where we were and what time we were doing what."

"I've got the whole guest list in the file. I guess I could interview all 300 people. God knows how I'd find them all at this point."

"Well, if you want some help, you should call Ermina first. I'll forewarn her. But no doubt she'll be thrilled to reminisce about the old days. Just be careful she doesn't make a pass at you. She's a black widow, you know. You might be Husband Number 5."

"I think I'll be safe."

"And you could track down Trevor's school friends—some of them were at the party too, if I recall."

"Laura said he went to a lot of different schools. And Ramir suggested I phone Dr. Bhandari. Do you think he could have been involved in what happened?"

"That would certainly make an interesting scenario. But I can't imagine his motive."

"You told me that he bought the house for a steal."

"That wouldn't be reason enough for a double murder, would it?"

"He just seems so suspicious."

The nurse returned. "I think Mr. McPhee has had enough for now."

"I'll decide when I've had enough," Cortland said. "And, in fact, I think I have. But I really do think you're on the right track with your screenplay, Mitchell. Keep me on top of the investigation."

I still had my portfolio case with me. I took out the two-page outline that Aaron hadn't wanted.

"Here's a copy of what I've done so far—if you're interested."

"I'll read it with relish, thank you."

"And I'll come back this afternoon, OK?"

"Please do." Abruptly Pisces jumped up on the bed and snuggled against Cortland's hand. "Perhaps you could pop out to the video store and bring me back a few old movies. You know the sort of thing I like—Bette Davis and Katharine Hepburn."

"You could always watch The Shopping Channel."

"Why would I waste my time on such foolishness?"

I found Rosemary perched uneasily in the splendour of the living room, flipping through a back issue of *Architectural Digest*.

"Do you think he's going to be all right?" I asked quietly so Cortland couldn't hear.

"Brain tumours are funny things."

"But does he seem OK to you?"

"He might come back to normal, or he might have another seizure. Just have to wait and see."

"That's the way it is with everything, I guess." I waved an awkward farewell. "I'm just down the hall in 1611, if you need me."

"I'm sure we'll manage just fine."

MONDAY, OCTOBER 19
—LATER—

Ramir and I were back on our barstools in the maroon gloom of Byzantium.

"If you want to see that $800,000, I think you need to keep your Hollywood movie producer on the hook."

"How am I supposed to do that?"

"Drive him wild in bed."

"Oh yeah, I'm an expert at that."

"I can give you a few tips." Ramir pressed his thumb down the length of my spine. Which felt very good, but I twitched my shoulders to make him stop.

"I don't want to play any games with him. He was playing enough already."

"You should invite him to Gabriella's concert. Lots of people are flying up from L.A. He'll fit right in."

"We'll see." I ate the cherry from my Rob Roy. "You'd think I would have learned by now that you can never trust movie producers."

"Can you trust me?" Ramir asked with a glint.

"I can tell that's a leading question."

"It is."

"Where's it leading?"

"It's just that I'm a producer now myself. I might be directing as well."

I put things together. "They're giving you an episode of *Station Centauri*?"

"No." I could sense this was still a sore point. But Ramir rose above it. "I'm making a documentary about the Seven Gateways."

"You're making a movie for them on top of planning the party?"

"I've always wanted to direct. This is a great way to get some experience."

"Are they paying you?"

"I volunteered."

"Ramir, you must know how bad that sounds."

"I know. But it's only going to be 15 minutes long."

"It's still work that you're doing for free."

"It's going to be easy. It's a project they've had on the back burner for ages. Dr. Bhandari sent out a letter, asking people for testimonials, but nobody's ever taken charge and done anything. So I'm just going to interview Dr. Bhandari and get clips from all the people coming in for Gabriella's concert. Ask them how the Gateways have changed their lives. Then I'll edit all the stuff together, and they can send out the tapes to people who are thinking about joining."

"So it's like an infomercial?"

"Everything always comes back to The Shopping Channel."

"But don't you think they're taking advantage of you?"

"Just spending time there is good for me, Mitch. For example, I heard from my agent this afternoon. I didn't get that Mexican bandit movie."

"Ramir, that's terrible. I'm so sorry."

"It's no problem. I'm fine about it."

"But you wanted that part so much."

"I told you, Mitch, I'm able to handle things really well now."

I didn't have to ask why.

TUESDAY, OCTOBER 20

Ingrid and I were both procrastinating, avoiding our artistic endeavours. We were lounging in Daphne's card shop, drinking cans of cream soda through red licorice straws—while rehashing my conundrum with Aaron.

"You deserve somebody better than that, Mitchell," Ing said.

"I know."

"You can never trust men," Daphne said. "Or women for that matter."

"I know."

"Is money more important than your own morals?" Ing asked.

"Is it bad that I can't answer that question right away?"

Ingrid was sticking to her point. "I remember when Pierre and I were married and I found out he was cheating—"

Ingrid's sentence was brought to a hormone-induced stand-still.

A woman with a baby carriage had just entered the premises.

Like she was trapped in a KerrZavian mind lock on *Station Centauri,* Ingrid developed a misty, glazed smile. She deposited her can of cream soda on the counter and turned away from us zombie-style, gazing down into the carriage.

"He's so cute," she cooed.

"Thanks so much," the mothered cooed in reply.

"What's his name?" Ing simpered.

"Tucker," the mother whimpered.

"He's so adorable."

I looked down at the sleeping infant. A standard example of a 3-month-old boy. Baby Gap clothes. (I could tell because he was wearing the exact same thing I was.)

"How old is he?" Ing asked.

"Eleven months."

Clearly I am not a good judge of babies.

Ingrid and the young mother began an intense discussion of baby haircuts. Shags. Bobs. Mohawks. It sounded like a cult in itself. And I knew Ingrid was eager to belly up.

"I'm not much of a baby person myself," Daphne whispered over my shoulder.

"I can only relate to kids after they learn to talk."

"That only makes them worse," said Daphne.

The door to the shop opened again. A woman in a dark-blue trench coat bustled in, holding a giant leather carryall. Dark hair fell in front of her face.

"Ingrid," I said. "Look who's here."

With a shake of her head, Ing recovered consciousness. "Laura!" And she let the young mother carry on her shopping.

Laura Donnington curved her upper lip in what I think was supposed to be a smile. "I made some cards, like you said I should."

"You're the girl from Mitchell's story?" Daphne exclaimed. "Wow, I heard all about what happened to your family. It sounds awful!"

"I only told her because I knew you were coming in," I explained.

"It's no big deal," Laura said. "It's all ancient history."

Ingrid smiled broadly to get things back on track. "I can't believe you made the cards already."

Laura shrugged. "What else do I have to do with my time?"

Which was another conversation killer.

"I'm dying to see them," Daphne said.

"It's OK if you don't like them." Laura reached into her carryall. "I brought about 50. I've got so many lying around the house, I figured I might as well do something with them or throw them out."

She plunked five bundles down on the counter—each held together with a thick elastic band.

Daphne, Ingrid and I each picked up a pile.

"I glued them on card stock, just like Ingrid said."

Laura had done a beautiful job. Her finely drawn pictures were carefully positioned on rectangles of heavy cream vellum. Each drawing was framed with a neat black key line.

The three of us examined variations of the nightmares on

paper. The ominous front door…the sharp angle of the Victorian Gothic roof…the broken gabled window.

Daphne was fascinated. "These are all the same house where Ramir's having the big party?"

"What party?" Laura asked.

"Our friend Ramir is helping to organize a big concert for Dr. Bhandari," I explained.

"And you think I should come?" Laura laughed bleakly at the thought.

"It's mostly going to be people who already belong to the Seven Gateways."

"Figures," Laura said, nodding cynically. "So have you had any more luck with your movie research?"

"Not really. Not yet anyway."

"That's too bad."

The four of us stood there, awkwardly silent.

"Do you guys always hang out here?" Laura asked, implying we might be pathetic losers who waste a lot of time.

"Sometimes," Ing said. Which definitely made us sound like losers.

"We were just discussing love-life problems," Daphne volunteered.

"And babies," I added. "Not that they necessarily go together."

"So do you have a boyfriend or a girlfriend?" Daphne asked, in the spirit of camaraderie.

"It'd be a boyfriend, if I had one. But listen, I'm on my way to work. Do you want any of the cards or not?"

Daphne bounced her head up and down in an exaggerated version of a nod.

TUESDAY, OCTOBER 20
—LATER—

This afternoon I phoned Ermina Milenska.

She assured me in her potent Polish accent that "of course I remember you from the Courtyard Café" and "it was so frightful to see Cortland take ill on the plane—I'm so happy he's getting better."

At my mention of the Donningtons, she bubbled with excitement. "Never do I ever tire of talking about a scandal."

She insisted that I come to her apartment for lunch on Thursday.

More progress. Good.

Then I called my agent, Rebecca, to give her a censored version of my mega-deal maneuvering with Aaron.

"He called me yesterday out of the blue," I fabricated. "He said he wanted to apologize for running out of the meeting last week, so we went for a coffee."

"You didn't sleep with him, did you, Mitchell?"

"Of course not."

"It's one thing to flirt," Rebecca sagely warned, "but it's crossing the line to go all the way. Especially before you've got a signature. So what happened?"

"I told him about my murder-suicide story."

"The one that was so depressing?"

"Except it's not depressing anymore. I found a new angle. And Aaron really likes it. He said he might be able to get me $800,000."

"He said $800,000? Maybe I can bring him up to a million. I'll phone him right now."

"No! I think it's premature. He wants to see a 20-page treatment first."

"He should pay you up front if he wants you to write a treatment. This is Apex you're dealing with, not some small-time Canadian."

"But I still have to do more research—to make sure the script is going to work."

"For $800,000, you'd better make *sure* it works. My, oh my, Mitchell, you are quite an operator. I never would have guessed."

And my heart swelled with pride.

I was sharpening my background knowledge by rereading the old *Maclean's* magazine article when I heard three sharp raps at my door. Cortland's knock.

When I answered, there he was, smiling broadly, his blue eyes sparkling, resplendent in one of his best tweed jackets.

"You're out of bed," I said.

"I've always been quick to recover. I just sent the nurse home. Dreary woman. And I needed to see you right away. Because I have a brilliant idea."

"You always have brilliant ideas."

"You inspired this one yourself."

"I did?"

"With that outline you wrote for the screenplay. When the main character gathers all the people together for the party in the house at the end."

"How did that inspire you?"

"I've decided to help Ramir organize the party at the Donnington house."

"But I thought you didn't want to work anymore."

"I've made an exception. It's going to be a night to end all nights."

"I know Ramir could use the help."

"He won't need to lift a finger once I get my hands on the job."

"Won't it get in the way of finishing your book?"

"That's why it's such a brilliant idea, Mitchell. I'm putting it *in* the book. We'll take pictures of every detail. Show the party then, the party now. I called my publisher this afternoon, and he's extremely excited. It's the perfect dramatic finale."

"It could be amazing," I agreed.

"My darling, you should be more excited yourself. I'm doing this for you just as much as me."

"How do you mean?"

"This gives you the chance to go back to the house. Interview Dr. Bhandari. Explore the scene of the crime." Cortland clapped his hands to summon me to action. "Call Ramir. Get him on the phone right now."

WEDNESDAY, OCTOBER 21

At 2 o'clock, Ramir's highly priced, highly prized Land Rover pulled up in the narrow crescent driveway in front of my apartment building. Ingrid was in the front seat, so Cortland and I climbed into the back.

I fastened my seat belt as Ramir careened onto Prince Arthur on our way to our appointment with Dr. Bhandari.

"We're off to see the wizard," I declared.

"Ingrid, you get to be Dorothy," Cortland said, "though there was a day when I would have fought you on that."

"I should have worn my red shoes," she said.

"And Mitchell is either the Scarecrow or the Cowardly Lion," Cortland continued.

"The Cowardly Lion," Ramir said, nodding with amusement.

"I am not a coward," I said. "But Ramir needs to be the heartless Tin Man. And he's definitely getting rusty."

"That leaves me as the Scarecrow," Cortland harrumphed. "'If I only had a brain tumour.'"

Ramir and Ingrid were silenced.

"Cortland, not everybody finds your morbid sense of humour as funny as you do."

"You'll all be forced to laugh at it eventually."

"Why shouldn't people laugh in the face of death?" Ramir said, playing along now. Then he screeched to a stop at a red light, throwing us all forward off our seats.

"So are you trying to make us laugh with your driving?" I asked.

He ignored that. "You know, Cortland, Dr. Bhandari did have a couple of special requests. He said he wants to make sure the decorations are totally different from the Donningtons' party—so they don't bring back any memories of the murder."

"No problem at all."

(I decided not to mention that I'd brought along my portfolio, containing Cortland's file folder with all his old photographs of the Donnington event.)

"And even though the concert's on October 30th, Gabriella

doesn't want it to look anything like Halloween."

"Of course not," Cortland sniffed. "She might be mistaken for the Wicked Witch of the West."

Ramir stayed on track. "You know, Cortland, I was thinking you might want to go through the Seven Gateways yourself."

"I've never believed in therapy. Why dredge up old muck that's perfectly settled into place?"

"But the meditation techniques are really helpful to keep you relaxed."

"In the face of imminent death, do you mean?"

"No, I didn't mean that."

"I don't intend to trade my services with Dr. Bhandari, if that's what you're implying. This is a special personal project for me. That's why I'm willing to waive my fee."

"He said he could give you some free tickets to the concert."

"That's very generous, I suppose. Though I don't know why I'd want to subject any of my friends to that tawdry sci-fi queen. The Diva of Deep Space."

"Wait until you hear her. You're going to be really impressed."

"You could always give the tickets to us," I suggested.

Ingrid passed a black hardcover folder to the backseat. "I did an illustration for the front of the program."

I opened the folder, and there was Gabriella in a loose black line drawing—not dissimilar to Laura Donnington's style, though not nearly as creepy. Gabriella's hair was loose and flowing like that famous Botticelli angel or a model in a shampoo commercial.

"She'll love it," Ramir said.

"No doubt she will," Cortland said. "You've taken 20 years off her."

"I just had a publicity picture to work with. I wanted to make her look more relaxed than she does in her *Station Centauri* outfit."

"Ingrid, you know, Mitchell's just been telling me about your show in Berlin," Cortland said. "If you're too busy getting ready, I could find someone else to paint the banners. Though I do love that swirly look of yours."

"My famous swirly look," Ing said dryly. "Actually, I'm not feeling very inspired right now. And I wanted to see the house for myself. After Laura told us the story, I'm as curious about the place as Mitchell."

"I wish you'd brought me along to meet Laura too," Ramir said. "She sounds bizarre."

"I still might call you up for one of my other research expeditions."

Ramir sped up and cut in front of another car. I discreetly gripped the door handle as we turned left off Bloor Street to Park Road. Within seconds, the high-rise office towers and condos disappeared, and we dipped into the lush park of the ravine.

Then in another moment we rose into Rosedale, the ultra-wealthy residential neighbourhood in the middle of the city. It's a complex web of oddly angled, curving streets with huge mansions battling for ultimate prestige. Overblown Tudor, Georgian, and Southern Plantation styles. Most are peculiar concoctions only remedied by huge trees and expensive landscaping. Some were cornily decorated for fall with pumpkins on doorsteps and sheaves of wheat framing driveways.

Ingrid shifted sideways on her seat so she could get a better view into the back. "So, Cortland, what do you think really happened with Trevor and Jackson?"

"I suppose I thought it happened just as the police said. Trevor killed his father and then killed himself."

"So why is Trevor speaking to Mitch from beyond the grave?" Ramir asked.

"I never said he was doing that," I said in my own defense.

"I'm not sure what to make of that phenomenon, I'm afraid," Cortland said. "I went to their funeral, you know. Terribly tragic. I don't intend to be buried myself. I want to be cremated and turned into very expensive potpourri."

We all grimaced.

"Mitch, I don't mean to sound skeptical," Ramir said, "but I don't see how you'll come up with a better solution than the police did."

"Maybe it *was* a murder-suicide," I said, feeling ganged-up on.

"I just think there might be a good reason why Trevor did it. Maybe this is a *why*dunit, not a *who*dunit."

Ramir smirked. "Being insane is a pretty good reason why."

"Mitchell could be right after all," Cortland said. "It could have been a double murder."

"Anyway, I want to ask Dr. Bhandari a few questions about Trevor. I'm hoping he'll show me where the whole thing happened—Trevor's old bedroom on the third floor."

"Can I come too?" Ing asked.

"That might be a problem," Ramir said. "Dr. Bhandari doesn't let anyone up to the third floor. It's his private living space. He keeps it locked up."

"Even if I ask nicely?"

"Definitely not going to happen."

We swerved around another corner.

"My dear, please don't kill me now," Cortland exclaimed. "I've escaped the Grim Reaper longer than even *I* could have expected."

Then, abruptly, we stopped in front of Thornfield Manor.

Standing there at the curb, we all looked up at the massive red-brick mansion with its gables and chimneys. Even on such a bright, beautiful day, the house looked dark in its grandeur.

I imagined its awesome creepiness filling a movie screen.

Cortland stood stock-still, staring at the house.

"It's awe-inspiring," Ing said.

Cortland nodded. "One of the finest examples of Victorian Gothic architecture anywhere in North America. Built in 1882, if I remember correctly."

I pointed to the second floor. "See that little balcony just to the right of the front door? That must have been Laura's room."

"Can we see Trevor's room from here?" Ramir asked.

"It's in the back over the kitchen," Cortland said.

"Do you think it'd be all right if we take a look from the outside?" I asked Ramir.

"I don't see why not. Now you've got me hooked too."

I noticed he was carrying a tiny high-tech video camera. "What's that for?"

"The documentary. I'm taping Dr. Bhandari every time I talk to him, in case he says something I want to use."

Cortland headed across the lawn around the right side of the house, as spry as if he were leading a walking tour of the English moors. The three of us followed behind.

I had a sudden vision of the ghost-chasing gang from *Scooby-Doo*.

Jutting from the side of the house was a small, single-storey octagonal room—all windows and empty, thank God.

"That's Dr. Bhandari's office," Ramir said. "That's where he does all the therapy."

"It'd make a fabulous studio for painting," Ing said.

"Vivienne called it the conservatory," Cortland explained. "She added it on to match the period. It was always filled with lovely exotic plants."

Behind the conservatory, the wall straightened back and there was a line of windows looking into the kitchen. Fortunately, that room was empty too, so no one noticed our snooping.

A 10-foot-high wrought-iron fence led out from the back of the house, protecting the backyard and then continuing along the lot line. Thick trees and bushes were planted along it to provide privacy, but the four of us pressed our faces through the yellowing greenery to look into the backyard.

We could just see the back wall of the house.

"That was Trevor's room up on the top floor," Cortland said, "just under the V of the roof."

"I think that's Dr. Bhandari's meditation room now."

"Is that the window Trevor jumped out of?" Ing asked.

"Just wide enough, unfortunately. And if you look down, at the edge of the kitchen patio there, you'll see the low wall around the pool. Vivienne had that built too, to match the house—red-brick capped with limestone. It used to have a line of wrought-iron fencing along the top—like this fence here, but only two feet high. That's where the boy landed."

I looked up at the fence in front of us, topped by six-inch arrowhead spikes.

No wonder the spikes cut right through him.

"Vivienne had the fence removed immediately after."

Ramir grimaced. "And he lay there for an hour before anybody noticed?"

"It was very cool that night. Not many people went outside, and those who did stayed on the other side of the house in the garden by the ballroom."

We stared in silence.

"It's hard to believe something like that could have happened here," Ramir said. "It's so peaceful now."

"It's more creepy than peaceful," Ing said.

We walked back around the house toward the front door. Ramir knocked this time, and a moment later the Christ-like Kevin opened the door, wearing a clingy white muscle shirt.

"Welcome," he said with a warm grin and an immediate hug for Ramir.

"*Greetings from KerrZavia,*" Ramir intoned with no urging. "Kevin, you remember Mitch." Kevin hugged me. "And this is our friend Ingrid Iversen."

"Hello," Kevin said. He gripped Ingrid in a hug, then he shook her hand as well. "Nice to meet you," he said. Was that an extra sparkle in his eye?

"And this is Cortland McPhee, who's going to help design the party."

"No hugs. I'm here on business." Cortland stepped into the all-white entry hall. "Oh dear Lord," he cried out, "they painted the woodwork!"

"I told you," I told him.

"It didn't sink in. Vivienne would die all over again. It's anemic! The white sucks out all the character. They didn't paint the ballroom too?"

Cortland immediately charged through to the back of the house, the rest of us chasing behind. He swung open the tall double doors. The ballroom was empty but still arranged with the rows of white chairs. Sun streamed in through the French doors, giving the white walls an otherworldly glow.

"Even the ceiling? Carved cherry wood and they painted it over? We had the walls covered in blue silk brocade. Not this plain white plaster."

Nonetheless, Ing's eyes were filled with wonder: "Can't you just imagine a party here when the house was built? All those Victorian men and women pirouetting around the dance floor."

"We hold a formal dance on New Year's Eve just like that," Kevin said.

"It must be so beautiful," Ing said. And the two of them started chatting.

Cortland ran his hand across a door frame nostalgically. "I suppose the wood can be stripped down again. But it's still a terrible crime."

"Our intention was to fill the house with light." We turned and there was Dr. Bhandari, looking handsome and serene in a brown cashmere sweater. "Before, the house felt too dark and foreboding."

"Forgive me. I'm Cortland McPhee."

"Yes, I remember you very well. We met on the night of that ill-fated party."

The two men shook hands.

"I gather Ramir has explained my proposal."

"It's a very kind offer."

"I was certain that a man in your profession would understand my desire for an appropriate swan song."

"And I hope Ramir has explained to you that I do not wish the night of the Donningtons' party to be echoed in any way."

"Not to worry, I don't like to repeat myself," Cortland said. "It's an ambitious deadline, but I've already contacted my suppliers. It's quite achievable if we make the right decisions today."

"Perhaps you should all come to my office." Dr. Bhandari moved toward the double doors.

"Do you mind if I stay here in the ballroom?" I asked. "I just want to absorb the atmosphere."

Dr. Bhandari turned a laser-like smile on me. "Ramir has told me you're interested in writing about the Donningtons."

"I've been doing some research. I talked to Laura Donnington the other day."

"Ah yes, Laura. I haven't seen her since her mother's funeral."

"She gave me permission to write about what happened, if that's what you're wondering."

"You should do what you wish. My one request, Mitchell, is that you portray the family with dignity. They were very good friends to me, and I wouldn't want their memories to be tarnished."

"Maybe I could ask you a few questions about them later?"

Dr. Bhandari looked me carefully in the eye. Then nodded. "Enjoy the room. Perhaps you might use this extra time for meditation."

They all headed off to the conservatory.

I was alone in the huge ballroom.

All the white was starting to feel disturbing. Too blank. Devoid of soul—even though that was probably the opposite of the intention. It was like whitewash, covering up all the detail and history of the house with a flat, even surface.

I sidestepped through the rows of chairs and sat in the very middle of the room to soak up the atmosphere.

I took a deep breath, then another. My own loose interpretation of the meditation from the intro night. I don't know why I was obeying Dr. Bhandari. To invoke that weird dream again?

I actually carried on for a minute or so. Then I felt something unusual—like a lead weight dropping inside my head. Like my brain had fallen out of place.

I opened my eyes and shook my head to get my brain back into position.

That was strange. Because otherwise I felt perfectly normal.

I opened my portfolio to Cortland's stack of photos, showing this same room more than 20 years ago. The walls were trimmed with dark wood and paneled in blue silk, just as Cortland had described. Garlands of pink orchids, red hibiscus, and yellow bougainvillea hung along the ceiling—creating the effect of a vivid tropical jungle, sensual and mysterious.

There were detail shots of the garlands above the door and beside the windows. I held up each photo and walked around the room, figuring out the relationship to the now-blank white walls.

I made my way to the far end of the room—to the lectern in front of the fireplace where Dr. Bhandari had stood at the intro night. There was a doorway on the right. I pushed it open. The pantry, and down the passageway, the empty kitchen. That must have been the servants' entrance when they were hosting large dinners.

I flipped through more of the photographs. At the bottom of the pile was the page of floor plans of the three-storey house.

I stared at the diagrams and determined that the main staircase in the front hall went only as far as the second floor. The back staircase led from the kitchen down to the basement, and up to the second floor and the servants' quarters on the third.

Holding the floor plan in front of me, I went back to the front hall to orient myself. The conservatory was far enough on the right side of the house that I couldn't hear my friends' meeting with Dr. Bhandari, nor could they hear me.

Dare I look around a bit? Even if the third floor was locked up, I still wanted to see Laura's old bedroom. And maybe Jackson's office. Dr. Bhandari wouldn't mind. He'd never even know.

Holding the floor plan in front of me—as if it were a planchette from a Ouija board—I started up the stairs.

My footsteps didn't make a sound. Obviously, the house was well built. Not that I was doing anything so bad. Just looking for the washroom, if anyone asked.

I made it to the central hall on the second floor. No sign of anyone.

I began exploring.

On the floor plan, the master suite took over one whole side of the house. Now the suite had been turned into a series of meditation rooms. Most of the doors were open. A white padded exercise mat lay on each hardwood floor. A few luxury rooms included a narrow futon.

Looking at the diagram again, I figured out which was Laura's old bedroom, positioned at the front of the house. The small Juliet balcony confirmed I was in the right place. A mat, no futon.

I tried to picture a 12-year-old girl, maybe in a pink-lace canopy bed, asleep like a princess after a fairy-tale party. Awakened by her mother's bloodcurdling screams.

I returned to the central hall and followed the map to the back of the house. To Jackson's office. Right under Trevor's room.

The door stood open. I went in. This room held a massage table, wrapped in fresh white sheets. The air was crisp and chilled.

I went to the window and looked down. The rectangular swimming pool—closed for the season and covered with a blue plastic tarp. The low brick wall.

I imagined Laura standing in this same spot, looking down and seeing her big brother impaled on the arrowhead spikes. Then Laura would have sat at her father's desk in the middle of the room, straightening his knocked-over possessions in an innocent attempt to be helpful.

I remembered Laura had said Trevor's fingerprints were found on the outer doorknob. I took hold of the handle and imagined Trevor's hand in the exact same position.

For a moment I thought I heard creaking. Footsteps on the stairs? I stood perfectly still. But no. Still no noise from the main floor.

I went back out into the hall. I looked at the floor plan again. Across from Jackson's office was a narrow cupboard-like door— the discreetly designed entrance to the back staircase. Downstairs was the kitchen. Upstairs was Trevor's room. I was so close.

Cortland's meeting could go on for another half-hour.

Laura had said Trevor didn't like people going into his room. Just like Dr. Bhandari. Not that I could get in if the door were locked. And if it did happen to be open, it's not like I'd touch anything. Except for a little peek in that hole under the floorboards that Laura had mentioned, to see if Trevor might have left anything behind.

All in all, no one would ever know I was there.

I pulled open the narrow door and found a cramped staircase, dim and claustrophobic with the same cold dry air. Don't ghostly spirits create a chill? I think I'd read about that in *The Exorcist* or *The Amityville Horror*.

I imagined what it must have been like on that night years ago. Jackson calmly climbing these stairs to check on his beloved son. And never coming down again—at least not on his own two feet.

I turned a corner on the staircase, up another short flight, and found a landing with a closed door. I tried the doorknob. Locked. As expected.

Suddenly I felt dizzy. That lead weight dropping inside my skull again. I leaned against the wall and shut my eyes.

CUT TO:

INTERIOR. DARK ROOM—NIGHT

Looking up at the fine crack of light at the top of a door frame. From the angle, the viewer must be lying down. Restless camera motions. The sound of heavy, rapid breathing.

A TALL FIGURE steps into frame, looming above. The room is so dark, the TALL FIGURE's face can't be seen.

A low grunting sound.

The TALL FIGURE bends forward, swiftly lowering a hand.

The camera jerks and everything goes black.

CUT TO:

I shook my head and opened my eyes to see the door in front of me opening.

WARREN DUNFORD

"Mitchell," a calm voice said.

Dr. Bhandari.

I blinked. "I was just looking for the washroom," I said.

"There are two on the main floor. I'll show you."

"Sorry, I can find it myself."

I turned to flee. I wanted to be alone. I wanted to figure out what had just happened—why I'd had the dream again.

"Hold on a moment." Dr. Bhandari held up a file folder of his own. "I came upstairs for some notes to give Mr. McPhee. We can walk down together."

But he didn't begin walking. We both stood perfectly still.

"Is this little exploration related to your film?"

"I thought it might help to see the room where it happened."

"There's really nothing to see."

"It's just that when Laura described everything, she made it sound so real."

"I would have hoped that Laura had let go of the past, as we all did. When Vivienne sold me the property, she asked me to clear the house of negative energy."

"I don't want to bring back any negative energy. I wouldn't know how."

Dr. Bhandari scrutinized my face, as though judging my paltry worth. "These are my private rooms, Mitchell. This is a sacred place for me."

"I'm sorry. I didn't know."

"Do you not feel well, Mitchell?"

"A little dizzy, but I'm OK."

Dr. Bhandari closed the door to the third-floor landing, then tried the doorknob to confirm it was locked. He motioned with his hand down the stairs. "Let's find somewhere more comfortable where we can talk."

I would have preferred to just escape. But I followed him. Strangely, he exited the staircase at the second floor and led me back into the massage room—Jackson's office.

Dr. Bhandari sat on the massage table, leaving me to stand.

"Mitchell, I am interested in what you said in your decree on

166

the first evening we met. You said you want to write a 'blockbuster screenplay.' Can you tell me why?"

"To make money?"

"And is money the only measure of success?"

"Of course not. But it can make life easier."

"Rewards come in various forms, Mitchell. If we were to have a proper session together, I could show you other ways to achieve spiritual success."

"Do you mean that whole idea about 'do what you love and the money will follow'? Because I've been doing what I love for years, and I'm still not making any money."

"And you think the Donnington story will help you make a better living?"

"It might. If I do a good job." I had to turn this conversation around. "Can you tell me what Trevor was like?"

"He could be a sweet boy, but his spirit was deeply troubled."

"Do you have any of his files?"

"That is confidential material."

Even though Trevor had been dead for more than 20 years?

"Laura thinks her brother might have been innocent."

Dr. Bhandari raised his eyebrows. "Perhaps in many ways he was."

"How do you mean?"

"Jackson was too indulgent with his son. He would seek out various treatments, then abandon them as soon as Trevor rebelled—before they had time to take effect. I believe that the lack of support and direction is what led Trevor to kill his father. Then the boy was driven by guilt to commit suicide."

"So you think he really did do it?"

"I have no doubt." Dr. Bhandari looked at me steadily. "You resemble Trevor somewhat, you know."

"That's what I've heard."

"Mitchell, I genuinely believe that the Seven Gateways would bring you a great deal of peace. It's not necessary to struggle as much as you do."

"I don't struggle."

Dr. Bhandari smiled as though he could see right through me. "Every individual struggles. Life is an ongoing balance. When the soul's balance is perfected, that is when the spirit leaves the body."

"You mean that's when we die?"

"Precisely."

"So why did Trevor die?"

"Apparently he had learned as much as he could learn." Dr. Bhandari stood. "Perhaps we should go downstairs. Your friends will be wondering what has become of me."

I practically tripped I rushed so quickly down the main stairs to the front hall.

"Now perhaps you'd like to join our meeting?" Dr. Bhandari said.

"I think I'll wait outside instead." But I held back a second. "There's one other thing I was wondering about. Isn't a house where a murder happened an odd place for spirituality?"

"On the contrary. That makes it the perfect place for healing."

I went out to the driveway and leaned against Ramir's Land Rover, looking up at the house—deep-breathing and trying to recover from that peculiar encounter.

There was definitely something suspicious about Dr. Bhandari.

And that dream again. It didn't seem to have anything to do with the murders, but it must. I'd been right outside Trevor's room. Could he really be trying to communicate through me? And if so, what's he trying to say?

A moment later the front door opened, and Kevin and Ingrid stepped outside. Was she being thrown out too? They stood there chatting. Longer than I would have expected.

Ingrid came toward me, smiling.

"Is the meeting over already?" I asked.

"They finished picking the locations for the banners. And Dr. Bhandari told me you were outside, so I thought I'd come out too."

"I bet he wants you to keep an eye on me. He caught me try-ing to sneak up to the third floor."

"Mitchell, don't you think you're getting too carried away with this thing?"

"There's definitely something weird going on, Ing. Just before I got up to Trevor's room, I had that dream again. About the tall, dark man. Except this time I wasn't sleeping."

"Did you ask Dr. Bhandari about it?"

"Of course not. He treated me like enough of a freak as it was."

"Because he didn't want you sneaking around his house? You wouldn't want him hunting through your apartment."

"My apartment wasn't a crime scene—except for the occasional crime against nature. But I really think Dr. Bhandari knows something about the murders."

"You'd better not try to accuse *him*. Ramir would never for-give you."

She was right.

"Can I look at those pictures you brought?" Ing asked. "It really is a fascinating place."

I gave her my portfolio, and she started flipping through Cort-land's photographs.

"What were you and Kevin talking about?" I asked, trying to sound casual.

"He was saying he liked my illustration of Gabriella. So I told him about my paintings and about the Human Bean cards I did for Daphne."

"I think he was flirting with you."

"Don't be ridiculous, Mitchell. He's just an interesting person. He teaches public school normally. Grade 3. He took a leave of absence to spend more time with Dr. Bhandari."

"Whatever you were talking about, he was still flirting."

"It doesn't make any difference. It's not like I'm available."

"So is everything really better between you and Pierre?"

"Mitchell, you don't like Pierre, do you?"

I was taken aback. "Of course I do."

"It's probably my own fault for telling you about that fight we had. But we really do have a good relationship deep down. We're still just getting used to living together again."

"I only want the best for you."

"I know. And things are going to be fine."

She attempted to close the subject by flipping through the pictures again.

I looked up at the house. I really have to be more careful about Pierre.

And I noticed a curtain move on the second floor.

"Did you see that?"

"What?" Ing glanced up from the photographs.

"Someone was looking at us."

"Where?"

"From that window on the second floor. Laura's old room."

We both stared at the house now.

The curtain moved again and we caught a glimpse of a face.

"It's Kevin," Ing said.

"He's watching us. Or watching you..."

WEDNESDAY, OCTOBER 21
—LATER—

According to my calculation of time zones, it was still the workday in Los Angeles. Aaron would still be at his office. And I was determined to keep it all business.

"Is this a good time to talk?"

"Just let me shut my door—get some privacy." At least he wasn't at home with the divine Ryan lurking nearby. I heard the door close, and then he was back. "What's up?"

"Aaron, you're still serious about the screenplay, aren't you?"

"Of course I am. Have you finished the treatment already?"

"Not yet. But I'm starting to think Trevor might really have been innocent. Not just for my screenplay. But for real."

"That'd make a pretty terrific publicity angle."

"But what if it really is true? Should I go to the police?"

"Not until you find some solid evidence, I guess."

"And if I do?"

"Then you've got a blockbuster on your hands."

My determination strengthened. I might be able to uncover the truth. Vindicate Trevor. Put the real killer behind bars…

"Aaron, exactly what day do you come back to Toronto?"

"Let me check my book—Friday the 30th."

Another coincidence. "That's the same day as Gabriella Hartman's concert at the house where it all took place. Do you want to come with me? Visit the scene of the crime for yourself."

"Sure, I'm putting it in my calendar right now."

"And I'll find out about getting tickets."

"But you know, Mitchell, it's still more than a week before I see you again."

"It's not that long."

"Actually, it is."

I chuckled uncomfortably at his crass sexual innuendo.

Aaron cleared his throat. "You know, Mitchell, I'm sitting here in my office with the door closed. Nobody can see in. I'm thinking…have you ever tried phone sex?"

It was great.

THURSDAY, OCTOBER 22

"Such an attractive young man," said the honey-blonde Ermina Milenska as she greeted me at the door of her luxury condominium. I leaned down to give her an air kiss, but she surprised me by planting a full dewy smooch right on my lips. "Now, what is that cologne you're wearing?"

Her hands remained clinging to my neck, allowing me to gaze down her lilac silk blouse, past the strands of delicate gold necklaces, deep into her cleavage.

"I think it's Aveda shampoo."

"Very sexy, yes?"

"Yes?"

Cortland had warned me that she's a fearless flirt. But hadn't he warned her that I'm homosexual?

"Just a few more things to prepare for lunch," she said, rolling every R. She placed her hand on my behind and pushed. "You wait a moment in the living room."

Would I be able to fight her off?

Elegant Chopin piano music floated through the apartment, decorated in yellow and white in Cortland's signature English-country style. On the walls were numerous framed sketches of ballet costumes. Cortland had said she was a dance aficionado.

I stood at the floor-to-ceiling window and admired her penthouse view. Her building was on Bloor Street East. Rosedale spread out at my feet, sheltered beneath a blanket of autumn leaves.

Ermina returned from the kitchen carrying a silver tray set with a plate of sandwiches, two champagne glasses, and a bottle of Pol Roger. She placed the tray on a tiny antique table for two, positioned flush against the window.

"You're trying to find Vivienne's house, yes?"

"Yes. But I don't think you can see it from here."

"Of course you can see it! It was one of the very first things I looked for when I bought the apartment." She gently took my hand and guided my pointing finger. "Look up Mount Pleasant Road. You see the bridge at Crescent Road. Just to the right.

Above the trees you can see the roof—black, like an upside-down ice cream cone."

"Or a witch's hat."

"That's very cute. Very funny." She lightly squeezed my bicep. Not that I have one.

"Cortland's actually there today, measuring everything and sorting out the details for the big concert."

"Yes, I know all about it. I've asked him to buy me a ticket. It will be so interesting to see the house again. I have so many good memories of the place. And some not so good." She fluttered her fingers as if to scurry away any less-than-appealing thoughts. "Now sit and we can nibble at our lunch. Would you like some wine?" she asked, pouring the champagne. "I hope the sandwiches are fresh. I had them sent over from Dinah's Cupboard. Thank goodness for Dinah's Cupboard, or no doubt I would starve absolutely to death."

We clinked flutes. "To new friends," she said.

"Your apartment's lovely. I can tell Cortland designed it."

"He's so finicky, he scolds me if I move even a chair. But of course, you know what he can be like. So nice that the two of you are having a little romance."

I set down my curried chicken salad on rye. "We're not having a romance."

"Don't be shy, you silly. It's very healthy—older people, younger people."

"Cortland and I aren't having an affair. Did he say we were?"

"No, he denied it as well. But hearing it from you, I suppose I must believe him." She smiled with a devilish twinkle. "I should be careful what I say. Cortland warned me on the phone that you write down every word. If I don't behave myself, you might put me in your script in a very unflattering way."

"I wouldn't do that," I promised.

"Oh, but please, you must make me the most fascinating character. I want Meryl Streep to play me in the movie. Because you know, I *am* the one who introduced Cortland to Vivienne in the first place."

"He told me that. Where did *you* meet her?"

"At the old McGill Club. Wonderful place. Closed now, of course. Me and Vivi would do our exercise classes together every morning. We had so many traditions. We'd go to Robert Gage to have our hair done. Go shopping at Creeds. Lunch at Fenton's. The garden room was always so pretty. They were such marvelous times in Toronto. We were always in Zena Cherry's society column. That reminds me, I have a photograph to show you." Ermina went to a bookshelf and handed me a silver picture frame. "Me and Vivi on a ski trip to France."

Both women wore massive fur coats and fur hats. Both smiled broadly. With her black hair and finely boned white skin, Vivienne looked icily beautiful. Ermina in her youth was a blonde bombshell in the Elke Sommer school.

"Vivi and I were best friends. But after what happened that night, she was a different woman. Who wouldn't be? It was never the same between us."

"She must have been very young when she got married."

"Just 19 or 20. She and Jackson were both from very good families. Very English. Very Old Toronto. It should have been a very good match. But they were never happy."

"They weren't happy?" I asked, my mouth full of sandwich. "When I talked to Laura, she talked as if they were the perfect couple."

"Oh, but Laura was just a little child. She wouldn't know the truth, except what Vivi told her. Jackson was so full of himself. All he did was work. Always away on business trips. Out for dinner with clients. Though he was always very good with Trevor. Jackson could be very charming when he wanted to be. He was a very attractive man. He was quite a ladies' man too."

"You mean, he fooled around?"

"Every chance," Ermina chortled. "He even made passes at me. Not that I told Vivi. But I'm sure she must have guessed."

"So Vivienne knew he was cheating?"

"She was always complaining to me. That's why she was in therapy—seeing that Indian guru. She was trying to accept the way Jackson was. I told her she didn't need to accept it. She should get a divorce! But Vivi didn't want that. They were married 20 years. She was very proud. She was so devoted to the children. She wanted them to have a normal family."

"Except Trevor wasn't exactly normal."

"But he *was* really, when he was young. I watched him grow up. I have a daughter the same age. Trevor was very good-looking. He would have been a handsome man. Something like you, yes?"

"So I've heard."

"And Vivi loved him so much. But he was exhausting her. Always in trouble. Always being thrown out of schools. Finally she was hoping her guru could do him some good too."

"So did you ever meet Dr. Bhandari?"

"Once or twice, at the house. Then at the party as well. Very nice man. Very gentle. Quite attractive for that exotic type. This was before he started the crazy cult, of course. He was a psychiatrist. Completely legitimate. But he liked those mystical ideas. And Vivi was always interested in far-out things, going to psychics and astrologers. She started seeing Dr. Bhandari first for herself. Three sessions a week. Then she thought he might help Trevor."

"*Did* he help him?"

"Not enough, apparently! Jackson didn't approve of the doctor. He said the mystical things were foolish. Near the end, Vivi and Jackson were always arguing."

"So if they weren't happy, why were they holding a big party for their 20th anniversary? Wasn't that sort of hypocritical?"

"We are all a bit hypocritical sometimes, yes?"

"Yes."

"You must understand, Vivi wasn't stupid. The party was for Jackson's business more than anything else. She knew it was smart to keep up a good image. And Vivienne was the perfect hostess. The house was so beautiful that night. Cortland was a genius. He *is* a genius. I've never seen anything like it, before or since. All the guests had those flower necklaces from Hawaii. I forget the name."

"Leis?"

"Leis, yes." (How could she forget a word like that?) "But of course, I was not in the best frame of mind at first. I was married to my second husband then—just a few months before we separated. He owned shoe stores. Nothing I would ever wear myself, but very successful. We had a tiff just before the party, and he refused to come. So I went by myself. And of course, I was cheered up very quickly. So many interesting people. Disco dancing. There was a bit of drug sniffing, but nothing very much. Mostly I was talking with Cortland."

"Did you see much of Jackson and Vivienne?"

"I danced with Jackson at the beginning, and he was as charming as ever. But then later, when he was missing, Vivi came to me in tears. She thought he'd gone off with another woman."

"You mean, somewhere in the house?"

"Or maybe he'd driven off to somewhere. Let's just say it wouldn't have been anything new."

"Did Vivienne have any idea who he might have been seeing?"

"It could have been any number of girls. Jackson was always very discreet, thank goodness. In any case, Vivi went upstairs to look for him. And a few minutes later, we heard the screaming. I can't even describe the sound. Then Vivi ran downstairs into the backyard. When we heard all the commotion, Cortland and I went into the kitchen, and we saw Trevor outside on the fence, all covered in blood. It was horrible. Poor Vivi. I tried to make her come inside, but she wouldn't leave the boy. I tried not to look myself, but you couldn't help it. So much blood. Then the police came and took our addresses and phone numbers. They called me the next day."

"What did they ask you?"

"They wanted to know what I'd been doing every minute. If I'd gone upstairs. If I'd seen any strange things. Of course, they arrested that terrible drunken man. Then they let him go, the stupid fools."

"You mean Bill Zale? But the police decided it wasn't him."

"Vivi believed he was guilty, and I could certainly see why. He was like a mad dog that night. He could have done anything.

So drunk, he was out of his mind. I saw when they argued in the ballroom. Bill swung his arm and tried to punch Jackson. Then they went upstairs. A while later, I saw Bill stumble out the front door. He could barely walk. No doubt he waited outside, then came back in and did those horrible things. Stupid man to begin with. He couldn't keep the company running after Jackson died. Then he tried to sue Vivi. All ridiculous."

"But I don't think the police found any of Bill Zale's finger-prints in Trevor's room."

"Maybe it wasn't him. But that's what Vivi believed. She couldn't imagine Trevor would kill his father. And it didn't make any sense, if you ever saw the two of them. They were very good friends. Always playing tennis. Neither of them were easy men to know, but together they were very happy."

"So that's why there was so much speculation about it being a double murder."

"Exactly. Of course, Vivi was destroyed by the whole mess. The double funeral. The stories in the paper. At first, she went into hiding. Moved in with her sister. Even *I* didn't hear from her for two months. Then suddenly she announced she was selling the house to her guru friend and she was getting married. I took her to lunch. I told her she was foolish to marry so quickly. But her heart was broken. She was desperate. She wanted a new life. And I could understand, of course."

"Did she know the man before?"

"No. She met him on the plane to Palm Beach, she told me. He was very wealthy too. An American from Philadelphia, living here, working for one of the banks. Patrick Stern was his name. I remember at the wedding, seeing little Laura at the front of the church in tears. Still in grief. Then more tragedy with the car accident that killed Vivi and her husband. Everything ended so badly. At the same time, my third husband was dying of cancer. But that's not what you want to hear about. Would you like more wine?" She refilled my glass with bubbly.

"So do you really think Bill Zale might have done it?"

"Well, no one can be totally certain."

"Were there any other suspects?"

"Everyone was a suspect at first. But there was *another* theory."

"There was?"

"Everyone was gossiping so much in those first few days. I'm sure the theory has some holes. But what if Trevor caught his father fooling around with another woman?"

"The way Vivienne suspected?"

"Maybe a little liaison upstairs. These things happen. Every party has many little dramas when you scratch beneath the surface."

"So Trevor killed his father because he was mad at him for cheating?"

"Perhaps. Or it could have been the woman who did it."

"She might have been worried Trevor would tell Vivienne?"

Ermina nodded. "So she killed them both and made it *look* like a murder-suicide."

"She'd have to have been a pretty strong woman to kill two men."

"Yes, that's one of the holes in the theory."

"Could Jackson have been with another man?"

Ermina was quick to shake her head. "They say everyone was swinging in the '70s. But not Jackson. He was too busy with women."

"So which woman do you think it might have been?"

"That's another hole. I went over all the guests in my mind. But I have no idea which woman it could be."

I was picturing the *coitus interruptus* scenario. "It'd make a good scene in the movie."

"Everyone likes the sexy bits, yes?"

"Yes," I agreed.

I noticed that Ermina had touched neither her sandwich nor her champagne.

She tapped her chin. "Who knows? Maybe Trevor stabbed his father to death for no reason at all. That's possible too." She tiptoed two fingers up my knee. "Now tell me something, if you're not dating Cortland, who *are* you dating? You must have someone—an attractive young man like yourself."

"Actually, I'm sort of seeing a film producer. He lives in Los Angeles."

"He must be very helpful for your career. I understand completely. Now could I tempt you with a teeny snifter of brandy?"

☆

I excused myself politely after one teeny snifter.

As I walked home, my head was gyrating with questions.

Should I start checking through the guest list for all the women Jackson could have been sleeping with? But if an expert gossip like Ermina couldn't figure it out, what hope could *I* have? What if it was Ermina herself who was with Jackson and she was just playing coy? But no, she was too petite to kill them both, and she'd been with Cortland the whole night.

Definitely I should contact Bill Zale. Though the idea of interviewing a suspected murderer doesn't thrill me. Then there's Dr. Bhandari's role in the whole scandal.

And what if Ermina is right in the end? What if there is no startling surprise revelation after all?

THURSDAY, OCTOBER 22
—LATER—

"Would you mind coming over to my studio again?" Ing asked.

"Did you try another version of the painting in the painting?"

"I don't want to say anything until you see it."

"Did you try the new style that Max wanted?"

"I'm not saying anything else."

As I headed out the door, it occurred to me that, of course, Ingrid had finished the painting of *me*.

But she'd sounded worried that I wouldn't like it. Maybe she'd portrayed me nonrepresentationally and literally put my foot in my mouth.

But this was serious art. I couldn't take it personally.

I doubled my pace and rushed right past the window of Daphne's store. But after pressing Ingrid's door buzzer, I did a double take back to The Paper Gallery. All eight easels in the window displayed drawings by Laura Donnington. Her spidery renderings of broken windows and spear-like fence posts and Gothic castle peaks.

And the cards must be good for business. Inside I could see three or four customers bustling about.

Then I heard Ingrid's footsteps as she rushed through the inner hallway to greet me.

"This is wonderful," I said, pointing.

"They look good, don't they?"

"You should be so proud, helping Laura get started like this." I had a shimmer of nostalgia. "Remember when you did the big mural in the coffee shop and you called me because you were scared to show people?"

"I was just remembering the same thing, actually."

"And that's what led to your whole career. Maybe the same'll happen for Laura."

Ingrid didn't say anything—just raised her eyebrows quizzically. She led me inside, but stopped abruptly once we reached the kitchen.

"Mitchell, I'm not really sure about this painting. But I figure I shouldn't say anything. I should just show you and get your gut reaction."

It occurred to me that I must look really hideous. "Whatever it is, I'm sure it'll be great."

"You have to be totally honest though, OK? Promise? Close your eyes."

She took me by the hand. I steeled myself. How must Picasso's friends have reacted when he showed them the new locations of their noses?

"Now open your eyes."

I prepared to gush with compliments.

But it wasn't me.

It was Thornfield Manor. A huge rectangular canvas. Ingrid's soft swirly brushstrokes were gone. No squiggles or curlicues. The Gothic architecture took shape in stark swaths of black and white—as if it had been captured in a flash of lightning.

"Ingrid, it's fabulous."

"I went back with my Polaroid yesterday afternoon." Ingrid pointed to a row of photographs she'd pinned to an adjacent bulletin board. "I've been working on it ever since."

"But how could you ever doubt that this is good? This is exactly what Max Friedrich was talking about."

"So you like it?"

"Of course I like it."

"But it's not just whether it's good or not," she explained. "I thought you might be angry."

"Angry about what?"

"That I'm painting the same thing you're writing about."

"Oh. I hadn't thought about it that way." I thought about it. "Of course it doesn't make any difference. Maybe we can use it for the movie poster."

"But the other thing is—do you think Laura Donnington might be angry?"

"Hmm, I see. But it's nothing like Laura's style."

"That's how I was rationalizing it too."

"Why would Laura ever need to know? You don't need to show it to her."

"The thing is, Mitchell, I want to do a whole series. All those photographs from the night of the party—they've stayed in my imagination. All those people, having a marvelous time, not knowing they're about to be part of a terrible tragedy."

"It sounds creepy. I like it."

"But what if it's not really inspiration? What if I'm just copying you and Laura? I mean, Pierre said I'm too easily influenced."

"Friends are always influencing each other. That's what friends are for."

"Maybe it's because you've talked about it so much. And because of meeting Laura and doing the banners for the concert."

"Those are perfectly good reasons. And maybe this'll push you into something else eventually. Something totally different. This could be an important developmental stage. That's what you'd say to me."

Ingrid nodded her acceptance of this logic. "Do you think I could borrow Cortland's file with all the photographs? I'll grey out their faces. No one'll recognize them."

"It sounds like me changing everyone's names."

The phone rang.

As Ing went to answer, I stood and stared at this strange interpretation of Thornfield Manor, wondering about the house and all its mysterious power.

"I can't hear you." Ingrid scrunched up her face. "OK. I'll be right there." She hung up the phone.

"Who was it?"

"Daphne. Whispering. She said to come into the store. A customer says he knows me."

"Who?"

"She tried to describe him, but I couldn't hear what she said. You'd better come with me for protection."

We didn't bother pulling on our jackets. We zipped down the hall and out onto the sidewalk—peeking in the corner of the front window to see who the mysterious visitor might be. Inside,

Daphne used one of those powdered candy Pixy Stix to point out a guy standing with his back to us at the card rack. All we could see were jeans and a denim jacket. Then a glimpse of short strawberry-blond hair and beard.

"It's Kevin," Ing said.

"I didn't think Dr. Bhandari let him out of the house."

"What's he doing *here*?"

"I told you he was interested in you."

"Do you think that's it? Oh God, Mitchell, I hate situations like this."

"It's a compliment."

"It *would* be if I was single."

"Maybe he was staring out the window again when you were taking pictures of the house."

"Nobody saw me," she said. "At least I don't think anyone did."

I pointed to Laura's cards on the display easels. "I wonder if he realizes these are all pictures of the place where he lives."

"You can't tell him."

"And I guess you'd better not show him your new painting either."

"You're right, I can't." For a moment, she looked stricken. Then she slapped my arm. "I'm not inviting him into my apartment, Mitchell. You're just trying to make this more complicated than it needs to be. Don't embarrass me, please?"

We sauntered into the shop, posing as casual shoppers.

Daphne tried to act spontaneous—"Mitchell, hi! Ingrid, hi! What are you doing here?"—revealing herself as a terrible actress.

Kevin turned. His face burst with a smile. "What a coincidence."

He enveloped me with a full-body-contact hug—which still felt incredibly good. Then he moved on to embrace Ingrid.

"You told me you lived around here," he said. "I wondered if I'd run into you."

"My apartment's just in back."

"The store's just as great as you said." He picked one of Ingrid's cards off the shelf. "So are these what you were telling me about? The Human Beings?"

"Human Beans," Ing corrected. And she began her explanation of the origin of the species.

"Who is he?" Daphne asked me in a mumbled whisper. Something large now bulged within her left cheek, making her resemble a squirrel.

"He's from Ramir's cult."

Daphne slid two fingers into her mouth and extracted a multicoloured jawbreaker which she held aloft right beside her mouth, poised for re-entry. "He's cute. He looks like Jesus."

"I think he's stalking her."

"I wish *I* had Ingrid's problems. Want some candy?"

Daphne offered me the ever-present bag, and I reached in for a gummy octopus. "Can I take a gummy cell phone for Ramir?"

"Grab all you want."

I did. "Thanks."

"You know, Laura's come by the store every day since that first time." Daphne gazed into her candy bag as if it were a crystal ball. "I think she's really lonely."

"I can't imagine what her life's like," I said, through stuck-together teeth.

"Pierre was in here yesterday, and they started talking. He was suggesting she should get into graphic design or something."

"It'd be nice if she could do something with her art."

"I think she mostly needs a haircut. I hate her bangs."

"So are people buying Laura's cards?"

"She's even topping Ingrid this week."

Though that looked as if it could change at any second. Kevin's enthusiastic grin persisted as he loaded his hand with a complete selection of Human Beans.

Daphne had to go serve a customer, so I browsed. I noticed a line of cards for women who've been treated badly by men. I opened one: "Liar, liar. Wish your pants were on fire."

Over my shoulder, I heard Kevin mention something about showing the Human Beans to a friend at an animation studio.

I've heard promises like that myself.

THURSDAY, OCTOBER 22
—MORE—

After Ingrid finally pulled herself away from Kevin, we went to the Future Bakery down the street. The sky was clear and sunny, which warmed the air enough for us to sit outside on the patio, amid all the other artsy types in their bulky Peruvian sweaters.

Ingrid picked the poppy seeds off a Danish. "He seems pretty normal for being so spiritual, don't you think?"

"Don't tell me *you're* going to get recruited next."

"He's just a nice person. Anyway, I told him I'm romantically involved."

"You said 'I'm romantically involved'?"

"I did that thing where you casually slip it in. I said 'My boyfriend Pierre and I are coming to Gabriella's concert.' And he was telling me that he's been married before too. He has a 4-year-old son who lives with his ex-wife. Actually, Gabriella is his son's godmother."

"The kid must get good gifts."

"But Kevin's cute. Isn't he cute?"

"Very cute."

We dwelled on his cuteness as we sipped our respective hot chocolates.

"Maybe we could set him up with Daphne," Ing suggested. "We could bring her to the concert with one of Cortland's extra tickets."

"Daphne'd probably be easy for Kevin to brainwash."

FRIDAY, OCTOBER 23

Back to my investigation.

Last night I flipped through the phone book again and found a listing for "Zale, William" on Huntingwood Drive, another street I'd never heard of. With its prestigious Britishy sound, I figured it must be somewhere in Rosedale. But when I searched in my handy pocket map book, I discovered it in the distant suburban reaches of Scarborough. Not a very glamorous neighbourhood for a 60-something executive—a former partner in "one of the most successful firms in the Canadian printing industry." It might not be the same guy.

Nonetheless, I downed a shot of tequila and dialed.

A soft female voice gave a meek "Hello." In the background I could hear a television blaring.

"May I please speak with Bill Zale?"

A deafening metallic clatter as the woman dropped the receiver into the giant garbage can she apparently kept by the couch. The television again. The peppy theme music from *Wheel of Fortune.*

Then a gruff "Yup?" on the other end of the line.

"Is this Bill Zale?"

"Who's this?"

"Um, well, this might seem a bit odd, but my name is Mitchell Draper, and I'm wondering if you might be the same Bill Zale who used to be in business with Jackson Donnington?"

"Jackson Donnington," he said slowly. "Why the fuck do you want to know about him?"

"Oh, well, um, you see, I'm a writer—"

"A writer?"

"Yes, and I'm doing some research, and I was hoping to ask you some questions about what happened with him and his son."

"Some questions?"

"Yes."

"The police thought I killed the fucking bastard—did you know that?"

"I'd heard a mention."

"I didn't do it." A caustic grunt. "What else do you need to know?"

"The thing is, I'm working on a screenplay—"

"You're making a movie?"

"I'm just doing some research at this point—getting some ideas about what happened."

"The bastard got what he deserved is what happened."

"Why would he deserve to get killed?"

"You really don't know much about him, do you?"

"Apparently not."

"I tried writing a book about Jackson a couple of times myself. Tell *my* side of the story. Never could finish the god-damned thing."

"Maybe you could tell *me* your side of the story?"

Bill paused as he considered my proposition.

"Buy me a martini and I'll even tell you who killed him." He coughed into the phone, allowing me to hear every ounce of phlegm. "I'm coming downtown tomorrow—have to make a fucking delivery that's two weeks late. Say 4:30. The Library Bar at the Royal York. I'll be the fat guy in the back."

☆

I called Ramir.

"You have to come with me."

"I'm busy tomorrow, Mitch."

"You said you wanted to help me with the investigation. You practically promised."

"I'll be at Dr. Bhandari's all day, interviewing him for the documentary."

"I don't want to do this alone. He said to look for the *fat guy.* What kind of person calls himself the *fat guy*? And he swears all the time. He's got a mouth like a sewer."

"Mitch, you used to write pornography. It's not like you don't know some dirty words yourself."

"That was different. It was in context. But this guy was the number-one murder suspect."

"Mitch, calm down. You're meeting in a public place. Nothing's going to happen. There'll be witnesses."

"There were witnesses at the party when he got into that fight with Jackson."

"Why don't you call me right after you're done? You can tell me how it went."

"If you don't hear from me by 6 o'clock, you can phone the police and tell them to start searching for my body."

FRIDAY, OCTOBER 23
—LATER—

I took the subway down to the Royal York. It's one of the oldest hotels in the city—a massive faux French château across the street from the train station.

In years gone by, this was Toronto's centrepiece of style, with fancy restaurants specializing in prime rib and the legendary Imperial Room showcasing Peggy Lee and Nancy Sinatra.

Somehow it still feels lost in time.

Tucked off the side of the lobby, The Library Bar is a dark-brown cave—dim to the point of murkiness—with a soundtrack of gentle Muzak and the scent of cigar smoke recycled through the air-conditioning system. It's the perfect locale for illicit romance and surreptitious business dealings.

When I arrived at 4:30, the room was spattered with suspicious executives. And, sure enough, in the back corner beside a wall of never-read leather-bound books, I spotted a fat guy on a rust-coloured velvet couch. His baggy pinstriped shirt was unbuttoned one button too far, revealing a spray of grey chest hair and a heavy silver chain. His grey hair was thinning on top yet shaggy in the back. Heavy half-moons of fat sagged beneath each of his watery blue eyes.

"Bill?"

"That's me."

Impossible to recognize him from the old magazine photograph in which he and Jackson had held aloft a trophy, smiling victoriously.

We shook hands. On his pinkie was a silver ring set with a chunk of turquoise.

"Tell the waitress what you want. I'll have another gin martini. You're paying."

"Dry Rob Roy," I said. Did that sound macho enough?

"You're younger than I thought you'd be," Bill said.

"I'm 30."

"A kid."

"I never felt like a kid even when I was a kid."

"When you're as old as I am, you'll look back and realize you were a kid." He drained his previous martini. "I wanted to take a look at you first before I decided whether I'd talk to you."

"Do I pass?"

He grunted a laugh. "You don't look too dangerous." Then he thrust his finger at me in a fierce accusation. "I want one thing clear about this goddamned movie of yours. Don't make it look like *I* killed those two. Because if you pull any shit like that, I'll drag your ass straight into court."

"I'd never do that," I quavered. "I'm going to change all the names. Change the city even. No one'll ever think you had anything to do with it."

"I *didn't* have anything to do with it."

"Slip of the tongue. Sorry."

"But I know who *did*," he said.

"That's what you mentioned on the phone. So who did it?"

"First, I want you to put what you just said in writing."

"What did I just say?"

From a shabby briefcase on the floor, he brought out a yellow legal pad and a Bic pen. "I should have got people doing this a long time ago. Write down what I tell you."

"Could you tell me what you want me to say first?"

"Just write: 'I—' What's your name again?"

"Mitchell Draper."

"'I, Mitchell Draper, promise not to write anything that implies Bill Zale was the murderer of Jackson and Trevor Donnington.' Now sign it and date it."

I complied—all the time wondering about the implications. What if Bill Zale really *was* the murderer? I'd never be able to reveal the true story. But if I could find proof that he was guilty, then this little piece of paper would be worthless.

At the same time, I wanted to hear what Bill had to say.

The waitress delivered our drinks in big round goblets—certain to get me plastered—which were then poured into individual glasses.

Bill toasted. "May the rotten bastard burn in hell."

"To burning in hell!"

We each took a swig.

"If anyone deserves it, it's him."

"Jackson must have been a very complicated person," I suggested delicately. "I've already talked to three or four people—his daughter and some friends of the family—and I've been getting lots of different impressions."

"Jackson was a fucking expert at that—giving people different impressions. Always made himself look like the perfect nice-guy gentleman. And he was always screwing everybody behind their backs."

"So what happened that you hate him so much?"

"He stole a million bucks from me. How's that for a start?"

"A million?"

"And he died at a very convenient time. He left me with a pile of shit to handle. If I'd ever known what was going to happen—" He stopped himself. "Something else I want to know. How'd a kid like you ever hear about Jackson in the first place?"

"A friend of mine was at the party that night."

"Everybody says they were at that fucking party. It's like people telling you they were at Woodstock. There would have been 2,000 people in that house if everybody was telling the truth. It hit legend status for a while. Jackson would have loved that."

The waitress delivered a plate of chicken wings—ordered prior to my arrival? I presumed I was paying for those as well. Bill dug in.

"How did you two meet?" I asked.

"We were both working at another printing house, Newsome & Gilbert. Both sales reps. Jackson was the slick type. I used to work on the floor, so I know the business hands-on. Anyway, we heard about another plant that was up for sale. We went out drinking one night and started bullshitting about setting up our own shop. I thought it was all just talk. But the next morning Jackson handed in his resignation. So I did the same. Day after that, we had our business cards: Donnington-Zale Lithography. We were booming in three months."

"What year was this?"

"Nobody remembers—is that what you're trying to say? We opened in '75. We did some fancy brochures. The Eaton's catalogue. Won some big awards. Rolling in dough. I bought a place in Rosedale too—not as big as Jackson's. But he always cared more about that kind of thing than I did. Of course, he had money in his blood. His wife did too."

"Did you know Vivienne?"

"Sure, I knew her. Coldhearted bitch. We hated each other on sight."

"Everybody I've talked to said she was charming."

"Typical ice princess. She looked at me like I was dirt, and she treated my wife the same way. But she was the kind of high-class bitch you need if you wanted to travel in certain circles, and those were the circles Jackson liked. Of course, he was still fucking around on the side."

"Do you know with who?"

Bill coughed out another laugh. "Who could keep track? A couple of afternoons a week Jackson would disappear. We always said he was 'having lunch at the Park Plaza.' But he and Vivienne had their arrangement." (That word again.) "She was always out with her society friends, decorating the house, throwing those huge parties, schmoozing the clients."

"I guess the parties were tax write-offs?"

"And I was the stupid fool paying for them. But that party would have been the last one. The thing nobody knew that night was that Donnington-Zale was going to be closing its doors on Monday morning."

"You and Jackson were splitting up?"

"I caught him embezzling. I was planning to call in the cops. Then Jackson would have been the one to get arrested—not me. Of course, the bastard died like a martyr before the shit hit the fan."

"Is that why you had the big argument at the party?"

"Exactly. That very afternoon—it was a Friday—our auditor called me over to his office. Just me. It turns out they'd found

$2 million in payouts to another printing company nobody had ever heard of. But they couldn't find any cost estimates or invoices to back them up. Jackson had signed all the cheques. He was draining the accounts."

"Why?"

"That's what I wanted to find out that night at the party. I thought Jackson was my best friend. We'd known each other for 10 years. I didn't know what to do. Call the police? Talk to Jackson? When I left the accountant's office, I was in a god-damned daze. I was supposed to go home and pick up my wife so we could show up at the party. Neither of us wanted to go in the first place. But I didn't want to tell my wife about the whole embezzling situation until I knew what I was going to do. So I sat in my car and drank half a bottle of Scotch to calm down."

"And that's when you went to the house?"

"Fucking brilliant, right? I charged in, screaming my lungs out, saying I wanted to see Jackson. And I found him, waltzing around in that fancy ballroom of theirs. He just stood there, calm as anything, saying, 'We'll talk about it on Monday, Bill.' I nearly slugged him in the mouth, and then he knew I wasn't going to shut up. So he took me upstairs to his office. He played dumb—acted like the accountant must be wrong, like I was crazy to believe it. I kept asking where was my half of the $2 million. Afterward, the police kept questioning me. How far did the fight go? Did I punch him? Where did I punch him? Did I push him onto his desk?"

"His daughter Laura said his desk was all messed up."

"We might have knocked into it—who knows. I stormed out of the house, making as big a scene as I could. I said I'd be calling my lawyer. Then I drove back to the office and got even more plastered. Which was the worst thing I could have done, it turns out. I should have gone home to my wife or gone to a bar so I'd have had an alibi. Another reason you should never drink alone." He raised his glass in a one-sided toast. "At 4 in the morning, the police came to the office, and they took me into custody. Interrogated me for eight hours nonstop. What route did I take to the office? Did I go anywhere on the way? Did anyone see me? Of course, no one did. Just my luck."

He reached for another chicken wing.

"They wanted me to confess that I'd gone back to the house, stabbed Jackson, then pushed the son out the window because he saw what happened. But what would the two of us be doing up in his son's room in the first place? None of it made any sense. They said I'd wiped the fingerprints off the knife before I threw it in the pool. But then they found the kid's prints on the back of a broken chair in his room. That's what finally made them let me go."

"Did you ever meet Trevor?"

"Jackson gave him a summer job at the company. The kid liked writing, so Jackson told him to come up with some form letters to send to new clients. Nothing we'd ever really use. But the kid stole some money out of a secretary's purse—like father, like son— and I told Jackson I didn't want him coming back."

"You're sure it was Trevor who did it?"

"Of course we were sure. He was a good-looking kid. Quiet. But you could tell he was the type you couldn't trust. He could fly out of control at a moment's notice."

"Did you ever meet his therapist, Dr. Bhandari?"

"I never even knew the kid had psychiatric problems."

"So you didn't know he was taking medication?"

"That was typical of Jackson. He liked to keep up appearances. Not good for business to have a nutcase for a son. Jackson was the biggest two-faced bastard you ever met. So polite and arrogant and condescending about it, you'd always be the one who comes out looking like an asshole. It's no wonder his kid went crazy. But still, I don't think Trevor was the one who did it."

"What about his fingerprints on the chair?"

"Sure, the kid was up there having a fit about something. But nobody ever found the 2 million bucks Jackson stole from me." Bill smiled cockily. He pulled a package of Camels from his shirt pocket and lit up.

"You think somebody killed them for the money?"

"Not just somebody. His wife."

"Vivienne?"

"She got married six months after Jackson died. What does that tell you about how much she loved him? She was fooling around just as much as Jackson. She and her lover came up with a plan. Get rid of the unfaithful husband and the screwed-up kid in one whack—then start a new life with Jackson's money, plus a million of mine."

"So she stabbed her husband and pushed her own son out the window?"

"I'm not saying she did it herself. She gets the lover to sneak into the house during the party. Perfect opportunity. Lots of noise downstairs. Nobody'd notice a stranger. He finds Jackson and Trevor up in the kid's room, and takes care of them both."

It actually sort of made sense. "Did you ever tell the police this?"

"Of course I did. They never followed up. But they never found my money either."

"It'd be hard to prove," I said.

"Don't I know that? I tried for years. I sued Vivienne, but I never got anywhere."

Bill consumed his final chicken wing.

"So what happened to the business after Jackson died?"

"A couple of months later, they gave me a pile of money from the partnership insurance. That almost made up for what he stole. But all the clients were still in love with Jackson, and the accounts pulled out, one by one. I had to shut down in 18 months. Ended up working at the shit place I am now. Trade printer. The work is crap. But at least I always know where I stand."

"So I'm just trying to sort this out. You think Jackson was hiding the money and Vivienne found it after he died?"

"Maybe he had it stashed in some Swiss bank account."

"In Switzerland?"

"That's where they tend to be. Of course, Vivienne eventually got what was coming to her in that car crash. Burned alive, from what I heard."

"I hadn't heard that." My stomach turned. "And what do you think happened to all the money after Vivienne died?"

"The daughter must have got it."

"Laura?"

"With everything that girl inherited, she must be a multi-millionaire."

"That's what I figured."

"She'd make a pretty good catch for some poor guy."

I didn't know how to respond. We both stared into our drinks.

"It's funny," I said, "when I started working on this screenplay, I had no idea the whole thing was going to be so complicated."

"Everything in life is always complicated," Bill said. "Do me a favour, kid. When you write about Jackson, make him look like a fucking bastard."

"I'll do my best."

"And remember…" He held up my signed promise. "I have this."

I downed the rest of my drink in a single gulp.

SUNDAY, OCTOBER 25

I'm confused.

MONDAY, OCTOBER 26

INTERIOR. SECOND-FLOOR HALLWAY—NIGHT

TREVOR is listening outside the door to his father's office. He hears loud voices as his father, JACKSON, argues with his business partner, BILL ZALE.

> BILL'S VOICE
> What did you do with the fucking money?

> JACKSON'S VOICE
> Bill, I told you. I don't know what you're talking about.

TREVOR puts his hand on the doorknob and edges the door open a crack. He sees BILL shove JACKSON against his desk. Papers and pens go flying.

> BILL
> So is it all stashed away in some Swiss bank account? Tell me where you put it.

> JACKSON
> Bill, I want you out of my house this second.

The arguing men don't notice TREVOR watching...

Or do they?

And then what?

After that conversation with Bill Zale, I've been completely stymied.

At first I was so sure the Mysterious Killer was Dr. Bhandari. Then Bill Zale. Then some nameless tramp. Or perhaps Ermina. Then Vivienne Donnington. Even though Laura might have benefited in the long term, I can't imagine that a 12-year-old girl could have killed two men—especially not her beloved father and brother.

So this afternoon, for lack of better inspiration, I decided to commune with the dead.

Naturally Jackson and Trevor Donnington are occupants of one of Toronto's most renowned burial grounds, St. James' Cemetery, established in 1844. Nestled on the side of a ravine, it offers convenient proximity to illustrious Rosedale—though its entrance is across the street from a block of bleak white apartment towers.

Inside the main gate, I stopped at a tiny office building designed to look like a quaint cottage in the English countryside. The inside had been modernized, offering the bland pastel greys of a franchised funeral home.

An equally bland, grey-haired man came to the counter.

"I'm hoping you can help me find some people," I said. "Dead people."

"That's mostly what we've got."

"They're old family friends. My mother asked me to drop by and pay my respects."

"The name?"

"D-O-N-N-I-N-G-T-O-N. Trevor and Jackson."

"Do you know the dates of death? Sometimes that makes it easier to narrow things down."

"July 13, 1979."

"Both?"

"Both."

The old man looked at me strangely for a moment.

I half-expected him to grab me by the collar and accuse me of being a blood-thirsty tourist out to torment the souls of the dead. Instead, he hobbled off around the corner. A moment later he returned and planted a map of the cemetery on the counter.

"They're down here," he said and marked the spot with an X.

So I set out on my hunt.

Cemeteries always give me the creeps. And this one is particularly creepy. Especially since I seemed to be the sole visitor.

As I walked along the gravel roadway, littered with orange and yellow leaves, I passed a miniature Gothic cathedral/crematorium, the Chapel of St. James-the-Less. (I presume they gave St. James-the-More a larger namesake.)

Behind the church spread a dense forest of moulting trees with an equally dense forest of ornate tombstones. Pillars and statues and mossy blocks of red granite. Family mausoleums that looked like miniature Parthenons. They had probably cost the same as a starter home today.

Every few steps I noticed another family name that I knew was somehow linked to Toronto history. Stollery, Jarvis, Gooderham, Cawthra. Not a graveyard with many new arrivals. But Jackson was of old Toronto stock, so he'd probably had his place reserved before he'd even been born.

I found the small wooden sign for Section H-H, which evidently was on a lower level. I took a staircase down to an area that felt like a separate cemetery. Bargain basement. A sloping hillside where all the graves were on a steep precarious angle, veering down to the bottom of the ravine.

Most of the gravestones were stained and blackened. The names and dates were hard to discern but the majority seemed to be from the early twentieth century. Crosses were broken off at their pedestals. Some stones were toppled over entirely—perhaps by the homeless people who sleep in the ravine at night. At the end of the centre aisle stood a headless stone angel.

Ahead I saw a pink granite obelisk, reaching at least twelve feet high—the tilt of the ground making it resemble the Leaning Tower of Pisa. I knew even from a distance that it was theirs. When I drew closer, I saw the limestone block at the base, etched with imposing letters: DONNINGTON.

On the front were names I'd never heard of. Jackson's grandparents and great-grandparents who'd died in the early 1900s. Then on the far back side I found them:

JACKSON HILLIARD 1935-1979

HIS SON
TREVOR NICHOLAS 1962-1979

So this was where all that drama and tragedy and publicity had ended up.

I stared at the earth beneath my feet and wondered how both

bodies could be squeezed into such a tight space. Were their coffins stacked one on top of the other? Had they been cremated?

I ran my hand across Trevor's name and dates. The dusty black paint was already flaking in the engraved letters.

I imagined the climactic moment from *Carrie,* with Trevor's hand parting the earth and reaching up to grab my ankle.

But nothing so paranormal occurred.

I sat on a bench-height tombstone across the aisle—thoughtfully provided by the Bramford family—and I stared at the Donnington clan.

Jane Choy had said I have latent psychic potential. Could Trevor Donnington be coordinating the universe and planting coincidences? Using me as a channel from the other side? And if he's going to so much trouble, there must be something important he wants me to say.

I closed my eyes and tried to connect with the spirit world.

I tried to imagine Trevor Donnington's face.

I tried using his name as a mantra.

I tried to imagine he was speaking to me.

He didn't.

When my rear end was sufficiently chilled by the granite, I got up and left.

It was just after noon.

I was walking home along Bloor Street in that bland cluster of cement high-rises just west of Sherbourne. In the midst of all the concrete desolation there's one charming little café—a bastion of warmth in gold and aubergine.

When I glanced in the window, I saw Pierre. I didn't know his new office was around here. He was laughing and chatting, dispersing his sexy French allure. And he was sitting with someone. A woman.

I was even more startled when I realized it was Laura Donnington.

Laura laughed as well. I hadn't seen her actually laugh before. The tight, strained expression had lifted from her face.

They didn't see me. And I didn't want to interrupt.

☆

Naturally I called Ingrid as soon as I got home.

"They met at Daphne's store," Ing explained.

"Oh right, Daphne told me that."

"Laura took him to lunch to ask him about getting into graphic design."

"I figured there was some rational explanation."

"Be honest, Mitchell, you were hoping to cause a scandal," Ing said, chuckling at her own mock-offense. "Did you think Pierre was cheating on me again?"

"It just surprised me, that's all."

"Well, he's not. I think it's great if they get along. Pierre needs more friends if he's going to feel like Toronto's home. And I bet Laura could use more friends too."

MONDAY, OCTOBER 26
—LATER—

All the detectives in books and movies and in those British police dramas on TV always travel efficiently from suspect to suspect, from discovery to discovery. They make it look so easy.

I don't know what to do next.

TUESDAY, OCTOBER 27

Once again I climbed the steps to the front porch of Jane Choy's ivy-covered house.

Last night, as I was rolling around in sleepless confusion, I remembered Jane mentioning her psychic-training workshops every Tuesday afternoon. After all, she'd been the first to sense something hovering above me when I met her at Dr. Bhandari's house, and maybe she could help me understand what these dreams and all the other coincidences actually mean.

As I stepped onto the porch, I fully expected Jane to swing the door open instantaneously as she had the first time. But I knocked and waited. Then I knocked again. When Jane finally opened the door, she was out of breath, and she wore a silly giggling grin on her fuchsia lips.

"Sorry, Mitchell. Just back in the kitchen. Telling stupid jokes."

"Am I too early?"

"No, no. Perfect timing. Only one other person today. You brought the hundred bucks?"

I reached into my pocket for my wallet and removed my five $20 bills—fresh from the bank machine. All this research is getting expensive.

"Come on in, sit down."

No sign of my fellow student. The floor of Jane's multiethnic living room was readied with three plump red cushions, arranged in a triangle. But Jane perched on one of the red silk chairs, and I sat across from her on the floor-level zebra couch.

"I hope you have a good time at this thing," she said. "I try to make it fun. Now what were you saying to my housekeeper on the phone? You told her about a tall guy?"

"Remember when I came for my psychic reading, you said I'd meet a tall, dark, and handsome stranger."

"You met him already? Having a big romance? See, I told you I'm good."

"Well, I *think* I've found him. But the problem is he's dead."

"Not very romantic."

"Remember I told you I had that weird dream about a figure standing above me? Well, it's happened twice now at Dr. Bhandari's house. And I found out that there was a murder-suicide there—or a double murder—and the guy the police think was the killer was tall, dark, and handsome. And now I think he wants me to prove he was innocent."

"Slow down, you're confusing me. People died in Bhandari's house?"

"Up on the third floor. I tried to see the room where it happened, but—"

Just then the other student entered the living room.

"Hartman, come listen to this."

"Forgive me," Gabriella Hartman said, "I was just freshening up." She patted and puffed her luxuriant auburn hair. Then she saw me, and her face erupted in an expression of exaggerated delight. "Mitchell Draper! What a *thrill* to see you again so soon."

"A thrill to see you too."

I felt ill and relieved at the same time. It's a good thing I hadn't said anything bad about Dr. Bhandari.

Gabriella hugged me and kissed me on both cheeks. "Isn't it *extraordinary* how the universe can arrange itself when something is *meant* to happen?"

"Mitchell was just telling me about people getting killed in your buddy Bhandari's house."

"Don't be *absurd*, Jane."

"No surprise to me," Jane said. "I could tell it was a spooky place."

"Nigel's never told me about *murders*," Gabriella said, as though personally offended.

"They happened over 20 years ago," I explained apologetically. "There was a big party at the house. A son stabbed his father and then jumped out the window. Or at least that's the official police version."

"And Mitchell thinks one of the guys is contacting him from the spirit world to prove he didn't do it."

206

"I know it sounds insane," I said.

"It sounds *fascinating*," Gabriella effused.

Suddenly, I saw the enormous potential of Gabriella Hartman's fascination. "Actually, I'm turning the whole thing into a screenplay."

"A *screenplay*?" Gabriella's eyes instantly took on the seductive glare I'd seen her use so often on *Station Centauri*. Like a lioness closing in on her prey, she moved close beside me on the zebra couch. "You know, Mitchell, my manager and I are actively reestablishing my career in feature films. I'm flying back to L.A. next week for meetings. All the big studios."

"In fact, I already have some serious interest from Apex."

"Apex? Really? Why don't you tell me the plot? Tell me the plot right now."

I recounted my latest scenario for *A Killing Upstairs*.

"It's positively *operatic* in scale," Gabriella gushed. "I'd *kill* to play the wife."

"Frankly, I've always thought Vivienne is the most interesting character."

"You give her some dialogue to win me an Oscar, and I'll sign up right away."

"Calm down, Hartman," Jane said. "That's your whole problem. You only think about your career, when Mitchell here has a serious psychic problem. So tell me again what exactly you saw in your dream."

Just then a scrawny man in a purple bathrobe entered the living room. His head was topped with a small quantity of stringy wet hair. "Honey, where are the new razor blades?"

Jane became coy and kittenish. "Silly, you can't find your right arm if it's not screwed on." Jane took him by his removable arm, and they disappeared down the hall.

Gabriella smiled indulgently. "*Soulmates* if I've ever seen a pair."

"They seem like sort of an unlikely couple."

"Oh, Mitchell, you *couldn't* be more wrong. The two of them spend hours together in their sensory-deprivation tank."

WARREN DUNFORD

"Doesn't that sort of defeat the purpose?"

"Jane says it makes them feel like the only people in the world."

I shuddered. "That thing reminds me of a coffin. I get claustrophobic just closing my eyes."

"I can't stand it myself. All that salt water is torture on the hair."

Gabriella put her arm back around my shoulder, and her face transformed once more, this time into something almost human. "Now, Mitchell, I think it's more than a coincidence that I've run into you this afternoon."

"Because of the screenplay?"

"No. Though that's wonderful, of course. But because I've been *terribly* worried about our dear mutual friend."

"Ramir?"

"He is so *devastated* about losing that movie role."

"He is?"

"Completely."

"We talked about it more than a week ago. He said he was handling it all right."

"Maybe he was trying to save face in front of you. You mean so much to him. But he just fell apart when he was talking to me last night." Last night? It was bizarre to hear about Ramir from someone else. Like Daphne telling me about Ingrid.

"He's been sort of fragile all year," I said, "after what happened with his father."

"At least we know he's in good hands with Dr. Bhandari."

"Right."

"I just want to make sure all his *closest* friends are watching out for him. Such a strange karma we artists must endure. Always putting ourselves up for rejection and criticism. And now here I am, stepping out on a limb again with my singing."

"But you've sung professionally before."

"Never this way. Never so vulnerably. To be completely honest with you, Mitchell, I am petrified."

And for a change, I could tell she genuinely was.

208

"Ramir says you're fabulous."

"That's very dear of him. So typical. But in only four days, I could become a public laughingstock."

"You won't—"

Jane returned. "Sorry about the disappearing act. Good thing it's you two and not some of those big fruitcakes who come sometimes."

"You were gone a *suspiciously* long time," Gabriella pointed out, her confident persona resurfacing.

"You be careful, Hartman. I know all your secrets too. OK, let's get to work on our ESP. Come sit on the floor."

Jane and Gabriella automatically dropped to the floor and twisted into lotus positions. They looked like yogic monks with their bolt-upright posture, hands on knees, thumb and forefingers touching and pointed up. I followed their lead, though my legs wouldn't quite cross that far.

"I can feel the vibrations already," Jane said. "I can tell this is going to be a very good session."

"Now, Mitchell, please don't be intimidated," Gabriella said. "This is only my fourth of Jane's psychic-training workshops. I'm hardly a pro."

"I'll try to keep up."

Jane began: "The important thing in developing psychic power is to let your mind be open. You have to know what you want, but keep open to whatever comes, so you don't let your brain get in the way of the messages. So both of you now, tell the universe what you want to happen."

"May I interject?" Gabriella interjected. "Mitchell, this approach is very similar to Dr. Bhandari's concept of decreeing."

"Don't compare me to Bhandari," Jane snapped. "I hate it when you do that. You know I came up with this stuff before I ever heard of that guy. Just shut up and tell the spirits what you want."

Gabriella cleared her throat and settled back into her lotus pose. "I want to allow the music of the universe to flow through me and resonate in others. I want to tap the healing power of sound vibrations. I want to connect with the life force that inspires me to sing."

"Very good," Jane said.

Gabriella nodded, because she knew it was.

"I don't know what to say," I said.

"Just say why you're here."

"I want to find out what really happened at Thornfield Manor."

"More specific."

"I want to find out what the tall, dark man wants me to say. And if there really was another killer, who was it?"

"Good. Now breathe deeply. Feel the breath move in your nose and down your throat, fill your lungs, expand your chest. Now let your mind go loose. Pretend your brain has been jumping up and down doing Tae Bo. It's so tired, it feels like a lump of mush."

And that strange sensation happened again. Like a lead weight dropping in the back of my skull.

"My brain really does feel like mush."

"Be quiet. Now breathe deeply and feel your brain go all runny, dripping down through your body. Your mind is flowing down your neck into your shoulders, into your right arm, into your hand. Now your left hand. Now your mind is running down your leg, into your right foot. Pretend you're thinking with your foot."

I rolled my eyes, even though they were closed.

"OK, now bring your mind back up your body into your head. Focus on the left back part of your head. Now the left front. Now right front. Right back. OK, now imagine there's a fountain coming out of the top of your brain. Energy coming out of your head, but also flowing back down in. Sit up tall. Feel like the fountain is pulling you up."

I sneaked a peek at Gabriella and Jane, still rigid with their perfect vertical posture.

"OK, now we're almost ready. Focus on your forehead. Think of it like a little door. Like the glove compartment in a car. Put your left forefinger in the centre of your forehead. This is your third eye. This is how your psychic mind can see. Now push hard with your finger, like you're pressing the button on the glove compartment. Push hard. Now take your finger away."

                                                                    CUT TO:

INTERIOR. DARK ROOM—NIGHT

Looking up at the fine crack of light at the top of a doorframe. From the angle, the viewer must be lying down. Restless camera motions. The sound of heavy, rapid breathing.

A TALL FIGURE steps into frame, looming above. The room is so dark, the TALL FIGURE's face can't be seen.

A low grunting sound.

The TALL FIGURE bends forward, swiftly lowering a hand.

The camera jerks and everything goes black.

A moment later, there's a shift in angle and the hand appears again, reaching forward in a caress. The face of the TALL FIGURE comes closer, but still no features can be distinguished.

Suddenly, the crack of light widens, illuminating the darkness. The door is opening.

ANOTHER FIGURE is revealed in the doorway, standing in silhouette.

The TALL FIGURE straightens and turns to the door.

                              MAN'S VOICE
What the fuck are you doing?

The door slams.

                                                                    CUT TO:

I opened my eyes.

My heart was pounding.

Jane and Gabriella were both staring at me with their mouths wide open.

"Why are you staring at me?"

"You spoke," Gabriella said.

"I spoke?"

"But it wasn't your voice," said Jane.

"What did I say?"

"*What the fuck are you doing?*" Gabriella quoted.

"I said that out loud? I thought I just heard it."

"You could be repeating what you heard," Jane said. "That happens to me sometimes in readings. What did you see?"

"It was like the other dreams—"

"Not dreams," Jane said. "You can't have dreams that fast. Your brain doesn't have time to make them."

"Then what are they?"

"Psychic visions. You're seeing something that really happened. Tell me what you saw."

"Well, it was like what I saw before, but it went further. It was like I was lying down flat on my back in a dark room. And there was a person bending over me."

"The dark man? What was he doing?"

"At first I thought it was a murder scene. Like strangling. But now I'm definitely sure it wasn't that. It was like we were having sex."

"I can picture it perfectly," Gabriella said.

"And you were seeing from the point of view of the person on the bed?"

"I don't think it was a bed," I said.

"Then what was it?"

Ideas fell together. "I think it might have happened upstairs at Dr. Bhandari's house. The second floor. Jackson's old office. The massage room."

Gabriella nodded excitedly. "I had a massage there just yesterday."

"People could have been fooling around on Jackson's desk," I said. "That's how everything got knocked over."

"And *you* were one of the people?" Gabriella asked.

I nodded, because that sort of made sense. "Then the door opened, and there was a figure standing in the light."

"A man or a woman?" asked Jane.

"I couldn't tell. That's when I heard *'What the fuck are you doing?'*"

Jane was impatient. "Which one of you said *'What the fuck?'* "

"I'm not sure. But it was a man's voice. Then the door slammed, and I woke up."

"Frankly, I don't care *who* was fucking *who*," Gabriella declared, her eyes fiery with excitement. "All I want to know, Mitchell, is when you can show me the fucking script."

As I was pulling on my jacket to leave, Gabriella went to the kitchen to make a phone call. Jane took me aside.

"You feeling OK? All that psychic power can tire you out when you're not used to it."

"I think I'm fine."

"Mitchell, let me give you a bit of a psychic reading for free."

"I'll take all the help I can get."

Jane shut her eyes and spoke slowly. "The solution to your problem is getting upstairs in that house. You need to visit the scene of the crime."

"But Dr. Bhandari keeps it all locked up."

"You have to find a way to get in."

"The next time I'm going back there is for Gabriella's concert on Friday night."

"That's going to be a very powerful night, Mitchell. I can feel it. It's there at the house that you're going to get your answers."

TUESDAY, OCTOBER 27
—MORE—

I walked home from Jane's. But I made slow progress, because every few feet I had to stop, pull out my notepad, and scribble down another idea—trying to see how I could make all my theories fit together.

As expected, I found Ramir, Cortland, and Ingrid at work in the basement party room of my apartment building. Cortland had paid off the superintendent to allow Ingrid to paint the banners down there because she required a large unobstructed space.

Calling the windowless pit a party room is an act of ridiculous hopefulness, since there's not an iota of festive atmosphere. It's just a blank beige box with eyeball-vibrating fluorescent lights.

When I walked in, the floor was covered in black plastic tarp, and that in turn was blanketed with 30 or more 10-foot-long rectangles of diaphanous white fabric. The banners were lightly swirled with various shades of white and gold. Ingrid crouched amid them, three cans of paint at her hip, while Ramir and Cortland sat ensconced at a long banquet table—artificial wood grain with collapsible legs. Both of them had cell phones pressed to their ears.

Cortland pointed to the receiver and mouthed "Jim Jones." Then he carried on: "I simply believe that at $500 a ticket, people will expect better beverages than carrot juice and fizzy water."

Ramir blew me a kiss, then covered his free ear so he could concentrate fully on his conversation—which sounded like a detailed discussion of the video shoot for the concert.

He didn't seem devastated, as Gabriella had suggested. He seemed perfectly normal.

I hopscotched between the rectangles of fabric. "I didn't think there'd be so many of them."

Ing stood up and gave me a hug. "They're supposed to create a path from the front door to the ballroom."

"Back to the swirls, I see."

"Can't escape them. But, Mitchell, I've had some really good

214

news. Because Geoffrey and his assistant from the gallery came over this morning and they loved the painting of the house."

"They think you're on the right track?"

She nodded—proud, relieved, excited. "I can't wait for you to see what I was working on last night. It's based on one of Cortland's photographs. A close-up of Jackson and Vivienne, standing in a doorframe."

"I know exactly the picture you mean."

"And I want to do another one looking through the fence at the back of the house. It's like I'm becoming possessed by that place too. Hey, didn't you just come from your psychic?"

"I was just going to tell you—"

Cortland had finished his call. "Another crisis averted," he announced. He gracefully stepped between the banners and handed me an envelope.

"As promised, the dear doctor gave me 10 tickets to the concert. Rather tardy, I must say. Ermina's already purchased her own. She's desperate to see Vivienne's old place again. But you can distribute these as you see fit. The event's already sold out, you know."

"All 300 tickets?"

"Dr. B. has a captive audience. But I must say that everything is coming together brilliantly. All the best people in the city are on the job. Florists and rental places and such. White on white is the theme, accented with touches of gold. I've ordered a truckload of candles and stands and candelabras. Very misty and spiritual. Everyone will think they've died and gone to heaven."

"Maybe that's a poor choice of words."

Ramir finally ended his phone call and sauntered over cockily, as though he had some especially delicious secret. Which he did. "So, Mitch, I was just talking to Gabriella. She said you had a pretty wild time at Jane Choy's."

I smiled painfully. I knew I was about to be teased mercilessly. "I was planning to tell you myself."

"She said you experienced some kind of psychic vision?"

"You've become a *psychic*?" Cortland asked.

"No, of course not." I felt like an idiot. "I just had a weird little dream. Actually, it was a vision. It's the same thing I saw when I was at Dr. Bhandari's house—during the meditation and when I sneaked upstairs."

"You never told me about a vision before," Cortland said.

"Because I didn't want you to think I'm insane."

"Which I obviously now do."

"Only this time the vision went on longer. It's like I'm lying on a table or a desk and this tall figure is bending over me—like we might be having sex. Then someone opens the door, and some-body in the room—a man, I'm not sure who—says, '*What the fuck are you doing?*' and then the door slams closed."

"You've seen all that in a dream?" Cortland looked dumb-founded.

"Mitchell, do you realize how nutty that sounds?" Ing said delicately

"I know. I now officially declare myself a New Age flake. But even if my subconscious mind is making it all up, what's so good is that it's helped me develop a theory of what really happened that night."

Ingrid nodded at me doubtfully, speechlessly.

"So are you going to tell us your theory?" Cortland inquired.

"That's why I came down here in the first place."

The three of them sat behind the long table, and I was left standing, like a lawyer pacing before a jury.

"OK, well, first you have to go along with me about the vision. Because now I think it really might have happened. It's like I'm really seeing through somebody else's eyes."

"Trevor Donnington's eyes?" Ing asked.

"That's what's so confusing. Because if I'm lying down and I'm seeing through Trevor's eyes, then who's that above me? At first I thought it was a man, which means Trevor must have been gay. But it might be a woman. I'm not sure anymore. Anyway, my basic theory is that during the party there was some kind of sex scene going on in Jackson Donnington's office."

"That sounds intriguing," Cortland said.

"You mean like an orgy?" Ramir asked.

"Just let me spell everything out first, OK? You see, I've heard from both Bill Zale and Ermina Milenska that Jackson was cheating on Vivienne."

"I remember those rumours as well," Cortland said.

"In fact, Ermina said that when Vivienne couldn't find Jackson at the party that night, she thought he might have been upstairs fooling around with another woman. And Laura told Ingrid and me that her father's desk was messed up. Everything was knocked over. The police thought that could have happened during the fight between Bill and Jackson, but Bill doesn't remember it. That might be because he was drunk. But I think what really happened is that people were on the desk having sex, and that's how everything got pushed over."

"Which fits with your psychic vision," Ing said.

"But there's more. Laura also said that Trevor's fingerprints were found on the doorknob to Jackson's office. The police thought Trevor came downstairs when he heard Bill and Jackson fighting. But what if Trevor went to the office for another reason? This is where my theory splits into two possibilities. The first possibility is that Trevor walked in on his father and another woman."

Ramir held up a finger to interject. "Remember when you told me Bill Zale said *Vivienne* was cheating on *Jackson*?"

"I never heard anything about that," Cortland said.

"Couldn't Trevor have found his *mother* going at it in the office?" Ramir persisted.

"Vivienne was downstairs at the party the whole time," I said.

"Except for when she was looking for Jackson," Ing reminded. "And when she took that plate up to Trevor's room."

"Oh damn, you're right. But just go along with me for now, OK? Because this is the second possibility—and it's based on my vision being through Trevor's eyes. What if the fingerprints were from when Trevor took his *own* love interest into the office? Trevor was lying on the desk. Then Jackson walked in and caught them, and somehow they all rushed up to Trevor's room, and that's where the killings happened."

"How extraordinary," Cortland said.

Ingrid squinted as she worked the whole thing through. "So this mysterious sex partner witnessed the murder-suicide and didn't say anything," she concluded. "Wouldn't this person have come forward afterward?"

Cortland shook his head. "Would you want the world to know that two men are dead because you were caught fooling around at a party?"

"I guess it wouldn't do much for your reputation," Ingrid agreed.

I waved my hand to get their attention again. "Or what about the more interesting possibility—that the mystery person killed Trevor and Jackson and then made it *look* like a murder-suicide. And totally got away with it."

Ing tilted her head at a skeptical angle. "So you think this mystery person killed Trevor and Jackson just because he or she was caught having sex with one of them?"

"They could have been embarrassed about it," Ramir suggested. "They wanted to keep it quiet."

"A double murder seems a little extreme," Ing said.

"That's what made me think Trevor might have been with another man," I explained. "He didn't want people to know he was gay."

"Has anyone said he was gay?" Ing asked. (She thinks I think everyone is gay.)

"No," I confessed. "And frankly, I don't really want to go that way for the screenplay, because people being shocked by homosexuality is so passé."

"This *was* 20 years ago," Cortland pointed out.

"Then I thought maybe it was something *really* shocking—like Trevor was having sex with his *mother* when his father walked in."

"Or having sex with his *father* when his *mother* walked in," Ramir suggested.

"I hadn't thought of that."

"There's no way Vivienne would have killed them," Cortland said with horror. "Besides, Jackson was as straight as they come."

"Or maybe he was having sex with his sister, Laura."

"That's nasty, Mitchell," Ing said. "You can't just make up things like that. Anyway, incest is overdone too."

"I'm not saying I'm going to write it that way. We're just brainstorming."

"What about that professional divorcée Ermina?" Ramir suggested. "Maybe *she* was with Trevor. Didn't you say she was a tramp?"

"You shouldn't be repeating stories like that, Mitchell," Cortland scolded.

"Maybe she was deflowering him," I suggested excitedly.

"Ermina may be many things, but I can't imagine her a murderer. Anyway, it's impossible. She was with me all night."

"What about Bill Zale?" Ingrid asked.

"He'd left the house already," I answered. "And I can't see him being gay."

"At least you're not suggesting Dr. Bhandari," Ramir said.

I didn't say anything.

"It *would* be pretty shocking if Trevor were having sex with his therapist," Ingrid said. I'm glad it wasn't me.

"But Dr. Bhandari wouldn't kill anybody," Ramir said. "He's totally nonviolent."

"You haven't seen him butcher my budget," said Cortland.

"All of these theories are very complicated," Ing said.

"And don't you need to come up with some actual incriminating evidence?" Ramir asked. "Psychic visions wouldn't exactly hold up in court."

"I didn't say it was a definitive solution. I still have to do more research—to find out who Trevor might have been with."

"Have you looked up any of his friends?" Cortland asked.

"Nobody seems to think he had any."

"Laura said his last school was Jarvis. You could check there," Ing suggested.

"Maybe I'll give that a try. And Laura told us about some loose floorboards under the window in his room. Maybe Trevor hid some papers under there. Maybe he wrote about who he was in love with in his diary."

"Do you want me to ask Dr. Bhandari to look?" Ramir offered.

"No, don't do that," I said quickly. "He'll think I'm even crazier." I realized that I shouldn't have mentioned that idea out loud. I didn't want Ramir to know I still wanted to get upstairs, in case he tried to stop me. "I guess I just like the idea of finding a hidden clue. It'd make a good scene in the movie."

"It always comes back to your screenplay," Ramir said.

"That's what started all this."

Cortland stood and placed his hands on his hips. "Well, I can see that the whole thing has terrific dramatic potential, Mitchell. I think you're doing a marvelous job. Congratulations."

"Thank you," I said. Maybe I could gloat a little now. "Ramir, did Gabriella happen to mention that she wants to *star* in my movie?"

"We tried it again three or four times, but I couldn't get back into the trance."

"Unbelievable," Aaron said.

I was lying on the couch, the phone on the floor beside me. "And Gabriella was so excited about the whole thing."

"If you can get a big name like her attached, Mitchell, the whole picture'll be easier to get off the ground."

"Technically speaking, she's about 10 years too old to play Vivienne."

"That shouldn't make much difference. But maybe you should rework the story so that Vivienne is the detective instead of Laura. Give her a bigger role. That's what she'll expect."

"Oh God, more work."

"Just an idea."

"You're still coming to the concert on Friday?"

"I've got appointments all afternoon. But meet me at the Four Seasons at 7. We can have a quick dinner first."

"Then I can give you a total up-to-the-minute report."

"But you know, Mitch, it's a long time to wait until Friday."

I could guess what he had in mind. "I don't think it's a good idea, Aaron."

"You will in a minute."

"I just don't want things to get too complicated."

"We'll keep it really simple."

"Is that possible?"

"Of course it is. Unzip your pants."

And I succumbed.

WEDNESDAY, OCTOBER 28

According to the logic of supernatural thrillers, I should invite as many people as possible from the original party to boost the spiritual energy in the house. Or at least bring all the suspects together for a classic whodunit climax.

Cortland, Ermina, and Dr. Bhandari were guaranteed to be there. Two of the 10 tickets would be for Aaron and me. Two for Ingrid and Pierre. One for Daphne, because Ing still wants to set her up with Kevin. One I put in an envelope for Laura Donnington. (In case she might be persuaded.) And two I addressed to Bill Zale and his long-suffering wife. (Not that I imagined he'd actually want to come.) Nonetheless, I called a delivery company for same-day service.

That left me with two tickets to spare.

☆

After a morning of phone tag, I spoke with the teacher in charge of the archives at Jarvis Collegiate Institute, the high school where Trevor Donnington had spent his final academic year.

"A friend of mine's birthday is coming up," I explained, "and we're planning this big surprise party, and we want to get pictures of him from when he was in high school. So I was wondering if I could take a look at the yearbook for 1978-79."

If the teacher had asked my friend's name, I was prepared to confuse her by saying Ingrid Martinez—because I didn't want her to think I was some morbid obsessive ghoul, digging up the school's nasty scandals.

But with no prying questions, she said the yearbook would be waiting for me in the library that afternoon. Around 2 o'clock was best, she said—after the lunchtime rush. And make sure to bring change for the photocopy machine.

At 5 minutes past 2, I approached the famous old high school. Broad and symmetrical, it's built of solemn rusty-brown brick with a broad stone staircase leading to its central doors.

In a corner of the church-like lobby, a group of six dark-clad boys lounged, all reading science textbooks, except for one who mournfully strummed a guitar. "Greensleeves," of all things.

I imagined Trevor sitting among them.

"Could you please point me to the main office?"

One of the depressive boys gestured down the hall to the left.

At the front desk, the receptionist phoned the librarian to alert her of my arrival—so I wouldn't linger in the boys' washroom, I suppose—then gave me further directions.

I went downstairs and followed a shabby locker-lined hallway to a nondescript door marked LIBRARY. In front of me was a short flight of stairs, featuring mottled beige-and-caramel broadloom, worn and matted. I climbed the steps and entered a vast high-ceilinged room with a narrow balcony wrapping around the second floor.

I stopped before the turnstiles and spoke to the appropriately bespectacled librarian. "I understand there's a yearbook waiting for me?"

She immediately handed me the book. No questions. No fuss.

"I was just wondering, would the library have looked like this back in 1979?"

"I suppose it did," she said, adjusting her glasses. "At one time this was the school gymnasium, but back in the '60s they turned it into the library." She pointed up to the balcony lined with study carrels. "The mezzanine used to be a jogging track."

She motioned to a table amid the jam of bookshelves and paperback racks. "Set yourself up there. You'll find the photocopier by the stairs. Ten cents per page."

I settled at a wide table, across from two Asian girls, both sorting through backpacks large enough for treks through the Himalayas. I placed a pen and notepad in front of me in order to look studious—or in case I gained any stunning insights into the mystery—and set to work.

The cover of the 1979 yearbook was metallic silver. Very disco.

I flipped through to find the student portraits. They weren't individual photographs in alphabetical order the way my high school yearbook had been organized, but full class shots of each home room. Groups of students were arranged in haphazard ranks, seated on the staircase outside in front of the school.

I found the section for Grade 12. On the title page, the year-book editor had thoughtfully included the Shakespearean quote: "Words, words, words." Whatever that means.

I started scanning through the photographs—12A, 12B, 12C—examining all the wholesome 1970s faces. Certainly, it was a more ethnically diverse bunch than we'd had at my high school in Willowdale. I noted an abundance of feathered and shagged hairdos with centre parts. A profusion of shirts with wing-like collars and even a few cowl-neck sweaters. All these young kids had since grown up to be doctors and lawyers, artists and alcoholics.

The sea of smiles quickly became overwhelming, and I realized I might not recognize Trevor anyway. So I started speed-reading the lists of names.

In 12K, I found Trevor Donnington. Seated in the back row, leaning forward, partially hidden by a tall girl in front of him. A plaid shirt and black feathered hair. I never would have identified him from the photographs or from Laura's painting.

He looked like a perfectly average kid.

That was anticlimactic. No startling insights. No profound revelations.

Maybe there'd be some other reference.

I thumbed through the rest of the sections, feeling like an interloper in all of these memories. Silly, vulnerable, cocky adolescents. A boy on his knees, proposing marriage to a department-store mannequin. A science class pretending to have a toga party. Four young toughs dressed as the gang from *A Clockwork Orange*—wearing bowler hats and white jeans with their jock-straps on the outside. Quite sexy, actually.

Near the front of the book was the inevitable section for school artsies, titled "Expression." Creative writing—poems and ultra-short stories—complemented by earnest photographs of pretty clouds and snowy mountains. Laura had said Trevor was

always writing, so I scanned the literary entries more carefully.
And I found this:

Danger: No Trespassing
by Trevor Donnington 12K

My smile is like a mirror.
It only shows
what I think you want to see.
Do not trust what seems to be reflected.

My words are like poison,
infected by the thoughts in my brain.
What I say may sicken you
and bring you down beside me.

My heart is like a jagged rock.
Don't fall on its sharp edges.
I can't be responsible
if you end up cut and broken.

Yikes.

That last stanza sent a chill through me. Almost prophetic.
Hard to believe the school would publish such a dark and disturbing confession in this otherwise lighthearted tome. (But then,
my school yearbook had printed a story I'd written about stabbing
my grandmother.)

The killings had happened in July—not that deep into summer vacation. Trevor's fellow students must have looked back at
this little literary entry as a warning sign and felt sick to their
stomachs. They must have gossiped like wildfire when they
returned in September for Grade 13—a grade that's since been
declared defunct.

The poem was well written, though. Intelligent. Mature. I slid
in a scrap of paper to bookmark it for future photocopying.

Laura had said her brother liked to play tennis.

I flipped to the portraits of the athletic teams. Football. Cross-country running. Tennis. And there was Trevor standing in the back row of the tennis club, looking tall, dark, and handsome in his white polo shirt. A bit gawky, as if he hadn't fully grown into his body. Strange to think he never would.

But this seemed much more the charismatic young man I'd been anticipating. A guy who looked so good must have had girl-friends (or boyfriends)—whether he was insane or not. In fact, his craziness should have made him *more* popular.

I really couldn't see that much resemblance between us.

Then I noticed the fellow beside him. A beautiful angelic face. Eyes that looked almost clear. The kind of prettiness that would stop traffic. I checked the caption to find his name.

Graham Linden.

It was so familiar.

Then I remembered. The gorgeous man Cortland had pointed out in the Courtyard Café. The Best Kept Boy in the World.

I went to the phone booth at the corner of Jarvis and Wellesley. The floor was littered with gum blobs and condom wrappers—clues that the pay phone was used predominantly by high school students and the nightly team of neighbourhood hookers.

I phoned Laura Donnington.

"I've been looking through old yearbooks at Jarvis Collegiate, trying to find some old friends of your brother."

"You're really taking this seriously," she said in her dry, cynical style.

"Do you remember if Trevor ever played tennis with a guy named Graham Linden?"

"Was he really good-looking?"

"Incredibly good-looking."

"Yeah, they knew each other. He came over for dinner a few times. I had a crush on him. Who wouldn't?"

"Did he know Trevor a long time?"

"If they met at Jarvis, it would have just been a year. But I remember they had some kind of fight."

"Do you know about what?"

"Probably nothing." She paused. "But Graham was at the house that night."

"He came to the party?"

"With his girlfriend. I can't remember why. Trevor wouldn't invite anybody—even though my mother told him he could. I remember Graham asked me to dance. Some old Bee Gees song."

"This might seem weird, Laura, but I've heard a rumour that Graham was gay."

"Does that mean you think Trevor was gay?"

"I'm just trying to cover all the angles."

"My brother was a lot of things, Mitchell, but he wasn't gay."

"Just checking."

"You know, Mitchell, I was planning to call you about that ticket you sent me this morning."

"I had an extra. I hope you weren't offended."

"I threw it in the garbage at first. Then I talked to my therapist, and he said maybe I should exorcise some more old demons. And Pierre said he's going to be there. So I've decided I want to come."

WEDNESDAY, OCTOBER 28
—MORE—

On my walk home along Bloor Street—wondering again about the peculiar new friendship between Laura and Pierre—I bumped into Cortland.

Slung over his shoulder was a green garment bag emblazoned with the high-end Harry Rosen signature. In his other hand, there was no mistaking the brown-and-red paper bag with the giant golden M.

"Cortland, you eat at McDonald's?"

"I have a strange weakness for the Filet-O-Fish sandwich. But if you tell a soul, I'll swear you're a liar. Now move along before anyone sees us."

"I thought you'd be doing last-minute work on the party."

"That's exactly what I have been doing. Choosing my wardrobe. All my other suits are far too baggy at this point in my declining physical condition, and I want to look my best on Friday. Thus…" He raised the garment bag. "Have you been making any more progress on your research?"

When I told him my discovery of Trevor's connection to Graham Linden, Cortland shook his head in amazement. "You are becoming quite the detective, aren't you?"

"Laura said Graham was at the party that night. Do you remember seeing him?"

"There were so many people. And I was so preoccupied with getting things organized and then busy talking with Ermina."

"Graham was only in high school back then, so it might have been before anyone knew him—before he earned his Best Kept Boy reputation. Do you think he and Trevor could have been lovers?"

"Graham Linden is a happily married heterosexual man, Mitchell. I'd love to see his face when you ask him that."

"I'll word it carefully. But maybe he'll be able to tell me about some of Trevor's other friends at school. Or who else Trevor might have been with that night."

"When you're talking with Mr. Linden, be sure to mention my name—though obviously he didn't recognize me at the Courtyard Café. And you could ask him about the lover he deserted on his deathbed. See what the ruthless bastard says to that!" Cortland pursed his lips in evil glee. "I want all the details, Mitchell— right from the first expression on his face to the name of his wife's china pattern."

THURSDAY, OCTOBER 29

As soon as I mentioned to Ramir that I intended to interrogate The Best Kept Boy in the World, he insisted on accompanying me. "Maybe we can pick up some tips."

"Do you think we should phone him first? Or should we just drop in?"

"They never phone on cop shows," Ramir said with convincing personal authority, since he's been arrested on dozens of them. "Besides, I want to see what he looks like. If you call him first, he might say no."

"What time should we go? We want to make sure he's home."

"Everyone's always home when they do it on TV."

"I wonder if he has a 9-to-5 job."

"Not if he's playing his cards right."

We decided on the 5:30 to 6 time slot. Just after work. Just before dinner. Just before Ramir had to go back to Dr. Bhandari's for more party planning.

I looked up Graham Linden's address in the ever-reliable Toronto phone book, and we set out on our mission in Ramir's Land Rover.

Now that sex was part of the scenario, Ramir was finally fully intrigued.

"So do you think Trevor and Graham were going at it when Trevor's father walked in? Two high school buddies getting drunk and fooling around—like the classic porno story."

"Except Laura doesn't think her brother was gay."

"What would a 12-year-old girl know about who's gay or not?"

"Even *I* have a hard enough time figuring it out."

"Maybe that's why Trevor has been trying to contact you. You're gay. He was gay."

"You're making fun of me again, I can tell."

"You could hold a séance and summon him from beyond the grave. Maybe he'll feel you up under the table."

"I'd prefer it if he did that automatic-writing thing. Then he could take control of my hand and write the script himself."

Ramir braked abruptly, and my foot crumpled the pile of mail on the floor. One torn-open envelope jumped out at me with its green block letters: CULTBUSTERS.

I picked it up. "What's this?"

"Junk mail."

"Discount coupons from Cultbusters?"

"Oh, that. Some guy found out I'm working on the documentary, and he wants equal time for his dissenting point of view."

"What's his point of view?"

"He doesn't say in the letter. But obviously, if he thinks the Gateways is a cult, we won't be using him. Just throw it back on the floor with all the bills."

"I thought your accountant dealt with those."

"Once I give them to him. We have a meeting next week. He's helping me get another loan from the bank."

"Why would you need a loan?"

"Because I'm in debt, why else?"

"How can you be in debt?"

"Don't act so shocked, Mitch. You're in debt yourself."

"But you get that huge salary."

"And I've got huge expenses. The car. Taxes I wasn't expecting. The new house. My mom's condo."

"She's not even living there."

"Then there's all the money for Dr. Bhandari."

"Maybe you should take a break from him for a while."

"I'm committed. I already paid for the Second Gateway."

"He could give you your money back."

"Mitch, he's helping me change my life. It's an investment." Ramir made a death-defying turn onto Spadina Road. "This afternoon Dr. Bhandari and I went to Gabriella's rehearsal."

"I hope she was good."

"Fantastic. Everyone's going to be blown away. And the crowd is going to be incredible. Her manager is flying in from L.A. I want to see if he'll represent me too. Plus, all the executives from *Station Centauri* are in town. I have a lunch meeting tomorrow with one of the producers."

"Sounds like a lot of serious networking."

"So is your Hollywood bigamist still coming?"

"Please don't call him that."

"I can't wait to see what he looks like."

"Just keep your hands off him." I felt a funny pride that Aaron was so attractive.

Ahead of us, rising among the trees on the escarpment, was Casa Loma, the massive Scottish castle that sits surrealistically in the centre of the city. It always inspires a moment of silent respect, wondering at the audacity it took to construct such a bizarre turreted monolith.

Just below Casa Loma sits Castle Hill, an equally surreal cluster of newish Georgian townhomes—all creamy stucco and stone block—like a street from a posh section of London lifted intact and transported across the ocean.

Ramir parked and we strolled up the single street. The three dozen townhouses curve perfectly around a tiny perfect park with perfect trees and benches.

"It's like a film set," I said.

"Or Disney World."

"I've heard these places start at $750,000."

"Obviously this guy's got it made," Ramir said. "Somebody told me once that the key to being kept is you have to pretend you have some big ambition you can't afford to pursue on your own."

"Would screenwriting qualify?"

"Then the rich old pervert can pretend to be doing a good deed by helping out the struggling youth. Gives the rich one a sense of dignity."

"I wonder what Graham Linden's wife gets out of it. Cortland said her family has a fortune from food importing."

"Maybe it's the same thing—if they were friends to begin with. He's gay. She's single. Getting married helps them achieve their ambition of looking normal."

"I guess there are worse reasons for a relationship."

☆

Amid the cloned townhouses, we identified Graham's street number and climbed the steps to the shiny black-painted door. Ramir rapped the reproduction brass knocker.

"He's going to think we're a pair of Jehovah's Witnesses," I said. "They always come around dinnertime too. I read someplace that they have all of North America mapped out, so they knock on every door at least once a year."

"Calm down, Mitch, you're starting to ramble."

Before I could declare that I was perfectly calm, the door opened and there stood the stunning Graham Linden.

We'd obviously interrupted him in the middle of a workout. He was dressed for exercise in a tight white tank top and loose blue nylon pants. His elegantly muscled arms glistened. His forehead was dewy, and his thick dark hair was tousled and tempestuous.

Slightly out of breath. "What can I do for you?" His smile and those clear green eyes were so dazzling, it was hard to stay focused. It was as if his face were flashing between the handsomeness of a man and the beauty of a teenage boy.

"I'm Ramir Martinez, and this is my friend Mitchell Draper." Why was Ramir taking over? Automatically flirting.

Graham looked at Ramir with those hypnotic eyes. "Haven't I seen you on TV?"

"That's possible," Ramir said, smiling his surefire coy/sexy smile.

"He's on *Station Centauri*," I said. "But his face is always covered in rubber."

"*Greetings from KerrZavia*," Ramir intoned as an audio clue.

"But I saw you in something else. *Traders*, I think it was."

"You remember that? That was ages ago."

"I guess you've got a memorable face."

Battle of the flirts.

I was waiting for Graham to say he recognized *me* from the

Courtyard Café. But apparently my memorable face had slipped his mind.

"So what brings a famous actor to my doorstep?"

It was time for me to take charge. "Actually, I was hoping—"

But Ramir cut me off. "My friend Mitch is a screenwriter, and we're working on a story—"

I interrupted. "I was hoping to ask you a few questions about somebody I think you knew back in high school. Trevor Donnington?"

Graham blinked, looked startled or confused for a moment. Then he smiled, beaming with those clear green eyes. "God, it's been a long time since I thought about Trevor. Pretty horrible situation. How'd you ever hear about *him*?"

"It's sort of a long story actually."

Graham opened the door wider. "Listen, why don't you two come in and have something to drink?"

"That'd be great."

He led us into a modern all-white kitchen. "Sorry—I was just doing some weights downstairs." His perfect high buttocks swayed gracefully, even in the baggy exercise pants. "Would you like some mineral water? Or wine?"

"Just water for me, thanks," Ramir said, still obeying the puritanism of the Seven Gateways.

"Me as well," I said, craving a glass of red.

Graham removed three miniature bottles of Evian from the fridge and distributed them. He leaned against the kitchen counter. "So let me get this straight. You're making a movie about Trevor Donnington?"

"I'm just in the research phase, before I start writing the script," I explained. "I'm gathering background information."

"Trevor was a strange guy, that's for sure. Not that I ever knew him that well. How was it you heard about him?"

"Do you remember Cortland McPhee?"

"Cortland McPhee," he said. I watched Graham's face carefully so I could describe his expression precisely to Cortland.

He looked blank.

"He's an interior designer," I offered.

"God, I met so many people back then. Honestly, I don't know how much help I'm going to be. All those drugs I took in my younger days." Graham smiled endearingly, making it seem like brain damage was the sexiest thing in the world.

"Mitch is doing his own investigation," Ramir said. "He's trying to figure out if somebody else could have killed Trevor and his father."

"I didn't think there was ever any question," Graham said.

"A lot of people seem to have other theories."

"Sounds interesting. How much do you know already?"

"Cortland just gave me the basic story about the murder-suicide. But I've already spoken to Trevor's sister, Laura. She's the one who told me you went to school with Trevor." That made for a simpler explanation. "And I've talked to some other friends of the family."

"I remember Laura. She was a weird kid too. Barely said a word."

Then Graham dropped his Evian. The tiny plastic bottle bounced on the white tile floor, splashing out its contents. "Don't worry, it's only water." Graham tossed a dish towel on top of the spill. "Listen, why don't you come into the living room and sit down."

He led us farther into the house.

The interior was an open environment of teak and white-upholstered furniture with a few 1970s globe lights for a tasteful note of irony.

"It's a beautiful place," Ramir said.

"My wife Carolyn and I bought it last year. I work in real estate in my spare time, so I always keep my eyes open."

I noticed a series of framed magazine ads on the wall. A youthful black-and-white Graham, shirtless in designer jeans.

"Richard Avedon did those," Graham said. "I keep telling Carolyn we should put them away, but she likes to remind me how badly I'm aging." Nothing could have been further from the truth.

"So you were a model?" Ramir asked.

"I wanted to get into fashion design, but that's as close as I got."

"That's pretty good."

"Some people said I should have gone into acting myself. But things have turned out OK."

"I can see," Ramir said, glancing around the room.

Graham sat on the white couch, leaning forward, his legs spread wide open. "I don't know if I can tell you much more than anyone else. Trevor and I were only friends for three or four months. But I guess I remember him pretty well."

I opened my notepad. "You met him at Jarvis?"

"We had a few classes together and we played some tennis. He used to get me in at his family's club in Rosedale. My mother could never afford a place like that. I grew up in an old apartment at Dufferin and St. Clair. I took the streetcar and the subway to school every day."

"What was Trevor like? Did he seem normal?"

"People thought he was weird. He was a loner most of the time. Didn't say much. He acted tough and streetwise, but everybody knew his family had money. And that made him seem even weirder. Sometimes he'd mouth off in class, make fun of other kids."

"Did you know he was schizophrenic?"

"I knew he had problems. He was moody. He had a bottle of pills he never took."

"Did you know he was in therapy?"

"He mentioned some appointments he didn't want to go to. He was embarrassed about seeing a psychiatrist. He hated it. I know he was seeing the same doctor as his mother."

"Dr. Bhandari?" Ramir asked.

"I think that was his name. Trevor always said he gave him the creeps."

Ramir laughed uncomfortably. "Why would he say that?"

"He thought he was a quack."

"I know him actually," Ramir said. "He's a really good doctor."

"I wouldn't take Trevor's opinion too seriously. He didn't like many people—including me in the end."

"You had a fight?"

"Around Christmas, I guess it was. We didn't talk for the rest of the year. I'd seen him blow up at other people before, but he never did at me. It sounds stupid, looking back. But the whole thing started with an emerald necklace. His mother had a big jewellery collection. Trevor took me into her room once and showed me. Hundreds of rings and brooches and necklaces in velvet drawers. Trevor was always stealing something and taking it down to a pawn shop on Church Street."

"So he was a kleptomaniac too?" I asked. How much more screwed-up could the boy have been?

"He only stole from his mother, as far as I know. And every time she found out, Trevor would get grounded. And his father would go buy the piece back, whatever it was. Then one day I was over there, and he pulled an emerald necklace out of the pocket of his jacket. I could tell it was expensive. He said we should go downtown, get some money, and go to Sam the Record Man to buy some albums. I told him he should put the necklace back. And he went crazy. He said I was a traitor—that I was spying on him and talking to his parents behind his back. Then he accused me of wanting the necklace for *myself,* and he said he was going to tell everybody at school that I was a fag." My ears perked up at the reference. "I thought he was going to beat me up. So I threatened him back. I said I'd tell everybody that he was seeing a psychiatrist. That stopped him, believe it or not. He told me to get out of the house. And he just ignored me every day at school after that."

"So how did you end up coming to the party?"

"It was through my wife's father. Not that Carolyn and I were married back then. But we've been best friends since high school. The way I think it worked was that Carolyn's father was invited by Trevor's father."

"Jackson Donnington."

"They had some kind of business connection. Carolyn's father insisted we go with him. I thought I might be a good chance to talk to Trevor. Maybe patch things up. But he never came down from his room. When I realized I wasn't going to see him, we left."

"So you weren't there when his mother found him?"

"I heard about it the next morning on the news. And then the police came and questioned me. Fortunately, Carolyn and I were together the whole night."

"I've been wondering what exactly Trevor was doing all that evening. I was thinking he might have been upstairs with a girl-friend."

"Or a boyfriend," Ramir added provocatively. "Do you think maybe Trevor might have been 'protesting too much' that time when he called you a fag?"

Graham laughed and shook his head no. "Trevor was totally straight, as far as I could tell. Homophobic even. He beat up another kid who called him gay once."

Ramir pressed again. "So you and Trevor never…?"

Graham arched a single eyebrow. "What else have people been saying about me?"

Ramir charmed him with a smile. "Nothing they don't say about me."

Graham chuckled. "Yeah, I got up to some pretty crazy things back in my youth. My parents were divorced. I lived with my mother. She never knew half of what I was doing. I dated girls…boys. I used to hang out at Bemelman's on Bloor. Quite a glamorous crowd. But I was still only in high school. I was scared. I didn't want anyone to know what I was getting up to at night. But I still had my share of fun."

"I bet you did," Ramir said.

"Then a few years later, I moved to New York to get into fash-ion." He motioned to the magazine ads.

"It must have been a wild time back then."

"It was for a while. Then AIDS started to happen. I'm lucky I got out of there alive. Fortunately, these days I've settled down. All the wildness is behind me."

"So Trevor never knew any of that stuff about you when you were in school?"

"Definitely not."

"Did *he* have any girlfriends?"

"He said he dated a girl he met at one of the private schools he went to before. I don't know whether he was making it up or not."

The front door opened, and in came the woman I'd seen Graham with at the Courtyard Café. Blonde hair smoothed back. Generous figure with a round face and a friendly smile. She set down her briefcase and pulled off her suede coat as she claimed, "I've just had the shittiest day at the office."

Graham greeted her with a peck on the cheek. The way I might kiss Ingrid.

"You should meet my wife, Carolyn. This is Ramir and...I forget your name."

"Mitchell."

"Are you guys buying a house?" she asked.

"You won't believe it, but they've been asking me about Trevor Donnington."

"Trevor Donnington?" Carolyn grimaced.

"They're making a movie about him. They wanted me to tell them what I remember. Which isn't much." Graham went into the kitchen and poured a glass of red wine.

"You knew him too?" I asked Carolyn.

"We all went to high school together," she said. "You must be making a horror movie, considering what happened. I had nightmares for months, and I didn't even see anything."

"Did you know him very well?"

"No, thank God. I wasn't in any of his classes, but I saw him around school. Nobody liked him."

"Graham said he beat up some kids..."

Carolyn nodded. "He was always teasing my friend Angie, telling everyone she was pregnant. Then she actually *got* pregnant. Which only made it worse. And then my father forced us to go to that terrible party. Honestly, I was hoping I'd never hear Trevor's name again."

Graham handed Carolyn the glass of wine. "They were just asking me if Trevor had any girlfriends."

"I remember people said he was sleeping with that tough girl who lived in the grey house on Chestnut Park," Carolyn said.

"I don't remember that," Graham said.

"What was her name?" I asked. "Do you know if I could get in touch with her?"

"Her family moved to Australia right after school finished that year—before Trevor died."

Graham sat down again, but Carolyn stood leaning against the wall. She took off one of her high-heel pumps—unmistakably Prada—and massaged the sole of her foot.

"I was just going to tell them about that thing you overheard at the party," Graham said.

"What thing?" I asked immediately.

Carolyn shrugged her shoulders. "I told the police, but I guess it didn't really matter in the end. It's just that I saw Mr. Donnington having an argument."

"I know he had a fight with his business partner, Bill Zale."

"Not him. This was another man. East Indian, I think."

"Dr. Bhandari?" Ramir asked.

"We were just talking about him," Graham said.

"What were they fighting about?" I asked.

"It wasn't an actual fistfight. Just an argument. I was in the front hall with my parents. Graham was off getting drinks. I'd just been talking to Mrs. Donnington, asking about Trevor. Mostly, I was being polite because I didn't really want to see him. But she said he wasn't feeling well. He was up in his room writing in his diary."

"Mitch does that all the time too."

"I remember at school Trevor always sat upstairs on the balcony in the library—writing all by himself. Anyway, Mrs. Donnington went off someplace, and I heard some people raise their voices behind me on the staircase, so I listened in. I only overheard a few sentences. I don't remember the exact words. But the point of it was that Mr. Donnington didn't like the way the doctor was handling Trevor's therapy. He didn't want him to come back to the house anymore."

"He was firing him?" I asked. "Right there at the party?"

"That's what it sounded like."

"What did Dr. Bhandari say?" Ramir asked.

"I didn't hear any more than that."

I was amazed. "And you told the police this?"

She nodded. "But I guess it didn't make much difference, once they realized it was Trevor who did it." Carolyn took a sip of wine and set it down on a glass table. "You know, I'm sorry to rush you two, but we have a dinner party this evening. And, Graham, I think you need to take a shower."

I reached into my pants pocket. "I know this is last-minute, and you might not want to come anyway. But there's going to be a concert tomorrow night at the Donningtons' old house. Gabriella Hartman's singing. I have two extra tickets. You're welcome to come if you want."

Carolyn took the tickets and stared at them doubtfully. "Let's just say we'll think about it."

Graham led us to the front door. "If there's anything else you want to know, feel free to give us a call."

"That was fun," Ramir said as we walked back to his car. "They never let me play detectives on TV."

"You acted as if you were starring in your own show."

"I liked both of them. They seemed really down-to-earth."

"For a while there, I wondered if you were going to give up your vow of chastity."

"You can see why he would have been The Best Kept Boy in his day. Those pictures on the wall? Very sexy."

"He's not the brightest guy I've ever met."

"Those eyes make up for it." Ramir unlocked the Land Rover. "It was interesting to hear how nasty Trevor could be. And you thought he was your little teen angel."

"I never thought that about him. But didn't you think it was interesting what they said about Dr. Bhandari?"

"You're not going to try to turn that into a big deal, are you?"

241

"There must have been *something* going on if Jackson was trying to fire him."

"But it can't have been that bad if Vivienne sold him the house afterward. I bet Carolyn just misunderstood what they were saying."

"It could be an important clue."

"I think it's a red herring. What *is* a red herring anyway?"

THURSDAY, OCTOBER 29
—MORE—

I asked Ramir to drop me off at Ingrid's instead of my own place.

I told him I had to pick up Cortland's file of old photographs, but really I wanted to tell Ing what the Lindens had said about Dr. Bhandari and commiserate about Ramir's blindness.

I'd already been buzzed in the front door and was standing in the kitchen quadrant before I realized what I shouldn't have forgotten.

Pierre wiped a paint-smudged hand across his already-spattered white T-shirt. Harsh instrumental jazz was blasting in the background. "Ingrid's at her sister's tonight."

"She told me that," I said. "I forgot. Sorry to bother you. I was just passing by. I thought I'd drop in."

"No problem."

A moment of awkward tension. Pierre and I had never before been alone together.

"I've been working on a painting," he said. "I got inspired all of a sudden. You want to take a look?"

I followed him through the messy apartment.

"Ingrid and I used to compete with each other all the time when we were in art school—see who was going to finish a painting first."

Leaning against the wall was a large horizontal landscape with a green-black cluster of trees in the foreground and a grey valley spreading out in the distance. Both traditional and modern at the same time.

"I like it," I said.

"I've always been more interested in landscape and architecture. Ingrid was always more focused on people."

On the opposite wall I noticed Ingrid's new canvas. She'd taken the photograph of Vivienne and Jackson smiling in the doorway and transformed it into giant scale. The detailing of the doorframe was done in precise bold strokes, but their faces were grey and vague—like ghosts.

"I'm not sure about Ingrid's new stuff," Pierre said. "I don't know if it's the kind of thing she should be taking to Berlin."

Who was *he* to decide? "I guess it's complicated. She has so many people to listen to now."

"She should listen to herself first," Pierre said with unexpected force. "But she won't even listen to me about that."

I tried to change the subject. "Did Ingrid tell you I saw you and Laura having lunch the other day?"

He frowned. "She didn't mention it. You should have come in and joined us."

"I was in sort of a rush."

"There's a job opening at my new company, so I'm trying to get Laura in. Do you want something to drink?"

"No, thanks. I should get home. I should do some work myself."

He nodded. "And I'd better use the studio while I can. So I guess I'll see you tomorrow night at the concert?"

"You will. Definitely."

Why does it seem so odd to me that Ingrid didn't tell Pierre I'd seen him with Laura?

FRIDAY, OCTOBER 30

I was still asleep when there was a sharp knock at my door. Cortland's distinctive three raps. I leapt from my pullout couch and realized immediately that the tequila I'd been sipping last night had caused a hangover. I jerked on my bathrobe.

There was Cortland. Sitting in a wheelchair.

"Why are you in a wheelchair?"

"Don't tell me you're still collapsed in bed at 9 in the morning."

"I was up late working. Why are you in a wheelchair?"

He patted the chair's arms affectionately. "I've been storing it in the back of the closet for just such an occasion. A bit unsteady on my feet this morning, so out it comes." He was smiling broadly, his silver hair slicked back, his blue eyes sparkling. He was dressed to be noticed in a trimly cut black suit with a bright-blue shirt and a yellow necktie.

"But you look good."

"I thought I'd splash out a bit." He wheeled his way into my apartment. "Honestly, I've had a delightful morning. Puttering around, tidying up, getting things in order. But tell me, did you manage to visit Mr. and Mrs. Linden?"

"They seemed like the perfect couple."

"A gay man and a straight woman always make the perfect couple. Did you mention my name?"

"I did."

Cortland chuckled. "And he didn't remember me?"

"He said he'd done a lot of drugs. He doesn't seem like the brightest guy I've ever met."

"I'm sure he can be—when his interests are at stake."

"He said he works in real estate in his spare time."

"Well, that says it all, doesn't it? Now I'm sorry to rush, but I must get over to the house to supervise. I have a cab waiting. Are you still eager to sneak upstairs and look under the floor-boards?"

"I'm not so sure anymore," I said. "Do you want me to help you get down to the lobby? I should put on some clothes first."

"Not to worry. You just apply some eye gel and concentrate on your script. If I uncover any clues, I'll let you know."

And he wheeled off with a flourish.

Last night I'd stayed up until well past midnight—catching up on my diary and then working more on the outline.

I'm still not sure what should happen at the end of the second act—the dramatic turnaround that pivots the story into the big reunion party that's the third-act set piece.

But I did come up with another idea for research.

It felt as if I were betraying Ramir.

Cultbusters was located in a side wing of an ancient, multi-denominational church on Bathurst Street. A creaky hardwood hallway on the second floor was lined with scuff-marked doors. Tiny signs named obscure public services and charities.

I sat in a small, windowless office with blank, dingy walls that once were white. The only furniture consisted of a plain pine table devoid of paper but equipped with a Macintosh computer and a multiline telephone.

Across the table from me sat a very large man in a brown plaid work shirt. His face was ageless, buried in an out-of-control black beard. He looked at me steadily. Amid all the bursts of hair, his eyes were dark and piercing.

"We have sources who keep us up to date on every organization." His voice was deep and intelligent.

"Spies?"

"Former members who maintain their connections."

"So someone told you about the documentary? That's how you knew to send Ramir the letter?"

He typed something into the computer and read the screen.

"Something to that effect."

"So you were already familiar with the Seven Gateways?"

"Very familiar. We've been monitoring them for nearly 10 years."

He tapped a few more keys, and the printer on the floor began spitting out pages.

"Is it dangerous?"

"Different cults are dangerous in different ways. The Seven Gateways asks for a major financial commitment."

"I'm aware of that much."

"It's standard operating procedure among these organizations. There's also the typical idealization of the leader to godlike status."

"Everybody seems to worship Dr. Bhandari."

"But what's uniquely dangerous about the Seven Gateways is the sexual component."

"Sex?"

"We had a young man come to see us last week. He left the doctor's house in the middle of a session. He told us everything that happened."

"I thought they made everyone sign a confidentiality agreement."

"That's simply to prevent former members from filing lawsuits."

"So what exactly is the sexual component?"

"We're not antisex in our mandate," the man said. "But we believe that sex should be between consenting adults for the purpose of pleasure. Dr. Bhandari states that sex is for spiritual development."

"You mean, Dr. Bhandari has sex with his clients?"

"Both men and women. He claims it's part of the therapy. For opening one of the Gateways he's invented."

"But Ramir said they told him to be celibate."

"That's one of the rules of the preparation period—getting ready for the sexual ritual." The man handed me the stack of pages from the printer. "You'll find a full description of the practice right here."

☆

I called Ramir. He was en route to his lunch meeting with the *Station Centauri* producers. He promised to meet me at his house at 2, before he headed to Thornfield Manor.

Then I called Ingrid.

FRIDAY, OCTOBER 30
—MORE—

I was back in Ingrid's studio. Against the wall was a rough outline of yet another new painting: an altered version of the Donnington family portrait in Laura's living room—the background soft grey and the figures black in sharp silhouette. It was dark and edgy and brilliant, and Ingrid bristled with excitement as she showed it to me.

Then we were curled up on her massive green couch, and she listened intently as I explained my discoveries—which made the Donningtons' story seem all the more macabre.

"Maybe Dr. Bhandari was already developing his psycho-sexual theories back when he was working with Trevor and Vivienne."

"It's like all those fundamentalist preachers who have sex with their disciples," Ing said.

"What if he was molesting Trevor under the guise of therapy? What if Jackson walked in on them that night and found them and that's why he was firing Dr. Bhandari? Then Bhandari killed them both to protect his career."

"So is Dr. Bhandari gay?"

"Ramir said his wife is studying in India, but I've never heard anybody else mention her. Maybe he just uses the wife story as a cover-up."

"Wow, Mitchell, this is the best theory you've had so far."

I flipped through the pile of pages from Cultbusters. "There are 15 different Web sites about the Seven Gateways. They all say it's a financial rip-off and dangerous sexual manipulation."

"Can I see that one?"

"This sheet says gay people are particularly vulnerable to joining cults. And after Ramir's father died…"

"He was falling for anything."

"Somewhere in here there's a list of all the teachings and meditations in each Gateway. All the secrets are spelled out in full. But I think you should look at this one." I held up another printout. "It says that Nigel Bhandari isn't even a real doctor. He has some kind of bogus degree from a spiritual therapy college in Arizona."

"I wonder if Vivienne knew that."

"I don't think Ramir knows."

"And you want to tell him?"

"We have to warn him about the sex ritual," I said.

"What if he knows already?"

"And you think he'd still go through with it?"

"Ramir's slept with men a lot worse-looking than Dr. Bhandari."

The idea crystallized. "What if he's been having sex with Dr. Bhandari all along?"

"No wonder he defends him so much."

More crystallization. "OK, I have another theory. What if Trevor *liked* having sex with Dr. Bhandari? What if they had a whole long-term relationship going on?"

"Why would Dr. Bhandari kill Trevor if he loved him?"

"To save his own reputation."

"I don't know if I buy that version."

"Neither do I."

"Mitchell, do you think Kevin has done that weird sex thing with Dr. Bhandari?"

"He must have if it's one of the Gateways."

Her shoulders shuddered. "That's creepy to think about."

"Why are you so interested in Kevin's sex life all of a sudden?"

"I was just wondering." She shifted on the couch, and now her shoulders took a skeptical stance. "You're not saying you think Dr. Bhandari would try to hurt Ramir, are you?"

"I don't know. He might."

"Don't you think maybe you're getting the truth confused with a good story for your screenplay?"

"I'm not doing that," I said. Then again, maybe I was. "But I still have to warn Ramir, don't I? What if he's in danger? I have to tell him. I'm meeting him at 2."

"And I guess you want me to come with you."

"Would you?"

"I guess it's inevitable," Ing sighed. "You know, Mitchell, you can come up with theories forever, but if you want to solve this thing, you need to find some tangible physical evidence."

"I know that. Of course I know that."

We heard a sound in the outer hallway. Then Pierre came in the door.

"This is a surprise," Ing said.

Pierre entered with a strange tentativeness. No rush to the arms-on-shoulders kissing routine. He nodded hello at me, then spoke to Ingrid. "I thought you were going to be with Ramir, putting up those banners."

"Cortland said he didn't need me after all. What are you doing home from work?"

"I forgot those sketches I was doing in bed last night. I have a big meeting this afternoon. I'll just go grab them." He headed to the sleeping quadrant.

"We were just leaving anyway," I said.

☆

The cab dropped us off in front of Ramir's house on Seaton Street. When there was no answer at the door, we sat on the two wooden cottage chairs permanently planted on the front porch.

"It's not that it's cold out," Ingrid said. "It's just so damp."

"I'm sure he'll be home any minute."

We sat there amid the blowing leaves, hugging our arms to our chests in an effort to stave off the cold.

"Pierre and I had another fight last night, if you couldn't tell."

"I thought there was something."

"Did you think it was odd—him coming home in the middle of the day?"

"Not if he really forgot something."

"It sounded like a bad excuse, didn't it?"

"It did."

Her lips tightened. "You know, I still remember when you saw Pierre with Laura."

"You think it might mean something?"

"He was acting different even before they met. But the thing is, Mitchell, I've been through this before. And I missed all the signs when he was fooling around the first time."

"Can you ask him?"

"No."

"Or hint?"

"If I'm wrong, it might ruin everything all over again." Her eyes were filled with tears. For avoidance, she reached for the folder of Cortland's photographs that was resting on my lap. I'd borrowed them back from her so I could show Aaron tonight. She started flipping through the party pictures yet again.

I picked at a chip of white paint on the arm of the deck chair. I didn't know what else to say to her.

I couldn't help but picture Laura and Pierre at the restaurant. Laura had looked so happy. And if Ingrid was actually interested in Kevin...

"Mitchell, look at this." She was pointing to the top right corner of a photograph—a crowd shot of the ballroom, everyone dancing and mingling. All the figures were barely half an inch high. "I never noticed before, but see right there—that's Laura standing in the doorway that goes into the pantry. You see, she's wearing that little grass skirt."

"You're right. That *is* her."

"And look at the face peeking through the door—just the profile."

"Trevor."

We were both silent a moment, comprehending the implications.

"She never said anything about Trevor coming downstairs," Ing said.

"Nobody has."

"It looks like he's sneaking into the party."

"Yesterday Carolyn Linden said Vivienne told her Trevor was upstairs in his room, writing in his diary."

"But Laura said Trevor wouldn't let his mother in his room. Remember, she left a plate of food outside his door. So how would she really know what he was doing?"

"Maybe he wasn't even in the room. Or maybe he was dead already."

"Mitchell, do you think Laura might have had something to do with the murders?"

"She couldn't have killed two men. She was only 12 years old."

"Remember she's the one who told you Trevor might not be guilty in the first place."

"You mean, she meant that as kind of a confession?"

"One thing's for sure, Mitchell. Laura knows more than she's saying."

Ramir's Land Rover screeched into an empty parking space on the street in front of the house. Ingrid and I both stood to greet him, eager to share our theories.

When he got out and walked toward us, his shoulders were hunched as though he was shivering. The warm brown of his skin looked grey.

"Sorry," he said, his voice flat. "I forgot you were going to be here."

"What's the matter? You look terrible," I said.

"I met with the *Station Centauri* people. It was bad." His voice cracked. He leaned against a column on the front porch.

"What happened?" I took hold of his arm.

"They're killing off my character. They're taking the story in a new direction. They fired me."

"Oh, Ramir, I'm so sorry." Ingrid hugged him.

"I don't know what I'm going to do. I need that job. It's the only good thing in my whole career."

"That's not true," Ing said.

"You'll get other work," I said.

"I've been doing the meditations from the Gateways, but my heart keeps racing. I talked to Dr. Bhandari on the cell phone just now. He's going to give me a special meditation tonight to help me get back in balance."

"Are you sure Dr. Bhandari is the answer?"

Ingrid elbowed me to shut up. And she was right. This wasn't a good time for deprogramming.

"I need to be alone. Pull myself together. But I'll see you both tonight, OK?" Ramir went into his house and closed the door, leaving me and Ingrid outside in the cold.

"You know he always likes to hide when he's upset," Ing said. She put her arm around me. "He'll be OK, Mitchell. We all will."

☆

Ingrid and I walked for a while, then I took a cab home, and she took a cab down to Queen Street to shop for a dress for tonight. We agreed to meet later at Dr. Bhandari's.

I typed for a few hours, recounting my day.

And I worked out my most likely scenario for the murder scene:

INTERIOR. SECOND-FLOOR HALLWAY—NIGHT

JACKSON is listening outside the door to his office. He hears the grunts and deep breathing of people making love.

He opens the door a crack. The light from the hallway illuminates the scene within.

TWO MEN are in a passionate embrace on his desk. In the fragment of light, he recognizes TREVOR and the boy's therapist, DR. BHANDARI.

DR. BHANDARI stands and turns to the door.

JACKSON
What the fuck are you doing?

The TWO MEN are too startled to respond.

JACKSON
Trevor, get up to your room this second.

JACKSON slams the door.

When Trevor left his father's office, he must have closed the door behind him. That's how his fingerprints came to be the last ones on the doorknob.

Then the double murder ensued—Dr. Bhandari killing Jackson in a rage of passion and pushing Trevor out the window to silence him as a witness.

Does that make sense?

Of course, if Dr. Bhandari killed Trevor and Jackson to protect his reputation, and he finds out that I'm about to expose him, he might try to kill me too this very night.

But that's probably as ridiculous as my whole theory.

I took two Tylenol to soothe my burgeoning headache and lay on the couch.

I thought about Ing and Ramir.

I don't like this phase of life. Watching our lives become more complicated—feeling distanced from my closest friends.

For a moment I drifted off into sleep.

I saw a figure descending. The tall, dark, and handsome man.

I snapped awake.

Was it another vision, or was it my imagination? Had it been my imagination all along?

I remembered what Ingrid had said: *"You can come up with theories forever, but if you want to solve this thing, you need to find some tangible physical evidence."*

I remembered what Jane Choy had said about tonight. I had to get upstairs at Thornfield Manor and visit the scene of the crime.

SATURDAY, OCTOBER 31

It was only last night that everything happened, but it feels like it must have been months ago. I need to write it all down to make sense of it.

Yesterday afternoon, after my nightmarish little nap, I came up with the notion of reading through my diary entries, sifting for any clues I might have overlooked. I started back at Friday, October 9th—the date of my first visit to Thornfield Manor.

I became so preoccupied that I didn't notice the time. Suddenly it was 6:45. I was supposed to meet Aaron at 7, after his afternoon of meetings. I dressed quickly in a black jacket and black pants—my own low-end version of a tuxedo—pulled on my trench coat and slipped our two tickets into my jacket pocket.

Then I rushed over to the Four Seasons.

When Aaron opened his hotel room door, he looked stern and businesslike, as he had that first day in my agent's office. "Sorry, I can't make it for dinner."

This took me by surprise. "But there's a ton of stuff I want to talk to you about."

"We start shooting *Niagara* next week, and another crisis came up. Did you bring the outline?"

"I haven't finished it yet."

"You said you'd have it done."

I was startled by his tone. More déjà vu. "That's why I wanted to talk to you. About some questions I still have. And tonight I'm going to sneak upstairs at the house to see the room where it all happened."

Aaron's manner finally softened. "Sorry, Mitchell, it's just that I sat beside Gabriella's manager on the plane this morning."

"You did? My friend Ramir wants to meet him."

"Gabriella already told J.D. about your project. She's really excited. I promised I'd give him your treatment tonight."

"I can finish it by tomorrow—I think."

Though Gabriella might not be so eager to work on the project once I'd proven my theories about Dr. Bhandari.

"If J.D. likes it, Mitchell, he could put together a whole package—bring in the right director, other actors. It'd be really good for you." Aaron grabbed his jacket from the back of a chair. "Anyway, I should get moving. I have to get out to the production office."

"Can you still come to the concert?"

"I told J.D. I'd see him there." Aaron gave me a kiss on the cheek. Our first physical contact. "Do me a favour tonight, Mitchell. Don't let anyone know we've been seeing each other."

I was taken aback again. "Don't people know you're gay?"

"Of course they do. That's not the issue. It's just that some of the people from L.A. might know Ryan."

"Ryan."

"And I like to keep my private life private."

He moved to kiss me on the mouth, but I stepped back. I pulled the tickets from my inside jacket pocket and handed him one. "The address is on the back."

"You understand, right?"

"Is it all right if I introduce you to my friends?"

"Please don't be angry, Mitchell. I'm under a lot of pressure right now." His cell phone rang. "I have to take this call. But I'll see you later, OK?"

I was dismissed.

I stood in the plush powder-blue hallway, waiting for the elevator, feeling like a gullible fool. Clearly, Aaron was an expert at dividing business and pleasure. I was an idiot to still be entertaining romantic notions.

From here on in, it would be strictly business.

Now, with no dinner plans, I wasn't sure what to do. Riding down in the elevator, I read the back of my ticket:

Drinks & Hors d'oeuvres, 8:00 p.m.
Welcome & Meditation, 9:00 p.m.
Concert by Gabriella Hartman, 9:30 p.m.

The Centre for Spiritual Success
Nine Thornfield Road, Rosedale

I didn't want to go back to my apartment and stew by myself. I had no decorating skills that would be of assistance to Cortland. Though if I did get to the house early, it might give me a better chance to sneak upstairs…

So I set off walking, hoping to fill enough time to make a somewhat appropriate arrival.

The night had a chill, and I hadn't dressed to walk such a distance. So I buttoned up my trench coat and shoved my hands in my pockets—feeling like Humphrey Bogart off to solve a case.

I started to formulate more of the details I'd gleaned from my diaries. Determined to impress Aaron.

I was still focused on the notion that Trevor was up in his room writing during the party. Laura had said Trevor burned his diaries a month before he died. But what happened to the journals he wrote in the final month of his life? And what about that final night?

If Trevor really was writing in his diary, as Vivienne had told Carolyn Linden, he might have been recounting what had happened with Dr. Bhandari—the sexual relationship that had motivated Jackson to fire him. Trevor might have explained why he went downstairs with his sister. And anywhere else he may have gone.

Maybe when Trevor was finished writing, he hid the diary under the floorboards, the way he always had before. Maybe the police hadn't searched there. It's possible—despite the skepticism of Cortland and Ingrid and Ramir.

If I can find Trevor's diary, it might provide the tangible evidence I need to bring Dr. Bhandari to justice.

After 10 minutes of walking, I was at Yonge Street, on the verge of entering Rosedale. I was hungry. And even $500 hors d'oeuvres can't be guaranteed to be filling. So I stopped at the Pizza Pizza joint just north of Bloor—squinting in the harsh lights and bright orange interior. I sat at a table by the window, staring out into the traffic and chomping on a pepperoni slice—totally unbefitting my elegant attire.

I ate quickly and nervously. As if it were my last meal before heading into battle. Then I continued up Yonge for several blocks and turned onto Crescent Road. Within five houses, the noise of the city was gone, and I was in the eerie palatial calm of Rosedale.

The sun had set, and the sky was a rich black.

There were hip-high piles of raked-up leaves beside the curbs, and clear plastic bags of leaves in mounds beside driveways. Leaves on the sidewalk crunched beneath my feet, while others made a dry rattle as the wind skipped them along the pavement.

The sweet warm scent of burning wood floated in the crisp night air.

On several front porches there were jack-o'-lanterns blazing orange. A group of children in Halloween costumes ran from a parked car into a house.

Despite the coolness, my back was hot and damp under the jacket. I felt a strange pressure in my temples. Caused by too much thinking?

What if the killings didn't have anything to do with sex? What if Trevor had been stealing something from his father's office—from his desk—when Jackson caught him? Then Trevor ran upstairs to his bedroom with whatever it was. His father followed him. And that's when the murder happened.

What could he have stolen that would have been so important? Anything from a pair of emerald cuff links to a false set of books for the printing company. Maybe it was the cash Bill Zale thought Jackson had been stealing. Maybe Trevor had hidden whatever it was under the loose floorboards in his room.

That hiding place has been nagging at me ever since Laura first mentioned it—promising a secret time capsule from that long-ago night.

And the moment when my detective discovers it—whether I make the detective Vivienne or Laura or anyone else—will provide my movie's perfect dramatic climax.

Now I just needed to get up to the third floor and discover it for myself.

☆

I crossed the Mount Pleasant overpass, the stream of cars below creating a whirr of lights. And suddenly, around the corner, rose the Victorian Gothic grandeur of Thornfield Manor.

The upper-floor windows were in darkness, but the main floor was alight. The curtains were drawn back, and inside was a surreal golden glow created by clusters of white candles in each window. The gas lamps flickered along the front walk.

I imagined how the house must have looked on the night of Jackson and Vivienne's party. Perhaps exactly like this.

The circular driveway was empty. On the street I noticed more than the usual number of cars—including a truck from the catering company, Vegan Vanguard. But there was no sign yet of the battalion of taxis that would soon deliver all 300 guests.

I checked my watch. It was still only 7:30.

I climbed the stone stairs to the front porch. Thick white candles in clear glass cylinders had been placed on either side of each step to frame the pathway.

Perhaps because of the occasion, I didn't feel obliged to knock. I pushed open the heavy wooden door. I'd expected to see a crowd of bustling workers, but instead the front hall was empty. Which made it all the more breathtaking.

The room was filled with white candles set on tall pedestals and in wrought-iron candelabras. More candles were piled on the marble fireplace in the corner, making it resemble the altar of a Catholic church. The white walls were draped with garlands of white flowers—orchids, lilies, and roses. Ingrid's ethereal banners were hanging on both sides of each doorway. Shimmering shades of white blended with the faintest swirls of gold.

The grand staircase was the focal point. The railings were wrapped in the same gauzy white fabric. Heavenly, romantic, and spooky all at the same time.

A small antique desk had been placed beside the front door, apparently for the purpose of ticket-taking. The desk was topped with stacks of programs, featuring Ingrid's lovely line drawing of Gabriella.

I could hear a constant murmur of voices at the back of the house. Everyone busy in the ballroom and the kitchen.

The emptiness around me was disconcerting.

Clearly, this was my chance to sneak upstairs. The opportunity coming so quickly made it almost anticlimactic.

I began to climb the stairs.

When I reached the first landing, I heard voices and footsteps below. I spun around to casually walk down again—prepared to offer a rational explanation—but they were just waiters carrying hors d'oeuvres trays into the dining room. They didn't pay the slightest attention to me.

I began my ascent once again, watching my feet so I wouldn't trip and noisily break both legs.

"Mitchell, you're early."

I looked up. Dr. Bhandari and Kevin stood at the head of the stairs. Dr. Bhandari was dressed in a traditional Indian-style shirt, knee-length, white with intricate red embroidery. Kevin favoured a form-fitting white sweater.

"I'm just looking for the washroom," I said.

"You seem to have a very bad memory for washrooms."

Change the subject. "Is Ramir here yet?"

"He was supposed to come an hour ago," Kevin said, "but he hasn't shown up."

"He was having a very bad day," I said.

"I'm sure Ramir will be fine," Dr. Bhandari said. Though I had no idea why he was so sure. "Kevin, would you take care of Mitchell for me?"

Take care of me?

"Certainly."

"Would you like me to check your coat?" Dr. Bhandari took my coat hostage and headed in the direction of his conservatory office.

"Come, I'll show you the washroom," Kevin said.

"What? Oh, right. It sure is quiet around here."

"Dr. Bhandari just did a meditation to calm the energy in the house."

"That must be it. Ramir was telling me that Dr. Bhandari lives upstairs."

Kevin nodded. "On the third floor."

"Does it have slanted ceilings and little garrets and cute nooks and everything?"

Kevin smiled apologetically. "I wouldn't know. The third floor is off limits. All locked up. I've never been up there."

"Not once?" Not even when he'd gone through the secret sex ritual?

"Not once. Here's the washroom," Kevin said in his soft, gentle, smiling voice.

Of course I didn't really have to go. I went in and made all the appropriate sound effects. Clattered the toilet lid. Flushed. Turned on the tap.

Maybe I'd be able to sneak upstairs later during the concert.

When I exited the bathroom, Kevin stood there waiting for me. It seemed that Dr. Bhandari had ordered him to stay glued to my side.

"Would you like to have a look at the ballroom?" he asked.

"Sure, just lead me to Cortland. I'm sure he can take me off your hands."

Kevin led me through the maze of hallways. He motioned to one of the walls. "Ingrid's banners are what makes the whole place so beautiful, I think." Then he stopped before the closed double doors to the ballroom. "Mitchell, can I ask you a personal question?"

"What kind of personal question?"

"About Ingrid. I've been wondering—is everything OK between her and her boyfriend?"

"For the most part, I think. Why do you ask?"

"Something she said the other day. It doesn't sound like he's treating her very well."

"They're just going through a bit of a rough patch."

"Never mind. I shouldn't even be asking," he said. There was no doubting his interest. "Anyway, you wanted to see the ballroom."

With an admirable sense of drama, Kevin swept open both doors at the same time, then stepped aside so I could appreciate the view.

The huge room radiated with hundreds of candles—shimmering from candelabras on stands and clusters on tables. In fact, a young woman was still at work, lighting more candles in the far corner by the passage door to the kitchen.

Ingrid's delicate banners were draped every 10 feet along the walls.

"It's breathtaking," I said.

"People have been setting things up since 9 this morning."

The rows of chairs were angled like a giant check mark with an aisle positioned off-centre on the left. Outside the French doors, fairy lights sparkled in the trees and bushes of the side garden.

The focal point was at the front of the room where two spotlights focused on the stage—a low podium, asymmetrically angled to the side of the magnificent fireplace. I walked to the front to admire the flowers atop the mantel. Three pots of white orchids, brimming with greenery that intertwined and wound the trio of plants together.

"I need more shots of the stage." From the door to the kitchen, Cortland came sailing in, still riding his wheelchair. Behind him followed a photographer with three cameras strung around his neck like chunky jewellery.

"Mitchell, my dear, so what do you think?"

"It's astounding," I said.

"Won't this make a magnificent final chapter for the book?"

"It was a brilliant idea."

Cortland motioned the photographer to the stage. "Now go take more pictures before the candles burn too low. Honestly Mitchell, we have enough pictures to fill a book of its own. I've been catching every stage of light all through the afternoon. Now, Kevin, shouldn't you be off at the ticket table?"

"I'm going there next."

"No dallying. Jump to it!"

Kevin stared me in the eye. "You'll stay around down here, won't you, Mitchell?"

"I'll stick with Cortland."

He nodded at me and headed off.

"I think Dr. Bhandari wants him to trail me. They caught me trying to get upstairs."

"We'll see what we can do about that later," Cortland said cryptically. "I'm so pleased with how everything's coming together."

"How are you feeling? You're not too tired?"

"Healthy as a horse. Frankly, I don't need this wheelbarrow contraption at all. But it's extraordinary how people have been falling on their knees to obey the crippled tyrant."

"They'd obey you no matter what."

"You know, I keep wondering what Vivienne Donnington would think if she could see the place now."

"She'd be proud."

"I hope so. It's been a very odd day. Filled with déjà vu. But enough nostalgia. Now follow me into the kitchen." I pushed open the passage door, and Cortland wheeled through the pantry. "I need to inspect what they're doing with the serving trays. And you can inspect the waiters."

"They're cute. I approve."

"Though all they're serving for drinks is fruit-and-vegetable purée—energy-boosting elixirs, they call them—with trays of vegetarian canapés. Delicious but more expensive than caviar. Now where's your Hollywood boyfriend? I thought we were finally meeting him tonight."

"He's coming. But please don't call him my boyfriend."

"A sensitive point, I see."

"The love affair is definitely over. Which just makes it more important that I make the script as good as I can." I knelt and whispered into Cortland's ear. "I think I might be able to solve the murders tonight—"

One of the cute waiters interrupted. "Mr. McPhee, we've finished refilling the baskets with the gold balls."

"I hope you used an odd number of balls this time. Even numbers are much too ordinary." Cortland wheeled to the counter for a ball count.

I took the opportunity to reconsider my exploration route. The back stairs, I noted, were entered beside the pantry in the midst of all the kitchen activity. Not good access if I wanted to sneak up unnoticed. I'd have to stick to the main stairs in the front hall. And keep Kevin away.

I went to the kitchen's glass doors. I tried to see out to the poolside patio to examine the spot where Trevor had fallen. But reflections from the kitchen's overhead lights blocked the view outside.

The photographer rushed in from the pantry. "Mr. McPhee, I think you'd better come back to the ballroom."

"Are the candles dripping? I paid for non-drip. I'll have someone's head if they're melting on the floor."

"Some woman is trying to move the stage."

"Over my dead body!" Cortland cried and careened his wheelchair off down the pantry hall. I stumbled into the ballroom right behind him.

One of the elegant side tables was now littered with a mammoth harp, as well as a jumble of microphone stands and sound equipment.

Gabriella Hartman was calling orders to a petrified man and a woman. She was still in street clothes—jeans and a tight white T-shirt showcasing her famously curvaceous figure. Gabriella pointed, as her plebes dragged Cortland's elegantly angled podium to the centre of the room right in front of the fireplace.

"What on earth are you doing?" Cortland cried.

"I don't know what *imbecile* arranged this room," Gabriella spat, "but I'm putting the stage in the centre where the audience will actually be able to see it."

"The audience will be able to see it exactly where I put it."

"Mitchell, my darling," Gabriella said, embracing me. "Do you *know* this obstinate man? Could you please talk some *sense* into him?"

"He's the one in charge," I explained.

"*I'm* the one in charge," she said.

"Should we move the spotlights too?" Gabriella's drone inquired.

"My dear woman, I am Cortland McPhee, the designer of this event, and I have personally tested the sight lines from every position in this room. Considering the angle of the chairs, the view is even better than if you were directly at the front."

"I am Gabriella Hartman, the *star* of this event. And my *next* project is straightening the chairs."

Dr. Bhandari appeared out of nowhere. Typical. "Is there some problem?"

Gabriella spouted tears on cue. "Nigel, this man is upsetting me *terribly*. He clearly has no understanding of *theatre*."

"I can see the *performance* has already begun," said Cortland.

Dr. Bhandari calmly sat in a chair in the front row. "Now please, Gabriella, come sit beside me."

She slouched toward him, like a spoiled little girl sucking up to her daddy.

Dr. Bhandari nodded to Cortland. "Would you please join us too?"

Cortland wheeled over. "I refuse to be swayed by feminine manipulations. I was given to understand that the 'entertainment' would be here at 4 o'clock. If she'd arrived then, I might have been able to accommodate her."

"I stated specifically that I would be resting at home until 7," Gabriella declared. "Obviously, I'm the one people have paid to see. And the way this 'designer' has arranged the room, half the people won't see a thing."

"If they really want to see you, they can watch a rerun of *The Love Boat*."

Dr. Bhandari raised his hands. "Let's pause a moment. Take a breath. Now let's sit together and decide how we can come to an agreement."

I didn't want to witness Cortland facing the indignity of compromise, so while they were keeping Dr. Bhandari busy, I casually meandered back to the front hall. A lineup of cute waiters formed a human barricade on the stairs. Kevin stood in front of them, giving instructions. Not a good moment for exploring.

I checked my watch: 10 minutes to 8. The flood of taxied guests would be arriving momentarily. I wondered about Ingrid and Ramir. They should have been here already.

I unobtrusively returned to the ballroom—where Dr. Bhandari was still conducting his negotiations—and slipped out the French doors to the patio that stretched along the left side of the house. Limestone paving stones tapered off to grass, which slanted down into the ravine. There were tall torches staked into the ground, ready to be lit. But the evening was too cool for anyone to want to linger outside.

I made my way across the lawn—the chilled grass crunching beneath my feet—around to the backyard. A Victorian-style pool house was nestled in the far corner amid the trees.

The only lights were from inside the house, giving the yard a shadowy gloom. Inside the kitchen, waiters were milling about.

I came to the low brick wall surrounding the tarp-covered swimming pool. I followed the wall, running my fingertips across the limestone cap. I could see the small indentations from which the wrought-iron fencing had once protruded. The holes had been carefully plugged with matching concrete. A detail that no one would think to notice, unless they knew the tragic story.

I reached the corner of the wall where Trevor had landed.

I imagined Trevor, lying face down in this very spot. Then I looked up to the third floor—to the window just under the V of the roof, the window from which he had leapt. Or been pushed. A dim light glowed inside his room.

"So, Trevor," I said to the air, "if you want to tell me what happened, tonight is your big chance."

Suddenly, I was surrounded by light.

The glaring backyard floodlights had been switched on. I was exposed. Had someone seen me and suspected me as a burglar? I immediately turned to flee back to the ballroom.

Dr. Bhandari opened the glass kitchen door and stepped onto

the patio. "Good evening, Mitchell. We didn't have a chance to speak earlier."

My heart was in my throat. I didn't want to be alone with him.

I decided to handle the situation proactively by totally ignoring the situation. "Did you get everything settled with Cortland and Gabriella?"

"I think everyone will be satisfied."

"It sure is getting cold out here. Maybe we should get back inside." I moved toward the kitchen door, but Dr. Bhandari stood still.

"Your curiosity can't be satisfied, can it, Mitchell?" His voice was sympathetic and a little sad, as if he felt sorry for me. "Why is that?"

"I'm not sure." Clearly, he wasn't psychic, because if he could read my mind, he would have thrown me out right on the spot. "I guess I just want to get to the bottom of what happened that night."

"Would you believe me, Mitchell, if I told you that our intentions are identical?"

"I don't know what you mean."

"I think you're right in your feelings about Trevor and Jackson Donnington. Their deaths are incomplete. In fact, I have felt that for many years."

"They're incomplete because you're not rotting in jail, you cold-blooded double murderer!" No, I didn't say that. Instead I politely queried, "What makes you feel that way?"

"I have sensed a disturbance in the house. It has been particularly strong since that first night you came for the introduction."

"You mean you think I brought back Trevor's spirit somehow?"

"Is that what you believe?"

"I feel some kind of weird connection to him, I guess."

"Clearly you do."

"Do you know if Trevor was gay?"

"That's a very peculiar question."

"Was he?"

"He never spoke of that with me."

"Was everything going all right with his therapy?"

"I felt he was making good progress. But as I mentioned to you the other day, his father was too impatient."

"I talked to someone who overheard you and Jackson arguing that night at the party."

Dr. Bhandari looked blank for a moment. "I had forgotten that myself."

"So did you argue with him?"

"Jackson was very worried about his son. He was intending to commit Trevor to a psychiatric hospital. I disagreed. There was much more I could have done. Unfortunately, I never had the chance."

Would a loving, overindulgent father really consider committing his son?

"You really think you could have helped him?" By having sex with him?

Dr. Bhandari shifted his posture. "Do you know why I agreed, Mitchell, to creating a party so similar—bringing back Mr. McPhee and so many of the original guests?"

"I did wonder about that."

"It is my intention to replicate the energy of that night in order to clear it once and for all. I have just said a prayer in my meditation room—which was once Trevor Donnington's bedroom. I will do another ceremony later this evening to elevate the energy in the house and release Trevor's spirit."

"I want to release it too. By finding out what really happened."

"No one will ever know what really happened, Mitchell. Unless Jackson or Trevor tells us." He said that with a sly smile. As if he were making fun of me. "Trust me, Mitchell. After tonight, the story will be settled. Trevor's soul will find peace at last. And I hope you will find peace as well."

Dr. Bhandari opened the kitchen door and waited for me to go inside first.

I should have confronted him about what I'd learned at Cultbusters—about him not being a real doctor. But I didn't want to risk being thrown out altogether.

"Shall we see how Cortland and Gabriella are getting along?" He led me through the pantry into the ballroom.

The stage was still slightly angled, but it had been moved closer to the centre of the room in front of the fireplace. Minions were in the midst of shifting all 300 chairs.

"It's not as though I didn't think the room was beautiful when I came in," Gabriella said. "Didn't I ooh and aah, Deborah?" The harpist nodded obediently, protected behind the string fence of her instrument.

Cortland must have escaped to the kitchen. At least he still had his photographs of the room looking the way he'd intended. Those would last much longer than the concert.

I didn't interrupt their work.

I headed back to the front hall to see if Ramir and Ingrid had arrived—and to see if the stairway might be clear. I knew I had to get up to the third floor before Dr. Bhandari's exorcism banished Trevor from the house permanently.

About a hundred guests were bustling between the front hall and the dining and drawing rooms on either side.

I watched the delight on people's faces as they entered the mysterious candlelit environment. I heard a few knowing whispers of "Cortland McPhee."

The chorus of cute waiters pirouetted about, balancing trays of herbal elixirs in champagne flutes. I grabbed a glass of something the shade of congealing blood.

Kevin was stationed at the little desk by the front door, taking tickets and handing out programs.

"I forgot to give you this," I said, pulling my ticket from my inside jacket pocket. "I gave some tickets to a few other friends. Has anyone been asking for me?"

He smiled. "No one yet."

An informal reception line had formed at the door with promi-nent Gateway Keepers greeting their fellow guests. No mere air kisses for this crowd. It had to be hugs. Every hug was rife with love, warmth, and spiritual healing.

I wandered into the drawing room—glancing up at the chunky chandelier with its telltale mismatched dish.

My drink tasted like mulched grass and beets. I set it on the credenza by the door and began to eavesdrop. All the guests seemed intent on explaining how intimately they were acquainted with either Gabriella or Dr. Bhandari.

"I still have her first eight-track tape."

"I remember when there were only *Six* Gateways."

I recognized a few of the nonalien cast-mates from *Station Centauri*. I could imagine how uncomfortable it would be for Ramir, facing them all after just being fired. With any luck, the cast and crew hadn't yet been informed.

I heard someone mention "Flying in from L.A." Was that J.D., Gabriella's all-powerful manager? But I couldn't figure out who'd said it.

Suddenly a video camera was pointing in my face. "What do you think of the party tonight?"

Wielding the camera was a reedy man dressed in a tattered blue denim ensemble, totally out of keeping with tonight's crowd.

Ramir appeared behind his shoulder, smiling buoyantly. "Hey, Mitch. Cortland did a great job. Things are buzzing already."

Ramir hugged me casually—as if he hadn't been in tears a few hours before. He wore a smart grey turtleneck and slim black pants.

"Everybody's been looking for you," I said.

Ramir motioned to the camera operator. "Go back outside and get some more shots of people arriving." Echoes of Cortland and his personal photographer. "I just needed time to regroup," he said brightly.

"So you regrouped?"

"I'm getting there."

"Can we step outside a minute too?"

"This isn't the best moment, Mitch. I need to squeeze in some interviews."

"Please," I said. And he could tell it was serious.

He followed me out the front door and around to the side of the house, beside the conservatory.

"I did something today you're not going to like."

He nodded as preparation.

"I called that Cultbusters place."

"Mitch, is this going to be what I think it is? Because I already know what you're going to say."

"No, you don't."

"Is this what you and Ingrid wanted to talk to me about this afternoon?"

"The man at Cultbusters gave me this huge pile of articles about Dr. Bhandari. Printouts from the Internet. I've read all the secrets in the Gateways. They're no big deal. Nothing you can't find in a typical self-help book."

"Everybody who goes through the Gateways signs an agreement of nondisclosure. Anybody who's writing that stuff on the Internet is breaking their word. So why should you trust them?"

"But I found out about a weird sex ritual that's part of the Second Gateway. That's why Dr. Bhandari wants you to stay celibate. It's preparation."

"I know that."

"You know about it? You're going to have sex with him?"

"It's not sex, Mitch. It's Tantric massage. It's part of the Eastern spiritual tradition. Like the Kama Sutra."

"But you shouldn't have a sexual relationship with your therapist. It isn't ethical. No medical board would approve of that. And he isn't even really—"

"Mitch, if you don't respect what Dr. Bhandari's doing, you shouldn't even be in his house."

"I'm worried about you."

"It's all just research for your precious screenplay."

"It's because I don't want you to get hurt."

"You think you're going to protect me somehow?"

"If I can," I said.

He looked at me with fragile vulnerability. "I can take care of myself, Mitch. That's why I'm seeing Dr. Bhandari."

The camera guy came up behind us. "We should get some shots in the ballroom before they open it up."

"Sure thing. I'll talk to you later, Mitch."

Cabs were now lined up in the street, dispersing glamorous passengers.

We went back into the house, and Ramir panned the front hall with his smile, so everyone would notice his good spirits— in case they'd already heard his bad news.

Right in front of us, Graham and Carolyn Linden were handing their tickets to Kevin. Carolyn wore a cream silk blouse and black pants. Graham sported a smart black suit. Matching understated elegance.

"Mitchell, I'm so glad to see you," Carolyn said, smiling. "We couldn't decide whether or not to come."

"Carolyn thought it would be too morbid," Graham said.

"But Graham insisted."

"All that talk about Trevor made me curious to come back." He grinned guiltily.

"I don't know how long we're going to be able to stay," Carolyn said. "But it certainly is beautiful tonight."

A tight-faced, beige society lady spun Carolyn away from us. "Carolyn Linden, I never thought I'd see *you* here."

Graham chuckled and lowered his voice. "It wasn't just the bad memories. She was worried about running into people she knows." He scanned the hall with those miraculous green eyes. "I'd barely recognize the place. Did that designer friend of yours put this together? What was his name again?"

"Cortland McPhee."

"I think I finally remembered who you mean. Is he here tonight?"

"He's in the ballroom, setting things up."

"I'll have to find him and say hello. So how's your script? Any more luck with your murder investigation?"

"Actually, I'm hoping to pin things down tonight."

"Sounds intriguing."

Carolyn returned from the society lady with an amused grimace. "We go to the same manicurist. Now she's going to tell the whole world that I'm a kook like her."

The two of them went into the dining room to peruse the trays of hors d'oeuvres.

Everyone in the crowd seemed occupied and distracted. Kevin was still busy at his little table, accepting tickets. I looked at the staircase. Could I just be blatant and let everyone presume I had free rein of the house?

I felt a hand clutch my shoulder.

"Is Pierre here?"

Ingrid was at my side.

"I thought you and Pierre were coming together."

Ing wore the same clothes she'd been wearing earlier in the day. Her eyes were red. "I have proof, Mitchell."

"About Dr. Bhandari?"

"About Pierre—and Laura."

I grabbed her by the arm and led her into the drawing room, to the nook in the bay window where we could have comparative privacy.

"What did you find?"

"They were in the apartment together when we were at Ramir's—when I was out shopping."

"You caught them?"

She shook her head. "When I got home, there was a message from Pierre on the answering machine. He said he had to work late—that he'd meet us here at the house. So I phoned him to see if he wanted me to go to his office so we could come together. But the receptionist said he'd taken the afternoon off."

"So he didn't go back to work after we saw him?"

"He was lying. He wasn't expecting us to be there, remember." Her voice quavered. "And then I sort of went crazy, and I started searching through the whole apartment, digging for clues. And there were two wineglasses in the sink."

"And one of them had lipstick marks?"

"No, but the bed wasn't made the same way as normal. And

there was an extra cushion on the couch. Which doesn't sound very convincing either, I know. But there were five of Laura's cards lying on the kitchen table."

"I see."

"And I had all my paintings of the Donningtons covered by a sheet. But the sheet was off. It was crumpled up on the floor."

"So you think Laura saw them?"

"Which makes me feel embarrassed on top of everything else." She started to cry, and I hugged her to my chest. "Mitchell, how could he do this to me again?"

"I don't know. But don't you think you should go back home? You don't want to confront them about it here."

Ingrid broke out of my arms, strong again. "Of course I'm going to confront them."

Other guests came and stood beside us, numbing our conversation.

"I need to put on some eyeliner. Where's the washroom?"

"I can show you," I said.

"Mitchell, you have to let *me* ask Laura what she was doing with Trevor when he came downstairs to the party. I want to see how she lies about that too."

"Whatever you say," I said.

We returned to the front hall. "The banners look good," she said unenthusiastically. "Have you talked to Ramir? Is he any better?"

"He still thinks Dr. Bhandari is going to cure all his problems."

"It'd be nice if he could," she said bleakly and disappeared into the washroom.

I examined the crowd, now crammed into the front hall shoulder to shoulder.

No sign of Aaron.

No sign of Laura, the two-faced bitch. But who was I to condemn her when I'd been dating a married man myself?

"Out of the way, out of the way." Cortland wheeled a path through the crowd and bumped into my shin. "I must say I've been getting rave reviews. A dozen people have asked for my card.

275

I could be planning parties for years—if it weren't for this both-ersome growth in my brain."

"Graham Linden was asking about you."

"He showed up, did he?"

"With his wife."

"Where are they?"

I pointed to the dining room, and Cortland craned his neck. "You'll have to help me snub them."

"Ing just got here—"

Ermina swooped in. "Cortland, darling, why are you in a wheel-chair?"

"I'm doing my impersonation of Joan Crawford in *What Ever Happened to Baby Jane?*" He stretched out his arms for a fragile air kiss. "I can't afford to overtax myself, after all."

"You're just begging for attention, yes?"

"And what are *you* begging for, baring all that cleavage? Advertising for a new husband?"

"I bought this just for tonight." Ermina wore a gold brocade jacket over a low-cut gold dress. (Cortland must have forewarned her of the white-and-gold colour scheme.) "Honestly, it feels like only yesterday that I was coming here to visit Vivi for a cup of coffee. Who would believe it's been over two decades?"

"Now, don't you get up to any of your funny business tonight," Cortland warned. "I won't be able to keep an eye on you."

Ermina tittered like a naughty little girl. "I hope you haven't been telling Mitchell about my reputation." She transferred her twinkle to me. "Don't you dare ask him any questions," she said, egging me on.

"Now come with me, darling. Let me give you a quick preview of the ballroom. We can enjoy it in peace—before that hideous creature from Mars begins all her shrieking." Ermina wheeled Cortland away.

Among the faces in the front hall, I spotted Jane Choy and her bland businessman husband.

"Hartman would cut my throat if I didn't come to this thing," she said.

"I'm glad you're here."

"There's powerful energy tonight, Mitchell. With your psychic sensitivity, you must be feeling it too."

"I have a headache. I can't feel much."

"That's the pressure. All the leftovers of the past coming together. I still think you'll find your answers tonight, Mitchell. You find me if you need me."

There was a burst of applause. Everyone turned to face the grand staircase. Dr. Bhandari stood on the landing. "Welcome, everyone."

More guests pressed out from the drawing room and the dining room. Ramir and the cameraman barged into position to record the guru's address.

"On behalf of the Seven Gateways, I would like to thank every one of you for your generosity in attending this evening's performance. We are all privileged to witness the new dawning of a great singer." A round of applause. "Gabriella Hartman has said that the Seven Gateways have transformed her life, and now they have transformed her voice as well."

Everyone chuckled and pooh-poohed the notion that Gabriella's voice ever needed transformation.

"I would like to thank most sincerely the individuals who have been responsible for organizing this event—Kevin McColm, my personal assistant, as well as Ramir Martinez and Cortland McPhee."

More enthusiastic applause. Ramir nodded to his public, acting his heart out to look cheerful and confident.

"Now I would like to invite you all to proceed to the ballroom for a special meditation, followed by our concert."

The crowd began to flow.

"My father made a speech in that exact same spot," Laura Donnington said, right behind me. "Dr. Bhandari must have remembered it from the party."

"History repeating," I said lamely. "How are you?"

"The place is so different. It doesn't seem real." She pushed the hair back from her face. She wore a close-fitting burgundy dress that revealed a surprisingly fine figure. But the serious lines across her forehead made the delicate clothes seem incongruous.

"Are Ingrid and Pierre here yet?" Laura asked.

Dare I interfere? "I thought you and Pierre would be coming together."

"He asked me, but I wanted to come by myself."

She seemed so matter-of-fact. Part of me felt sorry for her. I wanted to protect her from Ingrid's wrath.

"You know, Laura, you look sort of pale," I said. "Are you sure you want to be here?"

"It's just weird. I'll get used to it."

Ermina was back, reaching a hand through the throng of people to touch Laura's arm. "It's your Auntie Ermi, darling. We must have a chat later."

When Ermina was out of earshot, Laura was blunt. "I don't want to talk to her." She gave a tug on my sleeve. "Come with me, OK?"

Laura slipped between the tide of people and led me into the drawing room.

"This is all our old furniture," she said, mystified. "But it's all been reupholstered." She walked through the room, now empty of people, as though she were walking through a dream that might vaporize at any instant.

"Cortland says your mother had great taste, that she wanted everything historically accurate."

"She loved this house." Laura pointed above the fireplace to a bold modern collage. "That painting in my living room. It used to hang right there."

And Laura must have seen Ingrid's version this very afternoon.

She plonked down on the couch. "So is this your big night? You get to make your official pronouncement about the true identity of the murderer."

"I'm still trying to figure the whole thing out," I said. "You really don't remember anything else?"

"Laura?" Dr. Bhandari's voice echoed through the room. "I still recognize you after all these years. I was very pleased when

Ramir told me you would be here tonight. You know you've always been welcome to return."

Laura stared at him for a moment. Then she lowered her gaze, her bangs falling in front of her face. "Mitchell told me about your party," she said. "It seemed like as good a time as any."

"Is there anywhere in the house you'd like to see? For old times' sake? I give you free rein."

Was he saying that to taunt me?

"Maybe just my old bedroom," she said.

"We use it as a meditation chamber now. I think you'll find it very different."

"The more different the better," she said. "I'll see you in a few minutes, Mitchell."

Dr. Bhandari smiled at me patiently—or condescendingly. I couldn't tell which.

I followed them into the hall and watched as they climbed the stairs, side by side. Somehow, later, I'd be going up there myself.

But in the meantime, I had another crisis to deal with. I had to find Ingrid. Maybe I could encourage her to leave.

There were still a few other stragglers in the hall, sipping their mulched turnip greens with peach nectar.

No Aaron.

But Bill Zale had just arrived. He staggered up beside me, chuckling with apparently inebriated pleasure. "Jackson would shit himself if he saw this paint job. I can't wait to look around the rest of the place. Where can I find a martini?"

I left that for the waiters to explain.

Ingrid must still be in the washroom. I knocked. "Ing?"

She opened the door immediately—now dry-eyed and composed.

"Laura's here," I said. "But not with Pierre."

"They must be trying to cover their trail," she said bitterly.

"Maybe he's not going to show up."

"Then he's a coward."

I held her hand, and we went into the front hall together. Empty now. Kevin's little desk was abandoned.

"Everyone's already gone in for the concert," I said.

We both looked toward the staircase.

"I guess this is your chance, Mitchell. You can go up and find your clues."

"Actually, right now's not the best moment. Laura and Dr. Bhandari are up there."

Ingrid stared up the stairs. "I don't think I want to see her after all."

"That's probably for the best."

Then Laura began descending the staircase by herself, her gaze down, her hair falling in front of her face.

Silence.

"Hi, Ingrid," she said, finally seeing us.

Ingrid didn't say a word.

"Dr. Bhandari left me alone to look around. It was weird. All those pictures I draw, all locked up in this house. I wonder if now I'll finally be able to stop."

Laura stood at the bottom of the stairs directly in front of us. She looked Ingrid in the eye. "Is Pierre here?"

Ing was still speechless.

"I was hoping we could sit together for the concert," Laura said.

"With Pierre in between us?"

"Sure. Whatever."

"I *know,*" Ing said.

"Know what?"

"I know you were in my apartment this afternoon."

"I was at my therapist's this afternoon."

"You saw my paintings."

"What paintings?" Laura pushed the hair back from her face. "What are you talking about?"

"Why have you been spending so much time with Pierre?"

"We had lunch last week. What's the big deal?"

"What about this afternoon?"

"Do you think we're sleeping together or something?"

Ing was startled by Laura's frankness. "Aren't you?"

"Why do women always think that about me?"

Ingrid looked confused.

Laura's attitude was so convincing. And Ingrid's evidence wasn't exactly conclusive.

"Why should we believe anything you say?" Ing said. "You've lied before."

"When have I lied?" Laura said defiantly.

I took over my role as detective. "Why didn't you tell us that Trevor came downstairs during the party?"

"During the party..." Laura's brazen manner collapsed. Her mouth hung open. "How did you know?"

"We have a photograph," Ingrid said.

"There's a picture? Of me and Trevor?"

"It shows you both in the ballroom in the door to the pantry."

"I can't believe it."

"Did you go back upstairs with him?" Ing asked. "Were you there when they died?"

Laura stared ahead. "No."

"Then why didn't you tell us you saw him that night?"

"I never told anyone." Laura sank down and sat on the stairs, looking like the little girl she'd been all those years ago. "The police said Trevor was drunk when it happened. That was one of the reasons he went so crazy."

"The magazine article said there was a bottle of vodka in his room," I said.

"And I was the one who gave him the bottle."

"How? You were only 12 years old."

"Trevor came downstairs and asked me to steal it from the bar. I would have done anything for him, I loved him so much. And when the police said he was drunk, I knew what happened was partially my fault."

So much suddenly made sense.

Then the front door opened behind us and Pierre entered, debonair as ever. "Sorry we're so late."

Daphne followed him in, giggling, clutching her candy necklace and gawking girlishly. "This place is fabulous," she exclaimed. "It's just like the pictures."

Ing's eyes widened in realization. "Oh my God."

Daphne stopped giggling.

"Why are you all looking that way?" Pierre asked.

Daphne clapped her hands to her cheeks. "I'm so sorry, Ingrid." And she scurried out the door, leaving Pierre standing there alone.

"I get it now," Laura said. "Pierre's been sleeping with Daphne."

Only then did Pierre fully understand.

"I don't know what to say," he said.

"Is it true?" Ingrid asked.

"Only a couple of times."

"A couple of times? In my apartment? In my bed?"

"Daphne told me you were seeing another guy yourself."

"She made that up. She's lying."

"She told me some guy came to see you."

"Kevin? I've never done anything with Kevin."

"Ingrid, we should go home and talk." Pierre tried to seem the rational one.

"You're not coming back to *my* home."

"We can't go through this again, Ingrid."

"You're right. We can't."

Pierre was flabbergasted. "So that's it?"

"That's it," Ing said. "You'd better run after Daphne. If you can catch her."

Finally, Pierre turned. He opened the door and let it swing closed behind him.

I admit that I felt a certain vindication in that moment.

I never liked Pierre.

Ingrid slumped onto my shoulder. "I want to get out of here, Mitchell."

"I'll take you back to my place."

"No, you have to stay," she said. "Find out what you need to know."

"Don't leave, Ingrid," Laura said. "Watch the concert with me."

"I don't know if I can sit still long enough," Ing said. She looked into Laura's eyes. "I'm sorry for what I said to you just now."

"I've said worse things myself. Any time you want to leave,

we can." Then Laura gazed at me, deadly serious. "Dr. Bhandari told me you think Trevor is trying to communicate through you."

"It sounds ridiculous, I know."

Laura hugged me and squeezed as tightly as I've ever been squeezed.

Then Laura put her arm around Ingrid's shoulders and the two women headed into the ballroom.

And I realized I was alone in the front hall.

The perfect opportunity. Completely by coincidence.

I stepped toward the stairs.

I had to see Trevor's room. If I needed to, I could kick down the door. Not that I've ever kicked down a door before.

Then there was Kevin, appearing from the hall to the kitchen. "Mitchell, we're just about to start the meditation."

I stood at the back of the ballroom and surveyed the scene my friends had helped create, the crowd I had helped assemble.

Somehow the universe intended for me to play a part in this. All so I could write a movie and make some money? Or was there another more important reason?

Everyone was busy schmoozing. They seemed reluctant to take their seats.

I calculated. The 300 guests at $500 each. Gross of $150,000. Even minus expenses, Dr. Bhandari would still be making a huge profit. Not bad for a party arranged in two weeks with largely volunteer labour. He certainly had a lucrative *modus operandi*.

And he had a lot to lose.

Kevin had quickly been surrounded by a gaggle of similar disciples. He was out of my hair, at least for a few minutes. Jane was in the front row, absorbed in an intimate tête-à-tête with her hubby. Ingrid and Laura were in the third row on the far left. Cortland had parked his wheelchair at the end of the back row closest to the door. Graham Linden was crouched beside him, chatting. Cortland seemed to be acting particularly haughty.

And it looked as if Aaron definitely wasn't going to show up.

Ramir was fidgeting with the video camera, which had been placed on a pedestal at the back of the centre aisle.

"Don't tell me you're taking over the videotaping too?"

"The camera guy's on a bathroom break before we get started. What's the matter with Ing? She looks as if she's been crying."

"More weird news. Pierre was fooling around with Daphne."

"Holy shit."

"But I think she's going to be OK."

Ramir beamed out his serene smile. "After tonight, everything's going to be fine, Mitch. I can feel it."

He hugged me. Then, like an afterthought, he kissed me on the mouth.

"Thanks," I said.

"I bet tomorrow you'll sit down at your computer and nail that screenplay once and for all."

I nodded, somewhat less certain.

I joined Cortland in the back row.

"Reserved seat right here," he said, patting the chair beside him. "What did Graham have to say?"

"A lot of nonsense. His loving wife felt too 'edgy' being here in the house, so she went home. Then Mr. Linden got to the point and asked me to stop telling people about his sordid past."

"He didn't mind talking about it to me and Ramir."

"Deeply foolish fellow. I told him I'd shut up. But who can ever keep me quiet?"

Cortland stared off for a moment, watching Ramir in consultation with the camera operator.

"You'd do anything he asked, wouldn't you?" Cortland said.

"Ramir? Of course not. We argue all the time."

"You're in love with him."

"No, I'm not."

Cortland smiled patiently.

"Maybe I was a long time ago," I said.

"I've seen the way you look at him."

"We're friends."

"If Ramir snapped his fingers, your old boyfriend Ben and that Hollywood fellow wouldn't stand a chance."

His directness made me uncomfortable. "That's never going to happen," I said.

"Probably better for you if it doesn't. Friends are more important than lovers. And it's never wise to be so obsessed."

"Anyway, I'm too mature for all that now."

"Is anyone too mature? Look at our ridiculous Ermina over there, chatting up that young waiter. It's not as if he has two pennies to rub together. But bring her to a party, and she'll flirt with anything in tight pants."

I watched Ermina, and I thought about what Cortland had said about Ramir. Was it that obvious?

The gong donged. Kevin summoning our attention.

"And so the show begins," Cortland declared.

Dr. Bhandari took the podium, and the spotlight beam grew in strength to illuminate him. The crowd obediently became silent. Blissful, spiritually evolved smiles blossomed throughout the room.

"Thank you again for coming this evening. Many of you here are already familiar with the Seven Gateways. Some of you may not be. First, I am going to lead us all in a meditation that will enhance our enjoyment of the concert to follow. Utilize whichever Gateway to meditation is appropriate for you. Or simply close your eyes and concentrate on your breathing. We all begin in the same fashion."

"I don't know how much of this I can stomach," Cortland whispered.

"I hated all the meditation stuff at first," I said. "But it grows on you."

"I doubt that very much."

"Now please sit up straight," Dr. Bhandari commanded. "Uncross your legs. Close your eyes. Simply follow your breath. Feel it coming in your nose, down your windpipe, filling your lungs, expanding your chest. Now let it go..."

I started doing Jane's meditation instead, imagining my brain going loose, turning to mush, relaxing and draining through my body. Maybe it would help ease my headache.

I felt a poke in my ribs. "Mitchell, wake up."

"What?"

"It's over."

I opened my eyes, groggy. Everyone around me was standing, stretching. I stayed sitting. Confused.

Cortland yawned. "I had a nice little nap myself."

"I was asleep?"

Cortland checked his watch. "For nearly half an hour."

"I don't remember anything." I rubbed my eyes, trying to clear my head, shake my brain back into working order. I hadn't even been dreaming.

The crowd settled again. I noticed that Gabriella's musicians, armed with harp and flute, had taken to the stage.

Dr. Bhandari was standing at the front: "I hope you are all now refreshed and ready to enjoy this extraordinary musical event."

The last thing I felt was refreshed. It felt as if I'd drunk too much tequila.

Dr. Bhandari disappeared through the kitchen doorway. The crowd sat quiet and expectant.

A moment later Gabriella emerged through the same doorway—wearing a glittering white floor-length gown. She took her place in the spotlight and stood before the microphone.

Cortland whispered into my ear, "Notice how the orchids on the fireplace mantel look as if they're sprouting from her head? That's the reason I had the stage where it was. Now she looks like the goddamned Medusa."

He was right.

Gabriella stood there perfectly still and silent, looking at the floor. I imagined she would make some kind of self-congratulatory speech. But she was silent, moment after moment, to the point of worried puzzlement in the audience. I looked back over my shoulder to see Ramir's reaction, but the camera operator was alone.

And then an extraordinary note emerged from Gabriella's throat, followed by a single dramatic strum of the harp.

Gabriella's voice enveloped the room—a heart-swelling sound, notes so pure they pierced right through me.

I couldn't understand the words. Were they Celtic or Gaelic? Every rise of her voice seemed to draw me up in waves of energy. I felt a shiver through my shoulders.

I was hypnotized again, drowsy and overwhelmed.

And there was another poke in my ribs. "I can't stand another minute," Cortland hissed.

"It's beautiful," I said.

"I can't enjoy anything coming out of *her*. Help wheel me out of here."

"You can go by yourself."

"I'm too weak. Get me out, Mitchell. Now."

I wasn't in the mood for Cortland's games. But I couldn't concentrate enough to argue. Obediently, I stood and pushed the wheelchair out the rear doors. No one seemed to notice. They were all entranced by the music.

Once the double doors swung closed, Cortland groaned. "She's like a wailing cat in heat. Even my little Pisces could sing better."

I didn't respond. I felt dazed and dizzy.

"Take me to the drawing room. Far enough away so I can't hear."

I wheeled him through the dim and deserted front hall where the mountains of candles still flickered.

The drawing room was empty. A few leftover glasses and plates were scattered on the Donningtons' old tables.

"Take me over to the corner." I pushed him to the nook in the bay window, right beside a candle stand. "Pull back the curtain more so I can see out."

"Whatever you want."

"Yes, Mitchell, I must say that tonight has been a tremendous success. Perhaps there is some order to the universe after all."

"If there is, I still can't figure it out."

"I might be able to help you with that," he said. "I've got something you might appreciate." Cortland held up a key ring. "Dr. Bhandari gave this to me for letting in the service people. The big square-headed one is the master key for the house."

Finally, my mind came back.

I swallowed hard. "Thank you."

Reverently, I took the ring of keys from his hand.

"You see, old Cortland's been looking out for you. Now hurry along, Sherlock. Run up to the third floor and peek under the floorboards. See if you can solve your mystery once and for all. Myself, I need a cigarette." Cortland reached into his pocket for his silver case. He leaned toward one of the candles for a light. "Close the door behind you. I can still hear that howling."

I left the drawing room and gently pulled the door closed.

Gabriella's otherworldly singing resounded clearly from the far end of the house. Maybe I should go back and listen. Like Ulysses drawn to the mythical sirens.

Suddenly I had no idea why I'd wanted so badly to climb those stairs. Mostly I wanted to sit on the bottom step and listen.

The front door opened.

"Sorry I'm so late."

Aaron.

"This house is everything you said it was."

"What the fuck are you doing?"

"What? I thought you wanted me here."

"Did I say that out loud?" The words from the vision.

"Mitchell, are you all right?"

"I didn't think you were coming."

"The meeting went longer than I expected. But I've got some interesting news."

"This isn't a good time to talk."

"I have to apologize again that we couldn't have dinner."

"I'm busy right now."

"Are you going upstairs? Do you want me to come with you?"

"No," I practically shouted.

"All right, I won't. No big deal. Where's everybody else?"

"In the ballroom. Down the hall. I'll meet you later."

He headed off, looking bewildered.

☆

I placed my foot on the first step.

Suddenly, a splitting pain shot down behind my left ear.

I kept climbing. This was my only chance.

The second floor was dim, glimmering in the golden glow of candles casting shadows through the stairwell.

All the doors were closed.

Gabriella's haunting voice floated up from below.

I looked toward the back of the house, at Jackson's office door. Shut. Directly across the hall was the door leading to the back staircase.

First, I went to familiar territory. Laura's room. Where she'd visited not an hour ago. I tried the doorknob. Locked. What did Dr. Bhandari want to hide tonight? Did he expect his faithful followers would rob him? Play illicit party games? I sorted through the key ring and found the master key with its large square head.

It slid easily into the keyhole and turned.

All was normal. The padded mat on the floor, just as there'd been the last time. The window where Kevin had stood, watching me and Ingrid in the driveway.

I closed the door, and the automatic lock clicked into place.

When I came back into the hall, I could hear breathing. Loud and deep, exaggerated inhalations of breath.

It was like a drowning person, gasping for air. Like a woman giving birth.

Instinctively, my breath deepened as well, matching the pace.

Gabriella's voice was soaring below, and in front of me, I could hear these desperate intakes of breath.

The sounds were coming from Jackson's office.

Was I imagining it?

I walked toward his door.

Is this what Jackson had done on that night 20 years ago? Heard strange noises and headed to his office to investigate? Then he found Dr. Bhandari with his son?

Had Trevor entered the room willingly? Or had Dr. Bhandari forced him? A final tryst before he was barred from the house forever—or before Trevor was shipped off to the mental hospital?

I pressed my ear to the door. I heard low moans. A soothing whisper. Then back to the breaths.

I put my hand on the doorknob. It turned easily without the need for my key.

Slowly, I pushed the door open.

The light from the hallway lit the scene inside.

In his long white shirt, Dr. Bhandari stood at the massage table, his back to me. A naked man lay on the table. Dr. Bhandari's right hand rubbed the centre of the man's chest, while his left massaged his stomach, massaged lower...

The face of the man on the table was blurred by shadows, but the body was lean and muscular, the skin a light brown. His stomach rose and fell in giant breaths.

"What the fuck are you doing?"

The words had come from me.

Dr. Bhandari straightened and turned to look at me. His eyes filled with anger. "Close the door."

Ramir sat up on the massage table. "Who's there?"

"Leave us," Dr. Bhandari demanded.

"Who is it?" Ramir asked.

I slammed the door closed.

I had to get upstairs before Dr. Bhandari had a chance to stop me.

I went to the back staircase and opened the cupboard-like door. My heart was racing. My breath was hard and fast. This was my only chance. I ran up the stairs as if my life depended on it.

I tripped. Stumbled against the wall. Scraped my knee. Then I was moving again, running up the stairs, my shoulders bumping either wall.

I turned a corner on the stairs, and there was the landing with the closed door.

I heard Dr. Bhandari's voice at the foot of the stairs. "Mitchell, come down here!"

I fumbled with the master key and jammed it into the lock.

When I pushed open the door, I crossed a narrow hall and stepped into a small gabled room.

Finally I'd made it.

Trevor's bedroom.

But now it was Dr. Bhandari's meditation chamber. Startling in its simplicity. Totally bare except for a white padded mat on the floor and a low altar in the corner. A candle flickered in a clear glass jar.

I imagined Jackson lying bleeding on the floor, Trevor smashing through the glass.

I dropped to my knees, crawled to the window, and felt along the wooden slats until a board shifted under my hand. I lifted the panel of wood— 4 inches by 12—and there was Trevor's hiding place. A foot-deep gap between the wooden support beams.

I reached into the darkness and felt around in empty space. No papers, no books.

But in the back corner of the hole, I saw a square of white. I grabbed it. Crisp white fabric.

"You shouldn't have come here, Mitchell."

I stood up straight, still dazed, still dizzy.

"You shouldn't have interrupted us," Dr. Bhandari said.

"Where's Ramir?"

"You destroyed the ritual."

Dr. Bhandari moved toward me.

"Stay away," I warned.

He noticed what was in my hands. "What do you have?"

I'd barely looked at it myself.

"A handkerchief," I said. "I found it. Under the floor. It must have been Trevor's."

"I've looked in that spot many times. It was never there before."

"I was looking for Trevor's diaries. What he wrote on the night of the murder."

"The police found those. They were filled with nonsense— gibberish."

Ramir entered the room, still clumsily pulling on his turtle-neck. "What's going on?"

I unfolded the square of fabric. Inside were stains of reddish brown. Dried blood.

"Is this what you used to wipe the knife? Before you threw it in the pool?"

Ramir was angry. "What are you talking about, Mitch?"

"Dr. Bhandari had sex with Trevor in the office downstairs—like he was doing with you. Jackson caught them. Then Dr. Bhandari killed them both and made it look like a murder-suicide."

"Mitch, that's crazy."

Dr. Bhandari sneered in derision. "You think I would leave such evidence here for 20 years? Leave such a vile object in my sacred meditation chamber?"

That was true. It didn't make sense.

"Your ridiculous games have gone far enough, Mitchell."

I looked at the handkerchief more carefully. Fine white linen. Beneath the crusted blood, I could see the shine of gold embroidery.

"Oh my God."

"What is it?" Ramir asked.

"I can't believe it. It must have been—"

Suddenly, there was a deafening high-pitched buzz.

The three of us stood frozen.

"The smoke alarm," Dr. Bhandari said.

"A fire?" I asked.

"All the candles downstairs," I said.

I shoved the handkerchief into my jacket pocket.

Dr. Bhandari went first, hurtling down the steps of the narrow back staircase. Ramir and I followed inches behind.

A house this old. All the ancient wood. All the people crowded into the ballroom.

I couldn't smell smoke.

Yes, I could.

The three of us burst into the kitchen.

Kevin was pulling a fire extinguisher from a cupboard beside the stove. "We haven't found the fire yet," he said.

"Call 911," Dr. Bhandari ordered.

"I already did."

Kevin, Ramir, and Dr. Bhandari pushed their way toward the ballroom, fighting the crowds who were filing from the pantry, through the kitchen, and into the backyard.

Ermina Milenska and a young waiter burst forth from the door to the basement—their clothing disheveled.

"What's going on?" she asked.

"A fire. You have to get out."

Ermina and the waiter joined the crowd heading for the backyard.

I shoved my way into the front hall, where more people were rushing through the front door.

Smoke was seeping from beneath the closed door to the drawing room. I held my breath and pushed the door open. A black cloud billowed out.

The room was aglow with fire—vivid orange and yellow.

Cortland was in his wheelchair, a dark silhouette against the streaming flames of the curtains beside him.

From the way his head hung forward, I knew something was wrong.

I rushed inside. The heat of the fire dried my face in a flash. My skin felt crisp and tight. The roar of the flames was like a fireplace on high volume.

The cluster of candles in the window had fully melted.

"Cortland, wake up!"

I shook him by the shoulders. He slumped farther. Tears burst in my eyes.

I heard the door slam behind me.

"He was dead when I came in," the man's voice loudly announced.

In the dark and the smoke, I couldn't see who the tall figure was.

"We have to get him out of here," I shouted back.

Then the man did something inexplicable. He went to the credenza against the wall and shoved it in front of the door.

"What are you doing?" I cried. "We have to get help."

I grabbed the handles of Cortland's wheelchair. The palms of my hands blistered as the rubber melted in my grip. I shoved the wheelchair by its leather backing, heading to the doorway.

But the man stood in front of the door, blocking our path. "Now no one can get in until we're done."

Then I saw the man's face.

"It was you," I said.

He grinned, and his handsome face took on an evil twist. Then he reached into his pocket and flashed open a switchblade.

I pretended to ignore it. I couldn't believe what I was seeing. "We all need to get out of here," I said.

A floating fragment of burning fabric scorched my hand. I knew I had to push away the furniture so Cortland and I could escape.

The man came toward me with the knife. "Cortland promised he wouldn't say anything."

"He never did."

"There's no proof. Nothing left. Or there won't be after this."

The knife flashed in the firelight.

I heard a whoosh behind me. I looked back over my shoulder. A panel of burning curtains had folded onto the floor. Flames were eating into the ornate ceiling.

"Help!" I yelled, hoping someone in the hall would hear.

He was backing me toward the centre of the room. He pointed the knife at my throat. "After the fire, they'll think Cortland killed you."

"Nobody would believe that."

We heard a crack from above. We both looked up to the chandelier with its mismatched glass dishes.

"They'll decide it was Cortland who killed Trevor and Jackson too."

"Somebody'll figure out the truth."

The man smiled bitterly. "If you hadn't started meddling, Mitchell..." I could feel the cool sharpness of the blade against my throat.

A thunderous wrenching sounded above us. A chunk of sculpted plaster dropped from the ceiling. The man looked up, distracted for a moment, and I pushed him away.

Then the heavy chandelier broke from its supports. The man stared transfixed, his mouth opening in a scream, as the chandelier plummeted like a lead weight directly onto his forehead.

I rushed to the doorway. The credenza slid out of the way as easily as if it were weightless. I pulled open the door. Crowds of people were still flowing through the front hall. I shoved the wheelchair, pushing Cortland out of the burning room.

A woman screamed when she saw the mass of flames.

Kevin was brandishing the fire extinguisher.

"There's a man in there—on the floor," I said.

Kevin ran into the room, spraying a path. The rich fabrics of the chesterfield and chairs were alight. We heard another booming crack from above. Kevin backed toward the doorway just as the multi-layered plaster ceiling collapsed. Fire leapt up into the wooden beams.

"Close the door," Dr. Bhandari shouted. "We can't let it spread before everyone gets out." And Kevin pulled the door shut.

"Everyone please stay calm," Ramir commanded from his position on the stairs.

I joined the stream of people as I bumped Cortland's wheelchair down the front steps and out to the sidewalk. I put my hand to the side of his throat and felt for a pulse. I looked into his face, slack and peaceful. I pushed his silver hair back into place.

I wanted to talk to him. I wanted him to explain.

With a crash of glass, the flames burst through the front windows of the drawing room and reached up the brick façade. There was another rumble inside the house. Now the second-floor windows were glowing as well.

Two fire trucks with screaming sirens pulled up. A police car was right behind.

Ramir came over to me and Cortland.

"Do you think it was from inhaling all the smoke?" he asked.

"The tumour," I said, though I don't know why I was so certain.

"He must have dropped his cigarette."

"Or it might have been something else..."

We heard another crash inside the house.

The gas lamps on the driveway still flickered, and the candles on the front steps still burned as the firefighters rushed inside.

"Come away," Ramir said. "It's bad to breathe all this."

A moment later the paramedics arrived, and they wheeled Cortland away from me. It felt as though they were stealing him.

One of the ambulance attendants disinfected my blistered hands and wrapped them in bandages.

Laura and Ingrid came over to comfort me.

Ingrid hugged me. "You're OK?"

"Overwhelmed."

"I'm so sorry about Cortland," Laura said.

I nodded, and we all stared up at the burning house.

"But the fire's beautiful in a way, isn't it?"

I smiled at Ingrid's perpetual sense of aesthetics.

Ingrid had decided to stay at Laura's for the night.

"Do you want to come with us?"

"I want to stay here at the house a while longer."

I went out to the middle of the street where the crowd from inside had congregated. They stood looking at the house. Flames shot from the rooftop, licking across the shingles.

I wandered among the people.

I passed Bill Zale, smiling at the flames with bitter satisfaction.

Jane Choy was soothing Gabriella, who leaned against a parked car, coughing and convulsed in tears. Her white dress was stained with a long smudge of soot.

The video cameraman was capturing every dramatic moment.

I noticed Dr. Bhandari. He stared at his burning house as if hypnotized, his cheeks covered in sheets of tears.

"I'm sorry," I said. For my accusations. For my doubts. For my role in destroying his home. But he didn't pay any attention.

A third fire truck arrived. And now cabs were arriving to escort away the traumatized guests.

I sat on the curb and watched.

Aaron found me a few minutes later.

"I was worried. I knew you went upstairs."

"I'm OK," I said.

"Your hands. You won't be able to write."

"They'll be better in a day or two."

He sat beside me on the curb.

"I wanted to tell you some news before, but it doesn't seem like much now."

"Tell me anyway."

"My meeting tonight—it was because one of the actors dropped out of the picture. The casting director showed me the tape of your friend, Ramir. He's in our top three."

I smiled. "He'd be perfect," I said.

Maybe the Seven Gateways worked after all.

"Do you want me to take you home? Or do you want to come back to my hotel?"

"I'll stay here a while."

"Sure. Whatever. I'll call you in the morning, OK?"

Aaron headed off to find a taxi.

I sat looking at the grand old haunted house that had commanded such a tremendous influence—on Cortland, on Ramir, on Ingrid, on Laura, on me. Now fully ignited.

The crowd slowly began to disperse—people escaping to the comfort of home.

Ermina Milenska came and stood beside me.

"Cortland would have appreciated going out with such a bang," she said.

"A true Gothic finale."

She shuffled awkwardly from side to side. Her golden gown shimmered as it reflected the flames. "You caught me in a naughty moment," Ermina whispered, "coming out of the basement that way."

"Don't worry, I won't tell."

"A bit of silliness, for old times' sake."

"It's OK." I wanted Ermina to leave me alone—give me time to think.

"I was repeating a little history of my own," she said.

Which made me curious. "What do you mean?"

"I suppose it doesn't hurt to tell you now. Cortland wouldn't mind."

"Mind about what?"

"You see, at Vivienne's party, I became a bit tipsy, and I was flirting with a very attractive waiter. The two of us tiptoed off to the basement together."

She chuckled to herself, though it sounded tinged with melancholy.

"After the murder, the police wanted to know what everyone was doing all evening. Of course, I didn't want my husband to find out where I really was. So Cortland promised to tell the police that I was with him, gossiping all night. We never told a soul in all these years. Such jokes we've made about our silly little secret."

Ermina rattled on, and as she rattled, I realized what she apparently never had—that if her alibi was fake, Cortland's was as well.

I pulled the bloodstained handkerchief from my pocket. It was just like the handkerchiefs Cortland had given me—purchased at that exclusive men's shop on the Upper East Side. But this one was over 20 years old. Amid the dark-brown stains, when I looked carefully, I could see the initials embroidered in golden thread: *G.L.*

SATURDAY, OCTOBER 31
—MORE—

Finally, at midnight, Ramir drove me home. Our clothes smelled of smoke. There was a grey mask of ash on our faces.

I used Ramir's cell phone to call Cortland's sister, Beatrice, but the police had already informed her.

We drove in silence for a while.

"I guess the fire will make a good climax for your script," Ramir said. "But you still haven't told me what you think happened on the night they were killed."

"I'm still not sure," I said. It seemed disrespectful to start theorizing so soon.

"It was weird," he said, "having you see me like that."

"I've seen you naked before, remember."

"That was a long time ago. This was different."

"I'm sorry about…how I wrecked things."

Ramir explained that Dr. Bhandari had decided to show him the meditation for the Second Gateway as part of his plan to release the spirits of Jackson and Trevor. Gabriella's soaring voice added to the mystical power, while the ceremony itself was intended to enhance the spiritual experience for everyone at the concert.

Ramir said that during the Tantric massage of his second chakra, his body had been filled with an amazing electric tingling. It felt as if giant balls of energy were floating in the palms of his hands. He'd felt connected to the entire universe—until I so rudely interrupted.

"Do you think it was for real?" I asked.

He nodded. "I do," he said.

And at this point, I had to believe him.

Ramir pulled up in front of my building. More strange silence.

"I can spend the night at your place—if you feel weird about being alone."

I considered it for a moment. "It's probably better if you don't."

I kissed him on the cheek.

He nodded but didn't say anything.

"I'll talk to you tomorrow."

☆

I entered Cortland's apartment, using the extra key he'd given me. Pisces ran straight to my feet and looked up at my face expectantly, as though she knew something had happened and wanted to be informed immediately.

"He's not coming back," I said.

She meowed firmly until I picked her up.

With Pisces in my arms, I wandered through Cortland's rooms—all perfectly composed, pillows fluffed, as if waiting for a photo shoot by *Canadian House & Home*.

I remembered Cortland said he'd spent the morning getting things in order. Had he known somehow that he wasn't coming back?

The desk in his study was empty but for a large white envelope. Handwritten in the top right corner was my name.

Ungracefully, I carried Pisces and the envelope back here to my apartment. I poured a shot of tequila and stared at my burnt-orange walls. Painting them a gentle taupe would be my tribute to Cortland's impeccable taste.

I sat on my pullout sofa—Pisces curled beside me—and I opened Cortland's envelope.

Inside was a manila file folder. Paper-clipped to the top edge was a sheet of cream-coloured Tiffany's stationery inscribed with Cortland's elegant angular handwriting:

> *Mitchell, My Dear,*
> *I trust that by the time you read this, you'll have found my stealthily planted clue. Dr. Bhandari gave me the keys for the house yesterday, and I'm not nearly as wheelchair-bound as people may expect.*
> *I had often wondered whether I would take this secret to my grave, but after that chance encounter in the Courtyard Café—when the young man I had held in my heart stared through me as if I didn't exist—I knew I should never have agreed to protect him. If*

truth be told, of course, I was protecting us both. But that loyalty has cost me a great deal.

He phoned me, you'll be interested to know, immediately after you and Ramir paid your visit to his house. I assured him our secret was safe. I took great pleasure in telling that lie.

I am still mystified at how you came up with your psychic vision of that ghastly moment of discovery in Jackson's office. Perhaps you really are a mind reader. And who knows how this vicious tumour might be playing with my brain waves?

In any case, Mitchell, I hope I have supplied you with a juicy enough plot for your screenplay—complete with the necessary incriminating piece of evidence. (Please inform the police that they should test the handkerchief for two different blood types.)

My only regret is that I won't be able to attend your Hollywood premiere. Of course, you know I'll be there in spirit.

You will find my signed account enclosed.

Love always, C—

Inside the folder were six handwritten pages.

Before I read his account, I examined the rest of the folder's contents. A stack of 8-by-10 photographs showing the Italian palazzo in Barbados we'd included in Cortland's book.

But I'd never seen these photographs, I suppose because they showed the house unfinished, and Cortland's book was all about final polish and finesse. I turned one over. It was labeled "Montague House Construction, 1978-79."

There were photos of the red ceramic roof tiles being laid, columns half-painted with faux marbling, a line of seven elegant arches under construction in front of the poolside terrace.

I flipped through a dozen architectural shots.

Then I was surprised by a photograph of two men. More like a holiday snapshot than an architectural profile.

They were standing on the white-sand beach, the half-finished house rising behind them. Both were smiling, shirtless, and deeply tanned. Cortland's arm over the teenage Graham Linden's shoulder. Back in the days before Cortland's hair had turned silver, when it was still a rich, dark mane. The very definition of tall, dark, and handsome.

I took a sip of tequila and unfolded Cortland's pages.

THE SCRIPT

INTERIOR. OFFICE—NIGHT

Looking up at the fine crack of light at the top of a
door frame. From the angle, the viewer must be lying
down. Restless camera motions. The sound of heavy,
rapid breathing.

A TALL FIGURE steps into frame, looming above. The
room is so dark, the TALL FIGURE's face can't be seen.

A low grunting sound.

The TALL FIGURE bends forward, swiftly lowering a
hand.

The camera jerks and everything goes black.

A moment later there's a shift in angle, and the hand
appears again, reaching forward in a caress. The face
of the TALL FIGURE comes closer, but still no features
can be distinguished.

Suddenly, the crack of light widens, illuminating the
darkness.

The door is opening.

It becomes clear that we are observing TWO MEN in
disheveled tuxedos. ONE MAN is lying on a large
wooden desk, while the TALL FIGURE stands beside
him, bending over for a passionate kiss.

The door creaks as it opens farther.

The TALL FIGURE straightens and turns to the door.
His face now becomes visible. It's GORDON LINTON
(age 17), a beautiful young man with waves of dark
hair. Even in this small fraction of light, his eyes can
be seen as clear green.

GORDON watches as ANOTHER MAN is revealed in
the doorway, standing in silhouette.

MAN IN DOORWAY
What the fuck are you doing?

The door slams.

GORDON
Oh shit.

The MAN lying on the desk sits up. It's CORBETT McTEAGUE (age 37), handsome and elegant with thick dark hair swept back from his forehead.

CORBETT
Who was it?

GORDON
Travis Donnegan.

CORBETT
Dear Lord. Did he recognize you?

GORDON
(nodding sharply)
We go to school together. He'll tell everybody.

CORBETT
Did he see me?

GORDON is buttoning his shirt, fastening his pants.

GORDON
I have to talk to him. Tell him to keep quiet.

CORBETT
I'll come with you.

GORDON
That'll just make it worse. Travis can go crazy sometimes. Totally nuts.

GORDON exits the office. Through the door, we see him rush across the hall and open the door to the back staircase.

FOLLOW TO:

INTERIOR. SECOND-FLOOR HALLWAY—NIGHT

A moment later CORBETT is at the staircase door. He hears a scene unfolding upstairs.

> TRAVIS
> (screaming from above)
> Get away from me, you fucking faggot!

There's a crash of furniture.

FOLLOW TO:

INTERIOR. BACK STAIRCASE—NIGHT

CORBETT rushes up the dark, narrow flight of stairs.

> GORDON
> (from above)
> I just want to talk to you.

> TRAVIS
> (from above)
> Fucking freak. Fucking pervert!

Another crash as a bottle smashes against a wall.

CORBETT turns a corner on the staircase and comes to a landing with an open door.

FOLLOW TO:

INTERIOR. THIRD-FLOOR HALLWAY—NIGHT

CORBETT crosses the narrow hall and enters TRAVIS's room.

FOLLOW TO:

INTERIOR. TRAVIS'S ROOM—NIGHT

CORBETT steps into a small gabled room, decorated with rock band posters on every wall. The room is a mess. There's a huge mattress on the floor, sheets in a knot. The dresser is pushed over, drawers strewn. A vodka bottle lies in jagged pieces.

TRAVIS DONNEGAN (age 17) is dressed in a white T-shirt and jeans with bare feet. His face is twisted in total rage. He is hunched like a wrestler, ready to pounce.

GORDON makes a bizarre contrast in his formal tuxedo.

GORDON
You can't tell anyone, Travis. You can't tell anybody what you saw.

TRAVIS
What do you want to do? Fuck *me* now? You're both fucking perverts.

TRAVIS picks up a wooden desk chair and throws it at CORBETT. The chair splinters against the wall.

CORBETT
He's drunk, Gordon. Just leave him alone.

GORDON
You have to promise to keep quiet. You can't tell anyone.

TRAVIS stoops by his bedside and reveals a long, narrow butcher knife.

CORBETT
Put that down.

TRAVIS
Get the fuck out of my room.

Before they can escape, TRAVIS swings the knife and the blade scrapes GORDON's head. The knife is knocked from TRAVIS's grip and spins on the floor, stopping by the window.

TRAVIS bends to pick it up. GORDON pushes him fiercely from behind, rocketing him forward toward the window.

TRAVIS's head breaks the glass and, like a miracle, he's taken flight. His body disappears into the air. A strange short cry as he lands.

A moment of silence and stillness.

Then a large panel of glass drops from the window frame and shatters on the floor.

GORDON turns in horror. Blood drips down his face, a rivulet from his shiny black hair.

                    CORBETT
He cut you.

GORDON's hand flies to his face.

                    CORBETT
Your forehead.

GORDON reaches into his jacket pocket for a hand-kerchief. CORBETT takes it from him. Fine crisp white linen. CORBETT pushes the hair back from GORDON's smooth, perfect brow and wipes the blood away. The cut is hidden behind his hairline.

                    CORBETT
No one will ever notice.

GORDON glances to the window.

                    GORDON
I don't want to look. I don't want to see him.

                        CORBETT
We should get help.

                        GORDON
Maybe he'll be OK.

CORBETT goes to the ruined window and looks down.

In the shadows of the back garden, TRAVIS is lying
face down, his body folded over the spikes of the fence.
Blood has already darkened the back of his T-shirt.

When CORBETT turns, his horrified expression says
everything.

                        GORDON
They'll put me in jail.

                        CORBETT
Of course not. It was self-defense.

                        GORDON
I killed him. They'll say it was murder.

                        CORBETT
He attacked us first. I'm the witness.

                        GORDON
They'll want to know why. What if they find out what
we were doing?

                        CORBETT
We don't need to tell anyone.

                        GORDON
This could wreck everything. Wreck my whole life.

CORBETT takes GORDON in his arms to comfort him.

JEFFERSON DONNEGAN (age 42) enters the room,
dressed in a tuxedo with a tropical-pattern bow tie
and cummerbund. He is regal in his bearing.

He witnesses the men's embrace. They immediately part and stand awkwardly.

For a moment, JEFFERSON is speechless as he surveys the room, sees the damage, sees the broken window.

                    JEFFERSON
Where's Travis?

Neither CORBETT nor GORDON speak. They don't move. But GORDON's eyes shift to the broken window.

JEFFERSON goes to the window.

Before CORBETT can protest, GORDON bends to the floor, grabs the knife, and hides it behind his back.

                    JEFFERSON
               (looking out window)
My God.

His face is ashen when he turns. His expression is flat from shock.

                    JEFFERSON
How did it happen?

                    CORBETT
We just found him ourselves.

                    GORDON
He must have jumped.

                    JEFFERSON
What are you doing in his room?

CORBETT and GORDON are both silent.

Stricken, JEFFERSON turns to leave the room to go help his son.

With a movement too swift to stop, GORDON plunges the knife underhand into JEFFERSON's chest.

JEFFERSON stumbles backward. He clutches his chest, hands framing the knife handle jutting from his diaphragm. He looks down at himself in horror.

He drops backward onto the floor. His face goes slack as blood spreads across his white shirtfront.

The room is silent again.

CORBETT kneels beside JEFFERSON and puts his hand to the side of his throat to feel for a pulse.

                    GORDON
Is he dead?

CORBETT stares up at GORDON in horror.

                    CORBETT
Why did you...?

                    GORDON
It wasn't my fault.

                    CORBETT
Of course it was your fault.

                    GORDON
I did it for both of us.

                    CORBETT
We have to call the police. We have to explain.

                    GORDON
                  (shouting)
No!

CORBETT is startled by the outburst.

                    GORDON
It'd ruin everything forever. For both of us. Wreck our
whole lives.

CORBETT looks at the scene before him and ponders
the implications.

                    CORBETT
We can make it look like they killed each other.

                    GORDON
How?

                    CORBETT
              (pausing a moment)
I'll take care of it.

GORDON's eyes are locked on JEFFERSON's chest.

                    GORDON
My fingerprints are on the knife.

                    CORBETT
I'll clean it.

                    GORDON
We can't tell anyone what happened. Never.

                    CORBETT
You go downstairs. Find someone to give you an alibi.

GORDON approaches CORBETT for an embrace. COR-
BETT straightens GORDON's jacket. Smoothes his hair.
Gently touches the boy's beautiful face with the side of
his hand.

                    GORDON
We can't talk to each other. We can't let anyone see us
together.

                    CORBETT
Not until things blow over.

                         GORDON
Never. Never again.

CORBETT's eyes harden at the speed with which GOR-
DON's decision is made.

GORDON kisses him firmly on the mouth as if to seal
the promise, then leaves the room without looking back.
CORBETT stares down at JEFFERSON's body.

He kneels, grabs the wooden knife handle, and pulls.
The blade holds for a moment, as though it's taken
root. Then it smoothly releases.

He removes GORDON LINTON's handkerchief from
his pocket, and with a clean corner, he wipes the
handle and blade free of blood and fingerprints.

He leans out the window and pitches the knife into the
night. A gentle splash as it lands in the murky blue
waters of the swimming pool.

He looks down again at TRAVIS's body, his T-shirt now
almost entirely black.

CORBETT stares into the pattern of bloodstains on the
handkerchief. He touches the initials embroidered in
gold thread: *G.L.*

Then he carefully folds the handkerchief into squares
and slips it into his jacket pocket.

POSTSCRIPT

WEDNESDAY, MARCH 6

"The line of seven arches creates a sense of control and symmetry in vivid contrast to the lush vegetation that surrounds."

That's a direct quote from Cortland's chapter on Montague House, the faux Italian palazzo on the beach just north of Bridgetown, Barbados.

And it really is true.

As I write this on my laptop, I am sitting at a lovely wrought-iron table, directly behind those seven arches, sheltered in the cool shade of the loggia. Set before me is a spectacular swimming pool. Beyond that lies a strip of white sand and then the endless turquoise waves of the Caribbean.

It's consistently surreal, living in such a luxurious palace—all marble and antiques and formality—when right outside the window some exotic bird might be squawking or an iguana might dart along a tree branch.

What all this grandeur really means is that you end up sitting at a 16th-century antique dining table in a Speedo bathing suit.

Nonetheless, I felt compelled to dress in khaki shorts and a proper white shirt because it's 4 o'clock and time for tea.

"Afternoon tea is a charming tradition carried on faithfully in this former British colony." That's what it said in the tourist guide.

Hyacinth, the cook, has just brought out a silver tray with china cups and saucers. She'll deliver the pot of Darjeeling in a few minutes.

Montague House is still owned by Ned and Shirley Montague, the couple who hired the rising design star, Cortland McPhee, to work on it for them over 20 years ago. They run it now as a guesthouse. And in his will, Cortland left me a sum of money, along with explicit instructions that I should come here for a two-week holiday with Ingrid and Ramir.

"Everything is exactly the way Cortland originally intended it," the Montagues have assured me.

In the evenings over dinner, I've been asking them questions, learning more about their history and their connection to the tale.

They vividly remember Cortland flying down during their home's construction, joined on weekends by the youthful Graham Linden. Cortland was colourful and eccentric, so they weren't surprised that he might have a younger boyfriend. Though they thought Graham was a mature 21, not 17. Whatever his age, they found him irresistibly charming. In addition to being a great pleasure to look at, he was an avid player on their neighbours' tennis courts and an entertaining guest at dinner, talking enthusiastically of his ambition to become a famous fashion designer in New York City.

Then Graham abruptly stopped accompanying Cortland. The Montagues had been too discreet to ask why.

There's no doubt in my mind that Cortland had genuinely loved Graham Linden—enough to be willingly linked with him in such a terrible secret and then to be forever ignored because of it. No wonder Cortland had spoken of Graham so bitterly, as he watched a parade of other richer men (and women) indulge the young man's taste for luxurious living and international travel.

Now I look back and understand Cortland's subtle encouragements to search out Trevor's friends from school.

In subsequent police interviews, Carolyn Linden claimed she had no idea that her boyfriend was upstairs during the Donningtons' party—involved in a prearranged tryst with his *own* boyfriend, taking advantage of their mutual attendance at this glamorous party. Carolyn thought Graham was simply off getting drinks. Even though he *had* taken a very long while.

On the night of Gabriella's concert, Graham had encouraged Carolyn to leave the house, and once again she had no idea why. She was in absolute shock when the police explained her husband's true agenda of murder and arson to cover his past crimes.

Though, according to the medical reports, Graham didn't actually kill Cortland. His death was clearly attributable to the brain tumour. That's given me a measure of peace.

But it's been very disturbing for me, knowing the role I played in Graham's demise. Even though it was obviously in self-defense. Still, it's the second bizarre death I've been involved in—

after that disaster at Ramir's one-man show a few years ago.

But that's another story.

Ingrid has joined me on the terrace. She's been toting a sketch pad and a box of oil pastels everywhere she goes on the island. "There's a bougainvillea on the other side of the house. I've been sitting there for an hour."

She just showed me her sketch pad. Using oil pastels, she's turned a close-up of three blossoms into a fiery mayhem of reds and pinks with central bursts of yellow.

"If you keep up with those, you'll have a whole new show ready by the time we get home."

"I'm not sure what I think of them yet. They might be too Georgia O'Keeffe. But you never know where they might lead."

Ing is proceeding to refine her flowers, so I'll just continue typing.

Her show in Berlin last month was a huge success. At the opening-night party, Ramir and I were crowded away by admirers.

All of Ingrid's influences came together, and fire took over as the dominant theme, combining the Donnington paintings with paintings of the blazing Thornfield Manor. One of the show's highlights—according to a prominent German newspaper—was the pose of me with my arms outstretched, superimposed against the burning abstract mansion.

The seminal painting of her and Pierre didn't make the final cut. Ingrid decided to put it away in long-term storage.

Pierre himself has been totally thrown out.

The day after getting caught in his affair, Pierre packed up his possessions and moved in with an old friend from college. Daphne didn't want to see him again, we learned. Then, shortly after, things soured at his new advertising agency, so the weasel moved back to his parents' house in Ottawa. Ingrid hasn't heard from him since.

At first, Ingrid was concerned about the awkwardness of living so close to Daphne. But Daphne slipped an apology card—along with a pink candy heart that said KISS & MAKE UP—through Ingrid's mail slot and carried on waving hello as perkily as ever. Ingrid kept her distance.

The Paper Gallery closed just after Christmas, and there's been a FOR LEASE sign in the window ever since.

"Here's your pot of tea." Hyacinth has arrived with another silver tray, this one also stacked with coconut cookies, fresh-baked scones, clotted cream, and homemade mango jam. "You let me know if there's anything else you need."

Ing has already grabbed a coconut cookie. "These things are so good, I want to make sure I bring a few home to Kevin."

Yes, Kevin. He's proven to be one of the unexpected bonuses of the drama. After his position at the Gateways went up in smoke, he went back to his real job—teaching Grade 3 at a public school downtown—and he and Ingrid started dating. He's divorced. She's divorced. And he's got weekend custody of his completely cute 4-year-old son.

I think I actually approve of the whole thing. But they're taking it slowly.

The other gift is that Ingrid and Laura have become really good friends. In fact, Laura had us all over for dinner just before we came down here. She quit her job as a bookkeeper and has returned to school, studying graphic design with an eye on getting into advertising. She's even been dating a bit. A police detective she met during the reopened murder investigation.

A few days after the fire, I went out for a coffee with Laura myself.

When I showed her Cortland's account of what had happened that night—proving that her brother really wasn't a killer and that she herself really wasn't implicated—she didn't say a word. She simply nodded solemnly.

I'd felt a similar anticlimactic sadness.

For those intense few weeks, I'd felt so connected to Trevor. I'd imagined such a strong spiritual bond between us. And then, when the truth was revealed, Trevor simply disappeared into the story.

Ramir just sauntered up from the beach, bulging in his skimpy red swimsuit. His skin has tanned a dark chestnut brown, and he says he feels close to his Caribbean roots.

"I met some interesting people from Sweden at another house up the beach. Husband and wife and a bunch of friends. They invited me in for cocktails."

"So you've been drinking all afternoon?"

"No, I found a quiet spot under a palm tree and sat for a while by myself. Remind me to get one of those ocean-wave CDs when we get home. The sound is great for meditation."

He brushes some sand from the backs of his legs and takes a seat at the table beside Ingrid and me.

Yes, he's still practicing meditation. But he's carrying on independently, now that Dr. Bhandari has left town. The doctor saw the destruction of his home as a message from the universe that it was time to move on, and he relocated The Centre for Spiritual Success to Santa Barbara on the California coast. A few weeks ago, Ramir showed me an article from *Newsweek*, listing Dr. Bhandari's many famous alumni and proclaiming the remarkable effectiveness of his work. So I guess I never should have doubted him.

In the meantime, the lot on Thornfield Road sits bulldozed and empty under a blanket of winter snow. A new mansion will inevitably rise in its place come spring.

Instead of finding another spiritual counselor, Ramir sought the advice of a financial counselor, who offered the profound wisdom: "Much inner peace is lost because of outer clutter." As a result, Ramir has scaled back enormously, selling his mother's unlived-in condominium, remortgaging his house and taking in a roommate. Though he's kept his prized Land Rover.

And things are looking up career-wise. Last fall, he played the Latin lover in Aaron's production of *Niagara,* spending two memorable weeks in the company of Drew Barrymore. The movie should be released next summer. That might lead to more work. And he's become more interested than ever in producing and directing.

Celibacy is a thing of the past, of course, and he has a new boyfriend back home. Another actor. But frankly, I don't think it's going to work out. Ramir has been fooling around with one of the gardeners at the estate next door.

"Is the tea ready yet?" he asked.

"It needs to steep a while longer."

So Ramir now sits staring out, contemplating the sea.

The atmosphere here on the island is perpetually languid. Which is a nice change after the past few months.

Cortland's funeral was a grand society affair, attended by many illustrious clients and friends who flew in from around the world. Naturally, he'd prearranged every detail of the flowers and music and even the food.

It was such a lavishly beautiful affair; everyone in attendance was filled more with wonder than sadness. Which I'm sure had been Cortland's intention.

Shortly afterward, Cortland's publisher hired me to posthumously complete his book. I added the extra chapter showing the photographs of both the Donnington party and the Seven Gateways party. *Life of Beauty* should be coming out later this year.

Of course, at the same time I was working on the screenplay for *A Killing Upstairs*.

As promised, Aaron procured $25,000 in development money— saving me from the indignity of *Travels with Willie*. The two of us had dinner a few times when he was in Toronto during the *Niagara* shoot—though we kept the relationship strictly business. And I finished the first draft just before Christmas.

Gabriella Hartman has read it and loves it. Her manager has read it and loves it. But now Gabriella has become absorbed in her singing career—which was given an extra boost when the video-tape of the concert and fire was featured on *Entertainment Tonight*. My project seems to have dropped lower on her priority list.

But the Donningtons' story has received a lot of publicity, and there'll be more publicity once Cortland's book comes out. So maybe the script won't languish eternally.

In the meantime, I've been pruning and polishing my diaries into another roman à clef, so even if the film never gets made, I can tell my own version of the story. After all, it's got sex, death, rich people, celebrities, and the supernatural—all the essential ingredients of a commercial blockbuster.

Ingrid just closed her box of pastels and set them on the ground. "I think the tea must be ready now."

Ramir squeezed a slice of lemon into his cup in preparation for Ingrid's pouring. "How it's coming?"

"I'm just working on the postscript."

"Did you mention that Jane Choy is selling her psychic-training video on The Shopping Channel?"

"I will."

"And don't forget to put in that you adopted Cortland's cat." (My parents are taking care of Pisces while I'm away.)

"And say that *Station Centauri* went downhill after I left."

"Done." I took a coconut cookie from the tray. "One of the things I'm worried about is that this book doesn't have a very satisfying love story. Not like the first one when I met Ben."

Ing looked mystified. "Of course it's got a love story," she said.

"Aaron doesn't count."

"That was just cheap sex," Ramir added on my behalf.

"You're not going to say Trevor was the love interest."

I was scared she'd suggest it was Ramir.

"You and Cortland," she said.

"That's crazy."

Ramir nodded along with her. "Of course Cortland was in love with you."

"Like a friend maybe."

"More than that," Ramir said. "He gave you a movie and two books to write. How much more could you want from a man?"

"Didn't you ever notice how he looked at you, Mitchell?"

I tried to picture Cortland's expression. That wry smile and amused sense of patience that I'd come to see as fatherly.

Ingrid smiled philosophically. "You thought it was some mysterious force of the universe helping you—when it was really just your friend down the hall."

She was right, of course.

The three of us sat in silence for a while, waiting for the tea to cool, gazing out at the gently rolling azure waves.